KISS HER GOODBYE

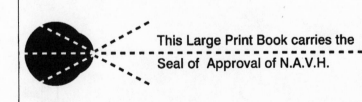

This Large Print Book carries the
Seal of Approval of N.A.V.H.

Wendy Corsi Staub

KISS HER GOODBYE

Thorndike Press • Waterville, Maine

Published in 2004 by arrangement with Pinnacle Books, an imprint of Kensington Publishing Corp.

Thorndike Press® Large Print Basic.

The tree indicium is a trademark of Thorndike Press.

The text of this Large Print edition is unabridged.
Other aspects of the book may vary from the original edition.

Set in 16 pt. Plantin by Al Chase.

Printed in the United States on permanent paper.

Library of Congress Cataloging-in-Publication Data

Staub, Wendy Corsi.
    Kiss her goodbye / Wendy Corsi Staub.
        p. cm.
    ISBN 0-7862-6740-2 (lg. print : hc : alk. paper)
    1. Teenage girls — Crimes against — Fiction.   2. Mothers and daughters — Fiction.   3. New York (State) — Fiction.
4. Suburban life — Fiction.   5. Large type books.   I. Title.
PS3569.T336456K57 2004
    813'.54—dc22   2004042275

Dedicated in heartfelt memory
of my cherished friend,
the gentle Big Man
Jon Charles Gifford
8/7/59–7/8/03
"Here's to you and those like you.
Damned few left."

And with love to William Pijuan,
aka Uncle Bill, who bravely carries on.

And, as always, to Mark, Morgan, and
Brody.

As the Founder/CEO of NAVH, the only national health agency solely devoted to those who, although not totally blind, have an eye disease which could lead to serious visual impairment, I am pleased to recognize Thorndike Press* as one of the leading publishers in the large print field.

Founded in 1954 in San Francisco to prepare large print textbooks for partially seeing children, NAVH became the pioneer and standard setting agency in the preparation of large type.

Today, those publishers who meet our standards carry the prestigious "Seal of Approval" indicating high quality large print. We are delighted that Thorndike Press is one of the publishers whose titles meet these standards. We are also pleased to recognize the significant contribution Thorndike Press is making in this important and growing field.

Lorraine H. Marchi, L.H.D.
Founder/CEO
NAVH

* Thorndike Press encompasses the following imprints: Thorndike, Wheeler, Walker and Large Pr int Press.

ACKNOWLEDGMENTS

The author gratefully acknowledges, in reverse alphabetical order for a change, Wendy Zemanski, Walter Zacharius, Steve Zacharius, Mark Staub, John Scognamiglio, Joan Schulhafer, Janice Rossi Schaus, Laura Blake Peterson, Laurie Parkin, Doug Mendini, Gena Massarone, Kelly Going, Kyle Cadley, and Danielle Boniello.

PROLOGUE

August

Her thoughts, that Tuesday night as she walks along the edge of the road, are mainly occupied by the first day of school tomorrow.

What she'll wear, who she'll have for homeroom, and whether she'll get third or fourth period lunch. Seniors always get one or the other of the later lunch periods. That'll be a nice switch. Last year, she had first period; who wants sloppy joes or egg salad at 10:20 in the morning?

The pothole pocked pavement of Cuttington Road shines in the murky glow of streetlights; the strip of ground that borders it is still muddy from this morning's hard rain.

Ma always reminds her to walk in the gutter, not the road, on her way home from her job at the fast-food place out on the highway. But she can't walk in the mud; she's wearing sandals.

And anyway, it's less than half a mile, and there isn't a lot of traffic on this old, winding back road leading to their apartment complex at this time of night. A year or two ago, there wasn't any through traffic at all; the only thing out here in the woods was Orchard Arms, a cluster of boxy, stucco, two-story buildings with rectangular wrought-iron balconies cluttered with potted impatiens, tricycles, and hibachis.

Then bulldozers rolled in and created a development where the woods used to be. They call it Orchard Hollow, probably because of all the apple trees they tore down to make way for the houses. Now, farther down the road, just past Orchard Arms, cul de sacs branch off from Cuttington Road like jeweled fingers on a work-roughened hand.

Two- and three-story houses with two- and three-car garages sprang up where there used to be only trees and brambles. In the garages are shiny cars and SUVs; in the homes are people who complain about the ruts and poor lighting along the old road that leads to Orchard Hollow. It's always been bad but nobody other than the apartment complex's residents ever cared until now. The construction equipment has torn up the pavement worse than ever, but they're still building back there.

The new houses have broad decks and brick terraces instead of wrought-iron balconies. They have real yards with raised beds of roses, wide gas grills, and elaborate wooden swing sets. Some of them even have in-ground pools.

On the hottest days of this summer, as she sat out on the balcony, she could sometimes hear the sound of splashing and gleeful shouts in the distance.

She often wondered what it would be like to make friends with one of the girls who ride her bus. Then she might be invited over to one of their pools to swim.

But so far, that hasn't happened. The girls from the development stick together, and she, as the only kid her age living in Orchard Arms, keeps to herself on the bus. Sometimes she eavesdrops on the other girls' conversations when they talk about things that interest her. Things like boys at Woodsbridge High and sales at Abercrombie & Fitch over at the Galleria. But when they discuss things to which she can't relate — like curfews and overly strict fathers and nosy mothers who are always home, always asking questions — well, then she tunes them out.

She sticks to the very edge of the pavement as she walks, doing her best to pick her way around the puddles that fill the potholes. Her toes are getting wet and dirty anyway.

Tomorrow, she'll have to put on regular shoes again for the first time in two months, she thinks with a tinge of regret. Regular shoes and regular clothes. In western New York, the days of sandals and shorts and tank tops are too fleeting as it is — you'd think Woodsbridge High would allow students to wear them through the warm days of early September, but nope.

What a waste of a pedicure, she thinks, remembering how painstakingly she polished her toenails pearly pink just this morning while she was sitting on the balcony watching the rain.

She hears a car splashing toward her from behind and steps farther off the road to let it pass.

It doesn't pass.

Gravel crunches beneath the tires as it slows; the headlights illuminate the road before her, casting an eerily long, distorted shadow of herself.

She wonders, as she turns toward the blinding lights, whether it's somebody she knows from Orchard Arms, stopping to give her a ride.

Her next thought, a belated thought, is that Ma always tells her to walk facing traffic, not with it, so that she can see what's coming toward her.

12

And her last coherent thought as the car door opens and she is dragged roughly inside is that she never, ever would have seen this coming.

PART I

OCTOBER

ONE

"Mrs. Carmody?"

Startled, Kathleen glances up at the orthodontist's bleached-blond receptionist.

"Yes?"

"We need your insurance card again."

With a sigh, Kathleen puts aside an issue of *Rosie* magazine — a relic of a bygone era when there actually was a *Rosie* magazine — takes her purse from the back of her uncomfortable chair and crosses the crowded waiting room. Her ten-year-old son Curran, absorbed in his Gameboy, is the only one who doesn't look up.

Kathleen fishes for the card in her wallet, hands it to the woman, and waits while she examines it, frowns, photocopies it, and frowns again.

"Is this new insurance?" the receptionist asks.

"Not since we started coming here in May." She wonders if the receptionist is new. She's never seen her here before.

"Not a new group number?"

"Nope." Kathleen sighs inwardly. What is it with insurance? It's been six months since Matt switched jobs and they moved to western New York, but every doctor, dentist, and orthodontist appointment brings another round of complications.

The woman spins her chair toward a computer, taps a few keys with her right hand while holding the insurance card in her left. The computer whirs, and she glances up. "It'll be a few seconds; I just have to check something, Mrs. . . . . *Katie?*"

Katie.

A name from the past. Which means that the unfamiliar receptionist is also a name, a voice, a face from the past.

It's Kathleen's turn to frown, in that vague, polite, *have we met?* manner she's perfected since the move.

"You're Katie Gallagher, right?"

Not anymore, thank God.

"I used to be." Kathleen forces a pleasant smile. "It's Kathleen Carmody now."

"I'm Deb. Deb Duffy, I used to be, but now I'm Deb Mahalski."

The name doesn't ring a bell. Not that it would. Kathleen did her best to block out just about everyone she used to know. It's easier that way.

"I thought you moved away years ago,"

18

the woman chatters on.

Kathleen wants nothing more than to grab Curran and his Gameboy and bolt, but that's out of the question. This isn't the first time she's run into somebody who used to know her. And anyway, the receptionist is still holding her insurance card.

"I'm . . . I did, but I'm back," Kathleen murmurs, absently noting Deb Mahalski's impossibly long, curved, crimson fingernails and wondering how she manages the keyboard.

"Where are you living now?"

"Woodsbridge."

Kathleen watches the woman glance down at her file on the desk; sees her overly plucked and penciled-in eyebrows rise. "Orchard Hollow? You've come a long way since Saint Brigid's."

So that's it. We were Catholic schoolgirls together in another lifetime.

"Did you hear they tore down the church and school a few years ago to build a new Wegman's?"

"I heard."

"That's your son?" Deb asks, with a nod at Curran.

"Yes."

"I have two girls, three and five." She gestures her poufy pile of hair, caught back in a

19

plastic butterfly clip, toward a framed photo on the desk. "Do you have other kids?"

"A younger son. And a daughter. She's . . . older."

"And you're married?"

"Mmm hmm."

It's not as though she can dodge the questions. After all, few taps of the computer keys would reveal everything anyone would want to know about her life.

Not everything.

Nobody knows everything. Not even Matt. Nor the children.

And they never will, Kathleen assures herself, clasping her trembling hands into fists within the deep pockets of her corduroy barn coat.

"I'm home! Sorry I'm late, Jen!" Stella Gattinski calls as she simultaneously steps from the attached garage into her kitchen and out of the brown leather pumps that have tortured her feet all afternoon.

"It's okay, Mrs. Gattinski."

Jen Carmody, the "bestest and most beautifulest babysitter in the whole wide world," according to Stella's two-year-old twin daughters, smiles up from the raised brick hearth in the adjoining family room, where a stuffed animal tea party is in progress.

The April day the Carmody family moved to Woodsbridge from the Midwest was one lucky day for Stella. Wholesome Jen is terrific with MacKenzie and Michaela, and she's at the perfect age: about thirteen. Old enough to be responsible for two small children, and too young for dating, driving, and most extracurricular school activities.

She comes every Wednesday to meet the twins when the day care bus drops them off. Wednesdays are Stella's late day at school; she's the French club advisor and that's the afternoon they meet.

Before Stella hired Jen, she was forced to rely on Elise Gattinski, aka the mother-in-law from hell, for Wednesday child care. Her own mother used to do it, but ever since Daddy's death last year, Stella hates to ask her. Mom's grown increasingly frail; she isn't up to caring for a pair of twin preschoolers.

Kurt's mother is hardly frail and she frequently offers to help out, but Stella always loathed using her as a regular babysitter. Not a week went by when Elise didn't make some dig about working mothers neglecting their children's needs — and, even worse, their husbands' needs. Thank God Stella no longer needs her help, unless she's in a pinch.

"Mommy, Jen doesn't have to leave now, does she?"

"Yeah, Mommy, she said we can play Candyland again after this," Michaela promptly joins MacKenzie's whining. "Can you go back to work?"

Stella grins. "Sorry, kiddo. You're stuck with me."

There's a brief commotion, then Michaela breaks off midwail to announce, "Mommy, guess what? Jen rescued a ladybug!"

"Yeah, the ladybug landed on her arm and I hate bugs so I wanted to kill it but Jen wouldn't let us," MacKenzie puts in.

"She says never kill anything," Michaela adds, "not even yucky bugs! Because they want to go home to their mommies."

"Jen's right," Stella says approvingly. "Did anyone call, Jen?"

"Just Mr. Gattinski." Jen doesn't seem to mind MacKenzie's hands attempting to braid her long blond hair. "He said to tell you he's got a late meeting and to eat without him."

Stella's grin fades. Another late meeting. That's the second time this week, and it's only half-over.

" 'Kenz, get your hands out of Jen's hair," she says absently, wondering who Kurt's meeting with tonight.

His promotion to vice president at Lakeside Savings and Loan seemed like a blessing, coming at the tail end of Stella's extended maternity leave. But that was almost two years ago, when money was scarce and family togetherness was not. Their household had just doubled in size, sweeping a dazed Stella from busy middle school teacher to invalid on bedrest to stay-at-home mom. Quite honestly, Kurt — with his banker's hours — was underfoot and on her nerves at that point, anyway.

Now she's back to work; he's a vice president; they've got a savings account, a Volvo station wagon, a weekly housekeeper, and this newly built center hall Colonial in Orchard Hollow.

Not to mention the most adorable little girls on the planet.

Life couldn't be better.

Really.

After checking the clock on the microwave — 5:26 already? — Stella fumbles in her wallet for a twenty and a ten. Jen's been here since three, and her hourly rate is only eight dollars, but Stella gives her ten an hour and always rounds up. The twins are a handful. Plus, it's only one afternoon a week.

"Girls, get off Jen's lap so she can stand up," Stella says.

Her daughters ignore her.

Jen giggles as Michaela throws her arms around her and gives her a bear hug.

Depositing her purse on the breakfast bar, Stella strides across the toy-strewn carpet, money in hand. She deftly plucks a wriggling MacKenzie off of Jen and pries Michaela's arms from around Jen's neck.

"I know you guys love Jen, but she has to go home. Her mommy is probably wondering where she is." *And your mommy is wondering where your daddy is.* "Please tell your mom I'm sorry it's so late, Jen."

"Actually, my mom's not home. She had to take Curran to the orthodontist in Amherst at four and they never get out of there for hours."

That's true. Kathleen Carmody was complaining about it just the other day when Stella ran into her at the supermarket. She mentioned that her older son has had three appointments with Doctor Deare so far and he's always running behind — and that his waiting room magazines are at least a year old.

"Maybe I should take up cross-stitch or knitting," Kathleen said, rolling her green eyes. "I've got years of this ahead of me.

Our dentist is already positive that Riley" — the youngest Carmody — "is going to need braces, too."

But not Jen. Stella finds herself admiring the teenager's perfectly even white smile. Add that to her wide-set brown eyes, fine bone structure, and willowy build, and she looks like a fresh-faced fashion model. She even has a quirky characteristic on par with Cindy Crawford's mole and Lauren Hutton's widely spaced front teeth: a thin streak of white hair running through the golden brown hair of her left eyebrow.

Next to her teenaged sitter, Stella feels frumpier than ever. Her own unruly dark blond hair is pulled back into a black velvet headband — the kind that went out of style more than a decade ago for all but New England finishing school students. The last twenty pounds of maternity weight still cling stubbornly to her hips and stomach, yet Stella refuses to acknowledge that they might be here to stay. That's why she's still wearing skirts and tops she bought a few months into the pregnancy, instead of something more streamlined and fashionable. She refuses to buy new clothes in size fourteen.

She notes with envy Jen's slender figure in jeans and a simple tucked-in T-shirt. Oh, to be young and skinny again. . . .

"Do you still need me on Saturday night, Mrs. Gattinski?" Jen brushes off her jeans and casually tosses her silky hair back over her shoulders as she stands.

"Saturday night . . . yes! We've got that Chamber of Commerce dinner. I almost forgot. Mr. Gattinski will pick you up at seven."

"I can walk over," Jen protests, and murmurs her thanks as Stella hands her the thirty dollars.

"You're welcome. And no, you can't walk over; it'll be dark by seven. In fact . . ." Stella glances over Michaela's red hair at the sliding glass doors that lead out to the deck and fenced yard. "It's almost dark now. Come on, I'll drive you home. Girls, where are your coats?"

"That's okay, don't do that, Mrs. Gattinski. By the time you get them bundled up and into the car seats, I'll be home."

"I don't know . . ." Stella looks again at the darkness falling. The thought of packing the kids into the car *is* exhausting, but —

"I'll be fine. I'll see you two on Saturday, okay?" Jen plants a kiss on each twin's cheek and heads for the front door.

As it closes behind her, Stella cuddles her daughters close on her lap and smooths their hair, the same shade and texture as her own. She sighs in contentment. Another long day has drawn to a close. All she wants to do is throw on sweats — even better, pajamas — and collapse on the couch.

"I miss Jen," MacKenzie laments.

"Me, too," chimes the inevitable echo.

You should have insisted on driving Jen home, Stella chides herself, glancing again at the shadows beyond the sliding glass door. *It isn't a good idea for a teenaged girl to be out alone after dark.*

Not that this neighborhood isn't the safest around. It isn't like their old street in Cheektowaga, where there were three car break-ins in the month before they moved. But still . . .

April Lukoviak.

The name flits into Stella's thoughts, sending a ripple of uneasiness through her.

April Lukoviak, who lived with her mother up the road at Orchard Arms, has been missing for weeks now — since right around Labor Day. There were fliers up all over the development back when school started. They were cheap, photocopied fliers made by the people who lived in the apartment complex, featuring a poorly reproduced black-and-white image of a pretty teenaged girl with long, straight

27

blond hair like Jen's.

At first, the other mothers at the bus stop were disconcerted by the fliers. They kept a wary eye even on their teenaged children, especially the girls. Then people started talking about how April didn't get along with her mother, who supported the two of them with food stamps, welfare checks, and by tending bar. People said that April was always threatening to run off to California, where her father reportedly last lived. The police seemed to think that theory made sense.

After awhile, September rains blurred the typed descriptions of April. Fierce autumn winds blew in off Lake Erie to tear the fliers from the development's lampposts and slender young trees, blowing them away altogether.

But every once in a while, when Stella passes Orchard Arms or goes through the drive-through at the fast-food restaurant where April worked, she finds herself thinking of her. She wonders what ever happened to her; wonders if she really did run away.

If anything ever happened to Jen, you'd be responsible. Next time, you'll insist on driving her home. After all, bad things can happen in safe neighborhoods, too.

★ ★ ★

Jen has always liked the sound of leaves crunching beneath her feet. So much that she goes out of her way to step in the piles that line the edge of the pavement along the cul de sac. There are no sidewalks here in Orchard Hollow, and the houses are bigger, farther apart, and newer than they were back in Ohio, where centuries-old trees scattered abundant drifts of leaves in October.

Here, there are leaves, too, but not many. There's only a scattering of old trees that weren't bulldozed when the houses were built, and the slender new maples and oaks that are still supported by stakes and wires barely have branches.

"I don't like it here," Riley announced on sunny moving-in day last April. "There's no trees and shade. I want to go home."

He had been whining in an annoying sing-song voice already for six hours in the overpacked Chevy Tahoe, making Jen long to be riding in the U-haul truck behind them with Dad and Curran. But this time, Jen secretly agreed with her little brother's sentiment. She desperately missed Indiana already. Even the trees. *Especially* the trees.

"There will be shade when the leaves pop out," Mom promised, as she put the car into

Park and turned off the engine, sealing their fate. 9 Sarah Crescent — a two-story, yellow-sided Colonial with blue shutters and stickers still on the windows — was officially home.

The house — and Woodsbridge — really *do* feel more like home now, six months later. Especially now that school and soccer are underway and the strangely cool, mostly cloudy western New York summer has given way to the more familiar and comforting chill of autumn.

Jen feels good about living here; good about the friends she's made and about her regular babysitting job for the Gattinskis. Mrs. Gattinski is so warm and nice, and the girls are adorable.

Too bad Mr. Gattinski gives me the creeps, Jen thinks with a twinge of guilt.

Okay, he's not necessarily creepy. It's just that sometimes, the way he looks at her makes her skin crawl. He seems to notice her more than somebody's husband — and somebody's father — should notice a kid her age.

But most of the time, he's not even around. And anyway, the job is worth the few minutes she has to endure in the car with him making stilted conversation whenever he picks her up or drops her off.

Realizing she's starved, Jen quickens her pace. Rounding the corner onto Cuttington Road, she walks along the edge where tangled vines, bushes, and trees border the still vacant lots. From here she can see the cluster of homes, including the Carmodys', that make up Sarah Crescent just ahead.

Jen inhales the sweet, smoky scent of leaves and somebody's fireplace, wondering what Mom has planned for dinner. Maybe she's got stew or chili in the Crock-Pot. And some of those brown-and-serve rolls that taste like the kind you get in a bread basket at a nice restaurant.

Back in Indiana, Dad worked late every night, and they ate a lot of grilled cheese and frozen pizza without him. But Mom's been on a cooking kick ever since they moved east, planning and preparing nightly family dinners like she's trying to transform herself into Martha Stewart or something. Over the summer, she was the queen of marinating and grilling; now she's into the Crock—

Jen jumps, hearing a noise behind her.

Probably a dog in the bushes, she thinks, scanning the seemingly empty road. Or maybe some kind of animal. What if . . .

Are there bears here?

Oh, please, she scoffs, even as her heart quickens its pace. *This is suburban Buffalo.*

Not the mountain wilderness.

She starts walking again, quickly, toward home.

Her eyes are trained on the loop of well-lit houses ahead; her ears on the thatch of bushes to her left.

Is something rustling in there? Another set of footsteps crunching in the leaves?

Feeling foolish, yet frightened, Jen starts to run. She barrels around the border of hedges onto Sarah Crescent — and slams into somebody.

Jen shrieks.

The other person cries out, too.

A high-pitched, female cry.

"Sissy!" Jen exclaims, recognizing Maeve's cleaning lady. "You scared me!"

"You scared me, too."

"I'm sorry."

"You're Erin Hudson's friend, right? Jane?"

"Jen."

"Oh, right. Jen." The girl — or is she a woman? — presses her hand against her navy sweatshirt as though she's trying to calm her heart. Jen notices a sheaf of colored papers in her other hand.

Fliers. She must be putting up more fliers for that missing girl. The thought of her reminds Jen why she was feeling so uneasy in the first place.

"Why are you running?" Sissy asks. "Is somebody chasing you?"

"No, I'm just . . ." Out of the corner of her eye, Jen spots one of her neighbors in a track suit approaching at a fast trot. Inspiration strikes. "I'm just out for a jog."

Yeah. Right. She always jogs in jeans and boots with a book bag over her shoulder.

But Sissy says, "I like to jog, too. It's good exercise. Keeps me in shape, you know?" She gestures at her thin frame in the baggy sweats Jen's seen her wear to clean over at the Hudsons'.

She's just being nice, Jen realizes. *She knows I was spooked.*

"Yeah, it's good exercise," Jen agrees, giving the neighbor a wave as she runs past.

She looks toward home. Theirs is the only dark house on the block. Mom isn't home yet. Reluctantly, she tells Sissy, "Well, I've got to get home."

"Yeah, me, too. Hey, does your mother need a cleaning lady by any chance?"

"My mother?" Jen laughs. "Nope."

She's well aware that they seem to be the only family in Orchard Hollow who does their own cleaning. But that's how Mom likes it.

"Can I give you one of my fliers?" Sissy

33

asks. "I've got reasonable rates, and I work for a few other families in this neighborhood who can give me references."

Oh. So this isn't about the missing girl after all.

Jen takes the flier Sissy offers and shoves it into her backpack, knowing she'll never bother to show her mother. "Night, Sissy."

"See you . . ." Sissy pauses, then closes her mouth in the manner of somebody who still isn't sure what the other person's name is.

"Jen."

"Right. Jen. I remember."

Back in Indiana, the only people they knew who had a cleaning lady were the Remingtons, and they were total snobs.

For a fleeting moment, remembering how Melina Remington used to look down her nose at the other girls, Jen almost wishes her mother would hire Sissy to clean their house after all.

But it's not like Melina Remington would ever know about it.

And anyway, doing stuff around the house keeps Mom busy. The busier she is, the less time she has to nag Jen.

This time, Jen doesn't run toward home. She's hoping that if she walks slowly enough, her mother and brothers will get home before she does.

That doesn't happen.

Jen turns on every light in the house as she goes, looking behind doors, inside closets, and under every bed . . . just to be sure.

To be sure what? she asks herself, returning to the living room and looking out onto the deserted street.

To be sure she's alone in the house?

Why wouldn't she be?

Who does she think she's going to find hiding in some dark corner, a crazed killer?

No.

Of course not.

Still, she stays close to the window — and the front door, her potential escape route — and she doesn't breathe easily until she sees the SUV's bright headlights turning into the driveway.

"Way to go, Jen! *Woo hoo!*" Blinking into the October morning sunlight, Kathleen waves a victorious fist in the general direction of her daughter on the soccer field.

"Mom!" Curran, sprawled on the ground before her nylon folding spectator chair, is clearly mortified. "Can't you keep it down? Geez!"

"Your sister scored again. I'm proud of her." Green eyes glinting with mischief,

Kathleen shouts another *"woo hoo"* for good measure, and grins when Curran cringes. He moves a few more feet forward to a new patch of grass and resumes pretending he doesn't know her.

Seated beside Kathleen in an identical folding chair, Maeve Hudson laughs. She pushes her designer sunglasses up to rest above her dark bangs and leans closer. "What are you going to do when he's starting quarterback on the high school football team? Show up with pompons and a bullhorn so you can really embarrass him?"

"Football? Curran?" Kathleen shakes her head, her auburn ponytail brushing against her fleece collar. She jerks it away, feeling it crackle. Static. Ugh. Static gives her chills. So does the ragged fingernail that's just snagged a strand of hair.

Her nails need filing; her hair needs trimming. Kathleen sighs inwardly. Some days, she's tempted to have it cut short, the way she wore it as a teenager. Short hair would be so much easier.

But Matt likes it long on her. On Jen, too.

Her daughter's blond hair had been neatly bound into a single braid when they left the house an hour ago. Now, long strands have worked their way loose, streaming behind Jen as she runs, falling into her wide-set brown eyes when she stops, causing her to distractedly shove impatient fingers through the deviant tresses.

Amazing how Jen can be such a tomboy on the field, then turn around and spend an hour in the bathroom putting on makeup and primping when people — namely her mother — are waiting to take showers.

Not only that, but Kathleen is fairly certain Jen has been going through her drawers again after several warnings not to borrow her mother's clothes without asking. Kathleen had noticed a faint ketchup stain on the collar of her favorite yellow sweater when she took it out to wear it this morning.

"Matt played football, right?" Maeve is asking.

Kathleen's gaze shifts from her daughter to her strapping husband, jogging down the field after the girls and the ball with a coach's whistle in his mouth.

Yes, Matt played football. Baseball and basketball, too. He's got two cartons full of trophies in the basement to prove it. They lined the shelves of his den in the old house, but so far, Kathleen hasn't found a place for them here. The family room off the kitchen is too cluttered as it is, between the television with its Playstation, DVD player, computer desk, and stereo — along with all of the games, disks, and CDs that go along with all that technology.

"Matt played football," she tells Maeve, "but Curran takes after my side of the family. He's built like a Gallagher."

The way things look now, wiry Curran doesn't have a chance of approaching his father's six-foot-three height or broad-shouldered build. Kathleen shudders just imagining her elfin son collapsing beneath a heap of brawny athletes.

Maeve sips from her paper coffee cup and comments, "So I guess Jen and Riley got Curran's share of Carmody blood."

Avoiding the comment, Kathleen focuses on her younger son, rolling pell-mell down a low hill several yards away. "Look at that kid. He's going to be covered with grass stains and I'm all out of Oxy Clean again. And if he survives childhood without broken bones, he's the one who's going to be the star athlete of the family."

"He looks just like Matt," Maeve says. "Acts like him, too."

Yes, Riley, with his dark curls and full throttle personality, is certainly the image of his father. And Jen . . .

Well, Jen doesn't look a bit like Matt. But she's the apple of his eye, nonetheless.

"So was that Jen's second goal this game?" asks Maeve, who missed the early part of the game, having made her ritualistic morning detour to Starbucks.

"Her third."

"Her third? Geez, what are you feeding her for breakfast?"

Kathleen can't quite keep from beaming as she turns her attention back to the field, where the pack of long-legged girls, knees bared above their soccer socks and shin guards, race down the green field beneath a piercing blue sky. There's a hint of wood smoke in the air, mingling with the sweet musk of damp earth and fallen leaves.

That's odd, Kathleen thinks, staring out across the field into the late morning glare.

Somebody is watching the game from the opposite end of the field, far from the rest of the spectators. Standing on the very edge of the clearing against a backdrop of peak foliage, he looks as though he might have just stepped out of the thatch of woods that border the park.

Or is he a *she?* The figure is draped in a long garment of some sort, making it impossible to discern gender from this distance.

There's a chill autumn wind blowing off the eastern Great Lakes, but an overcoat would be out of place in this crowd of fleece and sweatshirted, jean-clad families. Then again, so would a dress or skirt.

Her skin prickling with inexplicable apprehension, Kathleen squints into the sun, wishing she hadn't left her sunglasses on the dashboard of the Explorer in the parking lot.

The fact that somebody is standing on the "wrong" end of the field — and wearing a long coat or dress — is no reason to be suspicious.

"Way to go, Jen!" Maeve hollers as Kathleen's daughter barrels down the field toward them, expertly kicking the ball in front of her.

"All right, Jen!" Momentarily forgetting the oddly dressed stranger, Kathleen shrieks as her daughter approaches the goal again. She puts two fingers between her lips and whistles. "Come on, Jen!"

Curran flashes a glare over his shoulder. She ignores him, watching her long-legged daughter jab the ball with her right cleat. It sails into the air . . . only to be stopped by the other team's goalie.

"Almost." Maeve sighs. "I wish Erin were as into the game as Jen is. Look at her. It's like she can't wait for it to be over so that she can go home and crawl back into bed."

Kathleen watches Maeve's pretty blond

daughter trying to conceal a yawn behind a manicured hand. "She takes after her mom," she says with a laugh.

"Yeah, without the caffeine habit," Maeve agrees, lowering her sunglasses again. "Not that I wasn't tempted to give her a shot of espresso this morning to get her out of bed. You'd have thought I was torturing her. She's the one who insisted on playing soccer, but you'd think it was my idea for us to be out here in the cold at this god-awful hour on the only morning of the week I can sleep past nine."

Kathleen nods, but the hour is hardly god-awful, and she has little genuine sympathy for Maeve, whose existence seems as stress-free as a single mom's life can possibly be.

Maeve's ex is a dentist; her two-year-old four-bedroom Colonial and two-year-old Lexus are entirely paid for; she doesn't have to work, thanks to her hefty alimony and the child support she gets for Erin.

The girls take off down the field again, chasing the ball toward the opposite goal.

With an uneasy twinge, Kathleen glances back toward the trees, about to point out the lone spectator to Maeve.

The spot by the woods is empty.

Startled, she scans the perimeter of the

field, expecting to see someone striding away, coat or dress flapping about their legs in the gusting wind.

But there is no sign anywhere of the person she saw earlier. It's as though he — or she — has been swallowed by the dense woods once again.

A chill slithers down Kathleen's spine, and this time it has nothing to do with static electricity or ragged fingernails.

Naturally, the moment Lucy stops pacing the floor to perch on the edge of a hard-backed kitchen chair, the phone rings.

Heart pounding wildly, she leaps to her feet again and hurries across the worn linoleum, snatching up the receiver before it can ring again. Henry's working the night shift this week, asleep in the bedroom upstairs.

Lifting the receiver, she utters a hurried, hushed, "Hello?" and holds her breath, waiting.

The male voice is familiar, uttering a mere two words. But they're the two words she was half-hoping, half-dreading, she'd hear.

"It's her."

TWO

"So did you see him at the edge of the field again this morning, Jen?" Erin asks, flopping her long-limbed self on Jen's rumpled bed and unzipping the cosmetics case she brought with her.

"Did I see who?"

"That creepy guy we saw lurking around last weekend before the game, near the woods. I think he's some kind of religious freak. He's all huddled in some kind of long robe."

"I never saw a guy lurking last week," Jen points out, looking up from the manicure she's giving herself. "You and Amber were the only ones who saw him — or *thought* you saw him."

"We definitely saw him last week. And he was there again today. I think he's some kind of pedophile or serial killer. I bet he got that girl April."

April. The girl who ran away from the apartment complex back when school started. Jen didn't know her. Erin didn't

43

either, but she said she was trashy.

"I thought you said that girl April ran away," Jen points out.

"That's what my mother told me, but I don't believe her. I bet that creepy guy kidnapped her and raped her and killed her."

"I think you've been watching too many episodes of *CSI*," Jen tells her friend.

"It's not just me. Amber and Rachel saw him lurking today, too."

Lurking. It's such a dramatic word. Jen rolls her eyes.

Then she remembers something.

"Just because he was hanging around the soccer field doesn't mean he's some psycho stalker." Jen's voice is steady but the brush trembles slightly in her right hand, smearing wet red nail polish over the cuticle of her left thumb.

A few days ago, when she was leaving her after school babysitting job at the Gattinskis' home, she could have sworn she was being followed.

It was probably just her imagination.

Or maybe not.

Either way, the boogeyman didn't get her.

Not that time, anyway.

Maybe she was just lucky because the ladybug had landed on her arm just before that. Ladybugs are good luck. Mom always says that.

"Too bad you have to babysit tonight, Jen," Erin is saying as she files her own nails. "Me and Rachel are going to see *He Calls at Midnight*. It's supposed to be really good."

"My mom wouldn't let me go even if I didn't have to babysit," Jen points out. "It's rated R."

Erin tosses her long blond hair. "You want me to tell my mom to talk to her? Maybe she can get her to stop being so over-protective. My mom thinks your mom's kind of ridiculous."

Jen frowns down at the nail on her index finger as she paints it red, bothered, for some reason, by Erin's comment.

Not that it isn't true. Jen's mom doesn't let her do a lot of things the other kids are allowed to do. She won't even let her have a cell phone, which everyone else has, or a pager. She won't even agree to getting call waiting so that Jen can talk on the phone with her friends without her parents nagging her that they might be missing calls.

Nor will Mom let Jen get her own computer. She has to use the one in the family room, and it feels like somebody is always looming over her shoulder, especially when she's trying to IM with her friends.

Even worse, Jen's parents insist on kissing her goodbye whenever she leaves, even if she's just going to school or off babysitting.

It's frustrating, not to mention embarrassing. Especially being relatively new in town. The last thing she wants is for the other kids to think she's some kind of sheltered loser.

Still, Jen doesn't like the thought of Erin's mother talking about Mom behind her back that way — even if it's on Jen's behalf. Mrs. Hudson is one of Mom's best friends. They grew up together and went to Saint Brigid's all girls Catholic school together, then lost touch after graduation.

But as soon as the Carmodys moved to the Buffalo area last spring, Mom and Mrs. Hudson took up where they left off when they were kids. Which was lucky for Jen, because she found a built-in new best friend in Erin Hudson, one of the most popular girls in the ninth grade.

It was Erin who introduced her around, and Erin who got the coach to bend some rules and let Jen try out for the town's dive team after the registration deadline last spring.

But Jen won the MVP medal entirely on her own. She was even on *Eyewitness News*

— only for a few seconds, but a camera crew and reporter were there, covering the regional meet. It must have been a slow news day in Buffalo.

"Jen?" Erin prods. "You want my mom to —"

"No, don't say anything to your mom." Jen dips the brush back into the bottle of polish. "I'm totally used to my mother. And anyway, she's not going to change. She says she wants to keep me from making the kinds of mistakes she made when she was a kid. She said nobody ever cared where she went or when she got home."

"Lucky her," Erin mutters.

"Oh, like you've got it so tough." Jen shakes her head. "Your mom lets you do whatever you want."

"She won't let me go out with Robby."

"Well, duh. That's because he's a delinquent."

"He is not!"

"He does drugs."

"Not drugs. Weed. And everyone smokes it, so —"

"*I* don't. *You* don't." Or does she? Sometimes, Jen gets the sense that Erin is a couple of giant steps ahead of her.

"That's different. Robby's a senior. That's, like, practically an adult. And I don't see why everyone had to make such a big deal about him getting high."

"He wasn't just getting high, Erin. He got caught selling."

Erin rolls her eyes. "Well, I don't know how my mother even found out about it. You didn't tell your mother, did you?"

"I told you I didn't." Jen shakes her head. "It was probably in the paper."

"Not his name. They don't put your name in if you're not eighteen."

"Well, it's not like people don't gossip around here. Things get around. Like, the other day, I heard . . ."

No. Jen shouldn't say that. It wouldn't be nice.

After all, she really, really likes Mrs. Gattinski. She always gives Jen extra money and makes a point to buy special snacks whenever she's babysitting.

"What?" Erin asks, a cuticle stick poised in her hand like a cigarette. "You heard what?"

"Nothing."

It's probably not even true, anyway, Jen tells herself, reaching for a cotton ball and the plastic bottle of nail polish remover to wipe away the red smear on her hand.

A red, she finds herself thinking with a shudder, that is precisely the shade of fresh blood.

"Do you think she's babysitting too much?" Matt asks as the front door closes behind Jen Saturday night as she heads out to Kurt Gattinksi's car at the curb. "She's too young."

"She'll be fourteen in a few weeks."

"That's too young. She's never home anymore."

"She was home all afternoon," Kathleen points out, looking up from the latest issue of *People*. "Riley's the one who was out at a play date."

"For that matter, I think he has too many of these play date things for a little kid."

"He's popular." Kathleen shrugs, smiling. "And like I said, Jen was home, so I don't know why you're —"

"She was home, yeah — but in her room with Erin, and the door closed."

"Teenaged girls need privacy."

"What do you think they were doing in there?"

"Their nails. Their hair."

"Is the object to look like twins? Because when I saw Jen coming around the corner earlier, I swear I thought she was Erin. She was wearing the same outfit and her hair was parted in the middle in the same exact style."

"That's what teenaged girls do, Matt," Kathleen assures him with a laugh. "They like to copy each other and try to fit in."

"So it's just about looks?"

"And gossiping about their friends. And discussing boys they like. You know . . . the usual female stuff. At least she's here where we can keep an eye on her."

Matt sighs, aiming the remote control at the television. The college football game gives way to a home improvement show.

"Remember when we used to have family game night on Saturdays last winter?"

Kathleen laughs. "We did that once. Maybe twice. And it was total chaos. Did you forget how Riley insisted on moving his own piece and knocked over the entire board? And Curran kept accusing Jen of cheating . . . you really miss that, Matt?"

"I miss having all of our kids home with us on a Saturday night. Next thing you know, Jen is going to be going out on dates. And then away at college . . ." He shakes his head, reaching down to pull the lever that reclines his leather arm chair with a jerk.

"Then she'll be married . . . having babies . . . asking us to babysit her kids on Saturday nights . . ." Kathleen licks her forefinger and turns a page. J-Lo beams up at her, wearing a low-cut beaded evening gown. Kathleen shakes her head, imagining what she herself would look like in that outfit.

This tired thirty-two-year-old body has carried three babies and has the sagging stomach muscles — and breasts — to vouch for it. It isn't that Kathleen's overweight — she wears the same size as Jen, who has taken to "borrowing" her clothes and shoes lately, much to her frustration.

But Jen is taller and longer limbed, and she looks different in Kathleen's wardrobe. Her body is taut and lean; Kathleen's is flabby. She isn't motivated to get rid of the flab at the gym, as Maeve is. Nor is she motivated to give up fat grams or calories or carbs, or whatever it is that Maeve and the others are counting these days.

Banishing J-Lo — and thoughts of dieting — with a swift turn of the page, she asks Matt, "You hungry?"

"Are you?"

She shrugs. "I could eat." A few hours ago, after a late lunch of leftover beef stew and egg noodles reheated in the microwave, she swore she wouldn't be hungry again until tomorrow. Now, however . . .

"Want me to order some Buffalo Wings?" Matt asks.

She makes a face. "If you promise to stop

calling them that. Only out of towners say Buffalo Wings. Around here, you just say —"

"Wings. Just wings. I know. Okay, I promise I'll make more of an effort to sound like a local."

"And I promise I'll get some groceries into the house and start cooking again tomorrow."

"I never said you had to cook dinner every night, Kathleen. And I keep telling you that you can hire help around the house if you want. This place is bigger than you're used to. You don't have to do all the cleaning yourself."

"I know, but I want to. I want the kids — and you — to have . . ."

She trails off. She's said it enough times for Matt to finish her thought promptly.

"What you didn't."

"Right."

"They have a mother, Kathleen," Matt points out gently.

"I know they do."

So did she, long ago.

She closes her eyes and inhales, imagining the hauntingly familiar scent of tea rose perfume wafting in the air; glimpsing a pair of green eyes, twinkling, coke-bottle-green eyes — her own eyes, set in the face of a woman who died three decades ago.

Dad has green eyes, too. A murkier, mossier shade of green, and his have never twinkled. Not, for as long as she can remember, at Kathleen; not at his grandchildren; not at the few attractive nurses at the Erasmus Home for the Aged.

The twinkle, if ever there was one in his eyes, was snuffed out on the blustery November night that a tractor trailer jackknifed into oncoming traffic on ice-slicked Transit Road.

Kathleen was in the car with her mother; buckled in the backseat on the passenger's side of the car, she was pulled from the accident without a scratch. Barely eight years old. So young; too young, really, to remember. Surely the images — flashing red lights, flames, grim-faced strange men, whirling snow against the night sky — have been conjured by her imagination. She was in shock, after all — so traumatized after witnessing her mother's death that she didn't speak for weeks.

This she knows because Aunt Maggie told her. Mom's twin sister came from Chicago after the accident. There was a wake; a funeral, too. But no open casket. Pinned behind the steering wheel, Mollie Gallagher had been incinerated when the gas tank exploded as rescuers worked to free her.

Burned alive, fully conscious, Kathleen later found out. By the grace of God, she doesn't remember.

Aunt Maggie claims she wanted to bring Kathleen back to Chicago with her. But Dad wouldn't allow it. Dad, a middle-aged steelworker, insisted that Kathleen stay with him. Why, she'll never understand. As the years unfolded, he rarely looked at her, rarely spoke to her.

"It's because you're the image of your mother, Katie," Aunt Maggie would say in her faint brogue on the rare occasions Dad allowed her to visit. "It hurts him to see all he lost every time he looks at you."

Then why wouldn't he let me go? Why wouldn't he let me live with Aunt Maggie and Uncle Geoff and the cousins?

That she could have been raised in a loving home with four children, hugs, and laughter still stings after all these years. A home where somebody tucked you in at night when you were little — and cared what time you came in at night when you were older.

If Dad had let her go, so much would have been different.

But if things were different, she wouldn't have Jen.

"So . . . wings?" Matt asks, his recliner

squeaking as he raises it to the upright position again.

"With extra blue cheese," she tells him, smiling as he walks into the kitchen.

I'm so lucky. Lucky to have him, and the kids, and this house. Kathleen looks around the cozy family room, which she spent two hours cleaning this afternoon. She admires the burgundy leather sofa and chairs, the butter-colored rug with fresh vacuum marks in it, the creamy, textured beige walls she painted herself using a rag technique she saw on one of those cable decorating shows.

Maeve laughed when she popped over that day and found Kathleen on her hands and knees, covered in paint.

"You can hire somebody to do that, you know."

"I don't want to. It's fun."

Fun, for Maeve, involves salons and personal trainers.

She's always trying to get Kathleen to pamper herself more. Lately, she's been telling her that she needs to hire a housekeeper, though Kathleen protests that she finds cleaning therapeutic.

"That alone is evidence that you need therapy," Maeve declared.

Somehow, though, they're friends. Still friends, or friends again, depending on how you look at it. There were a few years when Kathleen lost track of her, along with everyone else from her old life in suburban Buffalo — Dad included. But you can't run away forever.

Rather, you *can* . . . but you might discover that you don't want to after all. You might conclude, when enough time and distance have buried the old hurts, and your husband has been offered his dream job at a Fortune 500 corporation in, of all places, your hometown, that it's time to stop running.

So.

So Matt accepted the job, and here they are. And everything is fine, after all.

She doesn't face unpleasant memories on a daily basis. She's stopped worrying that somebody is going to look at her and *know*.

What about Jen?

What if somebody —

But that's ridiculous. That can't happen. It won't happen. Nobody could possibly . . .

She frowns then, unsettled by the sudden memory of this morning's soccer match, and the person she saw — or thought she saw — standing on the edge of the field.

"Want another white wine?"

Stella glances at her husband, then at the

half-full glass in her hand, and the empty one in his.

She contemplates a playful wink, but settles on a suggestive grin. "Are you trying to get me drunk so you can have your way with me later?"

"Christ, Stella, what kind of thing is that to say?" Kurt's brown eyes are not amused. He looks over one suit-clad shoulder and then the other, as if he half-expects to find one of the bank's board members eavesdropping.

Embarrassed, Stella sips her wine and fights the urge to glance again at her reflection in the mirrored pillar beside them. She knows her cocktail dress won't be a size bigger and her hips won't be a size smaller than the last time she checked. Black is supposed to be slimming, and she skipped lunch so that she'd be able to get the zipper up without straining. But she can't stave off a self-conscious awareness that her dress is too snug, not to mention too dated. The other women in the banquet room — some of them bankers' and doctors' and lawyers' wives; many of them bankers, doctors, lawyers themselves — seem infinitely more slender and fashionable.

"I'm going to get another drink," Kurt says. "I'll be right back."

She refrains from telling him to go easy on the whiskey. He's already striding toward the bar.

But he has to drive them home. She can't see well enough in the dark to drive on the highway. Night blindness, Daddy used to call it.

Kurt calls it bullshit. He says that if she wears her glasses, she should be able to see just fine.

Stella sips her wine, silently cursing her husband, missing her father. It's been almost a year since Daddy's heart attack, but she still forgets sometimes that he's gone. Every moment that she remembers is a moment when she feels newly robbed. There is one less person in the world who loves her unconditionally.

But you still have Mom. And the girls. And . . . Kurt.

But Kurt doesn't love her unconditionally. Sometimes she wonders if Kurt still loves her at all.

She sips more wine, her eyes searching the three-deep crowd in front of the bar. Kurt is waiting for his drink, chatting animatedly with an older couple. His pale hair is receding at the temples and he, too, has put on a few pounds in the past few years, but he's still handsome. Back when she met him, she thought he looked like a Nordic ski instructor: tall, blond, gorgeous.

The same flattering adjectives could have described Stella, back then.

And they still do. You're still tall, still blond, still . . .

No. She's not gorgeous by any stretch of the imagination. These days, other adjectives crop up whenever she glimpses her reflection. Less flattering adjectives: dumpy, flabby, faded, weary.

No wonder Kurt doesn't want to get her tipsy and have his way with her. No wonder she caught him eyeing their beautiful teenaged babysitter tonight with more interest than he's shown his wife in years.

Caught up in her lousy self-image, it takes Stella a moment to realize that the faint sound of a ringing cell phone is coming from her black beaded evening bag. She hurriedly snaps the purse open, fumbling inside. The cap has come off the lipstick she tucked in earlier, and the hand that emerges with the cell phone is streaked in red. Lovely.

"Hello?" She must have dropped her cocktail napkin. Damn. There's no place to wipe her hand.

"Mrs. Gattinski?"

It's Jen. The connection is underscored

by static, but the sitter's voice is unmistakable, higher-pitched than usual. It sends a ripple of alarm through Stella.

"Jen? Is everything okay?"

The line goes dead.

"Want extra celery, too?" Matt asks, poking his head back into the family room, cordless phone in hand.

Kathleen nods. "And extra blue cheese, too."

"I know. You told me."

"Did I tell you to get mild this time? The mediums were too hot."

"No, but I will. Anything else I can do for you, your highness?"

Kathleen grins. "I'm sure I can think of something."

He raises a suggestive eyebrow. "Really?"

"Really. Don't look so surprised."

"Well, it's been a long time."

"Something tells me we're not talking about wings anymore," she says with a laugh.

"Pretty sharp there, aren't you?"

"Oh, I try."

Yes, and she also *tries* not to fall into bed too exhausted for anything but sleep every night. Not that he seems to mind that their once torrid love life has cooled to an occasional, fleeting fifteen minutes in each other's arms. It's not as though he's pulling out all stops to seduce her, either.

We're becoming middle aged and boring, she frequently wants to tell him. But if she acknowledges it, she — or he — will probably feel compelled to do something about it. And frankly, most of the time she's just too tired to care.

Footsteps pound overhead. "Mommy!" Riley bellows from the upstairs hallway. "He shoved me in the closet again."

Kathleen eyes Matt. "How about if I call for the wings and you handle that?"

"Too late. I already dialed." He holds up the phone, retreating toward the kitchen.

"Liar. You don't even know the number off the top of your head." She sticks out her tongue at him.

There's a thud overhead, followed by another shrieked "Mommy!"

"I'm coming." She starts up the stairs with a sigh, stepping around the heaping basket of folded laundry at the bottom. She'll put it away later; she's had it with housework today.

She's halfway to the second floor when the phone rings.

Kathleen rolls her eyes and grins, muttering, "I knew you were a liar . . ."

"Mom!" Curran is grunting from somewhere above. "Get him *off* of me!"

Moments later, she's on her knees prying her scuffling sons apart when she hears Matt's hurried footsteps and keys jangling below. He calls something up to her, his voice sounding oddly urgent.

"Shh!" Kathleen admonishes the boys. "Matt! I didn't hear you. What?"

Too late. Downstairs, the front door slams.

Kathleen's heart begins to pound. "Curran — Riley — did either of you hear Daddy?"

Her youngest shakes his head, still intent on poking his brother.

Squirming, Curran says, "Cut it out, Riley!" then, to her, "I think he said something about Jen."

Kathleen leaves the boys and hurries to the window in the front bedroom, just in time to see her husband take off down the street. Where on earth would Matt be going on foot?

The Gattinskis' house on the next block.

That was Jen on the phone.

Something is wrong over there.

Each piece of the puzzle seems to fall into place with a heavy thud, stirring billows of worry within. Her eyes fastened to her husband's retreating figure out the window, Kathleen attempts to quell the uneasiness.

Maybe the toilet is overflowing, or . . . or . . .

Maybe Jen can't get a jar of peanut butter open, or —

Matt is running now. Sprinting, as if his life — or God help her, Jen's — depends on it.

The trouble with events like this, Maeve decides, sipping her pleasantly chilled Pinot Grigio, is that she's bound to run into Gregory. As a prominent local dentist, her ex is always invited to these Chamber of Commerce affairs.

In the old days, Maeve reluctantly accompanied him, knowing they'd both drink too much, flirt too much, and wind up in a shrill argument on the way home.

"How is your wine?"

"It's wonderful." She smiles absently at her escort — Mo, as he likes to be called. His full name is Mohammed and she can't begin to pronounce his last name, but that isn't important. What matters, in Maeve's opinion, is the M.D. that comes after it. And that the exotically handsome Mo is better looking, and wealthier, than Gregory.

As Mo carries on a boring conversation

with a couple of boring businessmen, Maeve expertly feigns interest while scanning the crowded banquet room for her ex. Either Gregory isn't here yet, or he's not coming at all.

There are, however, several recognizable faces in the well-heeled throng: a few couples from the neighborhood, and one or two women she's seen at Pilates classes at the gym.

Maeve's eyes narrow in fascination as she spots Kurt and Stella Gattinski. She's met them once or twice since they moved into the development. The husband is charming; the wife could stand to lose a few pounds. At the moment, they appear to be in the midst of an argument. He seems irked and is obviously conscious of the spectacle they're making; she looks distraught and clearly doesn't give a damn who sees or hears them.

After a moment, Stella Gattinski spins away from her husband and strides toward the coat room.

Maeve watches Kurt shrug and turn back to the bar.

Trouble in paradise, hmm?

So what else is new? Is *anybody* happily married anymore?

Okay, Katie — er, *Kathleen* — and Matt

seem to be, she admits to herself, while nodding in blind agreement with whatever the hell Mo is saying.

She finds herself wondering what her old friend did right . . . and how on earth she managed to land Matt Carmody. There was a time when Maeve would have sworn that Kathleen was destined to wind up homeless — or dead. In fact, during the years when they lost touch, she was certain Kathleen had fallen off the face of the earth.

Then she heard that her old friend was back in town — more specifically, in Maeve's upscale suburb, as opposed to the blue-collar enclave a few miles away, where they'd both grown up. She was stunned to discover that Kathleen had a charming husband and three beautiful children in tow: the proverbial Phoenix risen from the ashes of a traumatic life.

There was no hint of the moody recluse Kathleen became in those years after high school. No, these days, she sounds like the same old Katie — aside from a few oddly skittish moments. She certainly isn't fond of discussing what happened to her before — and after — she left town.

Or rather, *disappeared*.

For that's how Maeve has always thought of her friend's departure from the sheltered world where they grew up.

One moment, Kathleen was there — on the fringes of Maeve's world, and running around with a crowd of losers, but *there* — and the next, she was, quite simply, *gone*.

Maeve knows why. She'd have figured it out even if she hadn't heard through the grapevine that people had seen Kathleen and she was obviously pregnant. Their daughters are about the same age: Erin a mere six months older than Jen. But Maeve was married to her high school sweetheart when she had Erin. Hastily married, yes — too hastily, and too young, and not permanently — but married, just the same.

Kathleen wasn't at the wedding. Though they had grown apart, Maeve sent an invitation to her father's address. Kathleen never RSVP'd. When she returned from her honeymoon, Maeve heard that Kathleen was pregnant and her father had sent her away when he found out. That wasn't surprising. Drew Gallagher was stern, old-fashioned, extremely religious. The last thing he'd endure was having a pregnant, unmarried daughter under his roof.

Maeve's parents weren't thrilled, either. But Gregory was almost finished with dental school at the time. He had an engagement ring on her finger before they told a soul she was expecting.

She's always wondered about the circumstances of Jen's birth. She assumes Kathleen met Matt while she was visiting her Aunt Maggie in Chicago as she did every Christmas; that she had gone back to the Midwest when her father sent her away. Presumably, Matt married her before the baby was born.

But she isn't sure about any of it. Nice Catholic girls like Maeve and Kathleen didn't talk about things like that back then. She doubts she'd have known the whole story even if their friendship hadn't drifted.

Still, you'd think Kathleen would be over it now. You'd think she'd be willing to talk about what happened to her back then with her newly discovered best friend.

Well, she doesn't. Every time Maeve tries to bring it up, Kathleen changes the subject.

Then again, does Maeve really need to know the details? She has other concerns.

Like whether Mo will want to sleep with her tonight when he drives her home. Erin is spending the night at Rachel's, so Maeve can't use her daughter's presence as an excuse.

It's not that she isn't attracted to Mo. It's just that he's *old*. Past fifty, if she had to guess. A far cry from the twentysomething personal trainer she was sleeping with last month. The trouble with younger men is cash flow; the problem with older men is . . . well, they're old.

Maeve again finds herself envying Kathleen's marriage. Matt Carmody is the perfect husband, the perfect father, the perfect man. If he weren't spoken for, Maeve would have no qualms about going after him herself.

Actually, if his wife were anyone other than Kathleen, she might consider it anyway.

Then again, back in the old days at Saint Brigid's, when Gregory was attending the all boys' brother school, she seems to recall Kathleen acting awfully flirtatious around him at times, and vice versa. At one point, Maeve actually confronted him and demanded to know whether he was fooling around with her best friend behind her back. Of course he denied it.

She didn't even bother to ask Kathleen, who had the sweet, innocent act perfected back then. Maeve figured she wouldn't admit to ever feeling a flicker of lust for the opposite sex, let alone for Maeve's boyfriend.

But now that they're all grown up, Maeve won't deny — at least, not to herself — that she occasionally feels more than a flicker of lust for Kathleen's husband. Hell, there are times when she sees Matt Carmody and a whole roaring inferno seems to ignite inside of her.

A delicious, forbidden fantasy slips into her mind: Maeve letting herself into Kathleen's empty house with the spare key her friend gave her, then waiting, naked in the master bedroom for Matt to come home . . .

But it's a fantasy, nothing more. She'd never hurt Kathleen, despite whatever may or may not have happened back in high school. And she suspects that Matt wouldn't hurt her, either.

The perfect man.

What on earth, she wonders again, did Kathleen do right?

Frantic, Kathleen pulls up in front of the Gattinskis' house, the SUV's brakes squealing when she jams on brakes.

"Just like the Batmobile," Riley says approvingly from the backseat.

"Stay in the car, both of you." Kathleen jumps out and hurries toward the two-story Colonial that, aside from the white siding, red trim, shutters, and front door, is a cookie-cutter duplicate of their own.

The place is lit up, inside and out, but there are no signs of flames or broken-down doors. Reassured, Kathleen tries the front door and finds it locked. The arched window is too high for her to see through.

"Jen?" she calls, knocking. "Matt?"

Footsteps tap across the floor inside. She finds herself staring at her husband as the door is thrown open.

"What's going on?" They say it in unison.

Jen appears in the background, holding hands with the miniature Gattinski twins.

Okay, so everyone's in one piece. Good. That's good.

Breathing more easily than she has since she glimpsed her husband tearing off down the street on foot, Kathleen asks again, "What's going on, Matt?"

"Jen called. She said —"

"Dad . . . shhh!" Jen motions at the children. "Girls, can you go change the Barbies into their dresses for the party? I'll be right there."

"My Barbie isn't going to wear a dress," one of the twins protests. "She's wearing pants."

"She can't wear pants!" her sister challenges. "It's a fancy party."

"They're fancy pants."

"Will somebody please tell me what's

going on?" Kathleen asks for the third time, losing patience.

"Dad will tell you. I'll be right back." Jen hustles the bickering twins out of the room.

In a low voice, Matt tells Kathleen, "She called me because she thought she saw somebody sneaking around outside the house."

"*What?*"

"I checked outside and I didn't see anything unusual, but she was really scared." He shakes his head. "Do we even know these people?"

"The Gattinskis? I know Stella."

"Well, I've never met her *or* her husband. For all we know, he could be in the mob or hooked up into something —"

"Listen to yourself, Matt. That's ridiculous."

"How do you know? Have you met him?"

"No," she admits.

"So we've been letting her spend all this time in a total stranger's house. Terrific. I *knew* she was too young to be babysitting."

"She's fourteen, Matt."

"Not for a few weeks. She still sleeps with her closet light on, Kathleen. She's got an active imagination, and —"

"Maybe there really was somebody sneaking around outside." She glances through the open front door at the SUV parked at the foot of the driveway, motor running. She had left the boys there without a second thought.

Seized by a disconcerting vision of the sinister prowler car jacking the Tahoe with the boys in it, she tells Matt, "I've got the boys out there waiting. I'll go get them and —"

"Don't do that. Just take them back home. I've got everything under control here, Kathleen."

"You called the police?"

"The police? No. I checked —"

"You didn't call the police?" She opens her mouth to tell him about the person she thought she had glimpsed on the soccer field today, but Jen is back, alone this time.

"Did Dad tell you?" she asks Kathleen.

"He told me. Why were you looking out the windows in the first place, Jen? Did you hear something outside?"

"No. I had gone into the living room to grab a video for the twins and I didn't turn the light on. The shades were up. I happened to glance out the window and I thought I saw someone standing by the bushes outside, watching the house."

"You thought you saw, or you saw?" Kathleen asks, keeping an anxious eye on the boys in the car.

Jen is hesitant. "I don't know. I'm pretty sure I saw someone. I turned on the light right away — I don't know why, because when I did that, I couldn't see out the window anymore. And when I turned it off again, whoever I thought I saw was gone. I didn't know what to do — I guess I freaked out a little. I started thinking about that girl, April —"

April? Kathleen frowns. Who's April?

"— and I called Dad," Jen finishes ruefully.

"I'm glad you did." Matt pats her arm. "I think it was just a trick of the light, or a low branch hanging down from that tree by the bushes. But I'll stay here with you until the Gattinskis get home."

Oh, April. That's right. The girl who ran away from the apartment complex down the road late last summer. Kathleen vaguely remembers hearing she turned up in California with her father.

Or did she?

Things are different here than they were back in Indiana. There, the neighborhood was so tightly knit that they knew everybody, and everybody knew them. Families, including Matt's, went back generations.

Here in Orchard Hollow, you can live a

stone's throw from somebody and still be strangers.

She opens her mouth to ask whether April did turn up in California, but Jen cuts her off, addressing Matt.

"You don't have to stay until the Gattinskis get home, Dad. They should be here in like, fifteen minutes. I'll be okay with the girls until then."

"Fifteen minutes?" Kathleen asks. "I thought they were out for the night."

"They were. I called Mrs. Gattinski on her cell phone. I was pretty freaked out, and she said to call in an emergency. I figured it was an emergency if somebody was creeping around the house. I didn't know what else to do." Jen looks increasingly embarrassed. "I just kept thinking —"

"About the girl who ran away? Do you know something I don't about that, Jen?" Kathleen asks.

Jen shrugs. "Erin thinks she got murdered."

"I thought they found her in California."

"Did they?"

"I don't know." Again, Kathleen considers how different the neighborhood is. Here her daughter is babysitting for virtual strangers and scared out of her mind. "You did the right thing calling the Gattinskis and

Dad, Jen. What did Mrs. Gattinski say?"

"We had a bad connection the first time I called and I got cut off, but she called me right back. She was really worried. She said they'll be home right away. You don't think they won't want me to babysit again, do you, Mom? What if they think I'm some wimp?"

"You're not a wimp," Kathleen firmly tells her daughter. She looks at Matt, wishing he were taking this more seriously, wishing she had told him about the soccer field.

But what did you see, really? Just a bystander watching the game.

Did April really turn up safe in California? Or did something horrible happen to her?

Darn Kathleen's imagination for conjuring a sinister stranger preying on young girls. But in this scary world, that's probably the fate of every mother of a teenaged daughter: feeling as though somebody is going to come along and snatch your precious child away.

Yes, surely other mothers feel that way.

Surely, when other mothers kiss their daughters goodbye, they secretly wonder if it might be for the last time.

But it's different for me, Kathleen tells herself grimly, looking at her beloved Jen. *I've*

been living with that fear for too, too long —
and it's been growing with every day that
passes.

We never should have moved back here. I
should have talked Matt out of taking the job. I
should've . . .

What?

Told him the truth?

She looks from her daughter to her husband. Both are unsuspecting. Both would be shattered if they knew . . .

No.

No, they'll never know. She's come this far without telling, and she'll carry her secret to her grave, just as she vowed on the day that began as the most tragic — and wound up the most blessed — day of her life.

THREE

Jen has never liked Mondays.

There's the whole thing about being extra tired Monday mornings because you slept in on Sunday morning and couldn't get to sleep Sunday night.

Plus the cafeteria always serves spaghetti on Mondays. Jen can't get the sandwich choice because it's always premade with mayonnaise, which is off limits due to her egg allergy. And she likes spaghetti, but the school's cook makes the sauce too garlicky. She sits next to Garth Monroe in biology lab right after lunch. He's cute — really cute — and the last thing she wants to do is breathe garlic fumes in his face.

And then there's the choir thing.

On Mondays, Jen has choir instead of gym. Back in Indiana, the school choir was made up of a select group of students, and they rehearsed while the others were in study hall. Here, choir is mandatory. Which would be fine — if you weren't one of the students who's been instructed to just move their lips during the upcoming fall concert. Jen has never been able to carry a tune.

So basically, Mondays suck.

Today was better than usual, though. Instead of making them sing during choir class, Mrs. Tylerson had them do worksheets on classical music while they listened to some opera. And Garth was absent, so her garlic breath didn't matter nearly as much as usual. It's just too bad she wasted her favorite pair of jeans and form-fitting black sweater on a day when he's not even here.

Now, as Jen heads to her locker to get her jacket and her backpack, she glances at the homework assignment her biology teacher just handed out. It's filled with little four-box grids that need to be filled in. Boring, boring. They're studying dominant and recessive genes. But that, she supposes, is better than the big reproduction unit that's looming. How will she ever get through *that* with Garth sitting only a few inches from her? Talk about embarrassing . . .

"Hey Jen!"

She turns to see Erin hurrying toward her, Amber Korth at her side.

"Hi, guys. What's up?"

"Robby said he'll drop us at the Galleria for a few hours and come back and pick us up at five-thirty," Erin says, falling into step with Jen, twirling a strand of her long blond hair around her fingertip. "There's a sale at Abercrombie. Want to come?"

"I can't."

"Why not?" Erin asks.

"Why not?" Amber echoes.

"I just can't."

"Her mother," Erin informs Amber, as though Jen hasn't spoken. "She doesn't want her hanging around with juvenile delinquents."

"That's so — I mean, God! We're not juvenile delinquents, Jen."

"I know you're not, Amber. And so does my mother. It's just . . ."

"Robby."

Erin's voice is flat, and so is Jen's when she replies.

"Right. Robby. My mother would kill me if she found out I'd been riding around with him. And so would your mother, Erin. She'd be so pissed."

"My mother *so* isn't going to find out, Jen. Is she?"

There's something almost . . . *ominous* in her friend's tone. Jen looks up to see that Erin's eyes aren't as warm as they were a few seconds ago.

Hurt, she says softly, "You know I

wouldn't tell your mother, Erin."

"But are you going to tell *your* mother? Because guaranteed if you do she'll tell mine."

"Geez." Amber shakes her head. "Why'd you even want to ask her to come with us, Erin? If my mother finds out —"

"Nobody's mother is going to find out anything. Right, Jen?"

Undigested spaghetti is churning in Jen's gut. She forces herself to look Erin in the eye. "I'm not saying a word to anybody."

"Good." Erin softens her tone. "I just . . . when I saw you I thought I'd ask because I figured maybe you felt like doing something fun for a change, Jen. I mean, I feel so sorry for you. All you ever do is go to school and play soccer and babysit. You never get to go anywhere or do anything."

"Yes I do."

"Oh, right. You forgot, Erin. Church. She goes to church with her family on Sunday mornings." Amber giggles.

"Cut it out, Amber." Erin flashes a sympathetic look at Jen.

Grateful they've reached her locker, Jen turns her back and works the combination with her right hand, clutching her books against her pounding heart with her left. Suddenly, she feels like crying.

"See you tomorrow, Jen," Erin says, behind her.

"See you tomorrow," Amber the trained parrot echoes.

"See you," Jen manages.

She opens her locker, blindly shoving her books into the backpack hanging on a hook. Oblivious to the din around her, she wishes they'd never moved here. Back in Indiana, she had plenty of friends. Friends who had known her — and her family — their whole lives. Friends whose parents were as over-protective as Jen's.

No they weren't, she contradicts herself. Not all of them. Nobody else had to be home by nine o'clock on a weekend night in Indiana, either. And almost everybody got to go to the Dave Matthews concert in Chicago last February. Everybody but Jen.

Her mother wasn't swayed by the fact that Dana Markowitz's parents were driving them into the city and staying for the concert.

Erin's words echo in her head. *I feel so sorry for you.*

Suddenly, Jen feels sorry for herself, too.

You never get to go anywhere or do anything.

Anger seeps in. Anger at her mother, and at herself, for allowing her mother to shelter her to the point where people are making fun of her.

Jen grabs her backpack and her barn coat, then slams the locker shut and looks around. Erin and Amber have stopped at Erin's locker at the end of the corridor.

Jen's sneakers carry her in that direction even as her mind wrestles with temptation. When she arrives at Erin's locker, she steps out of character long enough to say, "Is it too late to change my mind and tag along?" before wondering what the hell she's getting herself into.

Carrying a stack of still-warm-from-the-dryer jeans, Kathleen opens the bottom drawer of her dresser, then pauses in dismay.

The thing about getting caught up on laundry is that there's not enough storage space for clean clothes, towels, and sheets. What this house really needs, Kathleen decides, trying to jam the jeans into the already crowded drawer, is a large walk-up attic like the one in their old house. She used to be able to store off-season clothes up there in cedar-lined wardrobes. In this house, there's an attic, but it's more of a crawl-space, really, accessible only by a pull-down ladder through the ceiling in Jen's closet.

Kathleen forces the bureau drawer closed, then opens a top drawer to make room for her clean socks. It, too, is full already.

You could always clean out the clutter, she reminds herself as she rummages past several single socks whose partners vanished into clothes dryer oblivion.

Like these dressy black trouser socks — when does she ever wear them? And some of her gym socks are wearing thin at the toes. She removes several pairs from the drawer, then catches a glimpse of pink fuzz tucked into the back corner.

Kathleen's heart beats a little faster as she pulls out the familiar bundle: a hand-knit pale rose-colored blanket and a single matching baby bootee with lacy white trim. Swallowing hard over a sudden lump in her throat, she clutches the soft yarn against her cheek, remembering . . .

Until the faint, muffled sound of a ringing telephone startles her out of her reverie. She reaches for the bedside extension, only to find that the cordless receiver isn't in its cradle.

Damn it. Jen must have taken it into her room again last night to have a private conversation with one of her friends.

Frustrated, Kathleen hurries back down

into the kitchen, but by the time she reaches the phone there, it's fallen silent.

Four rings, and it goes into voice mail — that's the new system. In Indiana, they had a good old-fashioned answering machine, but that broke and Matt didn't see the sense in replacing it when they moved. Not when voice mail is so economical and convenient.

Or so he says.

Frustrated at having missed the call, Kathleen dials the voice mail access number. As she punches in her pin number, she glances at the clock. It's almost three. Curran and Riley will be getting off the bus in about five minutes, followed by Jen fifteen minutes after that.

"You have no . . . new . . . messages," a recorded voice says in staccato cadence.

Either that . . . or she dialed too soon.

Still holding the phone, Kathleen walks over to the counter, where she was mixing together a steak marinade between loads of laundry. As she throws a pinch of salt into the oil and vinegar combination in the bowl, she weighs the likelihood that the caller was her father's nursing home, calling to tell her he's run away again.

It's happened a few times lately. Somehow, her father manages to dress himself and slip out the front door. He never gets far. He's usually found by the Erasmus staff wandering in the same block, trying to find his way back to his old neighborhood and the house that was sold long ago.

"I just want to go back home, Kathleen," he says whenever she rushes over after one of those incidents. "Why can't I go home?"

The nurses have promised her — several times, now — that it won't happen again. But maybe it has.

Or maybe Drew Gallager himself was calling again?

Kathleen spoke to him less than an hour ago, and promised to visit first thing tomorrow morning — bringing the new socks and underwear he requested. That means a trip to Target on the way, unless she leaves the younger boys with Jen and runs out to the store this afternoon instead.

She bought Dad new socks and underwear right before Labor Day, when she was doing back to school shopping for the kids. She could swear she bought him some for his birthday in July, too. But when she asked him, he claimed somebody has been stealing them from his bureau.

For all she knows, he isn't just paranoid. The private Catholic nursing home isn't exactly a haven, but it's affordable.

Dad is proud of the fact that he worked

hard all his life and saved enough to take care of himself in his old age.

"You know, Katie, I never asked anyone for a penny," he likes to say, in his more lucid moments.

No, he never did. And she never asked him for a penny, either.

Sometimes, Kathleen is tempted to ask Matt if they can have Dad move in here.

Then she remembers what it was like to live under the same roof with him; remembers all the lonely, deprived years of her childhood.

She remembers *Get Out.*

Those were her father's final words to her on that awful March day; they rang bitterly in her ears as she closed the front door behind her, locked it, and pocketed the key. Not that she'd be needing it again. Drew Gallagher had made it more than clear that she — and her baby, when it was born — would not be welcome in his house.

Standing in her suburban kitchen, Katie is swept back to that day, remembering every detail, reliving it as she has so many times through the years.

She remembers the sting of the wind on her cheeks and the stink of sulfur from a nearby factory. Remembers how she raised the hood on her down parka, picked up her hastily packed suitcase, and descended the sagging front steps. How, when she reached the packed layer of recently plowed snow that marked the sidewalk, she paused.

Right or left?

Which way should she go?

Where the hell was she supposed to turn?

Aunt Maggie would have taken her in, without a doubt. But her aunt had warned her only months earlier, during Katie's annual Christmas visit to Chicago, that she was going to find herself in serious trouble if she didn't straighten out.

No, she couldn't go running to Aunt Maggie, Queen of *I Told You So.*

Who else was there?

Maeve O'Shea?

Her best friend lived only a few blocks from her father's house. However, Katie had all but ignored Maeve in the two years since they'd graduated from Saint Brigid's. The last she heard, Maeve was working at the Clinique counter at the mall and still dating her high school sweetheart, Gregory, who was in dental school — a far cry from the mess Katie had made of her own life.

She swallows hard over a lump that rises in her throat even now. The warm suburban kitchen has fallen away and she's once again standing on the street in the frigid dusk, feeling hot tears beginning to slide down her cheeks, stinging where the brisk March wind hits them.

There was nobody to turn to.

Nobody.

She was entirely alone in the world.

No. Not alone.

She remembers. She remembers what she promised the baby growing in her womb.

I'll keep you safe. I'll never let anything happen to you. To us. I'm going to be the best mommy in the world.

But how? And where? She needed help.

She remembers looking up at the sky, searching for answers there. She did that a lot when she was growing up, as though she expected to see her mother, the angel, looking down on her. But she never did. That night, she saw nothing but overcast twilight, heavy black clouds closing in over Lake Erie a few miles away. Katie instantly recognized what that meant. More lake-effect snow, rolling in quickly from the west.

She knew she couldn't stand out there on the street all night. She had to find some-place warm before the storm hit.

The answer came to her then, an answer so comforting, so *right,* that she almost dared to believe that it was actually sent from Mommy in heaven.

Wiping away her tears, Katie held her head high and turned toward the left, where the familiar steeple of Saint Brigid's rose high above the snow-covered roof tops.

Saint Brigid's is gone now.

So many things are gone.

So many things are different.

Katie has a family of her own. She's not dependent on Drew Gallagher for anything — and he's not dependent on her.

That's how it should stay, she tells herself firmly, dialing the voice mail access number again. She already has her hands full trying to keep up with the kids and the household. The last thing she needs is to move her elderly father in here.

This time, when she reaches the message center, the robotic voice drones, "You have one . . . new . . . message."

It's from Jen.

Surprised to hear her daughter's voice, Kathleen listens intently, her eyes narrowing as she realizes why Jen called.

"Mom, hi, it's me. I'm, uh, using Erin's cell phone. She and I and Amber are staying after school to get extra help in biology. Amber's mom will bring us home when we're finished. Okay? Um, that's it. Bye."

Bullshit.

Seething, Kathleen tosses the phone

aside, certain her daughter is lying.

"When is Jen coming over?"

"She's not coming today, 'Kenz, remember?" Stella tells her daughter for the tenth time in an hour. "Here, try the blue for the sky."

"I don't want to," comes the stubborn reply. Shooting her a defiant look, MacKenzie seizes a brown crayon and begins to scribble over the top third of her coloring book page, obliterating the one-dimensional outlines of clouds and a smiley-face sun.

Stella shrugs. "It's your picture."

With a groan, she pushes against the couch behind her to lift herself off the floor. She's been sitting cross-legged for so long that her knees are killing her.

I'm getting old. Old and stiff and . . . and fat.

"No! Mommy, where are you going?" Michaela protests.

"You said you'd color with us!" MacKenzie shouts.

"Well, neither of you will let me have a page to color, and I think you can both take it from here without my coaching."

"But Mommy! We need you! 'Kenzie is making her sky all dark."

"It's nighttime," MacKenzie says with a logical shrug.

"Then it should be black. Not brown. Tell her, Mommy."

"It's her picture. The sky can be brown if she wants." Stella brushes the Goldfish cracker crumbs off her jeans and glances at her watch, wondering how many hours stretch ahead between now and bedtime. Too many.

"I want Jen to come," Michaela declares.

Breaking news, she isn't.

Stifling a primal scream, Stella repeats her mantra through clenched teeth. "Not today. Jen isn't coming today."

"But Mommy —"

"Not today! Now finish coloring or I'll put the crayons away and make you . . ."

Make them what? Sit in time out? She doesn't have the patience to enforce the punishment and the squirming and whining that inevitably go with it. She doesn't have patience for much of anything today.

"I'm hungry," Michaela announces.

"I'm making dinner right now, so —"

"I'm starving," MacKenzie chimes in.

"You'll have to wait. I just said I'm making —"

"Can't we have a snack, Mommy?"

"A healthy snack."

Stella sighs. It's easier to comply than argue. "Fine," she says. "You can have an apple." God knows they have plenty of those. Kurt's mother brought them a bushel last week, suggesting that Stella make Kurt his favorite homemade strudel. She even brought the recipe, neatly copied on an index card, as a major hint.

Stella takes two apples from the crisper and hunts in a drawer until she finds the red-handled corer and a paring knife. The girls used to eat apples whole and unpeeled until her mother-in-law started babysitting. She does everything for them, just as she did everything for her son when he was young. Hell, she still coddles and waits on Kurt hand and foot, and she's made no secret of the fact that she thinks Stella should follow suit.

She holds an apple steady on a wooden cutting board and centers the corer over the stem, then pushes it down into the crisp flesh.

To think that Kurt frequently complains that the girls are spoiled rotten, implying that it's Stella's fault. If anyone is spoiled rotten, it's Kurt.

After coring, peeling, and slicing both apples into a plastic bowl, Stella plunks it down in front of the girls. Luckily, their whining tapers off fairly quickly and they go back to their coloring books, munching happily on apple slices.

Stella pads back to the kitchen in her socks, rubbing a knot in her lower back.

Other than the cutting board, the counters are spotless, and so is the sink. The entire house is, actually. Sissy was here while she was at work.

When school started again in September, Kurt finally agreed to let her get some help around the house. She knew just where to find it, having received Sissy's flyer in the mailbox, complete with neighborhood references and a special offer for 50 percent off the first few cleanings.

Kurt couldn't argue with a bargain like that, though he still grumbles about paying a cleaning lady once a week. Still, he grudgingly agrees that it's worth it. Stella was never much of a housekeeper in the first place — another sore point with her mother-in-law.

It's not even four yet, she notices on the microwave clock. The apple will hold the girls over for a while. Still, she might as well see what she can throw together for dinner. It's going to be just the three of them again tonight. Kurt told her when he left this morning that he has another late meeting.

It's just as well. Things have been chilly around here ever since Saturday night when he had to catch a ride home from the Chamber dinner with a colleague.

She can't understand why he didn't feel compelled to rush home with her after Jen called to tell them about the prowler.

Okay, so there's no evidence that there even was a prowler in the first place. Even Matt Carmody seemed to chalk it up to his daughter's imagination. Still . . .

April Lukoviak is still missing as far as Stella knows.

There was no way Stella was taking any chances with her daughters' safety, or with Jen's. And Kurt . . .

Well, Kurt just didn't seem to give a damn.

She was asleep when he showed up. She found him, still dressed, on the couch in front of the television yesterday morning. They didn't even discuss what happened Saturday night. She took the girls to church, and by the time they got back, Kurt's brother Stefan was there to watch the Bills game with him. Newly divorced and in no hurry to go back to his crummy apartment, Stefan lingered until late last night.

Not that Stella knows what she'd have said to her husband if they had the opportunity for private conversation. Certainly, there's nothing she hasn't said a hundred times before.

She removes a package of breaded chicken cutlets from the freezer and one of baby carrots from the crisper.

The bottom line is that her marriage is in trouble because Kurt's priorities are screwed up.

With a sigh, Stella dumps the carrots into a colander. This is the one vegetable the girls will eat — as long as they're steamed with plenty of butter and brown sugar.

Standing at the sink, she aims the sprayer over the carrots to wash them, telling herself that she should set half of them aside and eat them raw. Or at least, set half aside after they're steamed, before she glazes the rest.

She shouldn't be eating breaded chicken, either. She should buy plain, fresh cutlets, then bread and fry a few for the girls — and Kurt, if he's ever home for dinner again.

She should . . .

But she won't. She hasn't the energy to diet right now.

Gazing out the window into the backyard, with its sparse, newly planted shrubbery and towering wooden swing set, she tries to imagine somebody hiding there. Who on earth would do such a thing? A would-be robber? A neighborhood Peeping Tom? A serial killer?

Poor Jen. She looked more embarrassed than shaken when Stella rushed through the door on Saturday night. She kept apologizing for making her leave the dinner early.

"You did me a favor, sweetie. It wasn't any fun anyway."

"But what about Mr. Gattinski? He has to stay all by himself now."

She wasn't about to tell Jen that Mr. Gattinski probably preferred it that way.

Turning off the water and shaking the carrots in the colander, she finds herself almost wishing there really were some kind of prowler creeping around the neighborhood at night. Then maybe Kurt would be worried enough about her and the girls that he'd start spending more time at home.

She bites into a raw carrot.

Sure, she thinks wryly, munching, and maybe butter and brown sugar will be declared the next magic bullet for weight loss.

Kathleen's keys tumble from the pocket of her barn coat when she snatches it from the kitchen chair, realizing she's going to be late meeting the boys. She grabs the key ring and tosses it onto the counter, then hurries to the door. She never bothers to lock up the house when she's just going down to the bus stop at the end of the cul de sac.

As she steps out into the crisp fall afternoon, the breeze catches the door, slamming it behind her.

She wishes she'd slammed it deliberately herself. Lord knows she's in the mood to slam something.

Damn it, damn it, damn it.

Jen isn't staying after for schoolwork.

There isn't a doubt in Kathleen's mind. She knows, courtesy of pure instinct — the same maternal instinct that sent her speeding over to the Gattinskis' house Saturday night.

As she strides along the cul de sac toward a cluster of other moms, she wonders what the hell she's supposed to do now.

All her life, Jen has been trustworthy. Responsible.

As far as Kathleen knows, the only lie her daughter ever told — until now — wasn't even a verbal one. At seven, Jen scrawled Curran's name in crayon on the dining room wallpaper — clearly a hasty afterthought, as it was below a row of meticulously drawn stick people and flowers. At the time, Curran could barely scribble, much less create actual art complete with a signature.

That incident has become a family joke.

This one, Kathleen suspects, will not.

She sighs, slowing her pace as she nears the chattering neighborhood moms, envying the ones whose daughters are giggling toddlers or pink-bonneted infants safely tucked in their strollers. It will be years before they're out of their mothers' sight, free to sneak around and lie and take all the risks teenaged girls take in their growing independence.

Not *all* teenaged girls . . .

But look what happened to me.

The big yellow school bus pulls up, flashing its red lights.

As Kathleen welcomes her younger children into her arms, her hug is more fierce than usual.

"How was school, guys?"

Curran shrugs. "Fine."

"Stinky."

"Stinky? Why was it stinky?" she asks Riley.

"Somebody threw up on the rug after snack."

"Oh. That *is* stinky," she agrees, thankful that she still has a kindergartner, allowing her a moment's reprieve, whenever she needs it most, in a blessedly uncomplicated world.

"I hope you don't catch it," Curran tells his little brother.

"Catch what?"

"The throwing up thing."

"Mommy, am I going to catch it?" Riley's eyes widen with worry. "I don't want to throw up."

"You won't."

"You might," Curran tells him.

"Curran!"

"Well, he might."

Kathleen sighs, wishing Curran would leave Riley alone. There are times when he teases him unmercifully, preying on kindergarten fears of throwing up, the monster under the bed, the evil pirate in the closet.

As an only child herself, she's no expert at sibling rivalry. And Jen longed for a baby brother, so she was thrilled when Curran was born. Curran was outraged when Riley was born, usurping his position as baby of the family. He has yet to outgrow his disgruntlement.

Matt, who has three brothers, assures Kathleen that the intense jealousy is a normal reaction, especially with same-sex siblings who are five years apart.

When Riley was a newborn, Kathleen didn't dare leave him alone in a room with Curran for fear that he'd harm him. Even now, the boys inevitably end up scuffling if they spend too much time together.

"Riley, you aren't going to throw up," Kathleen tells her youngest child, ruffling his hair. "And Curran, cut it out."

"I'm just worried about him. I don't want him to get sick or anything."

"Gee, that's big of you," she says dryly.

"Hey, Riley . . ." Curran breaks into a run. "I'll race you home."

"No fair! You got a head start!"

Watching her sons scamper ahead of her, Kathleen wonders again where Jen really is.

Maybe she and Matt should have given in on the cell phone issue. After all, it would work both ways. If Jen carried a phone, Kathleen would be able to track her down any time she wants to.

A feeling of helplessness seeps in. Instinctively, she does what she was taught to do all those years ago at Saint Brigid's.

She prays.

She prays that God will bring her daughter home safely.

And she prays that He'll give her the strength to do whatever it takes to make sure it never happens again.

FOUR

Hearing the front door slam, Maeve hastily returns her half-full pack of Salem Lights to the drawer of the end table. Damn. After fighting off temptation for the past hour, she was just about to light up at last.

As far as she knows, Erin thinks she quit smoking last spring. Maeve isn't about to start smoking again in front of her. After all, her daughter is at the age when she might decide to pilfer a few cigarettes to sample.

That's how Maeve herself got hooked — about twenty years ago. You'd think seeing her own mother wasting away from lung cancer would destroy her own recent craving, but it hasn't.

"Mom?"

"In here," she calls, frowning as she notices a film of dust covering the table. Sissy was here all day yesterday. For what Maeve — ahem, *Gregory* — pays her an hour, you'd think the place would be spotless.

To be fair, Sissy is far more efficient than Marta, who broke her leg in a car accident back in — when? September? August? Time has been rushing by, as usual.

And unlike Marta, Sissy doesn't eat Maeve out of house and home while she's here. She never even touches the Atkins-friendly store-bought tuna salad Maeve keeps on hand and offers the cleaning lady weekly for lunch. Marta used to devour it, along with whatever else she could find in the fridge and cabinets.

Erin pops her blond head into the den.

"How was the biology tutoring?" Maeve turns down the television volume with the remote.

"It was good. What are you watching?"

"*Judge Judy*."

Erin rolls her eyes. "I'm going up to take a shower."

"Why don't you wait until later? I thought we could go out for salads at Ernesto's."

"I'm not hungry."

"You're not?" That's a switch. Erin is usually starved when she gets home from school at her regular time, let alone more than two hours later.

"Nah. I had a big lunch. It was spaghetti day." Her daughter disappears, her footsteps pounding up the stairs.

Damn. Maeve craves a chicken Caesar salad almost as much as she craves a cigarette. She could always drive over to the restaurant alone . . .

No, she can't. There's something pathetic about a divorcée dining out solo. Especially in a trattoria filled with couples and young families.

The phone rings just as she turns up the volume again. She presses Mute and trades the remote for the cordless phone on the end table. It strikes her that if she weren't so hungry, she could spend the rest of the night in this spot without having to get up.

"Hello?"

"Maeve?"

"Kathleen. Hey, want to go get chicken Caesar salads? It could be girls' night out."

Ignoring the invitation, her friend asks, in a low voice, "Is Erin home?"

"You want to talk to Erin?" Maeve asks, puzzled.

"No, it's just . . . Jen got home a few minutes ago . . ."

"So did Erin."

"Where did she say she was?"

"At school, getting extra help with biology. Amber's mother brought her home."

"Did you see her?"

"Who?"

"Amber's mother dropping her off."

"Kathleen, I did back-to-back spinning

and Pilates classes this afternoon. I haven't moved from this chair since —"

"Maeve, I think they lied to us. Jen said the same thing Erin told you. But I was watching for her to come home, and I didn't see a car dropping her off. She walked down from the main road. She said Amber's mother left her at the end of the cul de sac but why would she do that?"

"I don't know . . . maybe she's lazy?"

Kathleen is silent.

Maeve shakes her head. "Kathleen, they're fourteen."

"Jen's not."

"She will be in a few days."

"Weeks."

"You're nitpicking, you know that? Maybe they did lie. But how are we supposed to prove it? And what could we do about it? Anyway, who are we kidding? We did the same thing at that age. Worse."

All right, Kathleen wasn't that bad. Her father was too strict, and she just didn't have it in her to break rules the way Maeve did. Not back then. Kathleen's rebellion came later.

"Jen's not going to lie to me."

"Don't let yourself get all worked up over it, okay, Kathleen?"

"Too late," comes the bitter reply, followed by terse "bye" and a click.

Maeve stares unseeingly at the television. Oh, cripes, should she be more concerned about Erin? It never even occurred to her that her daughter wasn't at school working on her biology. But Erin wasn't hungry when she came in . . . so okay, maybe she went someplace to get something to eat.

And maybe somebody other than Amber's mother dropped her off.

Maeve isn't about to call the woman. She's only met her once or twice, and got the impression that she's one of those uptight family values types who frown upon divorce. The last thing Maeve wants to do is call someone like that to check up on her own daughter. That would give the impression that she's one of those single parents who has no idea what's going on in her child's life.

Nothing could be further from the truth. Erin tells her everything.

No. Not everything. *Not anymore.*

The truth is, she found out through the grapevine at the gym about her daughter going out with that pothead character, Robby Warren.

"Mom, God! Nobody says pothead," Erin laughed when Maeve met her with that accusation.

"I don't care what they say. And you're not dating him," Maeve retorted.

Actually, she *does* care. She likes to think of herself as more hip than the average mom — if hip is a word "they" say these days. She's certainly younger than most of Erin's friends' parents, who are in their forties. Only Kathleen is Maeve's age — but these days, she's about as cool as Sister Margaret, their old sixth-grade teacher at Saint Brigid's.

The phone rings again.

Still holding it, Maeve presses the talk button. "Hello?"

"I've got it, Mom," Erin's voice says from the upstairs extension.

"Already?" That was fast.

Maeve hangs up — then wonders, belatedly, who is on the other end of the line. Erin must have been right on top of the receiver, expecting a call. For a second, remembering what Kathleen said about the girls lying about biology tutoring, Maeve is tempted to eavesdrop.

But Erin would hear her pick up. And even if she didn't . . .

Well, it just isn't right.

Teenaged girls are going to tell the occasional lie. That's just the way it is. They're going to lie, and sneak around with their friends, and with boys. With any luck, they'll survive and become upstanding citizens, like Maeve. And Kathleen. With any luck, they won't hurt themselves — or anybody else — in the process.

Yup. That's the way it is. It doesn't give their mothers — or anyone else — the right to eavesdrop or snoop. If her own mother wasn't always checking up on her, Maeve might not have felt such a fierce need to grow up so fast. She's determined not to make the same mistake with Erin.

Still, she has a feeling she's going to have her hands full for the next few years.

Damn Gregory for walking out on her, making her a single parent when that was the last thing she ever wanted to be. Hell, that's why she married him in the first place — because she wanted her baby to have a daddy. A daddy with a lucrative profession.

Not that she'd welcome Gregory back now, the selfish SOB — but when it comes to child support, it would be nice to get something other than the financial kind. Not that the money that she does get is enough. Not by a long shot.

Maeve sets the phone on the end table again, then — with a sigh of resignation — reaches into the drawer for her pack of cigarettes.

★ ★ ★

Taking a deep drag of filtered menthol, Lucy remembers a film strip shown in her seventh-grade health class more than three decades ago. She visualizes the smoke filling her lungs, turning them hard and black, snuffing out healthy pink tissue.

They say smoking will kill you.

So why hasn't it?

Why is she still here, still breathing in and out, day after dismal day?

Gazing down at the faint pink scars that criss-cross the blue veins of her wrists, she tugs the sleeves of her green sweater so that they reach almost to her palms.

What was she thinking that day? Suicide, like divorce, goes against everything she was raised to believe. No matter what kind of life you've lived, killing yourself means being condemned to eternity in hell. Father Joseph said so.

Lung cancer isn't suicide. Emphysema isn't suicide. If you've lived a good life and you confess your sins, then get sick and die, you'll go to heaven.

Father Joseph said so.

Lucy started smoking the morning she was released from the psych ward.

If Henry noticed that his cigarettes were dwindling after she returned from the hospital, he didn't say a word. He was just damned glad to have her back home, where she belonged, the whole ordeal behind them. As long as she was under his roof, making his meals, doing his laundry, all was right in Henry's world.

He did complain when she started buying her own brand. He claimed they didn't have the money for that. But she persisted, with uncharacteristic obstinacy, and he relented.

That was years ago. Thirteen years; no, almost fourteen.

Fourteen years ago.

Sometimes, it seems like yesterday.

Other times, it was a lifetime ago.

The very eternity in hell she's forbidden by the church to escape through suicide or divorce.

Lucy taps the ashen tip of her Newport against the rim of the ashtray on the kitchen table, then pushes her chair back. Time to start Henry's dinner and pack his "lunch" — a sandwich he'll eat at two in the morning in the break room at the plant.

She glances at the clock. In ten minutes, the alarm will go off in the bedroom upstairs, and he'll get up for work.

One more week of third shift, and then he'll be back on days.

And so it goes, the familiar rhythm of their existence.

As far as she knows, Henry has no idea that something has changed. That her life was altered forever with the shocking phrase whispered over the telephone, confirming what she already suspected — or perhaps, deep in her heart, already knew.

It's her.

It's her.

It's her.

The words have echoed in her mind ever since, seeping into her every waking moment, into her dreams, into her nightmares. The nightmares never subsided, but they're back now, far more ferocious than they were fourteen years ago.

That's why she's thankful Henry's working third shift. She's had the bed to herself; there's nobody to witness her fitful sleep; nobody to hear her screams when she wakes in a cold sweat in the dead of night.

If Henry were here, he might guess. He might look at her — *really* look at her, for the first time in years — and read it in her eyes. He's perceptive — rather, he can be. He was, in that other lifetime.

And if Henry knew . . .

She shudders. He won't know. He can't

know. She'll make sure he doesn't find out.

It's her.

Yet how can it be? It doesn't make sense.

She's not supposed to be here, nearby, living in Woodsbridge. Orchard Hollow, of all places.

No, she's supposed to be dead. Dead fourteen years . . .

And she didn't go to heaven, as Lucy always believed she did.

Then again . . .

Orchard Hollow isn't heaven — but it's pretty damned close.

"Everyone asleep?" Matt asks from his recliner, looking up from the television as Kathleen sinks into the couch, her hair damp from the long, hot shower she just took.

"Riley and Curran are. Jen is finishing her homework. I told her lights have to be out at ten."

"Good." Matt turns his attention back to the episode of *Third Watch*.

"Matt?"

"Hmm?"

"We've got to talk."

"About what?" His gaze is fixed on the television, where a screaming ambulance is rushing to an accident scene.

"Jen. She lied to me today about where she went after school."

"What?"

She has his full attention now. Taking a deep breath, she fills him in on this afternoon's drama.

"So what did you say when she came home?"

"I didn't say anything. I didn't want to accuse her until I was sure."

"*Are* you sure?"

Kathleen shrugs. "Why wouldn't her friend's mother drop her off in our driveway? I think she's sneaking around with older kids who drive. And she smelled like cigarette smoke when she came home."

"Maybe her friend's mother smokes in the car."

"Maybe Jen is smoking."

Matt, the militant antismoker, cringes. "Get her down here. We're going to ask her about all of —"

"No. Not like that. She'll just get defensive."

"All right . . . then let's just hope you're wrong. Or that if you're right, it won't happen again."

"We can't ignore it."

Matt squeezes his eyes closed, rubs his

temples. "What do you want from me, Kathleen?"

"Some helpful input would be good."

"I gave you my input. You didn't agree with either thing I suggested. So . . . I don't know, do you want me to . . . what? Go up and talk to her? Leave you out of it?"

"No. I know we have to talk to her, but I don't even know how to approach it without alienating her right from the start. That's why I'm asking you."

He rubs his forehead again. "Look, I'm burnt out. Today was a lousy day at work, and it took me an hour to help Curran with his math homework . . ."

A dig at Kathleen, since she couldn't figure out fifth-grade fractions. Matt used to think it was charming that she isn't good with numbers; clearly that wore off some time ago.

"Plus then I had to read that story to Riley," he goes on, "and all I wanted to do now was sit here and watch TV for a few minutes before I fall asleep and it's time to get up and start all over again."

She stares at him. "So you're saying you can't be bothered with our daughter's issues because you're *tired?*"

"Not that I can't be bothered, just . . ." He sighs. "Kathleen, I know you worry

113

about her getting into trouble. I know you don't want her to end up the way you did."

She winces. She can't help it. Sometimes, she thinks that she told him too much.

Other times, she wonders if she should have told him everything, right from the start. Maybe then he'd understand.

Or maybe, if he knew the whole story, he'd stop loving her. Maybe he'd leave her.

Taking a deep breath, she looks her husband in the eye. "No," she says. "I don't want her to end up the way I did. I want to protect her. I just . . . I just don't know how."

"Well, I do."

Biology sucks even more than Mondays suck, Jen concludes, setting aside her homework, with its rows of four-box grids called Punnett Squares. This genetics stuff is incredibly boring. Not to mention confusing.

Mom has green eyes and so does Grandpa Gallagher. Dad has blue eyes and so do Grandma and Grandpa Carmody.

Jen has brown eyes. The chances of that are . . . um, slim?

Unless Grandma Gallagher, who died when Mom was little, had brown eyes?

That must be where I got them.

She glances at the Punnett Squares again,

then at the back of Sissy's flier, where she made several practice attempts at plotting her own heredity.

According to the diagrams, the chances of Jen having brown eyes regardless of her grandparents' eye color appear to be nil, which means she didn't do it right.

She sighs and crumples the flier into a ball. She probably should have stayed after school for biology tutoring. She stinks at science, and she's having an especially difficult time with this genetics unit, which has only just begun.

And anyway, if she had stayed after for tutoring, she wouldn't be dealing with this horrible guilt complex she's had all evening . . . ever since she got out of Robby's car over on Woodsbridge Road.

Lying to Mom's face about who had dropped her off was even worse than lying on the answering machine. Her mother said nothing, just nodded and told her to get washed up for dinner.

Mom was quiet throughout the meal, too. She gave Curran most of her steak, and she didn't even laugh when Daddy told the silly joke about the parrot and the old man. Even Riley cracked up at that, but Mom just smiled with this blank look on her face and looked like she hadn't even heard it.

Jen didn't laugh, either. Sometimes, especially when her father and brothers are laughing together, she feels like an outsider. She just doesn't have the same sense of humor — at least, not lately. She used to think her father's jokes were hilarious; now they're just corny.

Jen pitches the crumpled flier toward her wastebasket and misses.

She rises from her desk chair to get it, almost knocking over one of her swim team trophies on the shelf overhead. She grabs the wobbling trophy, which weighs enough to kill somebody if it fell on their head.

Good old Franklin Delano Roosevelt High, she thinks, reading the inscription on the bottom. Sometimes she misses her old school so much that she gets a lump in her throat.

She retrieves the crumpled paper from the floor and deposits it into her wastebasket. Then, swallowing hard, she tries to concentrate on the things she really likes about Woodsbridge High.

But all she can think about is that she wants to go back to Indiana and her old friends. Dana and Colleen would never dream of lying to their mothers and riding around in a car with a senior who also happens to sell drugs.

Not that Robby seems like a drug dealer. He's actually pretty nice. Funny, too. He had all three of them laughing all the way to the Galleria. And he didn't mind waiting while they shopped. Both Erin and Amber bought stuff at the Abercrombie sale but Jen was too nervous to shop. And anyway, all her babysitting money was here at home, tucked into the box set of Little House on the Prairie books, her secret hiding place.

"What if your mom sees that and wants to know where you got it?" she asked Erin as her friend crammed her new tops into her backpack.

"She won't notice. Or if she does, she'll think my dad bought it for me. He's always getting me new stuff."

True.

But the only person who ever takes Jen shopping is her mother. Mom would be suspicious right away if she saw her wearing something new.

Startled by the sound of two sets of footsteps coming up the stairs, she glances at the digital clock on her nightstand. It's not even ten o'clock yet — much too early for her parents to be coming up to bed. They never come up until the eleven o'clock news is over, at the very earliest.

The footsteps creak along the hall and

there's a knock on her door.

"Yeah?" Jen asks, as a chilling thought — *they know* — careens through her mind.

"We need to talk to you," her father says sternly through the door.

Yup. They know.

But how did they find out? Erin would never slip about it to her mother. And Mom doesn't even know Amber's mother. And Robby . . . well, no way does his mother — if he even has one — travel in the same circles as Mom.

"Come in," she calls, trying to sound calm. She hurriedly sits at her desk again, thinking it might help if they see that she's been studying.

The door opens and her parents step over the threshold. One look at their faces tells her that she was right. They know.

"I'm sorry," Jen blurts.

Her parents look at each other, then back at her.

The truth spills out. "I lied. I wasn't at school. I was at the mall."

"With Erin?" her mother asks quietly, the disappointment in her eyes more painful, even, than the blatant anger in Dad's.

Jen nods miserably. "With Erin and Amber."

"Who drove you?" Mom asks.

Dad has yet to speak. *When he does, it isn't going to be as calmly as Mom,* Jen thinks with a shudder. Aloud, she admits only, "A friend of Erin's."

"Which friend of Erin's?" her mother demands.

She hesitates.

"If you lie again," Dad's tone is ice, "you'll be sorry."

"His name is Robby."

"The drug dealer?" Mom is horrified. "You're driving around town with a drug dealer?"

When Dad puts it that way, it sounds so . . . *bad.* And it wasn't. She has to make them see that.

"Robby isn't a drug dealer." Not if you don't consider weed *drugs.* "He's really nice. He dropped us at the mall. We shopped for a little while. Then he brought us home. That was it."

"That was *it?*" Her parents echo in unison.

"I'm sorry I lied. I didn't mean to. I don't know what —"

"You're grounded," Dad announces. "For a month. You won't go anywhere except to school and to church. That's it."

"But — that isn't fair!"

"Life isn't fair," is the maddening reply;

one she's heard far too often.

"But what about soccer?" she protests. "The team needs me." She has to bite her lip to keep from saying it wouldn't be fair to inflict her punishment on the whole team, knowing what her father will say to that, even if he is assistant coach.

Her parents look at each other. "School, church, and soccer," Mom clarifies. "That's —"

"What about —"

"Jen, that's it!"

"— babysitting," she finishes, looking from one parent to the other. "Mrs. Gattinski needs me on Wednesdays."

"We need to discuss the babysitting thing, anyway," Dad says. "Mom and I aren't sure you're ready for that kind of responsibility."

"*What?*" Frustration and anger bubble up inside of her.

"Saturday night made us think that you might be too young to be alone in a strange house with two small children, Jen," Mom says gently, "and there's nothing wrong with that."

"But —"

"You're still a kid yourself, Jen."

"I am not a kid! I was scared. I couldn't help it. Mom would be scared if she looked out the window and saw somebody lurking there at night."

"If somebody was lurking in the Gattinskis' bushes, that's all the more reason we don't want you over there."

Jen opens her mouth to protest, then clamps it shut again. Not only is this unfair, but they're treating her like a baby. She'll be fourteen on November second, damn it. Fourteen.

How old was that girl April? she finds herself wondering, not for any good reason. What does some trashy runaway have to do with her?

"You can babysit this week," Mom relents, oblivious to — or choosing to ignore Dad's glare. Obviously, he doesn't agree.

"But what if Mrs. Gattinski can't find —"

"You can babysit until Mrs. Gattinski finds a regular sitter for Wednesdays."

Her father growls, "But absolutely no babysitting at night. And no play dates —"

"Play dates?" Jen echoes, outraged. "Dad, play dates are for preschoolers. I don't have play dates."

He shrugs. "Whatever you call them at your age — doing your nails in your room with your friends, or going shopping, or anything like that. When you're not at school, or soccer practice, or babysitting, you're here. Where we can keep an eye on you. Got it?"

"Yeah," she says miserably, turning her back.

"Good."

She stares blindly down at the ink doodles in the margins of the spiral-bound notebook lying open on her desk.

Her father leaves the room.

Mom lingers, standing behind Jen. After a moment, she puts a gentle hand on her shoulder.

Jen flinches.

The hand remains.

She shrugs it off, scowling.

Mom bends and kisses her good night, same as always.

Jen sits stiffly, ignoring her.

After a moment, she hears her mother's footsteps retreating into the hall, followed by the quiet click of the door closing.

He lowers the binoculars only when the last light has been extinguished on the second floor at 9 Sarah Crescent.

His breath puffs white in the night air; his legs are numb despite the trousers beneath his robe.

He doesn't know which room is hers; the shades are all down. That doesn't matter.

He knows that she's there, somewhere. Perhaps asleep already; perhaps lying awake in bed.

What is she thinking about?

Is she afraid?

Does she sense that he's here in the darkness, watching her?

The other night he was caught off guard when Genevieve — *think of her as Jen; they call her Jen* — seemed to look right at him through the window.

Instinct kicked in and he ducked out of sight.

But if she spots him again, he won't make that mistake. No, next time, he'll be ready.

Ready to do whatever it takes.

Just as he promised.

FIVE

On Wednesday afternoon Kathleen reluctantly joins Maeve for a "power walk" around the neighborhood. It's not that she doesn't desperately need the exercise; plus she's been hoping for a chance to discuss their daughters' Monday afternoon escapade. Still, Kathleen can't help feeling guilty as they stride along in the brisk autumn sunshine, and tells her friend as much.

"Guilty? Why?" Maeve asks, barely short of breath, her fists moving rhythmically alongside her ribs.

"Because my house is a disaster area and I should be home cleaning it." Kathleen huffs as she tries to keep up with Maeve's long legs and fast pace.

They've only been at it for ten minutes, and she's wiped out already. She can't even tell how far they've gone, or exactly where they are. Orchard Hollow's circular streets and big new houses are interchangeable, right down to the SUVs in the driveways and the pumpkins and potted mums on the steps. Even the campaign signs on the lawns tend to be for the same candidates — in this neighborhood, the Republican ones.

"You need a cleaning lady," Maeve declares, not for the first time. But this time she adds, "I'm sending you Sissy. She just told me she really needs more work to pay off a medical bill."

"Sissy?"

"My cleaning lady."

"I thought her name was Marcia."

"It was Marta, and she's out of commission with a broken leg or something. Sissy does a better job anyway, though. And she doesn't talk my ear off the way Marta did. She's very professional."

Kathleen hedges. "I don't know. I feel funny hiring household help when I'm not even bringing in an income."

"Oh, get over it. Matt won't care."

True. He's been urging her to get help, but Maeve doesn't know that . . . or need to. Sometimes, Kathleen gets the sense that Maeve thinks she makes Matt sound too good to be true.

For a long time, Kathleen believed that he was.

"Matt will do whatever makes you happy," Maeve is saying, in a voice laced with envy. "You know that."

Not necessarily.

Kathleen wonders if she'll ever get over the sense of being beholden to her husband — not for all he does for her now, but for saving her years ago, when she had nowhere else to turn.

Maeve says briskly, "Listen, Kath, I'm going to send Sissy over to do your house from top to bottom. My treat. Okay," she amends with a laugh, "Gregory's treat. Not that he'll even realize it."

"I can't let you do that, Maeve."

"I'm not asking your permission, Kathleen. Sissy really needs the work, and you really need the help. It's a win-win situation. And if you like her, you can hire her to do a few days a week for you. Okay?"

"A few days?" Kathleen shakes her head. She'd feel extravagant enough having a housekeeper here for one.

But Maeve is insisting, and anyway, Kathleen does need help. Her energy is utterly depleted this week, thanks in large part to her worry about Jen and to the old memories that have been intruding more frequently. She knew that moving back here would stir painful, long-buried emotions, but she truly believed she could handle the hurt after all these years.

"What do you say, Kathleen?" Maeve is asking. "Can I hire Sissy to do a day at your place?"

"Okay," she relents. "Is tomorrow too soon?"

Maeve laughs. "I'll find out. The house is that bad, huh?"

"Worse. Every time I turn around there are dishes in the sink and crumbs on the floor and the bathroom smells like pee. I swear, the boys can't aim to save their lives."

Maeve wrinkles her nose delicately. "Yuck. I'm glad I don't have sons. Girls are easier."

For some reason, that rankles.

"Not lately," Kathleen mutters.

A slight breeze stirs the tree branches overhead, sending dry leaves fluttering toward the ground.

"What did you say?" Maeve pushes a windblown strand of silky dyed-blond hair out of her eyes.

"I said, not lately."

"Not lately, what?"

Honestly, Kathleen wonders whether Maeve hears anything Kathleen's saying when she seems oblivious even to the words that spill out of her own mouth.

"You just said girls are easier. I said not lately."

Maeve's eyes widen. "Is Jen peeing on the floor?"

"Maeve! Of course she isn't peeing on the —"

"Relax, Katie, I was kidding."

She winces at the sound of her old nickname. "Oh."

"I know Jen doesn't pee on the floor. I guess you're talking about the lying and sneaking around thing, huh?"

With a sigh, Kathleen admits, "I can't get past it. How am I supposed to trust her again?"

"She's a teenager. You should never have trusted her in the first place."

"You're kidding again, right?"

"Wrong. This time I'm serious." Maeve shrugs. "She's going to lie and sneak around, Katie. That's what teenagers do. We did. And we're fine."

"It's Kathleen," she says churlishly. "Not Katie anymore. And what I did back then — which wasn't much of anything — has nothing to do with what Jen does now."

"It has everything to do with it. You're not being realistic."

"I won't have her lying to me, or riding around town with boys who smoke, or —"

"You don't have much say in it, Kathleen. What are you going to do? Lock her away until she's eighteen?"

"That would probably suit Matt just fine. He's already grounded her for a month. She's not allowed to go anywhere but school. And church."

"I thought she was babysitting for Stella Gattinski's kids after school today."

"She is. Just until Stella can find somebody else." Kathleen hesitates, then decides not to bring up Saturday night and the prowler Jen thought she saw. Maeve might mention it to Erin, and Erin will tell Jen, and Jen will feel betrayed.

Funny that Kathleen is worrying about betraying her daughter when Jen had no problem lying to her just two days ago. But she hasn't forgotten what high school is like and she can't help feeling protective of her daughter. The last thing Jen needs is for the other kids to find out she was spooked enough to call her parents while she was babysitting.

Kathleen wipes a trickle of sweat from her temple and looks at her watch, then remembers that it doesn't matter what time it is. She doesn't have to be at the bus stop this afternoon. Curran has a boy scout meeting after school and Riley has a play date at a friend's house.

"Want to go grab a quick Starbucks

before you have to get the boys off the bus?"
Maeve asks.

Rather than correct her, Kathleen shakes her head. "Sorry. Maybe tomorrow."

She's had enough of Maeve for today. Her friend means well, but Kathleen doesn't agree with her parenting style.

What Maeve considers mere adolescent mischief, Kathleen considers playing with fire — and she's hell bent to keep Jen off the self-destructive path she herself knows all too well.

"Okay, I'll call you later and let you know about Sissy."

Oh, right. Sissy. The cleaning lady.

If she can come tomorrow, Kathleen doesn't have to clean today. That leaves her with a few hours to kill . . . and, she thinks, as a chill slips down her spine, she knows exactly where she'll go.

"How's school going, Jen?" Stella asks, counting out several bills as the twins dive into the Happy Meals she picked up for them on the way home from work.

"School's fine."

Stella glances up from her wallet, noticing that Jen seems subdued today. "Is everything okay, hon?"

"Everything's fine. It's just . . . I, um,

can't babysit here anymore."

Stella's heart sinks, her initial reaction purely selfish. She knew Jen was too good to be true.

Then, catching the distress in the girl's brown eyes, she asks gently, "Why can't you babysit, Jen?"

Jen's chin quivers. Her gaze tilts down to her white Nikes. "My parents won't let me. They grounded me."

"Uh-oh. What did you do?" She probably brought home a rare C on her interim report card, Stella thinks, pressing several tens and a five into Jen's hand. Jen is such a model teenager she can't imagine that it was anything more extreme than that.

"I didn't do anything."

"They grounded you for no reason? Come on, Jen. What happened?"

"It was no big deal."

Aha.

"It was obviously a big deal to your parents. What was it?"

Jen shrugs, her gaze still averted. "Nothing. I just got a ride home from school with this kid who has a car."

"That was it?"

"Well, we stopped at the mall on the way, but that was it. My parents freaked."

"Because they don't want you riding

around in cars with other kids? I don't blame them, Jen. They're just making sure you're safe."

"No, they're just making sure I'm totally miserable. My mother won't let me do anything. She's ridiculous. She's always worried about where I'm going and who I'm with and what time I'll be back. I swear, she's smothering me!"

Surprised at the fervent outburst from mild-mannered Jen, Stella loops an arm around her shoulder, patting her reassuringly. "She's just being a mom, Jen. She loves you."

"Can you talk to her, Mrs. Gattinski? Maybe you can tell her that you really need me to babysit. And while you're at it, you can sort of tell her to lighten up."

"Oh, Jen, I don't want to poke my nose into —"

"But it's true, right? You need me to watch the girls, right? They'll be upset if I can't come anymore, won't they?"

Stella glances at her daughters, happily munching french fries at their little table in the corner. That they'd be bitterly disappointed if Jen doesn't come back goes without saying, but . . .

"Please, Mrs. Gattinski . . ." Jen lifts her blond head at last, her expression beseeching, "Can't you just tell my mom you really need me? It's really important to me to keep this job."

It isn't about the money, Stella realizes, looking into Jen's troubled brown eyes, and it isn't about the girls. Both undoubtedly matter to Jen — but this goes deeper. This is a power struggle between mother and daughter; one Jen is desperate to win.

Remembering her own sheltered adolescence, Stella is half-tempted to agree to talk to Kathleen on Jen's behalf. But another part of her — the protective, maternal part — feels compelled to tell Jen that her mother is right to keep a watchful eye. That the world can be a dangerous place; that every mother fears the worst that can happen and must do everything in her power to see that it doesn't.

"Never mind." Jen bows her head again, scuffing the toe of her sneaker along a line of grout in the ceramic kitchen floor. "You don't have to talk to my mom. That would probably be weird for you, huh?"

"A little," Stella admits. "But, Jen, if you feel that strongly, why don't you talk to her yourself? Explain how much the babysitting job means to you. Maybe if you have a rational conversation when you're both calm, she'll understand."

"Yeah," Jen says in a *whatever* tone typical of a teenaged girl convinced that all adults are clueless.

Stella isn't clueless. She remembers what it was like to be a kid. But things are different now. Thirteen-year-old girls want to grow up too fast. They dabble in things Stella didn't even discover existed until college. And even if they don't get into trouble on their own, they're prey for predators. They vanish from neighborhoods like this.

"Jen . . ." Stella begins, but trails off when Jen looks up expectantly — too expectantly. Stella doesn't know what she was going to say, but she's certain that Jen wouldn't want to hear it. She settles for, "I'll call your mom if you want me to."

"You will? Thank you!" Jen takes a pen and a spiral-bound notebook from her backpack. "Can I give you her cell phone number? If you call our house my dad might answer, and you don't have to talk to him."

Stella sighs. "Sure." She takes the number Jen scribbles on the sheet of paper, and tucks it into the drawer by the phone. "I'll call her as soon as I have time, okay?"

"No rush. I really appreciate it."

"Come on, Jen. I'll drive you home."

"I can walk."

"I'll drive you," Stella repeats firmly.

Now that the line has been drawn, she'll stay on the maternal side of it, if only for consistency's sake.

She doesn't blame Kathleen Carmody for wanting to keep Jen close.

She's willing to bet April Lukoviak's mother wishes she had done the same.

Mollie Gallagher's grave sits in a remote corner of the sprawling Saint Brigid's cemetery, sheltered beneath the spreading branches of an enormous red maple tree whose trunk is several yards away.

As Kathleen shuffles through the fallen red leaves toward the familiar gray stone, she finds herself noting that the tree's roots have likely snaked as far underground as the boughs have above. She wonders whether they've twined their way around her mother's coffin, around —

Stop it!

Kathleen swallows hard, shoving the macabre thought from her mind as she stares at the grave, toying with the green tissue paper wrapped around the stems of the crimson roses in her hand.

She always brings red roses. She has ever since she was a little girl. Back then, the parish priest Father Joseph was the one who brought her to the cemetery. Drew never did; not once. Aunt Maggie said he couldn't face it.

They came once a month, Father Joseph to visit his mother's stone, and Kathleen to visit hers. They would stop at the florist shop just outside the gates, and Kathleen would hand over her carefully saved allowance. Back then, she could only afford one rose. Now she brings dozens.

At the time, she was surprised that Father Joseph took her under his wing the way he did. Most of the kids at Saint Brigid's were afraid of the no-nonsense priest, who rarely smiled and was known for his fierce, thundering sermons.

But looking back, remembering the short span of dates on his mother's tombstone, Kathleen has gained insight. Like her, Father Joseph lost his mother when he was a child. Her predicament must have touched his heart.

Mollie Gallagher.
Loving Wife, Devoted Mother.

With a sob, Kathleen tosses the bouquet aside and sinks to her knees amidst the musty scattering of fallen leaves, tracing with her fingertips the letters etched into the gray slab, mentally adding her own.

Protective Grandmother.

The cemetery is deserted on this glorious

autumn afternoon. In the distance, she can hear the hum of the groundskeeper's lawn mower, and tires crunching along a far-off stretch of gravel. But here, there is only the occasional chirp of a bird overhead, and Kathleen's sniffles as she fumbles in her pocket for a tissue.

Finding one, she wipes tears that are quickly replaced with a fresh flood, wipes again and again until her tissue is soggy and her eyes are hot; her heart heavy with the grim weight of guilt-tainted memory.

If only she could turn back time . . .

No. It wouldn't matter. Nothing would change; she'd only have to relive every awful moment that led her here.

Father Joseph used to tell her that all things happened for a reason — both blessings and tragedies. He didn't just tell her — he preached it from the pulpit, in a booming voice of conviction that terrified Kathleen when she was a little girl reeling from the loss of her mother, and mesmerized her when she was older. Pounding the lectern for emphasis, fiery passion igniting his words, Father Joseph promised that even the most crippling tragedies could open the door to blessings, if you had faith. If you believed in miracles.

Kathleen chose to believe in miracles.

Now, she is blessed.

Blessed. Cursed.

Cursed to forever live with the almost unbearable burden of a secret so dark it threatens to smother her at times like this.

Breathe. That's it. Breathe. Deep breaths, in and out. You're okay. Nobody knows. Nobody will ever know unless you tell them . . . and you'll never tell.

Gradually, Kathleen becomes aware of the scent of damp earth and dying leaves wrapping around her like a shroud, just as it did on that long ago day. It was autumn then, too. Autumn, but the sky hung low and misty, the ground marshy from a recent rain.

Today, the sky is blue; the sun shines brightly.

Today, Kathleen is blessed.

A shrill ringing suddenly pierces the air.

Her cell phone.

Standing on shaky legs, she pulls the phone from her pocket and flips it open. As she does she checks the tiny digital clock in one corner of the screen, wondering if time has escaped her as it tends to do whenever she comes here. Is she late picking up the boys? Is a disgruntled scout leader or harried mom calling with an impatient reminder?

Noting the time, Kathleen feels momentarily reassured, until she remembers Jen. Jen, babysitting. Jen, lying. Jen . . . in trouble?

She answers with a wary, "Hello?"

"You're going to love me," Maeve's voice announces gleefully above the din of background voices and jazzy music.

Kathleen exhales. "Why am I going to love you?"

"Because I talked to Sissy and she'll be at your place first thing in the morning."

"That's great!" She feigns enthusiasm, but the fleeting thought of her daughter has filled her with an inexplicable uneasiness. "What time is first thing?"

"She said around nine."

"That sounds — wait, I have to be at the nursing home to meet with my father's doctor then. Can you let her in with your key?"

"Oh. I've been meaning to tell you . . . I lost it," Maeve admits. "It was in my purse and it must have fallen out. I've been looking all over the place, but . . ."

"Terrific. That was our only spare, other than the ones we keep in the doors."

The new house has the kind of deadbolts that need a key to lock from the inside. Kathleen insists that they keep the keys in the locks, rather than hiding them nearby, as Matt suggested. She isn't taking any chances of the kids being trapped in the house in a fire.

"I'm really sorry, Kath," Maeve tells her.

Kathleen shakes her head, thinking some things never change. Maeve always was queen of lost library books and misplaced homework assignments.

"Okay, tell Sissy I'll just leave the back door unlocked for her. It's no big deal. I usually do anyway."

"Maeve? Can you hear me?" she asks as static crackles on the other end of the line.

"Yes, I hear you. You're leaving the door unlocked."

"The back door."

"The back door. Got it. Is your address 11 Sarah Crescent, or nine?"

"Nine."

"Okay, great. I have to go. My order's ready."

"Where *are* you?"

"One guess."

"Starbucks," Kathleen remembers with a smile. "Where else?"

"You should have come with me. They have chocolate doughnuts today."

"You're not eating one, are you?" she asks in mock horror.

"Of course not, but you love them," Maeve points out as, somewhere behind Kathleen, the groundskeeper's lawn mower buzzes nearer.

"Where are you, anyway, Kathleen?"

"Running errands with the boys," she lies. "Listen, I'll see you later. And thanks for the cleaning lady."

Kathleen hangs up. More guilt. But she couldn't tell Maeve the truth about where she is. She doesn't want to get into the whole cemetery thing with her . . . or anyone. Nobody but Matt even suspects she comes here as often as she does . . . and he doesn't know why. Not really.

Brushing leaf fragments from her jeans, Kathleen spots the flowers she cast aside on the ground, still in their florists' wrapping. She bends to retrieve the bouquet and carefully removes the green tissue paper that hugs the stems. She takes a single red bloom from the bunch, then sets the rest carefully on top of the stone.

"I'm sorry," she whispers.

She presses her lips to the silken petals of the remaining rose and gently lays it on the leaf-strewn grass at her feet.

Then, once again, she looks at her mother's gravestone.

Protective grandmother.

"Watch over her, Mom," she says softly before turning and slowly walking away, tears rolling once more down her cheeks.

Sitting at her desk Wednesday evening, Jen stares absently at the open English textbook before her, thinking not about Renaissance poetry but about Robby.

He said hi to her when she passed him in the hallway today, flashing her a lazy smile from the radiator where he and his stoner friends like to lean as they linger between classes.

In that instant, feeling his eyes burning into her, Jen felt something utterly unexpected. Something she usually experiences only around Garth Monroe.

Okay, but she definitely has no business being attracted to Robby. For one thing, he's trouble. For another, Erin would be pissed.

Maybe Jen was imagining that Robby was looking at her longer — and with more interest — than he ever has before.

And even if she wasn't imagining it — even if Robby makes a move on her, which he won't — she's not about to go out with him. Robby is cute — really cute, in a dark, dangerous kind of way. But he isn't her type. He's older, and . . . and he smokes.

You're so lame, declares a voice in Jen's head. This time, it isn't Erin's voice, or even Amber's, but her own. *When are you going to stop being such a baby? You'll never have any fun, and you'll never grow up if you go around worrying about stuff all the time the way Mom does.*

As though summoned by Jen's subconscious, there's a sudden knock on her door, and a familiar voice calls, "Jen? I need to come in."

Immediately irked at the invasion, she says, "Go ahead."

The door opens and her mother carries a stack of clean laundry into the room. Looking around as she opens a drawer on Jen's dresser, she says, "Good. At least your room isn't a mess like your brothers'. It's going to take me at least an hour to get their toys picked up."

Jen shrugs. "So make them do it."

"They're helping, but you know how long it takes them to do anything. They keep arguing." Mom plops the clean laundry into the drawer and closes it with her hip. "And anyway, it's past their bedtime."

"So? Make them do it tomorrow after school."

"I can't. I've got a cleaning lady coming first thing tomorrow."

"Isn't it *her* job to clean?" Jen asks in the *duh* tone she knows her mother despises. But she can't seem to help herself. Mom is getting on her nerves lately, big time.

"Cut the attitude, Jen. Did you finish your homework?"

"Almost," she lies, turning back to the book.

She can feel her mother's eyes on her.

After a moment, Mom says, "We need to talk."

Jen doesn't turn around. "About what?"

"About you. I'm worried about you, Jen. That's all. I know it's not easy to be your age, and I just want to make sure you don't . . ."

"Get arrested?" Jen asks when her mother trails off.

"Or hurt. Or . . . pregnant."

Jen's jaw drops and her cheeks flame. "What do you think I'm doing, Mom? I'm not going to get pregnant. I mean . . ."

She falls silent, unwilling to confess that she's such a loser she's never even kissed anyone.

Now her mother is standing behind her chair, laying a hand on her shoulder. To Jen's horror, she feels tears springing to her eyes.

"I don't know, Jen. All sorts of things

went through my head the other day when you lied. I have no idea whether I can trust you."

"You can." Jen spins around in her chair to face her mother. "You can trust me. I didn't mean to lie. It's just . . . you won't let me do anything. I feel like a prisoner half the time. I mean, I can't even babysit?"

"You know why. You're being punished."

"But . . . That's so unfair. What's Mrs. Gattinski supposed to do? Why does she have to be punished? She's really upset. I had a commitment to her and now I have to break it. What kind of lesson is that supposed to teach me?"

Mom is silent.

Then, to Jen's surprise, she nods. "You're right. About that, anyway. You do have a commitment. And if there's anything Dad and I want you to learn, it's that you need to be responsible."

"Well, it seems like you're trying to do the opposite."

Anger flashes in her mother's eyes. "How responsible is lying and sneaking around behind our backs, Jen?"

Don't cry. Don't cry. Don't cry.

Too late. She's crying.

"I'm sorry." She sniffles. "I didn't mean to do it. I'll never do it again. Just . . . can't you tell Dad he's being ridiculous with this grounding thing? I mean . . . a whole month?"

"I'll talk to him."

"You will?"

"Only about the babysitting. And only because you're right. It's your commitment, and you should keep it."

"Really?"

"I'll see what Dad says."

"Thanks."

Mom bends to kiss the top of Jen's head.

Jen is tempted to throw her arms around her mother's neck and hug her. But something holds her back.

Instead, she merely says "thanks," again, and turns back to her book.

"Don't stay up too late."

"I won't."

Her mother's footsteps retreat across the rug and the door closes behind her with a quiet click.

Jen lets out a breath she didn't even realize she'd been holding.

She'll call Mrs. Gattinski first thing after school tomorrow and tell her she doesn't have to call Mom after all. What a relief.

Jen tries to focus on the John Donne poem she's supposed to have read and analyzed by tomorrow. Then something buzzes by her ear and she looks up to see a fly flitting almost drunkenly through the air, the way they do when they find their way inside this late in the season.

She pushes back her chair and walks over to the window to open it, hoping to shoo the fly out.

Glimpsing her reflection in the glass as she reaches for the sill, she pauses to study herself, trying to see herself as Robby might have today in the hallway. She's decent looking, she supposes, aside from the freakish white stripe in her eyebrow. Back in Indiana, the kids sometimes called her Skunky when she was younger. Here, nobody does that. But they do stare, sometimes.

Jen used to try to camouflage it with eyebrow pencil, but that never worked. Once, she combed the pale brow hairs with a dark mascara brush, which worked for a while. But she's so used to hiding her brow behind her hand that she accidentally smudged it during the day, and she wound up looking even more ridiculous.

Staring at herself in the window, she notes that you can't even see the white line in her eyebrow. Not from here, anyway.

Jen leans closer.

Not from here, either.

She leans toward the window, closer and closer until her face is almost pressed against the glass.

That's when she spots the figure standing below, just beyond the pool of yellow light cast by the street lamp overhead.

Startled, Jen squints into the darkness beyond the window, her heart pounding.

Somebody is there, watching her.

Or is he?

When Jen blinks, the spot is empty.

Either she was seeing things, or the lurker spotted her and scuttled off into the night.

Jen spins and hurries toward the door, opening her mouth to call for her father.

Then she stops short, remembering.

She can't tell him. Not after what happened last weekend when she was babysitting. No way will he agree to let her go back to the Gattinskis if she tells him this. He'll think she's a baby.

And maybe she is.

A big fat baby with an overactive imagination. Why does this keep happening to her? Last week, she was convinced she was being followed home from the Gattinskis for no reason whatsoever. Is she losing her mind?

But it isn't just me, she remembers. Erin saw somebody, too. And so did Amber and Rachel. At the soccer game. Or so they said.

For all Jen knows, Erin was just trying to spook her. But why would she do that? Just to be mean? Not Erin. She's not like that.

Slowly, Jen returns to the window and leans against the pane, gazing down into the street below.

Nobody is there.

Of course not.

Nobody ever was, Jen tells herself firmly, reaching within for confidence that refuses to settle as she stares out into the blackness.

SIX

Thursday afternoon, Kathleen steps through the unlocked back door to find the house spotless — and empty.

After setting down several bags from Wegmans and a folder containing her notes from this morning's meeting with her father's doctor, she dials Maeve's cell phone.

"Kathleen! I was just about to call you. Are you home?"

"I'm not sure." Kathleen walks across the shining tile floor in the kitchen. "The address is right, but this place is unrecognizable."

"I told you she was good," Maeve says with a laugh. "Do you want to hire her?"

"Definitely. I just have to check with Matt."

And if last night's agreeable mood is any indication, her husband will have no problem with it. She fully expected him to argue when she climbed into bed and approached him about letting Jen keep her babysitting job, but to her surprise, he was amenable. So amenable that when she thanked him and rolled over to go to sleep, he rolled alongside her and nuzzled the back of her neck.

A lackluster marital sex life might not be revived overnight, but they sure came close, Kathleen remembers with a smile.

"That's great," Maeve says, and it takes a moment for Kathleen to realize she's talking about the cleaning lady.

"Yeah, she really did do a good job." Kathleen runs her hands over the polished chrome of the kitchen faucet and inhales the sterile herbal scent of Windex and 409. "When you see her, thank her."

"You didn't see her?"

"No, I haven't been home all day. I had to be at the nursing home first thing."

"I forgot. How did that go?"

Kathleen sighs. "The doctor thinks it's Parkinson's. They have to do more tests."

"That sucks."

Used to Maeve's bluntness — and, after taking hours to digest it, to accept the tentative diagnosis — Kathleen says only, "It does, but he's close to eighty years old, Maeve. Something's going to get him sooner or later."

"Your mother was a lot younger than he is, wasn't she?" Maeve asks.

"Twenty years younger. Why?"

"I'm still dating Mo. He's growing on me, but I can't get over the fact that he's so old. I think younger men are more my style."

"Younger as in our age?"

"Younger as in younger." Maeve laughs. "A couple of fraternity boys checked me out at the gym today."

"Maeve . . . fraternity boys? That's just . . ." Kathleen shakes her head, laughing.

"It's flattering. Men that age are in their sexual prime, and so are we, Kathleen."

Again, Kathleen's thoughts flit back to last night in bed with Matt. Why don't they make love more often? Why hasn't she initiated it lately? She's been so damned tired, so overwhelmed . . .

But look at the house now. Spic and span, and Matt said he's bringing home pizza for dinner. There's nothing for her to do but put up her feet and wait until the kids get off the bus.

She thanks Maeve again for the cleaning lady. "Give me her number and I'll call and ask if she wants to come every week, okay?"

"I knew you were going to say that. Smart woman." Maeve gives her the number, then hangs up.

As Kathleen dials Sissy's number, she realizes she forgot to ask Maeve how much she charges. Oh, well. How much can it be?

After four rings, an answering machine picks up.

"Hi, Sissy, this is Kathleen Carmody. You did a wonderful job cleaning for me today, and I'm wondering if you can come every week? Please give me a call."

She leaves her number, then replaces the receiver in its cradle, noticing that the fingerprint smudges have been removed from the wall and light switch nearby. She makes her way through the house, pleased to see that the hardwoods and the windows are gleaming; not a trace of dust anywhere, not even on the leaves of the philodendron in the dining room. In the living room, the magazines are arranged on the coffee table in a perfect arc. The runner on the hall stairs bears vacuum marks, and the second floor smells of furniture polish and bathroom disinfectant. All of the windows are cracked to let fresh air in, and the bedroom and bathroom doors have been left ajar.

Having grown up in a house where all doors were kept closed, even on empty rooms, Kathleen has found the habit hard to break, to the point where Matt and the kids have adopted it, too.

Now, she finds herself appreciating the invigorating cross breeze wafting through the upstairs hall, and the light spilling into the usually dark corridor.

Kathleen pauses in the doorway of Jen's room, gazing at the ruffled white eyelet coverlet and curtains, the childhood classics lining the bookshelves, the collection of stuffed animals heaped on the bed. The room could belong to a girl a decade younger, she realizes with a pang.

When they moved, Jen asked if she could get a new bedspread and curtains.

"But these are almost new," Kathleen remembers telling her daughter. "I just bought them for you last year."

Jen didn't argue. She never used to argue. Not back then.

I should have let her pick out her own stuff, Kathleen thinks, stepping into the room and running her hand over the white ruffles at the window. *I never asked her what she likes. I just went out to Marshall Field's and bought these girly things.*

Erin's room, she recalls, is done in tones of bright orange and green and purple, with geometric patterns, painted walls, and retro blond wood furniture Maeve ordered from one of those upscale household chain stores. Jen thought it was cool; Kathleen thought it was incredibly ugly: a throwback to the seventies-style stuff that cluttered her father's house before the tag sale where he sold it all for pocket change.

Now, as she looks around Jen's traditional bedroom, she tries to see it through her daughter's eyes — and her daughter's friends' eyes.

Maybe we can update the curtains and coverlet, Kathleen concludes, realizing they're somewhat frou-frou. And Matt will probably be willing to paint the walls.

But not orange, like Erin's. Kathleen draws the line at orange.

Satisfied with her new resolve, she steps back out into the hallway just as the phone rings. She hurries to pick up the extension in her bedroom, hoping that, this time, the receiver is where it belongs.

It is. Either Jen is learning to put it back after she uses it, or the wonderfully efficient Sissy found it and returned it to its cradle.

Kathleen notes the absence of wrinkles in her freshly made bed as she perches on the edge with the phone, saying, "Hello?"

For the first few moments, her voice is greeted by silence.

Then she hears it.

The distinct sound of a baby crying.

"Hello?"

The cries grow louder.

A chill slips down Kathleen's spine.

"Who is this?" she demands, her hand trembling as she presses the receiver against her ear.

The only reply is a click, and then a dial tone.

Shaking, her breath coming in shallow gusts, Kathleen lowers the receiver.

She runs downstairs to the kitchen, where the Caller ID box is hooked up to the phone, and checks the digital window to see where the last call came from.

Private Name, Private Number.

It had to be a wrong number, she tries to tell herself. There wasn't anything ominous about it.

Just a wrong number, and nothing more.

"Hey, you! Where are you going so fast?"

Jen turns around to see Robby leaning on the low cement wall in front of the school, his thumbs hooked in the front pocket of his faded jeans. The sun casts auburn highlights in his unruly dark hair. For some ungodly reason she finds herself wanting to run her fingers through it.

"I have to get on the bus," she tells him.

"Why?"

She laughs nervously, gesturing around them at the hordes of chattering students streaming out of the school. "Because it's, um, time to go home."

He shrugs. "Is there a law that says you have to take the bus?"

Uh-oh.

Rather than answer his question, she offers, "Erin had to stay after."

Why did I say that? What does that have to do with anything? He must think I'm a total moron.

"Yeah, I know. She got caught skipping gym, right?"

Jen nods.

"You ever skip any classes?"

"Me? No!"

Did you have to sound so horrified? She notes his amused expression. *Way to go, Jen. Nothing like coming across as a prissy strait lace.*

She says hastily, "I mean, I never have, but . . ."

"But you plan to?" His grin broadens.

"Sure."

Robby kicks off the wall with one black boot and leans close to her, both hands jammed into his pockets now. "Yeah? Let me know when you're ready, okay?"

"Ready . . . ?"

"To cut a class. We'll skip together."

He makes it sound so . . . erotic. Jen's breath catches in her throat. She forces herself to exhale, to inhale. She can smell smoke clinging to his blue plaid flannel shirt and jean jacket: cigarettes and woodsmoke, an odd and intoxicating blend of decadence and the outdoors.

"Where . . . where would we go?" she dares to ask, though she doesn't dare to meet his dark gaze. "You know . . . if we skipped."

"You can decide. I'm easy. I'll go anywhere."

She looks from his boots to his face and finds him grinning at her.

"Whatever." She does her best to emulate Erin's coolly noncommital attitude, wishing she had gum to snap or — or a cigarette to exhale.

Not that she's ever smoked in her life . . . or intends to. Smoking is stupid.

And Robby . . . well, she always figured Robby was stupid as well.

Not anymore. Something about the way he's suddenly noticing her, talking to her, makes Jen wish she were capable of her friends' flippant nonchalance.

"Want a ride home?" he asks.

"Now?"

Duh, Jen.

"Isn't that where you're going?" he asks with a languid grin.

"I was going to get on the bus."

"And the bus would take you home. Right?"

"No, just, um, to the bus stop."

He actually laughs. But not at her. Not with her, either, because she's not laughing. No, she's just standing here feeling like an utter idiot and wondering why she's tongue-tied talking to her best friend's sort-of boyfriend, and why he's bothering to talk to her at all.

"Well," Robby says, quirking a black brow, "I'd take you right to your front door."

"Yeah, and my mother would freak."

"What, she doesn't want you hanging out with older guys?"

"I doubt it."

"So tell her I'm younger. Tell her I'm seven, but I'm very mature for my age." He laughs at his own joke.

This time, Jen laughs, too.

"So you want a ride?" he asks, grin fading, eyes taken over by an expression that makes Jen's lower belly cartwheel.

"I can't."

He shrugs.

"Not today, anyway," she adds as he prepares to walk away.

He looks intrigued. "Tomorrow?"

It's her turn to shrug. "Maybe," she says, as close to coy as she's capable of being.

She turns and heads toward the waiting yellow bus, wondering what the hell she's doing. She can't get a ride home from Robby. Her parents will kill her.

But only if they find out, she tells herself as she climbs up the steps, acutely aware of Robby watching her from a distance.

Totally oblivious to the fact that he's not the only one.

"Lucy?"

At the sound of her name, she spins slowly toward the booth in the far corner of the coffee shop, and there he is.

Fourteen years fall away in an instant.

His hair is still golden — that's the first thing she notices. Still golden, unless he's dying it.

Her hand goes to her own head, to the salt-and-pepper waves she hasn't bothered to color in years.

She regrets that as she cautiously walks toward him. Regrets a lot of things, actually; far more important things. But right now, letting her hair go gray at such a young age is all she can think of.

He stands as she comes closer, and she sees that he's as lanky as he was back then.

She wonders if he'll order the double bacon cheeseburger he always got when they came here, unless it was a Friday during Lent. It was the beer-battered fish fry then, with french fries *and* onion rings.

How he could eat, Lucy remembers, almost smiling despite her reason for being here. The man had a ravenous appetite.

Especially for her.

She feels her cheeks growing warm as she arrives in front of him, glad he can't know what she's thinking.

"Lucy. You look exactly the same." He reaches across the table, across fourteen painful years, to clasp her hands just as he used to.

"No, I don't," she protests, embarrassed.

"But you do."

It isn't a polite lie, not the way it was when he said it. Aside from the fine network of wrinkles around his eyes, he looks just as he did the last time she saw him.

"Sit down, Lucy. I can't believe you're really here."

She marvels that he manages to sound as though this reunion were his own idea, and not hers. As though it's something they discussed in advance, when the truth is, she hasn't heard his voice since he told her goodbye, and she believed, on that tragic day, that it was forever.

It would have been, too.

But everything has changed.

"I wasn't sure you'd show up." She sinks into the opposite side of the booth, remembering how they always shared the same vinyl seat all those years ago. It was an excuse to sit shoulder to shoulder, close together, but they always figured they should both sit facing the wall, just in case . . .

Just in case.

But this coffee shop is on the opposite side of the city. Nobody from the neighborhood was likely to wander in here, or so they managed to convince themselves.

We were reckless, Lucy realizes. *Incredibly reckless.*

Reckless, and in love. The two go hand in hand.

But age and sorrow have bred caution. She didn't dare to initially approach him in person after all these years, or even to call him. She wasn't sure whether his address was the same when she wrote the brief letter asking him to meet her here. Hell, she wasn't even positive he was still alive . . . although she suspects she'd have known if he wasn't.

When you love somebody, you sense things like that.

Or do you?

Maybe not, Lucy admits to herself, recalling the shock of a lifetime.

In any case, it took every ounce of her strength to come here today not certain what she'd find. For all she knew, he would bring his wife — or send her in his place, to tell Lucy to leave him alone; to leave them both alone, just as she promised she would.

"I can't believe it's really you, Lucy," he says again, and she realizes that he's staring at her. Not in dismay at what the years have done to her, as one might expect. He's looking at her just as he used to. Just as though . . .

"How's Deirdre?" she asks, to remind herself, as much as him, that neither of them is unencumbered.

"Deirdre," he echoes, and the light goes out of his brown eyes. "Deirdre is —"

"What can I get you folks?" A waitress stands above them, pad in hand.

"Coffee," Lucy says, when he looks expectantly at her.

"Make that two coffees. And menus."

Lucy opens her mouth to protest, and he smiles faintly, saying, "You don't have to eat. Let's just see what the specials are."

He used to say that back then, too. But he always ate, and she invariably wound up eating with him. Being with him awakened all sorts of fierce cravings within her.

"What's wrong?" he asks, looking up at her.

"Nothing, I just . . . I wish you could still smoke in this place. I need a cigarette with my coffee."

"Yeah, so do I. Some things never change, huh?"

"Deirdre," she says abruptly, again. "How is she?"

He shrugs. "She's fine. Henry?"

"Henry's fine. What about Susan? She must be grown up by now, or at least in college."

The question is as mechanical as his reply.

"Yes. She is. All grown up, and in college."

The waitress returns just long enough to deposit two laminated menus on the table. Lucy pretends to scan hers, but all she can think is that she has to tell him.

Now.

Before they sit here another minute pretending they're just old lovers saying hello. He has to know she contacted him for a reason. He may even suspect, or already know what it is.

She looks up at him; studies his face intently, as though it weren't indelibly etched

164

in her mind for all these years.

He still has the whitest teeth she's ever seen.

He still has those big brown puppy dog eyes.

And he still has the distinct tuft of pale hair running down the middle of his left eyebrow.

The dust, crumbs, and cobwebs might have been swept from the house, but there is a lingering tension with Jen that only seems to have escalated despite Matt's relenting about her babysitting job.

It's nothing that their daughter has said or done, Kathleen notes halfway through her third slice of mushroom pizza. It's more that she hasn't said or done anything, other than appear at last from her room after being called twice for dinner.

Now she sits picking at her first slice as her brothers vie for the stage, full of news about school and friends and sports.

"How about you, Jen?" Kathleen seizes a rare lull to ask. "How was your day?"

"Great," she says, without much enthusiasm.

"What did you do?" Matt asks.

"Went to school, came home. Don't worry, that was all. Why? Did you think I escaped when Mom wasn't looking?"

Kathleen and Matt exchange a glance. Kathleen shakes her head slightly. *Leave it alone, Matt. Don't make an issue out of her tone.*

Matt scowls but remains silent.

"How was school, Jen?" Kathleen asks brightly.

"I just told you, it was great."

"Be more specific."

"What's specific?" Riley wants to know.

"It's nosy," Jen informs him.

"Is Jen nosy?" Riley asks Kathleen.

"No, Mom is," Jen answers for her.

Matt plunks the remainder of his slice on his paper plate and glares at Jen. "Okay, that's enough with the mouth. Your mother asked you a question. Answer it."

"I did."

"Be . . . more . . . specific," Matt says darkly, and Kathleen wishes he would just shut up and let Jen off the hook.

That she's far more vexed with Matt than with their suddenly bratty adolescent makes little sense to her, but she can't help feeling suddenly protective of Jen. Maybe it's because there's an aura of vulnerability about her even now, a sense that she doesn't want to behave this way but is powerless to control her emotions or her mouth.

For a moment, there's silence.

Kathleen rescues Curran's teetering plastic cupful of grape juice before it spills, then almost wishes she had let it fall just to deflect attention from Jen.

"We're waiting," Matt tells her.

"I don't know what you want to know," Jen says, her sullen monotone giving way to high-pitched exasperation.

"How are your grades?" Kathleen asks quickly. "Are you doing better in biology?"

Jen hesitates.

Okay, wrong thing to bring up.

"We had a pop quiz today and I got a few wrong."

"Daddy's good at science," Curran pipes up, picking the pepperoni off another piece of pizza. "Maybe he can help you."

"Good idea. What are you learning?" Kathleen asks Jen, hoping they're not on the reproduction unit yet.

"Punnett Squares."

"Isn't that geometry?"

Matt rolls his eyes at Kathleen's question, and she retorts, "Hey, I was just kidding. I know what Punnett Squares are."

He laughs. "Are you sure?"

"Of course. I only stink at math, not science."

"So what are they?" Jen asks. "We're waiting, Mom."

Seeing the hint of a twinkle back in her daughter's eyes, Kathleen is tempted to pretend she's clueless, if only so that Jen will crack an actual smile.

"Punnett Squares are grids that are used to determine heredity, right?"

"Right," Jen says, apparently — and insultingly — surprised.

"See?" Kathleen playfully sticks out her tongue at Matt, then turns to Jen. "If you need help with your science, Jen, you can ask me, too. Not just Daddy. Do you have homework for tonight?"

"Yeah, more Punnett Squares." Jen makes a face. "I just can't get it right. It doesn't make sense."

"What doesn't?" Kathleen picks up her pizza again, crisis over and appetite retrieved.

"Genetics in general. I mean, your mom had brown eyes, right, Mom?"

The pizza turns to a sodden mass in her mouth. She can feel Matt's eyes on her as she reaches for her glass and gulps water to wash it down.

"Mom's mom is dead," Riley informs his sister, as if she didn't know.

"So? She still had eyes," Curran points out.

"You mean she doesn't have eyes now?"

"She's *dead*, Riley!"

"So dead people don't have eyes? Do worms eat them, or what?"

Heart pounding, Kathleen pushes back her chair. The wooden legs make a scraping noise on the tile; the bickering boys abruptly fall silent.

"Are you okay, Mom?" Jen asks, her voice laced with concern.

"I just have a headache. I'm going upstairs to lie down."

She walks into the hall and up the stairs on wobbly legs. She can hear Jen admonishing her brothers.

"What's wrong with you?"

"You're the one who brought up her mom," Curran protests.

"So? I didn't say worms were eating her eyes."

"Neither did I. That was Riley."

"Enough," Matt cuts in sternly. "Finish eating. I'm going to go see if Mom's okay."

No. Wishing he would just stay away from her right now, Kathleen goes into the master bedroom and sinks onto the bed, rubbing her temples. She doesn't want to talk about this with Matt. She just wants him — wants everything — to go away.

But his footsteps are treading up the

steps, and she hears the door creak behind her as he slips into the room. He comes to sit beside her on the bed. His weight slopes the mattress so that she has to brace her feet against the floor to avoid sliding into him. She doesn't want to touch him now, or be touched. She only wants to be alone, damn it.

"You okay, Kathleen?"

"No."

She swallows hard, still massaging her temples. His hand settles on the small of her back; it's all she can do not to flinch.

"We said we were going to tell her," Matt points out. "Remember?"

"We said when she was older."

"I think it's time. She's old enough if she's asking questions. We said that if she ever started —"

"That's not why she's asking questions," Kathleen cuts in tartly. "The questions are incidental. And we don't have to answer them. We can —"

"Lie?" He snorts. "After we grounded her for doing just that?"

"It's different."

He's silent, his hand a motionless weight at the base of her spine.

Kathleen turns to look into her husband's blue gaze, expecting the resignation — but not the sorrow — she finds there.

"You're not ready to let go, Matt. Are you?"

"Do you actually think I ever will be?"

"Nothing really has to change. If we tell her, I mean."

"Everything has to change."

"You're still her father."

"She'll want to find him."

Kathleen's jaw clenches so that she can barely force the words out. "I don't even know where he is."

"It would be easy enough to look him up in the phone book or on the Internet. She'll want to do that."

"I know she will, Matt." Her head is killing her. "Look, a minute ago you were trying to talk me into telling her. Now you're trying to talk me out of it?"

"I don't know. I don't know what we're supposed to do. All I know is that Jen deserves to know the truth."

"The truth about what?"

Startled by the voice, Kathleen turns to see her daughter standing in the doorway.

How much did she hear?

Enough to be wearing a look of confusion . . . and dread.

There's no turning back now, Kathleen realizes, her blood running cold.

Robby tilts his head and pours the last of the french fries from their greasy envelope into his mouth. They're unappetizingly cold and mealy, and they need salt. Ketchup, too.

But this isn't exactly a place where you'd expect fine dining, he thinks. He has to smirk as he glances around the fast-food restaurant, realizing that his idea of fine dining involves merely seasonings and condiments, not china and crystal — or caviar.

Caviar. He rolls his eyes, remembering how Erin once mentioned caviar and he assumed it was something to drink. He even bragged that he had a fake ID and could get some if she wanted it.

"You need a fake ID to get fish eggs?" she asked incredulously.

He managed to keep from sounding like a complete idiot by pretending that yes, you needed a fake ID to get fish eggs where he used to live, in Canada.

He never lived in Canada but Erin doesn't have to know that. Nor does she have to know that when it comes to things like caviar, Robby's clueless.

Burgers wrapped in paper — now that's where he's a pro. From the time he was old enough to drive, he's been eating most of his meals at this fast-food place or at Ted's Charcoal Hots down the road. Before that, he had to fend for himself at home, which usually meant cold cereal or peanut butter on crackers.

So, yeah, for Robby, this is the good life. Even if, at this hour on a weeknight, the only people in here besides him are a pair of overweight truckers and a miserable-looking mother with a bunch of runny-nosed, dirty-faced, squalling kids.

As Robby drains the last of his orange pop, he watches her slap the littlest one and call it — its gender is anyone's guess — a pain in the ass.

Robby's mother used to call him a spoiled brat, and she hit him, too. Not just with her hand. Lucky for her — and for him, too, he figures — that she cut out before he got bigger than she was. These days, if anyone dares to raise a fist at him, they find themselves on the receiving end of seventeen years' worth of pent-up vengeance. And if his mother ever dares to show her face again, she'll be in for it, too, he thinks, narrowing his eyes at the memory of her perpetual alcohol-fueled rage.

Dad, he doesn't get angry very often. Not even when he drinks.

Robby crumples the empty french fry bag

and pitches it toward the trash can. Misses. Shrugs.

Lately, Dad just stares off into space a lot and eventually passes out. This morning Robby found him sleeping in the bathtub, fully clothed — no water or anything. God knows the old man acts like he's allergic to soap.

It used to embarrass Robby, having a slovenly drunk for a father and a drunken shrew for a mother. He never brought friends home to their apartment in Orchard Arms back when he was a little kid in elementary school and cared what all the kids from the burgeoning new development thought. Now that he's in high school, there's more of a mix, so he can choose the kind of friends who couldn't care less what his home and his parents are like, as long as they get what they want from him.

They don't get it lately, now that he's on probation.

Getting caught selling weed shocked him almost as much as his old man's reaction to the news.

Dad cried. *Cried.*

The only other time Robby saw him shed a tear was when his mother walked out — and that time, Robby was disgusted by his father's blatant emotion. As far as he was concerned, his mother could rot in hell.

But his father . . . well, he must have cared about her. He must care about Robby, too, because when he showed up at the police station that night, he grabbed him and hugged him, tears rolling down his face. He was loaded, as always, blithering on about how he'd failed his son. Robby was throwing his life away, Dad slurred, and it was all his own fault. He wouldn't be able to bear it if Robby went to jail . . . or worse.

As they drove home — Robby at the wheel, at the cops' insistence — Dad made Robby promise that he'd never sell again.

He promised.

And Robby, who breaks promises like his mother broke seals on twist-off wine bottle caps, is hell-bent on keeping this one.

It won't be easy, that's for damn sure. It wasn't like he was a big time dealer making a shitload of cash, but at least it kept him in french fries and Marlboros and regular unleaded for his car. Now he figures he'll have to find a job. A real job.

Yeah, like people are just standing in line to hire a wise-ass kid with a record.

Okay, the record is sealed. All he has to do is stay out of trouble, and it will go away.

Yeah, that's *all*.

Needing a cigarette, Robbie plops the

empty paper cup beside the crumpled napkins on his plastic tray, stands, brushing crumbs from his jeans. He heads for the door, passing a trash can stacked high with empty trays.

Oh.

Right.

He left his garbage and tray on the table. Lately, he's been trying to remember to clean up his table, ever since some old guy made a comment about lazy kids expecting everyone else to pick up after them.

The comment was meant to be overheard, and Robby knew it was directed at him. At the time, his gut response was to shoot the man a belligerent glare. But for some reason, as he drove away from the restaurant that night, he felt guilty.

That's been happening a lot lately, and it bugs him. Life is easier when you don't give a damn what other people think of you.

Outside in the crisp October night air, Robby reaches into the pocket of his denim jacket and pulls out a pack of cigarettes. There are only three left. That will get him through the night, but he'll need to buy more in the morning. Crap. The cash stashed in a coffee can in the top of his closet will last him a few more days, tops.

Robby pauses on the concrete curb to

light a match, ignites the tip of the Marlboro, and takes a drag. Soothed by the rhythm of smoke drawn into his lungs, then exhaled slowly through his nostrils, he saunters toward his car.

Later, he'll remember how Jen Carmody popped into his head in that moment before he reached the car. He'll remember, and he'll wonder, feeling only slightly foolish, whether he might be psychic.

That his brain would suddenly conjure an image of Jen's face just then will seem eerily fortuitous, but now, when it happens, it doesn't strike him as particularly unusual.

After all, she's a pretty girl, and he enjoys busting her chops the way he did after school this afternoon. To his surprise, she isn't as straight as Amber said. Who would ever think that someone like Jen would agree to cutting class with him? Not that he believes it will actually happen. But wouldn't it be fun to show her that there's more to life than the soccer field and getting good grades?

Yeah, he thinks, cigarette clenched between his lips as he reaches down to open his car door, and Erin will be pissed as hell if she finds out that Robby's hanging out with her blond friend behind her back.

Erin Hudson is cute, but she sure can be

bitchy at times. She also likes to think she's got some claim on Robby. Yeah, right.

He slides into the driver's seat and closes the door, inhaling with another drag the familiar scent of his car: mildew and stale smoke. He turns the key in the ignition and after three tries, the engine roars to life.

Wondering how he's going to afford a desperately needed tune-up, Robby reaches down to tap the cinder tip of his cigarette into the open ashtray.

That's when he spots it.

A white envelope propped on the console.

Frowning, he reaches for it, wondering who put it there.

He left the car unlocked. He always leaves the car unlocked, knowing nobody would bother to steal a heap of junk in this neighborhood.

The envelope is sealed and he wonders, as he props his cigarette in the ashtray and slides a finger beneath the flap, whether it was meant for somebody else. It's not like his name was on the front.

Yeah, and it's not like Robby cares, once he sees what's inside, who the intended recipient was meant to be.

Cash.

And, according to the unsigned note, there's more where it came from. A lot more. All he has to do is show up at a designated time and place . . . and prove himself willing to earn it.

The house is dark when Lucy arrives home.

She wonders what Henry thought when she didn't get back before he left for work. He thought she was at mass. Was he worried that she failed to return? Did he even notice?

Probably not. She fixed his sandwich before she left, washed the dishes, swept the floors. She left nothing unfinished, almost as though she wasn't sure she'd ever be coming back.

That's a laugh.

What was she thinking? That she'd be running off to some paradise island with her long lost lover?

She pauses on the steps, fishing through her purse for her keys beneath the porch light, hearing them jangling somewhere in the bottom. It occurs to her that it probably isn't safe for a woman to be out here alone at night. The street is deserted, and the neighborhood has gone downhill these past few years.

She should have come home before dark. Why didn't she?

Why did she spend so many hours in church after she left the coffee shop? She prayed the rosary over and over, begging God's forgiveness, wishing she could turn back the clock, do things differently this time.

She's alive? What do you mean she's alive? How can she be alive?

His voice was a monotone when she broke the news to him, his expression one of disbelief, but she didn't miss the fleeting glint of fury in his eyes. It was almost as though he already knew, though when she questioned him about it, he said he'd had no idea. He thought she was dead all these years, just as Lucy did.

He didn't even seem to be listening as Lucy gave him the details. He nodded and he murmured his shock, but he seemed oddly distracted.

When the waitress came to take their orders, neither of them got anything. They didn't even finish their coffee.

What do you want to do about this, Lucy?

She shrugged. What was there to do?

She wanted to tell him how frightened she was, but something made her keep that to herself. She told him that she needed some time to think things through, and that he should do the same. They would meet again to discuss it. They didn't decide when, or where. They just left it at that.

Now, as Lucy shoves her key into the lock and turns it, she wants nothing more than to forget it for a little while — just put it out of her mind, at least until morning.

She steps into the house and locks the deadbolt behind her, then deposits her coat and purse on the hall tree.

Catching sight of herself in the mirror behind it, she frowns at her reflection. No wonder he didn't offer to run away with her. Look at her. She's gray and wrinkled and worn out, her beauty long faded, her eyes etched in a lifetime's worth of sorrow.

She reaches into her purse for her cigarettes and carries the pack toward the kitchen, deciding she'll make a pot of decaf and relax.

In the moment before she arrives in the kitchen doorway, the unmistakable smell of smoke reaches her nostrils.

Fresh smoke, not the stale lingering scent of an afternoon cigarette.

As she reaches for the light switch, puzzled, she spots it, and her heart stands still.

There, a few feet in front of her, is the glowing red ember of a cigarette, and the unmistakable outline of somebody sitting at the table, smoking it.

Jen is going to die.

She is. She's going to *die*.

She can't breathe. God help her, she can't breathe. In the terrible moments since her parents dropped their bombshell, her lungs have somehow forgotten how to do their job. It's as though she's being smothered, her chest burning and the room spinning and now her legs giving out, and she's falling, falling . . .

"Jen!" Mom catches her, pulls her onto the bed, wraps her arms around her. "Jen, sweetheart, it's okay. It's okay."

"Jen . . ."

Her father's voice.

Only it isn't.

She gasps for air.

It isn't her father's voice at all.

She's never even heard her *father's* voice. She's never seen her *father's* face. She's never known her *father* — her *real* father — at all.

Oh, God. Oh, my God . . .

An awful rasping fills the room. For a few seconds, Jen fails to realize that it's coming from her own throat as she struggles to take in oxygen, in and out, breathe, in and out. Her chest throbs frighteningly with the effort.

Her mother is stroking her hair, cradling Jen's head against her breast, rocking back and forth, sobbing.

Over and over, she's saying she's sorry. She's sorry. Sorry for lying.

Yeah.

Breathe.

In and out. In. Out.

Matt Carmody sits silently on Jen's other side, his hand leaden on her shoulder.

At last, Jen manages to force words past the stranglehold of revulsion; three words that are ridiculously innocuous, yet all she can muster with her world collapsing around her.

"How *could* you?"

The question is meant for her mother, but it is her father — rather, the man Jen was led to believe was her father — who replies.

"I didn't have a choice, Jen." His voice is ragged. "From the moment I saw you, I fell in love with you. I wanted you to be mine. And you were. You *are*. You're my daughter, sweetheart."

"No!" Jen wails. "I'm not. You lied. You . . . both . . . lied." Her body shudders with the supreme task of summoning each word; quakes in an effort to shake away the weighted vise of hands and arms.

"Calm down, Jen," Mom croons. "We'll

talk this out. We love you. We both love you."

In fury, Jen shakes her off, shakes them both off, leaping from their clutches with a violent, adrenaline-fueled jerk. She covers the distance between the bed and the door in a few quick strides, then spins around, trembling in rage.

"You love me? That's another lie. And I hate you. I hate both of you."

Her mother flinches as though she's been struck.

"Jen, you don't mean that," Matt Carmody's voice and gaze are unnervingly level.

"How could you?" Jen asks again, and this time the question dissolves into a help-less wail.

She clings to the door knob for support, refusing to allow her legs to give way this time.

She realizes that her mother has stood and is starting toward her, arms out-stretched.

Jen recoils, snarls, "Stay there! Stay away from me."

Mom stops short a few feet away, her green eyes pleading. "Jen, try to under-stand."

"I do understand. I get it, okay? I know

exactly what you —"

"No, Jen, you don't get it. I was young and alone with you, not that much older than you are, really . . . I wanted you to have what I didn't. I wanted you to have two parents. And Daddy came along, and he was crazy about you from the second he saw you. He's your father. The only father who matters."

Jen shakes her head mutely, in both disagreement and denial.

"We were going to tell you the truth before now," Mom goes on, the words tumbling from her mouth in a heated rush, "but there was never a good time. We knew that it would hurt you and we couldn't stand the thought of hurting you, Jen."

She snorts at that; at the thought of anything hurting more than this.

"Who is he?" she demands. "My father. I want to know who he is."

"I'm your father, Jen."

"No," she tells Matt Carmody. "You aren't. You only pretended to be. Who is my father?" she asks her mother again, pinning her with a steely gaze. "What's his name?"

Mom avoids looking at her daughter and her husband, bowing her head as she says quietly, "Why does it matter? He isn't your father, Jen. He signed away his parental rights after you were born so that Daddy could adopt you."

The latest blow slams into her with nearly as much force as the initial one. He didn't want her. Her own father didn't want her.

"You're lying," she accuses.

"No, Jen. It's true."

"Why should I believe anything you say?" she asks, her voice a mocking echo of theirs just a few nights ago, when they lectured her about violating their trust. "You're liars. Both of you. I hate you."

This time, her mother doesn't flinch. She merely comes closer, reaching toward Jen, saying, "You don't mean that, sweetheart. I don't blame you for —"

"Get away from me!" Jen shrieks, backing into the hallway, becoming vaguely aware of her brothers cowering there. "Don't touch me!"

"Jen —"

She wrenches from her mother's beckoning arms, turning and racing down the hall.

"Let her go, Kathleen," she hears Matt say, just before she slams the door to her room behind her.

Let her go.

He doesn't care.

Why should he? He's nothing to me. No

186

wonder I feel like I don't belong in this family half the time. The rest of them are blood relatives. I'm an outsider.

All right, that isn't entirely true. Her mother, after all, is still her mother, and her brothers are still . . .

No. Curran and Riley are mere *half* brothers.

A fresh wave of loss surges within Jen, along with the acrid, aching anguish of betrayal.

She sinks to her knees on the floor and buries her face in her hands, silent sobs wracking her body. She won't let them hear her cry, and she won't let them see her cry. She doesn't need their apologies or their concern; she doesn't need *them.*

From now on, she'll be isolated in her sorrow and anger, she thinks, lifting her trembling chin with firm resolve. Isolated.

The first line of the John Donne poem she learned for English class just days ago flits into her head.

No man is an island . . .

What did John Donne know, anyway? Nothing.

Jen wipes the tears from her cheeks and sniffles.

She slowly gets to her feet, finding strange comfort in the notion of herself as an island, buffered by an anesthetic sea of inner strength.

Nobody can reach me now, she tells herself as the tide of excruciating pain begins to ebb, giving way to stoic resolution.

Gradually, her heart slows its frantic pace; at last, the pain in her chest subsides and she catches her breath.

In. Out.

In. Out.

I'm going to be okay.

She hugs herself, rocking back and forth, cradled in her own arms, now, and not her mother's.

I don't need her.

I don't need anyone.

I'm an island.

Despite her newfound calm, a chill seems to seep in, settling over the room, over Jen herself. Huddled on the floor, she assures herself that the odd sense of foreboding means nothing — that the worst is behind her.

Yet for some reason, the words of the seventeenth-century poem have become a refrain in her head — this time, not merely the opening line, but the closing ones as well.

Never send to know for whom the bell tolls, Jen recalls.

It tolls for thee.

★ ★ ★

Everything has fallen into place this week with such simplicity and speed that one might easily become convinced that the fates are conspiring to aid this glorious plan for vengeance. Yes, it's almost as though it were meant to be.

But of course, it *was* meant to be. What was begun fourteen years ago will at last be carried through to fruition. There's no doubt about it.

And the sheer anticipation of that triumphant, long-awaited moment threatens to become excruciating if things stretch out much longer than they already have.

You can't afford to rush things along, though.

Speed breeds recklessness. Recklessness can easily lead to discovery — or, more disturbingly, to a tragic mistake.

Poor April. Her only crime was looking so much like Jen; same slender build, same long blond hair. The night was dark, and suddenly, there she was, walking along the side of a deserted road. It seemed too good to be true . . . and of course, it was.

Poor, poor April.

The moment she was in the car, it was obvious that she was the wrong girl. Yet it was too late to set her free. There was nothing to do but make sure she'd never tell.

What a waste.

A waste of time and energy disposing of the body in a remote forest more than an hour east of Buffalo.

And yes, even a waste of a young life . . . not that the girl's disappearance impacted many people, in the end. Not the way Jen Carmody's will.

She'll be mourned. They'll cry for her, and so will I. I'll say how tragic it is, how sorry I am. I'll hug the grieving mother, ask if there's anything I can do to ease her pain.

What delicious irony.

I can hardly wait.

But you have to. You have to wait until the time is right.

Patience. Yes, patience is the key to seeing this thing through to a satisfactory conclusion. Patience and clever and painstaking attention to detail. That's what keeps them all fooled.

Nobody must ever suspect the malignant intent that lies concealed beyond the most benign of facades. When the bloodshed is over, they'll all be left wondering how such a thing could have happened; wondering who among them could have been filled with such murderous hatred.

I'm the last person anyone would ever sus-

pect. I'm the last person Jen would ever fear.

That, in the end, is what makes it so perfect.

Being right here, among them; seeing them look through me, all of them, too caught up in their bustling lives to notice that nobody should ever be taken for granted . . .

And nothing is ever as it seems.

PART II

NOVEMBER

SEVEN

Kathleen hurries across the sidewalk toward Saint Mark's Church the morning of All Saints' Day, shivering in her black trench coat. The crisp breezes of October have given way overnight to the raw and incessant November wind.

She's late for the nine a.m. service, having spent an extra fifteen minutes searching for Riley's missing sneaker. It turned up tucked into the leg of his Winnie the Pooh costume, which he'd tossed behind his bed after trick-or-treating until well after dark last night. That, of course, was right before he threw up from all the chocolate he had pilfered from the bag of loot Kathleen mistakenly believed she'd so cleverly hidden inside the dryer upon their return.

"You hide our candy in there every year, Mom," Curran pointed out as she mopped his brother's vomit from the bathroom floor.

Okay, that's true. She does hide it there every year, after going through it to make sure there are no apples with pins or home-made cookies with razor blades.

"And you always steal all of our Milk Duds first."

Also true. This morning, she has a loose filling to prove it.

As she hurries up the steps of the church she runs a hand through her mussed hair, only to have a gust kick up promptly to tousle it again. What does it matter? She didn't even bother to put on lipstick or mask the blue-black circles beneath her eyes. These days, attempts at masking her exhaustion seem to be futile. She's never felt — or looked — her age until now.

There will be time after mass to run home and pull herself together before meeting Maeve for lunch at Ernesto's . . . *if* she feels like bothering. Big if. The last thing she wants to do today is sit in a pricey trattoria and make idle chit-chat, but her friend insisted. Kathleen broke two lunch dates with her last week, and screens most of her calls lately. She can't help it. Jen's hostility has been all-consuming these last few weeks, and she doesn't feel like discussing the situation with anyone but Matt.

Not that she feels like discussing it with him, either. He tends to shrug off their daughter's anger, saying she'll get over it sooner or later. And if she doesn't, he thinks they should all go to therapy together.

Therapy.

There is no way. Just no way. Kathleen can't sit in a stranger's office and have her emotions dissected. If she opens that door there's no telling what will come spilling out.

Stepping into the church, she carefully closes the heavy outer door behind her, abruptly curtailing the wind and street noise. As she tiptoes across the vestibule, she passes the door leading to the crying room, a windowed booth of sorts that allows parents of fussy infants to witness the mass without disturbing the congregation.

That's when it comes back to her — a snippet of the nightmare she had last night.

She stops short, gazing at the door, trying to recall it.

A crying baby . . . that's all she remembers.

Nightmare? That's not a nightmare. Not really.

But it was unsettling — as unsettling as that phantom telephone call a few weeks ago.

It hasn't happened since. But every time the phone rings, Kathleen's heart stops for a moment.

It doesn't help that the caller ID box broke last week and she hasn't had a chance to replace it. There's something eerie about picking up a phone without being able to anticipate who will be on the other end of the line.

A psychiatrist could probably have a field day with me, Kathleen tells herself as she shakes her head and moves on toward the double doors leading into the church.

Quietly, she slips inside and dips two fingers into the holy water font, then crosses herself. Organ music and the musty scent of incense wrap around her like a familiar shawl; she slips into a pew halfway up the aisle, sinks onto the kneeler, and exhales gratefully as she realizes she isn't as late as she feared.

Losing herself in the priest's intoned reading, Kathleen isn't immediately aware that somebody is watching her.

Only when the congregation stands to pray does she begin to feel it: the distinct sense that she isn't alone.

Of course you aren't alone. You're in church with a few dozen people, a priest, altar boys . . .

But it's something else, something as palpable as the wafting perfume of the old lady in front of her. She can feel a pair of eyes burning into her.

Kathleen turns her head slowly, from one side to the other, trying to catch a peripheral glimpse of whoever might be staring. All she can see are the empty pews directly across from her, on either side of the center aisle. She fights the temptation to swivel further, admonished by a decades-crossing echo of her mother's voice.

Don't ever turn around in church, Katie.

Strange how, with the little she is able to recall of her brief years with Mollie Gallagher, that gentle maternal warning always stands out. How many times has Kathleen used it on her own children, reminding them, as they squirm beside her in the pew, to always face forward during mass?

She bows her head obediently now, feigning prayer as the lector reads through the long list of intercessions, calling out names of the parish's sick and dearly departed.

One name jumps out at Kathleen, startling her from her reverie.

April Lukoviak.

Is she dead? Did they find her?

". . . and ask that you help to guide her safely home, Oh, Lord. We pray . . ."

"Lord, hear our prayer," Kathleen murmurs along with the rest of the congregation, wondering how April Lukoviak's mother bears the daily dread of not knowing. Surely that is the worst thing that can happen to a parent.

But is it worse, Kathleen wonders with a sick ache, than knowing with certainty that your precious child is dead? At least April Lukoviak's mother can hold out hope.

The skin on the back of Kathleen's neck continues to prickle with awareness as the mass proceeds. She bows her head, trying to remember who occupied the rear pews as she made her way up the aisle — and wondering why this is troubling her to the extent that she can no longer focus on a thing Father Edward is saying.

So somebody is looking at the back of her head. Who cares? There's no discernible reason for that to bother her. No reason at all.

Yet she can't fight a growing sense of apprehension as the priest moves through the solemn preparations for the communion ceremony. When at last Father Edward takes his place at the head of the center aisle, host in hand, Kathleen is poised for the opportunity to see who's behind her. She'll turn her head and scan the back of the church as she stands to join the shuffling procession toward the altar. Yes, that's what she'll do. She'll catch the eye of whoever is gaping at her and let them know that she finds their silent perusal ill-mannered, if nothing else.

She rises; turns her head . . .

And glimpses only a fleeting shadow of a figure disappearing through the double doors into the vestibule.

Utterly, yet illogically, unnerved, Kathleen clenches her fists at her sides.

It means nothing — not really. People leave during communion all the time. Back in the old days at Saint Brigid's, forthright Father Joseph repeatedly lectured the congregation about the importance of staying through until the end of mass, perpetually frustrated by the defiant parishioners who made a habit of escaping early.

As Kathleen makes her way up the aisle to receive the host, she can't keep a chill from creeping along her spine.

Somehow, she is certain that whoever just left was the same person who was watching her — and just as inexplicably certain that there was something far more sinister than rude about both their gaze and their premature exit.

"I can't believe I'm doing this," Jen tells Robby as she stashes her backpack in her locker.

"Yeah, me either."

She looks up at him, wondering where his enthusiasm went. Last night, when they discussed this plan on the phone, he seemed so into it. In fact, it was his idea. Now he seems almost . . . nervous?

His eyes are darting from side to side as she slips her jacket off the hook in her locker, as though he's suddenly afraid of getting caught. He, who assured her just yesterday that he could care less about the threat of detention.

"So you sit around for an extra hour after school," he told her with a shrug. "What's the big deal? Have you got something better to do?"

The truth is, unless it's a Wednesday — her day to babysit the Gattinski twins — she doesn't. Not anymore.

When she's not babysitting, Jen's sitting idly at home in the pink-and-white second-floor prison she resents more each day.

Mom, in a ridiculously feeble and transparent effort to bribe Jen out of her sullen state, has been offering to redecorate her room. "Whatever you want, Jen . . . you can even paint the walls orange, if you like Erin's."

That she once coveted her friend's room is almost ludicrous now that she's not only coveted — but won — her friend's boy-friend.

Erin isn't speaking to her these days, now that Robby has dropped her in favor of Jen.

Funny how things can change so drastically in just a few weeks. Funny how you can go so quickly from thinking cigarettes and beer are vile to frequently craving both; from never having been kissed to wondering how long you can possibly cling to your virginity, and why you're even bothering.

Jen slams her locker door shut and turns to face Robby. "Okay, I'm set."

"Shh." Again, he shoots a furtive glance over his shoulder. "Put your jacket back in your locker."

"But it's freezing outside."

"So? It's like a red flag that you're outa here if anybody sees us."

"Oh." She twirls the combination lock, feeling a little ridiculous for the nagging thought that if she goes out into the November wind without a jacket, she might catch a cold.

Robby's response to that would undoubtedly be derisive laughter. *You're afraid of a runny nose, Jen? Come on.*

I'm not afraid of a runny nose, she tells him silently as she shoves her jacket back inside the locker. These days, she isn't afraid of much. After what she's been through at home, there are very few things that could throw her, and the common cold isn't one of them.

So your old man really isn't your old man. So what?

That was Robby's response when she unburdened herself on him a few days into their relationship.

We've all got problems. My mother is a violent drunk who broke my arm when I was two, broke my nose when I was six, and left when I was ten. Big deal.

He said it matter-of-factly, but there was something vulnerable in his black eyes — something that touched Jen in the most profound way. If she had been hesitant about getting involved with the likes of Robby, it evaporated in that moment.

"Where are we going?" she asks him now, as she matches his purposeful stride through the locker-lined corridor, past book-laden students rushing to fourth period.

"I told you . . . it's a surprise."

"I know, but can't you at least give me a hint?" she asks playfully, disappointed when his reply is a terse *no*.

Why is he suddenly so uptight? You'd think somebody who cuts class every day of

204

his life would take it in stride. Maybe it's because Jen is with him, and it's her first time. Maybe she's making it too obvious.

She does her best to adopt a bored expression as they saunter closer to the exit that leads to the parking lot where Robby's car is waiting. *Ho-hum, another uneventful day of classes. No, sir, we're not up to anything.*

Yet as they approach the double glass doors, Jen's heart is racing with anticipation. All those years of following the rules — God, she had no idea what she was missing. Being with Robby has opened up a whole new world to her.

She reaches for his hand, is relieved when he squeezes hers back.

Looking up at him, she sees that he seems more relaxed now, as though he's done this a million times and it's no big deal.

"I can't wait to get out of here," she says with a grin.

A shadow seems to flit across his face before his lips quirk upward. "Yeah," he says, "it'll be great."

But again, she senses that his response is less than wholehearted. Maybe he's feeling guilty about corrupting her. She squeezes his hand again, to reassure him that she's as into this as he is.

Again, he squeezes back . . . tightly, this

time. So tightly that Jen's fingers ache as he opens the door and the icy wind hits her full force, along with a tidal wave of foreboding.

I shouldn't be doing this.

But there's no turning back now.

Looking into the mirror above the bathroom sink, Lucy cringes.

Holy Day of Obligation or not, church is out of the question this morning. She can't leave the house looking like this.

She's certain God will forgive her for missing mass.

She isn't so certain God will forgive Henry, though. She hopes not. Her husband can rot in hell, for all she cares.

She leans closer to the mirror. The swelling around her nose has gone down considerably in the past week or so, and she's fairly certain it wasn't actually broken. But the angry black and purple bruises that rim both eyes are still too dark to be concealed by makeup.

How did he find out where she was that day?

He claimed he found an anonymous note on his windshield, telling him that she had met her former lover at the coffee shop.

Lucy isn't sure she believes him. She confided in only one person where she was going — the one person she trusts more than anybody else in the world. And he would never have told Henry. *Never.*

For all Lucy knows, Henry followed her to the coffee shop when she left the house that afternoon.

But if he did, why wouldn't he have confronted her there? Confronted both of them, for that matter.

How many times, fourteen years ago, did her husband swear he was going to kill the man she loved?

She believed him, believed he was capable of murdering somebody with his bare hands. She still does.

So why, if Henry followed her and saw them together that October day, didn't he come forward right then and there?

Why did he go back home to wait for her, sitting in the darkened kitchen smoking, planning, preparing to pounce on her with his vile accusations — and with his savage fists?

Somebody must have tipped him off. Otherwise, he'd have had no reason to follow her that day. No reason to suspect, after fourteen years, that she was anything but a faithful, obedient spouse.

If Henry wasn't lying about the note, then somebody is watching her, following her every move . . . or somebody else found out about the meeting.

In either case, she'd better watch her step. And so, she realizes with a sinking heart, should Jen Carmody.

Maybe it's time to get this out in the open. All of it, and to hell with the consequences.

The trouble is, the decision isn't hers to make alone.

She spotted him. He's certain of it. In the moment before he ducked out the door into the vestibule, he looked back over his shoulder and saw Kathleen turn her head and look directly at him.

Did she recognize him in that instant?

Probably not. If she had, she probably would have come running after him.

He looks over his shoulder, half-expecting to see her there, chasing him down the boulevard. But the sidewalk is empty aside from a litter of dropped candy wrappers, Silly string, pumpkin guts, and bits of shattered orange shells.

The wide steps of the church are still deserted. Mass won't be over for at least another five minutes. He's heard that Father Edward likes to lengthen the service with endless announcements before the final hymn.

He assumes Kathleen won't leave until mass is over, that she learned her lesson well in all those years of Catholic school.

You shouldn't have left before communion, either, he tells himself, consumed by remorse so potent it's all he can do to keep moving.

But God understands. And God will forgive.

Overhead, branches creak in the gusting wind, the toilet paper draped there by Halloween pranksters fluttering noisily against the remaining leaves.

He quickens his pace as he hurries around the block, away from the church, away from the woman he once believed he would never see again.

Ah, Kathleen. It would have been better for you if you had never come back here. Better for all of us.

"My God, what happened to you?" Maeve asks, setting aside the menu she's been pretending to read as Kathleen slides into the seat opposite hers.

Kathleen's hand goes to her damp, tousled head. "You mean my hair? It's like a hurricane out there."

"I mean all of you." Maeve glances from her friend's drab gray sweater to her sunken eyes to her overall pallor. Only her cheeks have a faint splash of color, undoubtedly from the raw weather rather than rouge. "You look like hell."

"Thanks," Kathleen says dryly, reaching for her own menu.

"No offense," Maeve adds belatedly. "Is everything okay?"

"Everything's fine."

"No, it isn't. If I hadn't dragged you here today you wouldn't even be out of the house."

"Yes, I would. I went to church this morning."

"Church?"

"It's a holy day of obligation, remember?"

Maeve searches her distant memory, then nods. "All Souls Day?"

"All Saints."

"Right. Day after Halloween. Remember when we were kids, how we used to sneak trick-or-treat candy into morning mass on All Saints Day because we were starving and we weren't allowed to have breakfast before communion?"

That brings a smile to Kathleen's pale, chapped lips, albeit a fleeting one.

"So you went to church?" Maeve asks, watching Kathleen peruse the list of specials. "At least you got out for a change. I swear you've been hibernating. I haven't seen you in ages."

"I went to the soccer game on Saturday. You weren't there."

Maeve shrugs. "Erin didn't feel like playing. I didn't feel like going, so why force her, you know?"

Kathleen's mouth tightens. "Actually, we had to force Jen."

"Jen? Superstar Jen? Why didn't she want to play?"

"I guess she was just tired. I thought maybe she was coming down with something, but she seems okay now."

"I heard there's a nasty stomach flu going around. Which reminds me, they're having a flu shot clinic at my gym next week if you want to come. They said this season's going to be worse than last year. You can bring the kids if you want."

"Maybe I'll bring the boys. Jen can't get a flu shot. She's allergic to eggs."

"What about Matt?"

Kathleen makes a face. "He never gets one. He says he's afraid of needles."

"Big, strong, strapping Matt is afraid of needles?" Maeve shakes her head, then wonders if she shouldn't have described Kathleen's husband that way right to her face. Any red-blooded woman would notice that Matt is big, strong, and strapping, but Maeve certainly wouldn't want Kathleen to suspect that she has a thing for Matt.

To change the subject, she asks quickly, "What are you ordering?"

"Is the spinach wrap any good here?"

"I have no idea. I always get the same thing."

"Which is . . . ?"

"Chicken Caesar salad. It doesn't have any carbs." Maeve braces for the usual attack on her stringent dieting, but Kathleen merely nods and goes back to scanning the choices.

Maeve busies herself glancing around to see whether she knows anybody else in the cozy trattoria, with its blue-and-white checked café curtains, round wrought-iron tables, and white wainscot walls. She vaguely recognizes a few faces from the gym, and momentarily locks gazes with the male half of an attractive couple. Relishing his appreciative glance, she allows a tiny smile to play across her lips.

Too bad flirting gets old after awhile, Maeve concludes, looking away as the man's partner reclaims his attention. There are days — more and more of them, lately — when she wouldn't mind being married again. Days when she actually craves the casual, comfortable camaraderie that bored her when she was living it.

Back then, she envied the exciting lives of single women. Now she finds herself coveting what her happily married friends have. Kathleen, for example. That she has the freedom to go around looking like *this*, knowing that at the end of the day, big, strong, strapping Matt will come home to her no matter what . . . well, there's something to be said for that kind of confidence.

Yet, studying her friend as her friend studies the menu, Maeve suspects that something's wrong. Something serious. She can feel it. It isn't just that Kathleen has obviously neglected to put on makeup and fix her hair; she looks haggard and, Maeve notes jealously, she's lost weight recently.

What's going on? Is the perfect Carmody marriage really on the rocks? For the past few weeks that Kathleen's been avoiding Maeve, she's kept such a low profile that the neighborhood rumor mill has already kicked into gear.

A waitress appears, pad in hand, to take their order. The moment she leaves, Maeve leans forward, elbows on the table, chin in her hands. "So what's up?"

Kathleen looks startled. "What do you mean?"

"You're a wreck. I can see it." Maeve hesitates, then asks, with what she hopes is concern and not hopefulness, "Are you and Matt having trouble?"

A scowl crosses Kathleen's features.

"No," she says, so firmly that Maeve believes her.

Okay, so the neighbors were wrong about that. Chances are, they're also wrong about Kathleen having a problem with liquor or drugs. Maeve knew her when that was the case, and it was obvious. You could smell it on her; see the stupor in her eyes.

Now, she doesn't look stoned. She looks troubled.

"It's your father, isn't it?" Maeve realizes, wondering why she didn't think of that sooner. She kicks herself for not being a better friend. She should have called to ask Kathleen about his test results before now. "Did they diagnose him with Parkinson's?"

"Actually, the doctor said he's leaning away from that. Dad has been much better lately. The tremors aren't as bad."

"Good."

"Yeah."

So why doesn't Kathleen seem relieved? God knows she has every reason for contentment, Maeve thinks, wishing she could keep from begrudging her friend all that she suddenly longs for in her own life.

Maybe she's imagining trouble where there is none. Maybe she wants so badly not to be the only screw-up in suburbia that she's projecting her own discontentment.

The waitress sets down Maeve's black coffee and Kathleen's hot tea, along with a basket of freshly baked rolls that immediately assault Maeve's willpower with the tantalizing aroma of hot yeast.

She tries to focus instead on her coffee, but it just isn't satisfying without a cigarette to go along with it.

After stirring a packet of sugar into her cup, Kathleen looks up. "Maeve . . . since you asked. . . ." She pauses, takes a deep breath. "There is something that's been bothering me."

Forgetting all about the rolls and her salivating taste buds, Maeve nods triumphantly. "I knew it. When you've been friends as long as we have. . . . So what is it?"

"I thought maybe Erin mentioned it to you."

"Mentioned what?"

"I figured Jen told her . . ."

"Told her *what?*"

"I don't know how to say this."

Oh, for God's sake, just say it!

Kathleen stretches a sip of her tea into a

maddening pause before blurting, "Jen found out that Matt isn't her birth father."

Maeve sputters into her coffee cup. "What!"

"Please, Maeve, don't say anything to anybody."

"Who am I going to tell?" she asks, offended . . . although the neighborhood gossips would have a field day with this news. "I can't believe it, Kathleen . . . I had no idea."

"Really? Because I was sure Jen must have told Erin."

Maeve debates whether to reveal that Erin and Jen don't seem to be as friendly lately as they were at the beginning of the school year. In fact, Erin hasn't mentioned Jen at all. She's been spending most of her time with Amber, and with Michael, a lanky tenth-grade basketball player who seems to have replaced Robby, from what Maeve has been able to figure out.

"If Jen said anything to Erin, Erin kept it to herself," Maeve tells Kathleen, who nods, her expression desolate.

"What happened, Kathleen? Who is Jen's father? And does Matt know that he isn't?"

"Of course he knows!" Kathleen snaps. "I didn't even meet him until she was almost a year old. He adopted her when we got married, and we figured we'd tell her the truth as soon as she was old enough to understand. But then . . . we just didn't. It was just easier not to."

"It would be." Maeve reaches out and touches Kathleen's hand, finding her flesh icy despite her fingers cupped around the steaming mug of tea. Her mind is awash with questions she's dying to ask, but she settles on, "So you decided it was time to tell Jen now?"

"No. She overheard us talking. It was a horrible scene." Kathleen closes her eyes, as if to block out the memory. "Now she's barely speaking to any of us, not even the boys. All she does is lock herself in her room."

"Who's her father, Kathleen?"

"Do you remember Quint Matteson?"

"Should I?"

Kathleen's smile is bitter. "Probably not. He was older than we were, and he was a loser. He played the drums in a bar band that used to play over on the Elmwood Strip. We went out a few times, if you can call it that. I don't know if you remember, because you and I had drifted by then, but at the time, I wasn't exactly . . . together."

"I remember," Maeve admits.

"It's such a cliché, you know? Nice Catholic girl gets involved in sex and drugs and rock and roll, gets herself pregnant, and the guy wants nothing to do with her."

Maeve nods, thinking that she, too, was a cliché, minus the drugs and rock and roll and with a happier ending.

Then again, not really. Gregory might have married her when she found herself knocked up, but eventually, like Kathleen said, he wanted nothing to do with her.

"My father freaked out when he realized I was pregnant. I wasn't even going to tell him — I don't know how I thought I could avoid it, you know?" Kathleen laughs bitterly. "But I was sick as a dog, and getting fatter by the second, and he figured it out, of course. He threw me out."

"You went to live with your aunt in Chicago, right?"

Kathleen hesitates, her green eyes clouding over. "Eventually. But not until after I had the baby."

"You had her right here? I can't believe I never knew."

"No, not here. Do you remember Father Joseph?"

Maeve smiles. "How could I forget?"

"When I had nowhere else to turn, I went to him."

"You went to Father Joseph?" Maeve asks in disbelief. "He's the last person I'd have gone to in your shoes. He scared the shit out of me."

"Me, too," Kathleen admits. "But when my mother died, he was around a lot, and he told me that if I ever needed help, I should come to him. So . . ."

"So you did. That's unbelievable."

"I had nowhere else to go, Maeve. It was cold and stormy and I was alone and afraid and — and I had nowhere else to go," she repeats, a faraway look in her eyes.

"What did he say when you told him you were pregnant?"

"He didn't say much. He just . . . he let me stay at the rectory for the night, and he made some phone calls. The next day, he sent me to a home for unwed mothers near Albany."

"That sounds horrible."

"It was . . . but in a strange way, it wasn't. It saved me. Father Joseph saved me."

"And Jen."

"Yes." Kathleen looks down at her teacup, stirring, stirring, the spoon rattling against the porcelain. "When I left that day, I promised Father Joseph I would name the baby after him if it was a boy."

"Too bad it was a girl." Maeve is striving for levity, but her tone merely feels inappropriately flippant. "Then again, you could have gone with Josephine."

"Actually, she's named after Father Joseph's mother. I told him I'd do that if the baby was a girl."

Maeve conjures the image of a little old Italian lady huddled in a black shawl, then shakes her head in disbelief. "Father Joseph's mother's name was Jennifer?"

"It was Genevieve. That's Jen's name, too. I started out calling her that, but then Matt and I decided it was too big for such a tiny girl so we shortened it, but she's Genevieve. She doesn't know why. She just thinks we liked the name. And I don't know why I'm telling you all this, except . . ." Kathleen exhales heavily, looking up at Maeve. "I need to tell someone."

"That's what friends are for."

"Plus, I'm worried about Jen, Maeve. I don't know how to reach her now. I'm afraid she's slipping away from us. I'm afraid she'll want to find her birth father."

"Do you know where he is?"

Silence.

She knows, Maeve concludes, watching her friend over the rim of her coffee cup.

"He's listed in the local white pages," Kathleen admits at last. "I checked when we moved back. But I don't want to set her up for disappointment. The truth is, he was a drugged-out loser and fourteen years later he's not going to welcome with open arms this kid he didn't want."

"Maybe he's changed."

"Maybe."

"*You* have."

"I know, but . . ." Kathleen shakes her head. "You know, I wouldn't even recognize him if I ran into him on the street. For all I know, I have. The few times I was with him, I was so wasted . . . I mean, it's not like it was this great love affair."

"Not like you and Matt." Maeve means it sincerely, but somehow, the words emerge with a sardonic edge.

"Matt saved me, Maeve. I was on my own with a baby, living above my aunt's garage, working as a waitress. . . . If he hadn't come along and wanted me — wanted both of us — God only knows where I'd be now."

She'd be exactly where I am, Maeve thinks, as the waitress arrives with their order. *A bitter single mother raising a rebellious teenaged daughter.*

Maeve gazes moodily down at her plate, suddenly sick to death of chicken Caesar salad, sick to death of everything in her life. When did it become all about denial?

Almost without thinking, Maeve reaches into the basket for a hot roll. She breaks it open, and after only a moment's hesitation, takes a small bite.

Oh, God. It's delicious.

Maybe it's time to make a change. Time to start indulging in some of the things that have filled her with ardent longing.

Feeling gloriously defiant, Maeve reaches for the butter, slathers the roll, and wolfs it down in a few intensely ambrosial bites.

EIGHT

I can't do this, Robby thinks as he and Jen head through a cold drizzle toward his car on the opposite side of the parking lot. *I can't.*

He steals a peek at Jen as they cover the last bit of ground. The wind is blowing her long blond hair straight back from her face, revealing big brown eyes and her one facial imperfection, the streak of white that bisects her left eyebrow. She's shivering so badly her teeth are chattering audibly.

She suddenly seems younger than usual. More vulnerable.

So vulnerable that Robby's instinct is to protect her, not —

Stop it. You'll do what you have to do.

Oh, hell. Look at her, glancing up at him and smiling. He can see in her eyes that she's tentative, but excited, too. She has no idea she's walking into a deadly trap.

I can't do this.

You have to. Think of the money.

He envisions the growing stack of bills

223

stashed in the coffee can on top of his closet. By this time tomorrow, if he goes through with the task ahead, a coffee can won't be big enough to hold his cash.

He used some of it the other day to buy Dad a new shirt for his birthday. It wasn't expensive: twenty bucks on sale. But when Robby found it, he knew he had to get it. How long has it been since his father had a new shirt? Years. How long has it been since Robby was able to give him a birthday present?

Never. You've never bought him a present before.

The shocked pleasure on his father's face when his son handed him a gift was a high unlike any chemical one Robby ever experienced. Dad has been wearing the shirt every day since.

Yeah, and it needs a good washing. But some things never change.

He and Jen have arrived at his car. For some reason, Robby is compelled to go around to the passenger's side and open the door for her.

"Wow, what a gentleman," she says with a surprised smile as she climbs into the dim interior.

A gentleman.

He slams the door behind her and walks

around to the driver's side.

A gentleman.

There are some things he never thought he could be. A gentleman is one.

A cold-blooded killer is another.

He slides behind the steering wheel and looks over at Jen.

"Are you sure you want to do this?" he hears himself ask.

He holds his breath for her reply, telling himself that if she says no — if she decides to back out now — then he'll let her go. He'll forget about the plan, about the money; forget that he ever even opened the note that night in the parking lot.

Why did he follow its instructions? Why did he show up at the designated time and place to find out who had written the note, and what else they wanted from him?

Curiosity got the best of him, that's why. Curiosity, and the need for cash.

He waits for Jen to answer his question, and he prays that she'll say no.

Then he'll be off the hook. He'll give back the money he's already received, and he'll tell the creep to go to hell. He might even go to the police and report that somebody wants Jen dead.

Yeah, that's what he'll do. He'll be a hero. Not —

"Yes." Jen's voice shatters his thoughts. "I definitely want to do this."

Robby nods grimly, his jaw set as he turns the key in the ignition.

She wants to do this.

So be it.

Stella makes it as far as Cuttington Road before she has to pull over.

Jamming the shift into Park, she opens the car door and leans out into the wind and the rain that's been falling since noon.

She vomits into the muddy rut below, made even sicker by the sight and smell of a smashed pumpkin littering the ground. When she's finished, she leans back into the car, her stomach still churning, her forehead on fire.

When she felt sick upon awakening this morning, she assumed it was because she pretty much polished off the contents of Michaela's plastic pumpkin pail before bed. She figured that was what she got for gorging on one too many minipacks of Raisinettes and Milk Duds.

Welcome to cold and flu season, she thinks grimly now. It's starting off with a bang this year, just as the newspaper predicted it would.

She must have caught something from

one of the kids at school. Occupational hazard, and one that never seemed particularly perilous before she was a mother.

Now, as she reaches into the glove compartment for a napkin to wipe her mouth, she prays that the girls won't catch whatever it is she's got.

As for Kurt . . .

Well, the truth is, she wouldn't mind seeing *him* miserable.

After what he pulled last night . . .

"It was just a joke," he said.

"Well, it wasn't funny."

"You have no sense of humor," he accused.

"You have a sick one," she shot back, her heart still pounding like crazy.

She had returned from trick-or-treating with the girls only to have him jump out from behind the door, hideous in a rubber monster mask.

The girls shrieked and cried long after he made a big show of taking the mask off to show them that it was only their daddy.

In the end, he opened the front door and tossed it out into the night, telling his whimpering daughters, "There. The monster's all gone. See?"

They saw. They calmed down.

Stella didn't. Not for a long time. Not

even after his grudging apology.

Looking back, she wonders if she was too hard on him. Maybe he really did think it was funny. Maybe if she had more of a sense of humor, if she were quicker to forgive, he'd be nicer to her.

Guilt surges through her, along with another wave of nausea. She presses a wrinkled fast food napkin to her mouth until it passes. The nausea, not the guilt.

The guilt has become as pervasive as the resentment.

What the hell has happened to her marriage? How did she become this pathetic, vengeful person?

She catches sight of herself in the rearview mirror and cringes at the misery etched on her face. It isn't just the stomach bug. It's everything. Her whole life is falling apart because her husband doesn't want her.

He hasn't come right out and said it. Nor is she absolutely convinced he's having an affair.

But she does have her suspicions, based on . . .

Well, based on nothing other than intuition.

Oh, and the fact that he's late coming home every night, and he pretty much limits his contact with her to conversations about the kids.

It happens in lots of marriages, she supposes — this wall that goes up so slowly that you aren't even aware it's being built until one day, it's just there, looming like one of those enormous houses that are popping up all over the development.

She remembers what it was like at the beginning. Love at first sight. That's what she told her college roommates, anyway.

They met on a ski lift one weekend at Holiday Valley. He was skiing alone; her friend Emily chickened out just before they boarded the lift. So Stella found herself riding to the top of the mountain with a tall, good-looking charmer. By the time they reached the end of the ride, she was agreeing to ski down with him.

She assumed he meant the intermediate slope, but as it turned out, he had one of the difficult trails in mind. Standing at the summit, gazing at the steep incline before her, Stella wondered if she'd lost hers.

"What's the matter? Are you scared?" he asked, his brown eyes almost seeming to taunt her.

She shook her head, unable to speak.

"You want me to go first, or do you want to?"

She started to tell him that he could.

But before the words were out of her mouth, he was giving her a little nudge. Just a slight tap, really . . . not a shove. But it was enough to make her wobble, almost losing her balance. The only way to keep it was to tilt forward . . . and with that, she was off, careening down the trail at breakneck speed.

"Was he trying to kill you?" Emily asked her later, when Stella confided what happened.

"Of course not!"

Never mind that Emily was echoing exactly the thought that had raced through her head earlier as she struggled to negotiate the treacherous trail.

"It was just a joke," she assured Emily.

A joke. Just like the monster mask.

When she met up with Kurt at the bottom of the trail that day, he was laughing. "That was excellent," he told her. "You were great. It's a hard run."

His praise warmed her.

She was young, naive, and, all right, stupid back then. Too stupid to care that she could have been killed. Too stupid to tell him to get lost. Too stupid not to fall in love.

Well, she's not stupid anymore. Not

230

stupid, or young, or naive.

Stella starts the car again and drives slowly toward home, wondering whether she remembered to leave her lesson plan for the sub who's covering for her for the rest of the day. And she should have brought a stack of papers home with her to grade later, when she feels better.

If she feels better later.

With any luck, this is one of those twenty-four-hour bugs. God knows she can't afford to be out of commission for any longer than that. She has a busy week at school, and she has to chaperone the homecoming dance Friday night.

Stella pulls into her driveway and presses the automatic garage door opener. As it goes up, she spots wet tire marks on the concrete inside.

That's odd.

It wasn't raining yesterday, and even if it had been, any tire marks her car made would have dried overnight.

It's almost as though . . .

No. Why would Kurt come home in the middle of the day? His office is a twenty-minute drive away.

Spotting an election sign on a neighbor's lawn in the rearview mirror, Stella is momentarily relieved, thinking he must have come home to vote. Then she realizes that election day isn't until tomorrow.

Well, maybe he forgot something, Stella tells herself as she pulls the car into the garage and lowers the door behind her.

She steps out and makes her way to the door that leads into the house, her legs feeling weak and her stomach queasy.

All she wants to do is climb into bed and go to sleep.

The house is clean and quiet and smells of the chili she threw together last night right before she took the girls out trick-or-treating. Right now, it's enough to turn her stomach, as is the sight of the girls' plastic pumpkin buckets on the counter. She had guiltily dumped half the contents of MacKenzie's into Michaela's nearly empty one. With any luck, they won't notice that all the good stuff is missing.

Stella hurries from the kitchen after tossing her coat over a chair and her keys on the table beside a basket of gourds and apples. As she climbs the stairs, she spots something clinging to the runner halfway up. It's a small shred of maple leaf somebody dragged in on their shoe.

Which wouldn't strike her as odd if Sissy hadn't cleaned the entire place from top to bottom just yesterday.

And if the leaf weren't slightly damp.

In the master bedroom, Stella pauses, toying with the leaf in her fingers. She stares intently at the bed she made only hours ago, looking for signs that somebody has been in it. The pillows appear to be propped just as she left them, and the quilt isn't wrinkled.

If Kurt came home unexpectedly from the office today, it wasn't with a lover. Not unless he suddenly learned how to make a bed.

Or unless they did it on the floor.

Stella looks down, closes her eyes, sees her husband's naked limbs entwined with the lithe arms and legs of a stranger.

Pressing her hands to her mouth, Stella attempts to force back the bile that rises swiftly in her throat.

The effort is futile.

With a frustrated cry, she gives up and rushes to the bathroom, retching.

"You look good, Dad."

"No, I don't." Drew Gallagher waves off his daughter's comment with a gnarled old hand, scowling.

Juggling a bakery box and shopping bag, Kathleen bends over his wheelchair to press a perfunctory kiss against her father's cheek. His skin sags across his features like the hovering nurse's baggy, parchment-colored hose do around her ankles.

The nurse, whose name Kathleen can never seem to remember, tucks in his lap robe, then flashes a conspiratorial smile at Kathleen. "Don't let this old grumposaurus fool you. He's spent the whole day waiting for your visit."

"That's just because he knows I always bring him something. But Dad, you have to promise that you won't try to sneak out of here again." It happened just yesterday — he managed to dress himself and escape.

This time, it was a few hours before he was spotted by a policeman on patrol, nearly a mile away from the nursing home. And this time, Kathleen didn't even know he was missing until it was all over and he was safely back in his room.

In fact, if she hadn't happened to call in to check on him and learned about it from the nurse on duty, she might not know about his latest escape at all. It makes her wonder if the staff even bothers to inform her of his every attempt to break out. She vows to have a talk with the management. But not today. She's got other things on her mind today.

"Did you hear that, Mr. Gallagher?" the nurse is asking. "You have to stay put. Your daughter doesn't want you out on the streets. You could get hurt."

"Yeah, yeah, yeah." Drew scowls as the nurse leaves the room, then turns to his daughter with anticipation. "What'cha got for me today, Katie?"

She hands over the white bakery box and the plastic Wal-Mart shopping bag she just filled with candy corn and pumpkin-shaped marshmallow Peeps on clearance.

"Fried cakes!" he exclaims, peering into the bakery box. "I love these."

"I know you do." She smiles. She, too, adores the frosted, sprinkle-covered dough-nuts unique to western New York and this time of year. There's nothing like freshly baked fried cakes and hot apple cider on a brisk autumn day. She's missed that in the years since she left, just as she's missed true Buffalo wings, and beef on weck, and con-cord grapes . . .

Funny how she never realized she was homesick until she actually came home. Homesick for more than food, she acknowl-edges, a lump rising in her throat as she watches her father looking over the contents of the doughnut box.

Dad is homesick, too. That's why he keeps trying to run away.

I just want to go home, Kathleen.

"You got me a whole dozen?" he asks, delighted.

"A baker's dozen," she clarifies around the lump in her throat, and he chuckles.

"Good thing I'm not superstitious about thirteen."

"Good thing. And you'll have enough to share with all of your friends here."

"What friends? You mean the jail guards? I'm not sharing with them." A mercurial scowl dissipates once again when he sets the box aside and looks into the plastic bag. "Candy!"

"Yup." She watches him tear into cellophane as eagerly as Riley. Dad has a sweet tooth to rival any child's. He always has. One of her few happy childhood memories is of going to the five and dime with him, and being allowed to fill a big paper bag with all the penny candy it could hold.

"I forgot it was Halloween," he says around a mouthful of orange marshmallow goo. "Are the kids going out trick-or-treating later? Or don't they do that these days?"

"They do it, but they already did." Kathleen perches on the edge of the bedside chair. "Halloween was yesterday."

"Oh." He looks embarrassed. Why didn't she let him think that he knows what day it is? What difference does it make?

"Riley was Winnie the Pooh this year," she goes on with forced cheer. "And Curran was a baseball player."

"How about Jenny?"

Dad insists on calling her that, though nobody else ever does. Kathleen is never sure whether it's done out of affection, or if he simply doesn't bother to remember her name.

"She didn't get dressed up."

This was the first time ever. Back in Indiana, Jen wore a Halloween costume and went out trick-or-treating right up until last year, and Kathleen has no doubt that the friends she left behind still are. But here, the kids Jen's age don't wear costumes — at least, not elaborate ones. Sure, a handful of older kids showed up late in the evening with trick-or-treat bags, unchaperoned. And they had made only halfhearted attempts at disguises: a fake mustache, perhaps a wig, an eye mask at most.

"Don't give them candy," Matt advised Kathleen when she complained that they were running low on Kit Kats and Nestle's Crunch Bars.

"I'm afraid not to."

"Why? They're too old and they're not even dressed up."

"Yeah, but I get the feeling it's like black-mail. When they say trick or treat, they mean it."

Sure enough, this morning, she woke up to a neighborhood decorated with toilet paper and Silly String and strewn with smashed pumpkins. For the most part, the Carmodys' lawn and trees were spared, and they brought the pumpkins inside before dark, but there were eggs around their mailbox. It was easy to tell who had turned the older kids away without candy; those houses were hit hard.

"Jenny's getting too old for that kid stuff," her father says now. "How old is she, anyway? Twelve? Thirteen?"

"She'll be fourteen tomorrow."

"Already?"

"Already."

Kathleen falls silent as he crams another sugar-encrusted Peep into his mouth, his dark green eyes thoughtful. She wonders if he's thinking about the granddaughter he once refused to know; wonders if he has any regrets about all those wasted years.

It was Aunt Maggie who convinced Kathleen to invite her father to her small wedding in Chicago, just as she convinced her niece to have a priest officiate, rather than the justice of the peace she and Matt had originally chosen.

That her father decided to attend caught Kathleen utterly off guard.

That she found herself asking him to give her away did, too.

But in the end, she supposes, it all comes down to the fact that he is her only parent — the one who raised her. She loved him, loves him still, despite all of his mistakes. And deep down inside, she knows that he loves her despite her own.

So he walked her down the aisle, and she caught him wiping tears away as she and Matt exchanged vows. Later, she caught him holding his granddaughter's hand as she toddled around the reception.

He never did apologize for throwing Kathleen out when she told him she was pregnant; she isn't even certain that he *is* sorry. Nor is she certain that she forgives him for it.

But she does understand that he's a throwback to another era, to a deeply religious generation, at least in her family. Right or wrong, he did the only thing he was capable of doing under the circumstances.

If anybody understands that, it's Kathleen.

With an inner shudder, she forces her thoughts back to the present.

"What is that nurse's name, Dad?"

He looks around. "What nurse?"

"The one who was here a few minutes ago. She's always so nice, and I . . . I can't ever remember her name."

"Do you think I can? I'm lucky if I know what day it is, remember?"

She laughs, pretending it's a joke, knowing that it isn't.

"I went to mass this morning for All Saints Day," she announces, knowing that it's ridiculous to need her father's moral approval after all these years, but unable to help herself.

"That's good."

"I'm sure the priest will be by later to bring you communion."

"Father Joseph?"

"Father Edward, Dad."

Kathleen watches her father reach into the bag of candy again, selecting a package of candy corn. He opens it and pops a few pieces into his mouth.

She tries to think of something else to say. These visits can be excruciating. It's easier when one of the kids or Matt come with her, but they rarely want to, and she doesn't blame them.

"Father Joseph was here earlier."

"Dad, that was Father Edward," she repeats patiently. "Father Joseph retired years ago."

He frowns, looking confused. "Are you sure?"

"I'm positive." That's what she heard, anyway, on one of her visits back to Buffalo. She hasn't been in touch with the priest in years. Fourteen, to be exact. She couldn't bear to face him, not after all that happened.

"Well, I don't know about that, but he's been here a lot lately," her father says. "He comes in to check on me."

Kathleen holds back a weary sigh. It isn't easy to watch her father make the long, slow decline into senility. Most of the time he's utterly lucid, but other times he's hopelessly confused. That's why it's so scary that he manages to run away from the home as frequently as he does.

One day last week when she woke him from a nap, he called her Mollie. And he still claims somebody is stealing his socks and underwear.

Dad takes another handful of candy corn, munching it.

"I'll bring you some of Jen's birthday cake next time I come, Dad," Kathleen promises, glancing at her watch, wondering if she's done her duty yet.

"Whose cake?"

"Jen's," she repeats. "Her birthday is tomorrow, remember?"

"I knew that!" His expression is reproachful. "You just have to stop mumbling. I can't hear you."

"Sorry," she practically shouts.

"That's better."

Lord, this room is overheated. She could take off her coat, but then she'd feel obligated to stay even longer. The smell of institutional food wafts unappetizingly in the steam-heated air. Down the hall, she can hear somebody moaning in pain in one room, a blasting television laugh track in another.

Kathleen glances longingly out the rain-splattered window, and then again at her father. How does he get through the dreary days in this place? How can he stand it?

"Dad, Matt and I are coming to get you tomorrow," she hears herself saying.

As soon as the words are out of her mouth, she wants to take them back. What the hell is she doing? Why is she further complicating her life right now? Jen's birthday is always a difficult time for her, and this year it will be even harder, given the circumstances. The last thing she needs is to throw her cranky, confused father into the tense mix at home.

Maybe he didn't hear me, she thinks hopefully.

But he's looking up from his bag of candy with enthusiastic interest, asking, "Why are you coming to get me tomorrow? Are you taking me home?"

"To *our* home, yes. For Jen's birthday party," she says as gaily as she can manage. "You can come over for dinner and cake, and then we'll bring you back."

"I can't go anywhere without a wheelchair."

"Really? You seem to do just fine every time you make a jailbreak."

"I'm not supposed to go anywhere without a wheelchair," he repeats, looking stubborn.

He's given her an out, but for some reason, she won't let herself take it. Instead, she shrugs and says, "The home will let us use one for a few hours. I'll ask the nurse."

He considers it.

Then, to her surprise — and, truth be told, her dismay — he shrugs and says, "Okay."

Kathleen forces herself to feign enthusiasm, to say "Great!" and then forces herself to spend a few more minutes making idle conversation with him.

Then, when she can no longer stand it,

she says, "I have to get going now, Dad. I have a lot to do before the kids get home this afternoon."

A lie. She has nothing to do. Nothing but brood.

"All right."

"I'll see you tomorrow."

"Okay." He nods as she kisses the top of his head.

"Betty," he calls when she's halfway to the door.

She pauses. Sighs. Turns to say gently, "I'm Kathleen, Daddy. Katie."

"No, the nurse. You asked me what her name was. I just remembered. It's Betty. She was named after Betty Crocker because her mother loved to bake."

As she makes her way down the corridor, past the painted mustard-yellow cinderblock walls and withered residents visible through open doorways, Kathleen can't help smiling, telling herself that Dad might not be as feeble — or as far gone — as she thought.

"You're going pretty fast," Jen tells Robby as he steers around a corner, the tires squealing slightly.

"Yeah. It's no fun if you go the speed limit." He straightens the wheel, eyes focused on the windshield as the wipers bob rhythmically across the glass.

Jen wants to tell him to slow down, but doesn't dare.

He'll think she's wimping out, and she isn't about to do that. No, she's in this for the duration.

She stares out her window at the closely set, nondescript two-story houses, noticing how different this neighborhood is from her own. Here, the trees tower high above rooftops, fences are made of chain link, and driveways are occupied by cars and old pickups, not SUVs and Volvo Country wagons. Most of them even have rust spots around the fenders and tailgates.

She can't imagine what they're doing in this part of Buffalo, a good twenty minutes from Woodsbridge. She was expecting him to take her to the mall, or maybe out to eat, or . . .

Okay, a motel room did cross her mind once or twice, but she's pretty sure that isn't what he's got planned. In fact, if anything, he's been less amorous lately than he was when they first hooked up a few weeks ago. Maybe he's turned off by the fact that she's a virgin. Or maybe he's seeing somebody else behind her back. Somebody more experienced.

Somebody like Erin.

She winces at the mere thought of her best friend — former best friend, that is. Erin hasn't been speaking to her since Robby decided he liked her. Jen has been trying to convince herself that she couldn't care less — that Erin is shallow and disloyal. But now she wonders reluctantly whether she's the one who is both of those things.

Erin was her only true friend in Woodsbridge. Now, alienated from her parents and siblings as well, Jen has nobody.

Nobody but Robby.

"Where are we going?" she asks him yet again, noticing that he seems to be checking the street signs as they fly by. "Do you even know? Or are we totally lost?"

"We're not lost," is his terse reply. "And you'll see when we get there. It's a surprise."

She smiles. A surprise. For her birthday, no doubt. How he found out that it's tomorrow, she has no clue. She certainly didn't bring it up to him.

She tells herself that she should be exhilarated, not fearful. This, after all, is an adventure.

They take another sharp turn, this time on two wheels. She bites her lower lip to keep from crying out as he swerves to miss scraping a utility pole on her side. He's driving like a maniac, and she's starting to think he's trying to get them killed or something.

His hands are clenching the wheel so tightly that his knuckles are jutting white knobs, bringing to mind a skeleton's bones and sending another ripple of worry down her spine.

"Robby? Are you okay?"

"I'm fine."

But he isn't. His voice is laced with tension and an odd undercurrent of something else. Anger, maybe? But that doesn't make sense. Why would he be angry with her?

Jen sinks lower in her seat, her fingers reaching toward her left hip to make sure her seat belt is fastened.

What are you doing, Jen? Why are you doing this? This isn't fun.

She closes her eyes. Her mother's face flits into her mind's eye, and then her father's. Erin's, too.

You have to tell him to stop. Turn around, take you back to school.

Yes, and if she does that, she'll lose him. That's for sure.

How much does she care?

He's all you have. He's the only one who cares about you.

All right, she admits in a moment of clarity, Curran and Riley care, too. Her brothers have been watching her with worried expressions these last few weeks, trying unsuccessfully to lure her from her self-imposed exile.

Truth be told, Mom and Dad probably care, too. Despite their lies, despite their hypocrisy, despite the fact that she doesn't even have Dad's blood flowing through her veins, he must care about her. Mom, too. She hasn't missed the anguish in their faces or the hurt in their voices whenever she turns a cold shoulder on their attempts to win her back.

If they knew where she was now, they'd be upset. Upset, and furious.

Until this moment, she wouldn't have cared. Now, for whatever reason, all at once, she does.

This is wrong. All of it. Not just cutting class, but Robby, and —

A blast of sound shatters Jen's thoughts.

A siren.

Robby curses, jerking his gaze to the rearview mirror as Jen turns her head to see a police car emerging from a shrub-sheltered speed trap.

In moments, it's bearing down on them, red light spinning.

For a fleeting second, Jen wonders whether Robby is going to try to outrun the cops.

Then, abruptly, he brakes and pulls to the side of the road.

"You're going to get a ticket," Jen tells him, her heart pounding. "And we're going to get into trouble for being out of school."

"Yeah." He shoots a glance in her direction. "I know that."

Gone is the devil-may-care swagger. To her surprise, he looks almost . . . relieved?

Relieved to be nailed by the cops?

It doesn't make sense.

Jen frowns, realizing that she doesn't know him nearly as well as she thought.

She only knows that when the stern-faced uniformed police officer appears at the driver's-side window, she, too, is relieved. Their adventure is over.

At least, for the time being.

NINE

The baby!

Kathleen sits bolt upright in bed.

The baby is crying.

Heavy eyelids fluttering closed again, Kathleen automatically swings her legs out from beneath the warm covers, over the edge of the mattress into the inky darkness.

The moment her feet hit the chilly bedroom floor, she's jarred into consciousness.

I don't have a baby.

But . . .

She listens.

The night is still.

Beside her in the bed, Matt is snoring softly, his breathing deep and even. The only other sound she can hear is a water faucet dripping somewhere down the hall, and a faint breeze stirring the leaves outside their bedroom window.

She must have been dreaming again. Dreaming of the long ago nights when the boys and Jen were infants, waking her to nurse at all hours. Funny how the routine comes right back; how maternal instinct is so innate that you will rise to start the familiar sleep walk to the cradle, even when the cradle has been empty for years.

Kathleen settles her exhausted body back beneath the warm blankets.

Just as she is drifting into slumber, another faint cry pierces the night.

Her blood runs cold as she listens to the unmistakable wail of an infant. For a moment, she's paralyzed by fright. Then she clutches the arm of her sleeping husband and whispers frantically, "Matt! Wake up!"

His even breathing disrupted, he is jarred to alertness with a sputtering snore. "What? What is it?"

"Shhh! Listen!"

Silence.

"What?" he asks again.

"I heard something."

"Probably the wind," he mutters, rolling over again.

"No!" Kathleen pulls at his T-shirt. "Matt, I'm scared. Please."

"What did you think you heard?"

"I didn't think I heard it, I know I heard it. It was a baby."

"You were probably dreaming, Kath. Go back to sleep."

"I wasn't —"

She breaks off at the sound of another distant cry. The sound is muffled, but it's there.

Matt sits up, his body poised as he listens.

"You heard it, didn't you." Kathleen clings to his arm.

"I heard it. It's probably one of the neighbors' kids."

"The windows are closed, Matt. It's November."

"Kathleen, do you remember how loudly Curran used to scream? Somebody could have been a mile away and —"

"There it is again! Matt!"

"Okay, okay." He rubs his eyes, swings his legs over the side of the mattress.

"Where are you going?"

"To check on the kids. Maybe one of them is watching TV downstairs or something."

She nods, shivering beneath the covers, wanting desperately to believe that the sound came from the television. The explanation makes more sense than anything else her brain can conjure.

As she hears his footsteps treading down the stairs, she wonders if it's Jen who's up in the family room. She wouldn't be surprised if her daughter were having trouble sleeping after what happened yesterday.

The vice principal reached Kathleen at home just as she walked in the door after visiting her father. Fifteen minutes later, she was sitting opposite his desk, beside her silent daughter. Jen's eyes looked swollen and red, as though she'd been crying, but by the time Kathleen arrived her face was a sullen mask.

Robby, who had been caught cutting class one too many times, had been suspended. That the vice principal let Jen off with a week's worth of detention seemed generous to Matt when Kathleen broke the news to him over the phone while he was still at work.

"Maybe she needs to be suspended," was his grim reply. "Maybe that would snap some sense into her."

When he arrived home, he informed Jen that she would be grounded for an additional four weeks. She would have to give up the babysitting job, and soccer, too, was out of the question now.

Jen's response was a shrug, as though she couldn't care less about soccer, or about anything.

"We're losing her, Matt," Kathleen told her husband tearfully right before they fell asleep a few hours ago. "I don't know what to do."

"Neither do I," he admitted, and again brought up family therapy.

This time, Kathleen agreed to at least consider it, well aware that nothing matters now more than rescuing Jen from the frightening downward spiral.

Kathleen hears Matt's footsteps coming back up the stairs again.

In the hallway three bedroom doors creak open one by one and then close quietly again before Matt reappears beside the bed.

"The kids are all sound asleep in their rooms, and the TV is off downstairs," he informs Kathleen as he walks to the window, lifts the shade, and looks out. "I bet it was an animal."

"What kind of animal?" she asks incredulously, huddled beneath the comforter, unable to stop her body from trembling.

"I don't know . . . maybe a cat or something."

A fuzzy memory flits into her mind, a memory that makes her heart ache with longing for more innocent days. She sees Jen snuggled on her lap as a little girl; Kathleen reading aloud to her from the Little House on the Prairie books she herself had loved as a child. She recalls Jen's big brown eyes growing rounder than ever at the author's vivid description of a panther

254

crying out in the night, a blood-curdling sound that was almost human.

But this isn't the prairie. There are no panthers in suburban Buffalo. She tells Matt as much when he slips back into bed beside her.

"I know a baby's cries when I hear them," Kathleen informs him, her voice wavering on the verge of high-pitched hysteria. "And this isn't the first time, Matt. I heard it last night, too. But I thought it was just a dream. And —"

"And what?" he asks when she falls silent, suddenly reluctant to tell him about the phone call a few weeks ago.

"Nothing." She takes a deep breath, lets it out slowly. "Never mind."

"Go back to sleep, Kathleen. Whatever it was, it's gone now."

Moments later, he's snoring once again.

Kathleen lies awake, her body tense, hands clenched at her sides.

The phone call and the cry in the night were no coincidence. She's certain of it.

Yet the only explanation she can conjure is a supernatural one. Kathleen has never believed in anything like that, and it's not as though they're inhabiting some Gothic Victorian mansion. Even if she were inclined to go with an otherworldly explanation for the cries, this newly built Colonial is the last house she would ever imagine as haunted.

All night, she keeps a fearful vigil, her thoughts whirling feverishly over and over traumatic events — not just those that are recent, but the ones that torment her still, after all these years.

When at last the first gray light of dawn filters through the window, she silently bids her firstborn a happy birthday, tears trickling slowly down her cheeks.

"What are you doing still in bed?"

Stella stirs, roused out of a deep sleep by Kurt's voice somewhere overhead. Rolling over, she opens her eyes and then quickly closes them again, blinded by the glare of the overhead light.

"Can you turn that off?" she croaks, her mouth foul-tasting and so dry she can't even muster enough saliva to swallow.

She hears him cross the room to the light switch. "Okay, it's off," he says, sounding almost curt.

Kurt sounds curt. Imagine that.

Resentment mingles with the nausea that slips in to claim her once again, making her long for the blessed reprieve of sleep that was a long time coming. She was up far into the wee hours, most of that time spent huddled in misery on the chilly bathroom tile. Every time she dared to venture away from the toilet, she found herself racing back.

But of course Kurt doesn't know any of that.

When he came home — *if* he came home at all — he spent the night on the couch. He'll blame it on her being sick, but she has her suspicions.

It was only after she begged him over the phone that he left the office on time to meet the girls' day care bus. He fed them takeout pizza — its aroma wafting up the stairs and sending Stella running for the bathroom — then got them into bed and informed his wife that he had to head back to the bank to finish some paperwork.

Doubting his story and too sick to care, she asked him to pick up some ginger ale and saltines for her on his way back.

If he did, he never came upstairs to tell her, or to offer to bring her some.

Now, she looks up at him, wearing suit pants and a dress shirt, a tie looped through the collar. Clearly, he's headed back to work . . . and expects her to do the same.

"I can't do it, Kurt," she informs him, her stomach roiling as she tries to sit up. "I have to stay home. You'll have to get the girls ready and drop them off."

"I have a breakfast meeting at eight."

Breakfast.

Food.

She tries again to swallow, but her mouth is too dry. Nausea rides up her throat and she clutches her stomach. Her bed might just as well be a storm-tossed sea. Her efforts to fight the waves of seasickness prove futile and she bolts from the bed.

This time, she doesn't make it to the bathroom.

She vomits on the bedroom carpet — ironically, in the very spot she imagined her husband making love to a phantom mistress just yesterday.

He looks down at her in disgust. "Jesus, Stella. You're worse than one of the kids. This is going to stink to high heaven. By the way, I have a banquet I have to go to on Friday night, so you'll have to get a sitter if you're still planning to chaperone that dance."

Stella leaves the mess behind; leaves him behind. Staggering to the bathroom, she slams the door behind her.

"Bastard," she mutters as her jellied knees give way and she sinks to the floor in front of the toilet once again.

Her body wracked with dry heaves, she

wonders how on earth she wound up married to a stranger.

"Look, I already said I'm sorry," Robby snaps into the pay phone at the 7–11 store around the corner from Orchard Arms apartments. "It isn't my fault that I got stopped by the cops for speeding. They made me go with them and they got a truant officer to take her right back to school. There was nothing I could do."

"I paid you to do a job, and I expected it to be done."

"I know. It will be. Just as soon as I can figure out how."

"I'll tell you exactly how."

As the ominous voice murmurs in his ear, Robby watches a packed yellow school bus pass the parking lot out on Cuttington Road, filled with kids on their way to Woodsbridge High. He finds himself scanning the windows for Jen's familiar blond head, even as he listens to the carefully outlined plan for her demise.

"Do you understand?"

He hesitates. "I don't know. That seems a little —"

"Are you going to do it or not? If you're not, I'll need the money you've already been paid returned to me when we meet in a half hour, and I'll find somebody else. I can't risk another screw up."

Robby throws his head back to examine the overcast sky, contemplating the offer.

He needs the money. Needs it desperately. And yet . . .

He closes his eyes, seeing Jen's innocent face — and his father's beaming one.

His father made him promise that he'd stop dealing — that he'd stay away from drugs altogether. Robby is fairly — all right, completely — certain that the old man wouldn't prefer he convert himself into a murderer-for-hire instead.

Jen paged him last night, and again this morning. He ignored her, and finally turned his pager off. He feels guilty every time he sees her number come up, knowing she's probably worried about him.

She shouldn't be, damn it. She should be afraid of him. Is she really that clueless? That trusting? If she is, then she deserves what she gets.

Or so he tries to convince himself.

He lowers his head, his gaze falling on his new black leather boots. He paid full price for them, over four hundred bucks. He's always wanted boots like this, with thick soles and shiny silver buckles.

If he goes through with this, he can buy

the other stuff he's always wanted. A stereo with kick-ass speakers, a shearling coat, hell, maybe even a computer.

Yeah, right. What do you need with a computer? It's not like you're going to college or anything.

Okay, but if he had a computer he could IM like all the other kids do, and burn CDs, and surf the Web for stuff. Not just porn, but other cool stuff, too.

"Are you there?" asks the voice.

"Yeah. I'm here."

"I need to know. If you can't do this then tell me right now."

This is it, Robby realizes. *It's in your hands. This is where you get to decide which way your life is going to go.*

He squeezes his eyes closed again and he sees his mother's face, filled with fury, with resentment, with hatred.

Sees the cop gazing down at him through the driver's side window yesterday, wearing an expression of utter disdain.

Sees the vice principal's obvious contempt, his blatant surprise that a girl like Jen would become entangled with the likes of Robby.

He's seen it, seen all of it, so many times before, on the faces of the teachers and adults and the kids who inhabit the homes

261

of Orchard Arms. They judge him, all of them, based on where he lives, who his parents are — no, who they *aren't*.

Is it so surprising that they expect nothing of him? Nothing other than trouble. Is it so surprising that it's all he's given any of them all these years?

This is your chance. You can prove them wrong.

Or you can prove them right.

Everything is hanging in the balance.

Clenching the phone against his ear, he makes his decision.

"Look, I have to go," the voice says impatiently. "Meet me in a half hour. Either you'll have her with you, or you'll have the money."

Moments later, he's back in his car, heading back home to get the coffee can from the top of his closet, certain that he made the right choice.

He'll get a job. He'll start looking for one today . . . just as soon as he's handed over the money, then gone to the police to tell them that Jen Carmody's life is in danger.

So this is what it feels like to be fourteen, Jen thinks glumly as she shuffles into biology. So far, it sucks. If today is any indication of what the year ahead holds, she'd probably have been better off if Robby had rammed them into that utility pole after all.

Her parents and brothers wished her a happy birthday this morning when she came downstairs.

Only the boys seemed to mean it.

Dad is still obviously angry about the detention thing yesterday, his voice as cold as his expression whenever he speaks to her — which he does only when absolutely necessary. Even his birthday wishes were cursory. Not that she'd expect anything else from a man who isn't even a blood relative.

That isn't fair, Jen.

She frowns at the nagging, increasingly vocal inner spokesperson for her conscience, wishing it would shut up already.

So what if she isn't being entirely fair to the man who raised her?

Life isn't fair.

Yeah, Dad. Life isn't fair.

And then there's Mom. When she stumbled into the kitchen in her robe, she looked as though she hadn't slept all night, and she sounded slightly hoarse. She hugged Jen, but her arms felt stiff — especially when she felt Jen's whole body go rigid in her embrace. Jen *did* feel a pang of regret when she saw the hurt in her mother's eyes, but she couldn't help her reaction.

She knows she's the cause of her mother's exhaustion; her mother has been losing sleep over Jen even before she got herself into trouble yesterday. But that has been easy to ignore until now.

At least nobody has made Jen sit down and discuss the circumstances of her birth and adoption. Not yet, anyway.

She heard her parents discussing her last night after she was in bed. From what she could piece together, they're in disagreement over how to handle this. Her father wants the whole family to see a shrink. Her mother doesn't think that's a good idea, which is somewhat surprising, since Mom usually is a big fan of talking things out. She claims it's healthy.

When Jen was little and heard her parents arguing, she'd worry that it meant they were going to get divorced. She still remembers how her mother used to hug her and assure her that all mommies and daddies argued sometimes, and it didn't mean they didn't love each other.

That she is the direct cause of friction in their marriage now should probably bother Jen, but it doesn't. Not much, anyway.

You're beyond caring about them, she reminds herself.

She would probably feel differently if her

family were really the wholesome unit she had been duped into believing they were: happily married parents, three happy kids. That was something special, as far as Jen was concerned — something that set her apart from most of her friends.

She was different from Erin, being raised by a single mother. Different from their friend Rachel, the product of a third marriage with a trail of stepparents, stepsiblings, and half siblings along the way. Different from Robby, whose mother took off when he was a kid and whose father is an unemployed alcoholic.

Jen figured she was one of the lucky ones.

Boy, was she wrong.

At least her friends never had any illusions about who and what they are. At least *they* weren't blind fools, Jen thinks bitterly.

To find out that she herself was the result of her mother getting herself pregnant by some other guy, that her father isn't her father and her brothers aren't her brothers . . .

Well, who cares if their marriage doesn't last now? The family is already splintered, as far as Jen is concerned.

Wishing this miserable day were over, Jen slips gloomily into her seat at the lab table she shares with Garth Monroe, whose seat is still vacant.

"Hey, Jen, I heard about you and Robby," Rachel Hanson leans across the aisle to say. "Did you guys really get arrested?"

"Arrested?" Jen shakes her head, rolling her eyes. "No, we weren't arrested."

Rachel is obviously disappointed. Erin once told Jen that if Rachel were paid for gossiping, she'd be driving a BMW by now.

Erin, again.

The thought of her brings another little pang of guilt. Her former best friend is no angel — far from it. But Jen knows she's the one who trashed their friendship. She chose Robby over Erin.

Oh, who are you kidding? You stole Robby away from Erin.

Well, it wasn't something she set out to do. It's not like she was falling all over him, the way Erin accused her of doing when she found out. No, Robby was the one who came after Jen, and she tried to resist him. Really, she did.

Okay, she probably would have tried harder if her parents hadn't spilled their horrible secret and turned her world upside down. At the time, she was hurting so badly she didn't care who else she hurt.

And do you care now? that infuriating inner

voice asks, as Jen again pictures her mother's face when she pulled back from the hug this morning.

Life is easier when your conscience is obeying gag orders, that's for sure.

"I thought Robby was in jail," Rachel presses on.

"Well, he's not."

Not that Jen would know. She hasn't spoken to him since the truant officer ushered her away from the car. When she snuck out of her room to use the phone last night, nobody answered at Robby's apartment. She paged him again, too, but he never called back.

"Well, he isn't in school today," Rachel informs her.

"Yeah, I know." Jen shrugs. From what she overheard in the hallway this morning, he's been suspended — unless that, too, is a rumor. She has to figure out a way to get in touch with him.

Naturally, her parents have forbidden her to see him again.

Naturally, Jen has no intention of obeying their orders.

If she was momentarily scared straight yesterday afternoon in the moment before the cop pulled them over, she's long over it by now.

She watches Garth come through the door of the lab, laughing and talking to Jackie Chamberlain. Jackie is one of those annoying girls who has it all together, and whose biggest fault is that she knows it.

For a moment, Jen finds herself watching them wistfully, forgetting that she no longer has a crush on Garth. He's tall and well scrubbed in a cream-colored roll-neck sweater, neatly pressed khakis, white leather sneakers — the proverbial good guy dressed head-to-toe in pale shades that compliment his golden coloring.

Jen looks away, thinking of darkly handsome, devil-may-care Robby in his black leather jacket and new black boots.

Bad guys wear black.

Black.

White.

Yeah, right.

If only anything in Jen's world were that simple.

Okay, the kid is five minutes late.

Either it took him longer than he thought to convince the girl to come with him, or he's not going to show.

What if he's already gone to the police?

Yeah, sure. What's he going to tell them? That somebody hired him to lure Jen

Carmody to this deserted stretch of water-front and kill her?

Why would they believe a messed-up druggie?

There's no evidence.

He's got the cash, yes. But there are no prints on the bills.

He's got the typewritten notes. No prints on those, either.

None of the phone calls can be traced.

If the kid is smart, he'll finish the job he was hired to do.

Doesn't he realize that either way, Jen Carmody is going to die?

And that either way, so is he?

Ah, but he doesn't know that. As far as he's concerned, all he has to do is deliver her to this spot, collect the rest of his fee, and walk away.

Yeah. Right.

An elderly man with a schnauzer on a leash passes by with a nod and a smile.

Nod. Smile back. Look away.

Damn it. This is what happens when you stop paying attention to details for even a moment. You find yourself grinning like an idiot as you walk down the street, and the next thing you know you're making eye contact with a stranger. A stranger who might later be questioned by the police about whether they've seen anything unusual in this neighborhood lately. Anything, or anyone.

Well, look at that.

There's the kid after all, walking in this direction.

Alone.

With a coffee can clutched in his hands.

So the local bad boy has a conscience after all.

Oh, well.

As they say, if you want something done right, you have to do it yourself.

"What are you doing here?"

Maeve turns to see Gregory striding into his office in blue dental scrubs.

"Didn't Nora tell you I was here?" Nora is his longtime receptionist, an ill-tempered old biddy who blatantly dislikes Maeve. The feeling is mutual, of course.

"She said you were here, but she didn't say why. And you'd better make this quick because I'm taking molds on a patient and they'll be set in a minute."

"I need more weekly support from you. I can either do this through the lawyers, which will wind up costing you, or we can settle this like adults."

"Maeve . . ." He breaks off and exhales,

looking at the fluorescent-lit drop ceiling. "Do we have to discuss this now? Right this second?"

"Erin needs a new coat. She needs boots, and she wants to join a ski club."

"How much can that possibly be? I'll write a check for —"

"If she's going to join a ski club we're going to get her into lessons on Saturdays," Maeve goes on.

"I thought we were talking necessities, here, Maeve."

"I'm not willing to risk our baby's neck on the slopes. Are you?"

He sighs. "How much is all this going to cost?"

She hands him the notes she jotted this morning over a grande mocha latte and cranberry scone. "This is what I came up with."

He glances over the paper, his eyes narrowing to a frown behind his unfashionable aviator glasses.

"I could pay the mortgage on a ski chalet for this, Maeve. This is ridiculous."

She shrugs.

A hygienist Maeve has never seen before pokes her head into the doorway. "Dr. Hudson? The molds . . . ?"

He spins on his heel. "I have to get back to

my patient," he informs Maeve. "You and I will have to discuss this later."

"We definitely will, Gregory."

Watching him walk out on her without a backward glance, she reminds herself that all she wants is what she has coming.

Rather, what Erin has coming, she amends with a smile, as she rises and walks airily out of the office, unfazed by Nora's glare.

As Kathleen climbs out of the SUV, a frigid wind whips her hair across her cheeks. She pauses to button her wool peacoat against the chill, then reaches into the backseat for the tissue-wrapped bouquet.

Taking a deep breath to steady her nerves and prepare for what lies ahead, she inhales the scent of roses along with the promise of snow that seems to hover in the air.

November already, and Buffalo has yet to see its first snowfall.

As Kathleen closes the door and walks along the gravel path, she wonders idly if her hometown's legendary weather has changed that drastically since she left. She can remember taking her sled out in October and riding it well into April.

Not that she cares one way or another when the first flakes fall. Contemplating global warming is a way to keep her mind from registering where she is — and why she's here.

The path between the gravestones has become a familiar route in the six months since she came home again — back to the western New York suburbs, back to this place. By now, she's grown accustomed to the somber silence; she finds it more comforting than macabre.

But today is different.

Today is November second.

Today is supposed to be about life, not death.

Yet here, surrounded by countless epitaphs of lives lived long and well, of lives cut tragically short, it's impossible for Kathleen to think of anything other than profound loss. She's here not to commemorate the child she first held in her arms fourteen years ago today, but to grieve the life that was over far too soon.

She leaves the gravel path, the heels of her boots sinking into the marshy grass. She slows her pace as she approaches the red maple tree, its branches left nearly bare after yesterday's stormy weather. The bouquet begins to tremble in her wind-chapped fingers. Tears spill from her eyes, stinging her cheeks in the cold air.

Mollie Gallagher.

Loving Wife, Devoted Mother . . .

Kathleen brushes her coat sleeve across her damp face and the rough wool feels like an emery board against her raw skin and red, sleep-deprived eyes.

Protective Grandmother.

A shuddering sigh escapes her, a sigh that becomes a bitter sob. It's unfair. So unfair.

Life is unfair, Matt's voice calmly reminds her, and she hates him for it with a blaze of irrational fury.

Hates him because he's wrong. Life isn't unfair to everyone. Not the way it's been unfair to Kathleen Gallagher Carmody.

She glares at the cross etched into her mother's stone monument. All those years of doing everything right . . . of going to church, and saying her prayers, and giving up chocolate for Lent, and putting half her allowance into the poor box at Saint Brigid's.

Why is God punishing me like this, Father Joseph? Why?

Stop feeling sorry for yourself, Katie. Stop blaming God and start accepting what is. Start asking him for guidance.

Start accepting what is. Start accepting that she had a hand in her own fate.

Huddled in misery, she shifts her gaze away from the cross — and spies another set of footprints sinking into the muddy patches that dot the leaf-littered grass nearby.

They aren't her own prints from yesterday; a quick perusal confirms that these are larger, wider, deeper.

Clearly, they belong to a man.

Somebody just passing through?

No.

Tracing the footprints' path with her eyes, Kathleen sees that they lead directly to Mollie Gallagher's gravestone and then back again in the opposite direction.

Who, besides Kathleen or her father, would have reason to visit her mother's grave after all these years? Mom's family is in Chicago; Dad lost contact with all of her local friends after she died.

Contemplating the question, Kathleen feels oddly unsettled — until she realizes that it was probably just the groundskeeper. Maybe a tree limb came down in this spot, and he removed it.

The explanation is a logical one; her curiosity is momentarily assuaged.

Then, as she removes the tissue wrapping from the bouquet, her gaze falls on yesterday's floral offering. The bundle of roses she left on the stone yesterday have blown to the ground beside her mother's headstone, most of the stems having come loose from the bunch. The blossoms have faded to a deep maroon . . . all but one, its petals still lush and scarlet as a drop of fresh blood.

Frowning, Kathleen bends to examine it, her heart quickening its pace.

How could one rose retain its freshness and the others lose theirs? Is it the rose she symbolically separated from the bouquet?

No natural phenomenon Kathleen considers can possibly be responsible for that — and she refuses to entertain a supernatural one.

Still, her thoughts drift back to the middle of the night — to her fleeting thoughts of ghosts and hauntings. She doesn't believe in that stuff. Really, she doesn't. It's just a little eerie that one rose is still red, that's all. Just one.

Gazing down at the flowers, she doesn't even comprehend that she's counting the stems until she reaches a dozen — and is struck by something odd.

There's still one more.

She must have counted wrong. Quickly, she goes through them again, this time reaching to touch each flower.

Thirteen.

There are thirteen red roses on her mother's grave.

Yesterday, there were only twelve. The

florist's shop, unlike the bakery, does not give out baker's dozens.

Again, Kathleen looks at the muddy footsteps.

Somebody else was here.

Somebody else left a rose by Mother's grave.

Somebody knows.

The words are swept into her brain on a wave of sheer panic that leaves her desperate in its wake, desperate to believe that this has nothing to do with her. Nothing to do with her secret. Nothing at all.

Remembering yesterday's overwhelming sensation of being watched in church, she swivels her head from side to side now, her eyes darting warily around the cemetery.

The place is deserted, just as she expected. She doesn't feel that frightening awareness here; she hopes she'll never feel it again.

Maybe she was just being paranoid yesterday in church. Paranoid, too, about the cries in the night, about the phone calls, about the roses. Perhaps some of it is her imagination playing tricks on her, and the rest is her guilty conscience making itself heard after all these years.

Leave me alone, she begs the part of herself that refuses to forget — or forgive.

It was long ago, so long ago. I was somebody else then. Look at what I have now. Look how far I've come. What happened then can stay in the past. Nobody ever has to know.

She glances again at the single blood-red rose and closes her eyes, praying that nobody does.

Today, the doors at 9 Sarah Crescent are locked.

How amusing, really. A little too late to start exercising caution, isn't it? Rather like locking the barn door after the horse, or however that old saying of Mother's used to go.

Funny, too, how people go to the trouble of installing fancy deadbolts in their doors, then leave the keys right in the locks. Only on the inside, of course. As if that makes much difference. You'd think they'd realize how simple it would be for anyone inside the house to slip a key out of a lock, run it right down to Home Depot for a duplicate, and be back ten minutes later, before anybody even realized the key was missing.

The house is deserted, of course. That was to be expected with both the car and SUV missing from the driveway. The Carmodys never park in their brand-new two-car garage, but they will. When Buffalo snow starts falling in another few weeks, they definitely will.

Where is Kathleen off to? Last minute shopping, perhaps. Birthday presents for her oldest child?

So Jen is fourteen today. Isn't that amazing? Fourteen already. Seems like only yesterday that she was born.

The stairway creaks a bit on the ascent. You'd think stairs wouldn't creak in a fancy new house like this.

They probably wouldn't creak if you slowed down. But after this morning's unexpected complication, there's little time to waste.

"Here's your money. I've changed my mind."

So said pathetic Robby the would-be hero as he handed over the coffee can.

He was sweating despite the chilly wind. Sweating, as though he knew he was in over his head.

"Fine. You can't do it. No problem."

The look of relief on the kid's gullible face was priceless.

He actually turned his back.

He actually thought he was going to walk away.

He took three steps, maybe four, before he heard the gun click and froze in his tracks.

If you want something done right, you have to do it yourself.

Another old saying of Mother's. She had so many of them.

Bet you never expected me to put your advice to such good use, did you, Mother? Ha!

In the linen closet beside the master bedroom door, way in back on the top shelf behind a stack of neatly folded beach towels, is the tiny tape recorder.

It's tempting, so tempting, to press rewind, just to hear the baby's pathetic cries and imagine how that must have sounded in the middle of the night.

Did the whole family hear it?

Or just Kathleen?

It would be fun to leave it here, and set the timer for it to go off again tonight. Fun, but risky. This time, they might be lying awake, waiting for it. They might trace the sound to the closet, find the tape recorder, and . . .

And what? They'll never figure out where it came from even if they do find it.

No, but it's far more delicious, for now, to let them fret about the disembodied cries in the night.

That decided, it's on to the next order of business.

Only one other door along the hallway is closed. Closed, but not locked, because there are no locks on the bedroom doors in this house. Who needs locks in a perfect family like the Carmodys? They have no secrets from each other.

Do you, Kathleen? Do you have secrets?

Oh, dear. The daughter's bedroom isn't very neat, now, is it? She probably expects somebody to come along and pick up after her. She's spoiled. Daddy's little princess is spoiled rotten.

You have secrets, too, don't you, sweetie? Secrets from your parents, secrets from your friends.

Ah, Jen Carmody. You're just a regular teenaged girl, aren't you?

Fourteen.

Welcome to the last birthday you'll ever have. And I've got the perfect little gift for you . . .

Is the back door locked?

That's unusual. Maybe it's just stuck because the weather is damp. That used to happen sometimes back in Indiana.

Jen attempts to turn the knob again, even as she tells herself that this house is brand-new construction, not a quirky Victorian rattletrap. Doors don't stick here, not in any kind of weather.

Which means that it's definitely locked.

But Mom's SUV is sitting in the driveway, and she never locks the door when she's home in the afternoon. Sometimes, she doesn't even lock the house when she *isn't* home. In this neighborhood, nobody really does, not in broad daylight.

Well, today, for whatever reason, the back door is locked.

So, Jen realizes when she walks around the house, is the front door.

Uncertain why she feels so annoyed, she knocks — rather, bangs on the door, her palm flat. She bangs so hard that the cluster of Indian corn topples from the wreath hook and falls to the ground at Jen's feet.

Ignoring it, she spots the curtain fluttering in the window.

"Mom, it's me!" she calls, exasperated.

The door opens and her mother appears, looking frazzled. She's wearing frayed, outdated jeans, her hair is pulled back into a haphazard ponytail, and there's a smudge of flour on her cheek.

Jen mentally compares her to Erin's mother and hopes to God that Mom didn't leave the house looking like this. She wants to ask, but thinks better of it. No need to start a whole big *thing* right now. She's just not in the mood.

"How was your day?" Mom asks, stepping back to let her in.

"Why did you lock me out?" is Jen's peevish reply. She can't help it.

"I didn't lock you out. I locked the door."

"Same difference," Jen mutters, pushing past her.

"Watch the attitude," her mother replies tartly, already on her way back to the kitchen, where a buzzer is going off on the stove.

The house is warm, the air scented with sugar and cinnamon.

She's baking my birthday cake, Jen realizes with an unexpected pang.

Every year, her mother makes her a pumpkin cake with cream cheese frosting for her birthday. She has a special recipe that doesn't use eggs.

Jen was convinced that the cake would be store bought this year, purchased from the local health food grocery that caters to customers with allergies like Jen's. Mom frequently buys egg-free cookies and treats for her from the in-store bakery.

But for whatever reason, she's baking the cake this year, same as always. A wave of nostalgic longing sweeps over Jen as she deposits her heavy backpack on the bench by the door.

In the past, she would have gone right to

the kitchen, sniffing around for a batter bowl or beater to lick. She and Mom would have laughed together as Jen tried to talk her into giving her one of her presents before evening, when birthday gifts are traditionally opened in their family. Mom has almost always relented and given her one, just a small one, ahead of time.

That won't be happening this year, Jen concludes as she pushes back the unwanted wistfulness and the guilt that goes with it. This year, everything is different.

She tosses her down jacket over the hall tree and heads for the stairs.

Her mother's voice stops her in her tracks. "Jen, did you call Mrs. Gattinski and tell her you can't babysit tomorrow because of detention?"

"How could I call her? It's not like I have a cell phone," she grumbles, unable to resist the dig. Until everything blew up in her face, she had been hoping her parents might relent and get her one for her birthday. Now she's certain there's no chance of it — especially when she hears her mother's icy tone.

"There's a phone right here, so you'd better hurry up and do it. She's going to be in a bind."

Jen walks slowly into the kitchen, where

284

her mother wordlessly holds out the cordless phone.

Sure enough, several round cake pans sit steaming on the counter beside the stove.

Jen's mouth waters. She skipped breakfast and tossed her school lunch into the garbage uneaten.

But with Mom in the kitchen, she isn't about to start hunting down a snack. All Jen really wants to do right now is get the dreaded phone call over with, then escape to her room and wallow in misery.

Riding the late bus home was one of the most humiliating experiences of her life. Especially since she's taken it so many times in the past, having stayed after school for club meetings, for soccer practice.

Never for detention.

Riders of the late bus are a fairly balanced mix of wholesome extracurricular types and troublemakers. Normally, Jen would sit up front with the nice crowd. She's one of them, after all.

Not anymore, you're not.

Mr. Krander, the teacher in charge of detention, always waits to release the students until just before the bus is ready to leave — probably so nobody has time to land in more trouble between their lockers and departure.

The front of the bus was already full by the time Jen climbed onboard. She was acutely aware of the stares as she passed one occupied row after another. Fighting back tears, she wound up taking a seat halfway down the aisle. Alone. She couldn't quite bring herself to walk all the way to the back of the bus to mingle with her fellow detainees. She isn't one of them, either.

Really, she's not.

"Don't you know the phone number?" her mother asks, intruding on her thoughts. "Do you want the phone book?"

"I know it." Jen turns her back on her mother as she dials. When it begins to ring, she walks into the dining room, out of earshot.

Three rings . . . four . . .

Convinced — and relieved — that she's about to get the answering machine, Jen is dismayed when there's a click and a raspy-sounding "Hello?"

"Um, is Mrs. Gattinksi there?" she asks the unfamiliar voice.

"Speaking."

"Mrs. Gattinski? Are you all right?"

"Oh, Jen, is that you? I've just been sick. One of those flu bugs."

Jen senses her mother standing in the doorway behind her, and turns to find her

286

eavesdropping. She scowls, faces the wall, cradles the phone into her mouth as she says, "I'm sorry this is such short notice, but I, um . . . I can't babysit tomorrow. I have to stay after school for . . . for something."

Conscious of her mother listening, Jen wonders if she's expected to admit the reason. Well, she won't. She's not about to confess to Mrs. Gattinski that she got into trouble at school. That's none of anybody's business.

There's a pause on the other end of the line, and then Mrs. Gattinski says, "That's all right, Jen. I wouldn't want you to catch what I have, anyway. I'll probably still be home recuperating. But I was going to call and see if you were available Friday night starting at seven? I have to chaperone a dance at school and Mr. Gattinski has a banquet to go to."

"Oh. Um . . ."

Mom is still there, listening. Resentment floods Jen, along with defiance.

"Sure," she hears herself saying. "No problem."

"Great. One of us will pick you up at seven-thirty, okay?"

"Sure," Jen repeats, wondering what she's getting herself into. Her parents have forbidden her to babysit.

Well, she'll deal with it when Friday night arrives.

She hangs up and faces her mother.

"Was she okay with it?" Mom has the nerve to look concerned.

"I guess she has to be, doesn't she?" Jen thrusts the phone into her mother's hand and strides out of the room.

As she climbs the stairs two at a time, she can hear her brothers laughing at some cartoon in the family room. How many afternoons has she been right there with the boys, cracking up at *Sponge Bob* or *Ed, Edd, and Eddy?* For one impulsive second, it's all she can do to keep herself from retreating back down the stairs to join them.

Then she reminds herself that she doesn't belong there with them anymore.

The island.

Jen trudges down the hall and opens the door to her room, which is just as she left it this morning, unmade bed and all. So the cleaning lady wasn't here today. Good.

She doesn't mind having somebody else do the dusting and vacuuming, which means her mother doesn't bug her to do it. But she doesn't like the idea of a stranger being in here, and it bugs her that the woman always leaves the hallway door open when she's done cleaning. In fact, it's gotten so that the boys now leave their bedroom doors open on a daily basis, and now Mom and Dad sometimes do, as well.

Jen isn't about to leave her door open, whether or not she's in here.

In fact, it's too bad it doesn't have a lock, she thinks as she pulls it closed behind her.

She's halfway to the bed when she spots the package on the pillow.

A present?

She stops short, staring at it.

So Mom remembered that Jen always pestered her for one gift in advance. Did she do this to be nice? Or did she do it to make Jen feel guilty for not speaking to her earlier?

For a moment, she's tempted to leave the present right there on the pillow, to pretend she never saw it. That way, she won't feel obligated to go downstairs and thank her mother for whatever it is.

It's hard to tell, in a box that size. It's larger than a jewelry box, but smaller than a clothing box.

A cell phone would fit in there, definitely.

But there's no way. Absolutely no way.

Maybe it's a scarf, or gloves, or a cosmetic bag.

Nah, Mom wouldn't get her one of those,

even if Jen has been asking. She doesn't like Jen wearing makeup.

The gift wrap is a bit young, Jen thinks, walking over to the bed. She picks up the box and makes a face at the clown-printed paper. Well, what does she expect? Look at the frilly bedspread and curtains Mom picked out for her just last year.

The box doesn't weigh much, and it doesn't rattle. It probably is a scarf. Socks, maybe. Well, that's fine. Boring, but fine. She can always use another scarf or socks.

Jen slides a finger beneath the seam in the wrapping paper and pulls it apart carefully, then wonders why she's trying so hard not to rip it.

She tears the rest away and crumples it into a ball, tossing it across the room toward the overflowing wastebasket. It bounces out again. Oh, well. The cleaning lady can pick it up whenever she comes.

The box is plain white cardboard; no store name is embossed on the cover as a hint.

Jen shakes it a little and hears something shifting inside. Something soft.

A scarf?

She lifts the lid, and finds . . .

Not a scarf.

Not gloves.

Not socks . . . not the kind she'd expect, anyway.

What she finds is the oddest gift she's ever received: a lone pink baby bootee with lacy white trim.

TEN

"Happy birthday to you . . . Happy birthday to you . . . Happy birthday, dear Jen . . . Happy birthday to you."

"Blow out the candles, Jen," Kathleen urges her daughter, watching a trickle of pink wax drip into the cream cheese icing.

"Don't forget to make a wish!" Curran reminds her.

Jen scowls at that, but closes her eyes and releases an obedient puff toward the cake.

Kathleen's *yay* sounds forced and hollow to her own ears. She realizes belatedly that most of the candles are still ignited.

"Did you make a wish?" Riley wants to know. "Because if you don't get them all out in the first blow, it won't come true."

Jen doesn't even bother to acknowledge Riley's question. She merely sits staring at the cake, not sullen, exactly, but more . . . contemplative.

Kathleen glances at Matt. He's sitting with his arms folded, watching the proceedings with a level of interest he usually reserves for Father Edward's annual parish finance sermon.

At least the boys, standing on either side of their sister's chair, are enthusiastic.

"Can I take out the candles, Mommy?" Riley asks eagerly, stretching a hand toward the white-frosted layer cake. It's leaning precariously to one side, and there's a finger-sized bare spot at the base on one side where Kathleen neglected to spread the icing.

"Mommy?" Riley nudges her as she reaches toward the cake plate.

"What?"

"Can I take out the candles? I like to help."

"Mom!" Curran speaks up. "He only wants to take out the candles so he can lick off the frosting."

"Nobody's licking any candles," Matt says sternly from his place at the head of the dining room table, opposite Jen and the cake. To his right is Kathleen's father, who doesn't even appear to be paying attention. He's busy hunting through the pockets of his cardigan, frowning.

"But I want to help. Mrs. Egan says we should always help our olders." Riley frequently quotes — and often misquotes — his kindergarten teacher, much to the rest of the family's amusement.

Tonight, nobody is amused.

"I'll take out the candles, Riley." Ignoring his whine of protest, Kathleen plucks them, one by one, from the frosting. Normally she would have to resist the urge to lick the tips herself, but tonight she isn't even tempted.

She certainly hopes the cake tastes better than it looks. She's had no appetite all day, and her heart certainly wasn't in baking this afternoon. Cooking, either. The roast was dry, the gravy lumpy, the mashed potatoes the consistency of Elmer's Glue. Nobody complained except Dad, who grumbled that even the instant potatoes the nursing home serves were better than these.

"Does anyone want ice cream with the cake?" she asks, hoping nobody does. She had to muster every bit of energy to prepare the meal and set the table in the dining room with their best china and crystal. And after single-handedly carrying the dinner conversation — all right, with some help from the boys — she's feeling utterly depleted.

Unfortunately, everybody but Jen wants ice cream, and nobody else offers to go to the kitchen to get it.

Sighing inwardly, Kathleen shuffles into

the kitchen, not bothering to turn on the light. She opens the freezer, finds a half-gallon of Breyer's Vanilla Bean, and what's left of a pint of chocolate Haagen Daz, Jen's favorite. She turns to nudge the freezer door closed with her shoulder.

In the instant the appliance light is obliterated, plunging the kitchen once again into darkness, Kathleen spots a face pressed against the kitchen window.

Her shriek brings Matt running, followed by the boys and Jen. Somebody flips the wall switch on their way into the kitchen and the face vanishes into a reflective glare.

In the dining room, Dad, confined to his wheelchair, bellows, "What the hell is going on in there?"

"Nothing, I . . ." Kathleen shakes her head, gazing at the window, seeing nothing but the room behind her and her own anxious face.

"What happened?" Dad shouts again, and Matt echoes the question, touching her shoulder gently.

Kathleen turns to see her worried family hovering. Even Jen looks concerned, and Riley is downright frightened. She settles on the first lame explanation that enters her mind. "I just . . . I thought I saw a mouse."

"Cool! Where?" Curran asks, scanning the tile.

"Over there." She points vaguely in the direction of the sink.

"I'll set a trap," Matt says tightly, for the children's benefit, she knows. She can tell by his expression that he's aware there's no mouse.

"Thanks." She meets his gaze head-on, then shifts her attention to Jen. Her daughter is watching them with narrowed eyes.

Jen, the girl who literally won't hurt a fly. She steps around ants on the sidewalk; she sets spiders free outside. If she really thought there was a mouse, she wouldn't let Matt set a trap.

She, too, knows Kathleen is fibbing.

She knows more than that, Kathleen realizes, glimpsing something else in Jen's expression. Something far more telling.

"Good news! I don't see any mouse poop, Mom," Curran announces from the floor.

Riley drops to his knees beside his brother. "I want to look for mouse poop, too."

"Nobody's looking for mouse poop." Matt pulls them both to their feet and escorts them back to the dining room.

Jen starts to follow, but Kathleen calls her back.

"Is everything okay, Jen?"

"What do you mean?"

"You seem on edge."

"So what else is new? Finding out you're adopted does that to a person. And guess what? You seem on edge, yourself."

"That's not what I was talking about." Kathleen hesitates. "I mean you seem a little . . . anxious. About . . . the mouse?"

"What mouse?" Jen asks flatly.

"What do you mean, what mouse? The mouse that I saw."

"What mouse?" Jen repeats pointedly.

"What makes you think there wasn't a mouse?"

"Because once you've told one big lie, how am I supposed to believe anything else you ever say?"

She's paraphrasing Kathleen's own words, and her eyes dare Kathleen to call her on it. Still, she sees something more than blatant contempt there. The trepidation hasn't left; the fear has intensified.

Kathleen longs to pull Jen into her arms and comfort her, to tell her to stop worrying, that she's fine. That they're all fine, that everything will be okay.

How many times did she make that very promise when Jen was a little girl?

Too many times to count — too many

times to guarantee that the promise would be kept.

And now, Kathleen's lies — all of them — are catching up with her.

"Never mind," she tells Jen, and presses the cartons of ice cream into her hands. "Take these into the other room. I'm just going to get the scoop."

Jen obeys without argument, disappearing into the next room.

Kathleen takes the ice cream scoop from the drawer, then walks over and presses the wall switch.

Darkness swoops over the kitchen.

She returns to the window and looks out into the night, fighting the urge to turn on the floodlights. Even without them, she can see by the light of the moon that the yard is empty.

She must have imagined the face at the window, just as she imagined everything else. It isn't the only logical explanation she can come up with, but it's the only one she's willing to consider tonight.

Still, she tries the back door again, just to make sure it's locked. Whatever the reason, she hasn't felt safe all day, not even at home. Especially not at home.

"Where have you been?" Stella asks,

looking up from yet another opponent-slamming preelection commercial on television.

From where she's lying on the family room couch, she can see Kurt stepping into the house through the garage door. She can also see the mantle clock. "It's almost seven-thirty. How long does it take to run to the supermarket?"

"Too damned long," he snaps, plunking a paper grocery bag on the counter.

"Did you remember the crackers this time?"

Wearing a sardonic expression, he lifts a box of saltines from the bag and holds them up to show her.

Surprised, she asks, "How about the ginger ale? Did you get more of that?"

"They were out of regular Canada Dry so I got diet."

"Diet!" she echoes in dismay. Just what her weak stomach needs: chemical sweeteners and bitter aftertaste. She's finally stopped running into the bathroom every few minutes, but she's still not certain she can keep anything down.

Kurt says succinctly, "I just said they didn't have regular, Stella."

"They didn't have regular ginger ale anywhere in Wegmans? I find that hard to believe." She hates her brittle tone and the shrew she's become. But he's doing this to her. He was an hour late coming home from the bank, and his idea of feeding the twins dinner was to divide a can of Campbell's chicken noodle soup into two bowls and nuke it for a minute. The poor girls kept complaining about the saltiness and were dying of thirst by the time they were done eating. Only then did Stella realize Kurt hadn't even bothered to dilute the soup with water.

"They didn't have regular Canada Dry," he repeats now.

"What about Schweppes?"

"What *about* Schweppes? I didn't look for that. You wrote Canada Dry on the list."

"But you knew I meant ginger ale. The brand doesn't matter. Generic would be fine."

"You didn't say that, and I know how you are."

Exasperated, Stella throws the afghan off and rises shakily from the couch to face him. "Really? How am I?"

"Picky." He removes a large, deli-made sub sandwich from the bag, along with a package of Fritos and a large plastic produce bag filled with apples.

"What are those for?" she asks.

"What do you think they're for? They're for eating."

"The fridge is full of apples. We've got apples coming out of our ears. I can't believe you got those and you didn't get my ginger ale."

"I got it."

"Diet."

"Stella, trust me, diet ginger ale isn't going to kill you."

His disdainful expression speaks volumes.

She wants to tell him she's probably lost ten pounds overnight, thanks to the stomach bug. She wants to tell him that she knows what he thinks of her, anyway, and that it doesn't matter to her anymore. That as soon as she has the strength, she's going to kick him out of here.

But she can't bring herself to say any of that — in part because it does matter, and because she isn't certain she'll ever find the strength to kick him out.

She's had plenty of time for contemplation today.

The truth is, without Kurt, she would have two little girls to raise single-handedly while working full time. He would have to support the girls financially, but Stella certainly can't afford to quit teaching. And anyway, where would he go if he moved out? To an apartment?

She thinks of his brother Stefan, newly divorced and living in a dump that costs more than Kathleen and Kurt can spare on top of their mortgage payment.

Which means that if they were to separate, they'd probably have to sell the house. She and the girls would wind up back in their old neighborhood in Cheektowaga, or someplace like it.

The truth is, Stella loves living in Orchard Hollow; she loves her big, beautiful new house and her Volvo station wagon. She loves having a weekly housekeeper and an expensive private day care center for the girls. And, as much as she hates to admit it, there are times when she even thinks she might still love Kurt.

She has no illusions about it being mutual.

Sure, he agreed to go back out to the store for her tonight. So readily that she was surprised. But he must have had an ulterior motive. Most likely his own hunger, she thinks, watching him unwrap the sub sandwich.

Either that, or his mistress is a checkout girl at Wegmans.

"What are you laughing at?" he asks,

looking up from the bag of chips he's opening.

"Me? I'm not laughing. That was a sneeze," she lies.

"You sneezed on my sandwich?" He looks down at the sub in disgust. "You're all germy. What are you trying to do, get me sick, too?"

Yup.

Aloud, she says only, "Sorry."

"That was my dinner, Stella. Thanks a lot. What am I supposed to do now?"

"Sorry," she repeats sweetly, shuffling back to the couch, resisting the urge to tell him exactly what he can do with his sandwich.

"I so-o-o-o don't want to do this," Erin informs her mother as Maeve pulls up in front of the Carmodys' house.

"I know you *so-o-o-o* don't."

"Mom!"

"What?" Maeve takes one last satisfying drag of her cigarette, then stubs it out in the ashtray.

"Erin, you don't have a choice."

"But I can't stand Jen."

"I know you can't." Though she doesn't know why and Erin refuses to tell her. "You're not doing this for her. You're doing it for me."

"Yeah, and I thought you quit smoking for me."

"That has nothing to do with this." Maeve snaps the ashtray closed, beyond caring what her daughter thinks of her lighting up again.

"I just don't get why you care about Jen's stupid birthday."

"Because her mother is one of my oldest and dearest friends," Maeve retorts, shifting into park and flipping down the lighted mirror on the visor to check her lipstick.

"So why can't you do this by yourself?"

Maeve ignores her. Sometimes Erin reminds her too much of Gregory, what with the nasal litany of *whys* and *why nots.*

It would be so goddamned nice, she thinks, snapping the mirror closed, if just once she could make a request that wasn't met with a whining tirade by her daughter or ex-husband.

She pulls the keys from the ignition. "Let's go. Get the present."

"Can't you get it?"

"I asked you to get it, Erin."

Sometimes, when her daughter isn't acting like Gregory, she's acting like a total stranger. Maeve can look at her and see no sign of the happy-go-lucky little girl she once was; she has absolutely no idea what's going on in Erin's head.

She suspects there are times when she's better off not knowing.

Grumbling, Erin climbs out of the car clutching the large shopping bag from Lord & Taylor. Inside a gaily gift-wrapped box is the cashmere pullover Maeve picked out in Jen's size. Erin refused to come to the mall and help her, so she isn't entirely sure about the color or style.

Still, Maeve followed her own basic rule — when in doubt, go with classic black — and is fairly certain Kathleen's daughter will like the sweater. And even if she doesn't . . .

At least I tried, Maeve thinks, her heels clicking on the curved slate walk as she leads Erin toward the porch light.

As far as she's concerned, a black cashmere sweater is enough to lift anyone's spirits — even a girl whose life is falling apart at the seams.

Maeve tries the door and finds it locked.

"Don't you have the key?" Erin asks.

"How did you know that?"

"I don't know . . . I guess maybe Jen told me."

"Oh. Well, I lost it," she replies briefly, and presses the doorbell.

It seems to take a long time before somebody opens the door. Maeve is pleasantly surprised to find Matt standing there, darkly handsome in suit pants and a dress shirt without a tie, the sleeves rolled up to reveal muscular forearms.

He looks surprised to see her, too. "Maeve! Kathleen didn't tell me you were coming."

"She doesn't know. It's a surprise. Surprise!" She sails past him, catching a whiff of citrus aftershave as she goes.

"Come on in," Matt tells Erin, who is still hovering on the doorstep.

Maeve turns and shoots her the evil eye, and her daughter reluctantly crosses the threshold. She thrusts the bag into Matt's hands after he closes the door, mumbling, "This is for Jen."

"That's nice of you." He looks at Maeve. "Did you eat? Because I'm sure Kathleen won't mind reheating the —"

"Oh, we ate." Actually, she isn't certain about Erin, but she herself had two slices of Sicilian pizza at the food court earlier, followed by one of Mrs. Fields Snickerdoodles. The cookie was warm, right out of the oven, and she'd have gone back for another one if the line weren't so long.

Pizza. Cookies. Cigarettes.

Welcome back to the real world, darling,

Maeve tells herself, noticing that the guilty twinges have grown fewer and further between.

"We're just having cake," Matt informs them, leading the way toward the dining room.

"Really?" Nothing like forbidden pleasure to perk a girl right up.

Maeve smiles at Matt. "I'd love some."

"You would?" Erin asks beside her, wearing such a shocked expression that for a heart-stopping moment, Maeve fears she accidentally requested what she really wants.

"Cake," she says quickly, glancing from her daughter to Matt, who looks reassuringly unfazed. "I'd love some cake."

"I hope you like pumpkin, because that's what Jen always has on her birthday," Matt tells her. His tone is affable, but he seems a little tense.

Well, no wonder. Poor man.

Arriving in the doorway of the dining room, Maeve takes in the scene, from the bickering boys to Kathleen's obviously cross father in his wheelchair, from a brooding Jen to her mother, whose frayed nerves are evident in a glance.

Casting aside her last nagging doubt that coming here was the right thing to do,

Maeve pastes on a cheerful smile and goes over to embrace the birthday girl.

Erin is here.

Why?

Obviously, because her mother made her come. That much is clear to Jen as she sneaks a peek at her former best friend, glumly poking a fork at the slab of pumpkin cake in front of her.

Erin glances up and meets her gaze with a glare that's startling in its intensity.

Wow. She really hates me.

Jen tries to tell herself she doesn't care, but Erin's visual daggers are unsettling.

Mrs. Hudson is chatting with Mom about how great the house looks, going on and on about the centerpiece and the china. In a way, Jen is glad the Hudsons popped in, even if things are uncomfortable with Erin, because things were really getting tense around here right before they came.

Jen is positive it wasn't a mouse that made Mom freak out in the kitchen.

But what was it?

She didn't miss the way her mother kept glancing at the window, almost as though she was expecting to find the bogeyman lurking in the night.

It took every ounce of restraint for Jen not

to tell her mother that she's almost positive she's seen somebody watching the house.

And now she's not so sure the odd gift on her bed was from Mom, either.

She's been trying to convince herself since she opened the bizarre present that it's some kind of symbolism for all that's happened these past few weeks — her mother's way of telling Jen that she loves her.

Now she isn't so sure.

It just doesn't make sense.

One pink baby bootee?

She makes up her mind to swallow her pride and ask Mom about it later . . . if only just to make sure it's from her.

If it isn't . . .

Jen glances up from her cake to find her father's gaze on her.

He looks so wistful, she thinks. Wistful, but still angry.

I let him down.

She looks away, hating herself — and, stubbornly, still hating him.

So? He let me down.

How is she ever going to get past the betrayal? How is she ever going to get over the unsettling sensation that the man she thought she knew inside and out might just as well be a stranger?

It's like they're all strangers, Jen realizes,

looking around the table.

Again when she glances in Erin's direction, she finds Erin staring back at her.

I let her down, too, Jen thinks miserably, unable to break away from the blatant anger in Erin's eyes.

And for what? For Robby? Robby, who let her birthday pass without acknowledgment? You'd think he'd at least have called her back after all those pages she sent him.

Maybe he was too intimidated, after what happened. Maybe he's afraid to risk talking to her parents.

The thing is, she's never known Robby to be intimidated before.

Then again, how well do you know him, really? Jen asks herself, and again looks around the table at her so-called family and friends. *How well do you know anyone?*

Kathleen is in her bedroom, about to change at last into her pajamas and collapse into bed, when there's a knock on the door.

Matt wouldn't knock, and the boys would just barge in.

"Jen?" Kathleen calls, anticipation sweeping over her. "Come in."

The door opens. Sure enough, her daughter is on the other side.

In a too-big long-sleeved T-shirt and

flannel boxer shorts, her face scrubbed and her hair pulled back in a scrunchy, Jen looks like a little girl again. Kathleen's first instinct is to rush over and pull her into a fierce embrace.

The memory of her daughter's reaction to her happy birthday hug this morning in the kitchen stops her.

Maybe Jen is going to thank her for the birthday dinner, the cake, the gifts. She had murmured her appreciation as she worked her way through the stack of presents Kathleen had assembled for her: the usual assortment of clothes and books and a couple of CDs from the boys. Though Jen was far more low key than on birthdays past, she seemed genuinely pleased with the gifts, especially the elegant black sweater from Maeve and Erin. To Kathleen's surprise, even Dad had a card for his granddaughter, and he'd tucked a fifty dollar bill into it.

As Kathleen drove him back to the nursing home, he said he'd had Betty go out and buy the card for him that afternoon. Impressed that he still remembered the nurse's name, Kathleen was touched that her father had made the effort not to show up empty-handed — even if the card was addressed to *Jenny*. He seemed grateful to have been included in the birthday dinner, and asked for leftover cake to take back to Betty.

All in all, the evening she had so dreaded was a success. Maeve showing up with Erin was a lifesaver after Kathleen's episode in the kitchen. Clearly, the relationship between the two girls has become strained, but Kathleen hopes they'll get over it. Maeve seems to think so. In the kitchen, as she helped Kathleen load the dishwasher, she pointed out that all teenaged friendships have their ups and downs.

"Remember how we used to argue?" she asked Kathleen. "We always made up sooner or later."

Which is true, of course.

Grateful for her friend's unexpected presence, Kathleen confided in Maeve about the face she thought she'd seen in the window earlier. Maeve was convinced she'd imagined it, thanks to stress, guilt, and being overtired. The more Kathleen considers the past few days, the more she's certain Maeve is right.

Stress. Guilt. Exhaustion.

Her friend doesn't know the half of it. Is it any wonder Kathleen is feeling paranoid?

"What's up, Jen?" she asks, forcing herself to remain casual.

"I need to ask you something."

Kathleen's heart sinks.

Based on pure instinct, she knows that whatever it is, this isn't going to be easy.

Jen holds up a rectangular white box. "Did you put this on my bed this afternoon?"

"No. What is it?"

"A birthday present. Are you sure you didn't put it there? It was wrapped in clown paper."

"Clown paper?" Kathleen shakes her head. "It wasn't me."

"It looked like it was supposed to be for a little kid. Maybe it was from one of the boys. Or Daddy."

"Maybe," Kathleen agrees, though she's fairly certain Matt didn't leave a gift for Jen on his own. Why would he do that and not mention it to her?

"I'll go ask Curran and Riley if it's from them," Jen says, turning slowly toward the door.

"Wait, Jen . . . what was it?"

"The present?" Jen shakes her head. "That's the thing. It was just kind of . . . strange."

"Strange?"

Jen lifts the top of the box, saying, "I guess it's some kind of gag gift, but I just don't get it. See?"

Kathleen is speechless.

Lying inside the gift box is a single pink bootee edged in white lace.

OhmyGodohmyGodohmyGod . . .

Who took it out of her bureau drawer?

And why was it wrapped in a box for Jen?

The room seems to have lurched into motion. All Kathleen can do is shake her head mutely as Jen puts the lid back on the box with a shrug.

She opens her mouth to stop her as Jen turns toward the hallway, but she can't find her voice. She's left to stand helplessly by as her daughter leaves the room, closing the door behind her with a quiet, " 'Night, Mom."

Kathleen rushes to the dresser, jerks open the top drawer. She feels around inside, pushing recklessly past heaps of socks until she finds the familiar bundle at the back.

Thoughts, impossible thoughts, screech through her brain as she pulls it toward her.

She unwraps the pink crocheted blanket, already knowing it will prove to be empty.

But what she finds is far more chilling . . . and utterly unexpected.

The pink bootee is still there, just as she left it.

Meaning . . .

The one Jen showed her was the other half of the pair.

A pair Kathleen never had in her possession at all.

From the start, there was one. Just one.

At this time of year, with a stiff wind blowing off Lake Erie just a few blocks away, it always becomes increasingly challenging to find shelter for the night.

Sometimes, Gary is lucky enough to remain undiscovered in the public restrooms of the nearby park, but most of the time, the security guards find him and kick him out when they lock up. That's what happened tonight.

"Move along, Buddy," the uniformed man said unsympathetically, impatiently jangling his keys with a hand that wears a wedding band.

If Gary were a woman, he could probably attempt to bribe the guard into letting him stay, wedding band or not. He's heard stories. He knows most of the guards aren't beyond accepting sexual favors in exchange for turning a blind eye on the homeless occupants of the ladies' room.

But Gary's not a woman. Nor is he the kind of man who caters to the sick bastards who prefer his gender — unlike some of his cohorts who are willing to do whatever it takes to survive on the streets.

No, as far as Gary's concerned, you have to draw the line someplace. You have to keep your self-respect. That's all you really own that matters, when you're living on the street.

He wanders barefoot and shivering in a tattered blanket down toward the waterfront. With any luck, he'll find an unlocked parked car, or even a couple of packing crates in a deserted alleyway — anything to block the wind so he can get a few hours' sleep. It's well past midnight and he's been up almost twenty-four hours now.

He turns a corner and makes his way down another block, past a couple of restaurant-tavern type places. The dank air blowing off the lake mingles with the smell of greasy food, cigarette smoke, stale beer.

Hearing a banging noise, he spots a restaurant employee closing the lid on a Dumpster on the far end of a restaurant parking lot. He waits for the man to retreat through the restaurant's back door again before approaching the Dumpster.

Gary isn't foolish enough to consider spending the night inside it. The streets are rife with legends of the poor unfortunate who crawled into Dumpsters to sleep off their liquor and wound up crushed to death in a garbage truck.

However, the Dumpster is worth a temporary visit. There's likely to be something edible in whatever the busboy just tossed. Not just uneaten food scraps, either; at this time of night, restaurant kitchens are closing down and discarding whatever can't be salvaged for tomorrow's menu.

His mouth watering, Gary picks his way around broken glass in the parking lot, wishing he knew what happened to the sneakers he had until yesterday. They were a size too small and hurt his feet, but better than nothing. Too bad he made the mistake of taking them off while he was sleeping in a doorway. He woke to find them gone, along with the half-loaf of bread he'd saved for breakfast.

He scuttles across the remaining stretch of glass-free pavement to the Dumpster. After opening the lid, he eagerly hoists his small, wiry frame over the edge.

Amidst the sickening stench of rotting food, his nose detects the appetizing scent of some type of seafood, and something deep fried. Once, Gary found an entire cooked lobster discarded in the trash here, and other times, he's come across perfectly good fried chicken.

He pokes around the top layer of the Dumpster, aided by the light of an overhead streetlight, until he figures out which bag was most recently tossed.

As he takes a step forward to pull it toward him, his bare toes encounter some kind of cloth. With any luck, it will prove to be an old coat. Wouldn't that be something?

The food bag momentarily forgotten, Gary bends to move several pieces of cardboard away from his ankle, uncovering whatever he's standing on.

It *is* a coat!

A coat, and . . .

And jeans, and —

Oh.

Wrinkling his nose, Gary bolts back a few steps, realizing the clothing is still occupied by its owner.

He shakes his head. Apparently, this guy hasn't heard the horror stories about sleeping in Dumpsters.

"Hey, Buddy." He leans forward to poke the guy, who is lying facedown, motionless. "Wake up."

Whoever it is refuses to stir.

It takes a few moments for Gary to understand why.

He's dead, Gary realizes when he spots dried clumps of blood matting the dark hair around an entry wound at the back of the skull.

Well, that's a damned shame. But this isn't the first murdered corpse Gary's stumbled across on the street, and he doubts it will be his last. In no time, he overcomes his squeamish hesitation and gets down to business.

First, he bends and slips his hands into the guy's pants pockets, front and back, looking for a wallet — and, with any luck, cash. Nothing. He checks his coat pockets, too. Empty. Damn.

Well, there's always the coat itself, Gary thinks shrewdly. He tugs at the sleeves, trying to remove it. But he quickly gives up; the body's arms are bent in a way that makes it impossible. Rigor mortis has long since set in.

Gary gingerly kicks more trash away from the body, wondering if it's worth trying to get the jeans off. The legs are straight out, so maybe —

Well, look at that.

A slow smile crosses Gary's face.

This cowboy died with his boots on.

Brand-new boots, from the looks of things, and just about the right size. The thick soles are barely worn, the black leather is shiny, and the polished silver buckles glint in the streetlight's glow.

ELEVEN

A rapping sound startles Jen out of a dead sleep.

Is somebody knocking on her door? Did she forget to set her alarm and oversleep?

Aside from the glow coming from the overhead bulb beyond the open closet door, the room is barely light. She lifts her head to glance at the clock — sees that it isn't even six yet. She must have been dreaming.

She's about to snuggle back into the blankets when she hears the rapping sound again.

Who would be knocking on her door at this hour?

"Jen?" her mother calls softly. "I need to talk to you."

"Come in." She sits up, rubs the sleep from her eyes as the door opens and her mother slips into the room.

Even in this dim light, Mom looks horrible. She's wearing pajamas beneath a flannel robe, but she doesn't seem to have slept a wink.

"What's wrong?" Jen is too worried not to ask, too dazed to remember to keep her voice — and her emotions — detached.

Maybe something happened to Grandpa. He didn't look very good last night. Jen wonders, with remorse, if he died. She could have been nicer to him. He gave her fifty bucks, even if he did address the card to *Jenny*, which bugs her. She could have spent some time talking to him during dinner, instead of selfishly —

"Did you ask the boys about that gift?" Mom's voice cuts in abruptly.

For a moment, Jen is confused. Then she remembers. The pink bootee.

"They said they had no idea where it came from," she tells her mother, relieved that this isn't about her grandfather, or anything earth shattering.

"You asked both of your brothers?

"Yes." Jen pulls the covers up to her chin in the early morning chill. "And they both said they didn't put it there. Why?"

"What about Daddy? Did you ask him?"

"No. Did you?"

"No." Her mother's expression is impossible to read. "I didn't mention it to him at all."

Jen wonders why not — especially since Mom's making this into such a big deal.

A chill slips down her spine, just as it did last night when her brothers denied leaving the odd present on her pillow.

At the time, she chose to conclude that they were lying . . . or that her so-called father did it, for whatever reason. But she still isn't speaking to him unless it is absolutely necessary, so she isn't about to ask.

Now, realizing that her mother is rattled enough to be in here at dawn asking questions, Jen can't help feeling uneasy.

Somewhere in the bowels of the house, the furnace rumbles to life.

Jen burrows deeper under the white eyelet bedspread. "What's going on, Mom?"

"Just tell me . . . where exactly did you find that bootee? And tell me the truth, Jen."

The phrase *this time* remains unspoken, but her tone blatantly implies that Jen wasn't telling the truth before.

It's infuriating enough to shut down Jen's emotions once again.

"I told you where I found it," she says icily. "It was in a gift-wrapped box on my bed. On my pillow, to be 'exact.' "

"Where is it now?"

"What difference does that make?"

"I just . . . I need to see it again."

"For what?"

"Just give it back to me, Jen, okay?"

"Back to you?" she echoes incredulously. She should have known. "So you *were* the one who gave it to me."

Her voice rising unnaturally, Mom protests, "That's not what I meant. I didn't give it to you; I'm just trying to figure out who did."

Jen watches her mother hug herself, shivering, and suspects she isn't just trying to ward off the early morning chill. Why is she so worked up about a baby bootee? You'd think it was a gun or drugs or something.

Whatever. This is her mother's peculiar game, and Jen's willing to play. Especially when she realizes she's the one who's in control, for a change.

"I'll give it to you on one condition," she hears herself saying.

"What's that?"

No going back now, Jen. Just ask her. You've been dying to ask her.

She takes a deep breath, then plunges in. "You have to tell me about my father. My real father."

"Oh, Jen . . ." Mom sighs, falters.

"Tell me about him, Mom."

"You don't want to know. Trust me."

"I do want to know. Trust *me*."

For a change.

Mom is silent.

Jen clenches her hands beneath the sheet, willing her to talk.

Finally, her mother sits on the edge of the bed, facing the window instead of Jen. "There's not much to tell. His name was Quint. Quint Matteson."

"Madison?" Jen echoes, wanting to make sure she knows how to spell it. "Or Madsen?"

"It's Matteson," her mother replies with obvious reluctance. "With two t's."

Matteson.

Quint Matteson. Two *t*'s. She memorizes that detail.

"I always thought it was ironic," Mom is saying, a faraway expression in her eyes. "Your father's first name is so similar to his last. Matt, Matteson."

What's ironic, Jen thinks, is that she's chosen to phrase it that way. Shouldn't she say "your father's *last* name is so similar to his *first*"? The *his*, of course, referring to Matt Carmody, who isn't her father.

"What else?" she prods, still disgusted with her mother's deception, yet unwilling to alienate her further. Not when she needs to know more about Quint Matteson.

"He was a musician," Mom continues with a shrug. "And I didn't know him for very long. I was young, and naive, and, what can I say? The whole thing was a big mistake, Jen."

Jen's eyes fill with tears. She can't help herself.

Mom turns to look at her then, and cries out, "Oh, sweetheart, not you. You weren't the mistake. I meant getting involved with him, thinking he was . . . But you, you were . . . I wanted you more than anything."

She reaches for Jen.

Jen allows herself to be pulled, sobbing, up into her mother's arms.

"I'm so sorry." Mom is weeping, too, her tears soaking Jen's hair. "I'm so sorry, for everything. I never wanted to hurt you. I always meant to tell you the truth."

"You should have."

"The older you got, the more I knew it would hurt you."

"You were right."

The floodgate opened, Jen is crying uncontrollably now.

"I know. Jen, please forgive me. Please, sweetheart."

"I'm trying."

The familiar scent of herbal soap and fabric softener wraps around her, as comforting as her mother's embrace.

"It's okay, Jen." Her mother heaves a shuddering sigh, stroking Jen's hair. "Everything is going to be okay."

"I just don't feel like it is." She pulls back to look up at Mom's face, seeking reassurance, finding only uncertainty.

"It will be," Mom says unconvincingly, sniffling, digging in the pockets of her robe for tissues and handing a clean one to Jen. "It just takes time, that's all. We have to get used to this. We all do."

Jen nods, doubting she ever will.

"I still want to know more about my real father," she says, when she can speak again without her voice breaking.

Mom's eyes cloud over. "I know you do, Jen, and I can understand that. But just . . . not yet, okay? Promise me you'll give it some time. You're not ready for that. I don't even know where he is."

She's lying. Staring at her mother's face, Jen senses it. For whatever reason, Mom is unwilling to tell her the truth.

And in that moment, she makes up her mind.

"Do you promise, Jen?" Mom asks. "Promise you'll wait awhile before you want to meet him?"

"I promise."

Her mother nods. Pats her on the arm. Inhales, exhales, looks around the room expectantly.

That's when Jen remembers. The pink bootee.

"You can take it," she says, sinking back against the pillows, finding that she doesn't have to work very hard to feign physical and emotional exhaustion. "It's in the top drawer of my desk."

Mom wastes no time in crossing the room, opening the drawer, and taking out the white box. She pauses again by the bed to lean over and plant a kiss on Jen's forehead. "I love you, sweetheart."

"I know," Jen murmurs, unable — unwilling — to say it back.

"Daddy loves you, too. You know that, don't you?"

Jen shrugs.

Her mother's gaze is shadowed. "Just remember one thing, Jen. Love is thicker than blood."

She says nothing, just turns her head into her pillow and yawns, as though she's about to doze off again.

Her mother leaves the room and closes the door behind her.

Jen waits until she hears her footsteps retreating down the hall.

Then she bolts from the bed, pulls on a robe, and hurriedly slips downstairs to the kitchen.

Taking the weighty volume of Buffalo white pages from the bottom drawer, she hides it inside the fold of her robe, just in case.

Back in her room, she sits in the chair and turns on the lamp.

She blinks impatiently as her eyes grow accustomed to the light, her fingers already blindly flipping pages. She holds her breath in anticipation as she zeroes in on the *M*'s, then the *Ma*'s, then finally, the *Mattesons*.

She scans down the list, telling herself that even if there's just a *Matteson, Q,* she'll call the number.

Yeah, great. What will you say?

Are you a musician and did you get your girlfriend pregnant almost fifteen years ago?

That sounds ridiculous.

Well, then, what *will* she say?

It doesn't matter, because she's in luck.

Matteson, Quint.

She stares at the listing for a long time.

He's my father, she tells herself. *My father.*

It doesn't feel real. It won't until she speaks to him . . . or maybe, until she actually lays eyes on him.

There's an address, too.

With trembling fingers, Jen copies it carefully onto a scrap of paper.

★ ★ ★

Back in the master bedroom, Matt lies snoring peacefully beside the rumpled spot where Kathleen tossed restlessly throughout the night. Her ears were trained on the stillness, her body tense in anticipation of the phantom baby's cries.

They never came. Not this time.

Clutching the white box in one hand, Kathleen steals across the room to her dresser. She slides the drawer open quietly and feels around inside. It takes her a few heart-stopping moments to locate the bundle she hurriedly jammed back inside when she heard Matt coming to bed last night.

There it is.

She slips out of the room carrying the pink crocheted blanket, stealthily making her way along the dim hallway and down the stairs.

The heat hissing from the baseboard vents does little yet to warm the house; the lights she turns on along the way fail to dispel the gloom of a stormy November dawn. In the kitchen, Kathleen flips the overhead light switch, then sets the pink bundle and cardboard box on the table, resisting the urge to examine their contents right away.

Instead, she first measures coffee into a filter. She's running on empty, desperately needing an artificial energy boost. Fueled by caffeine, she might be able to make it through another day without collapsing. The cleaning lady is coming so she'll have to clear out of here for at least a few hours, and Curran has an orthodontist appointment late this afternoon.

As she runs cold water at the sink, she stares intently out the window at the backyard. Her eyes scan the clumps of shrubbery, search the blue shadowed nooks beside the boys' wooden swing set and Matt's shed at the back of the property.

Was somebody really out there in the night, looking in at her?

Or, God help her, is she finally cracking beneath the burden of the secret she's kept all these years?

With a trembling hand, she sets the automatic drip pot to brew and returns to the table.

Carefully, she lays out the blanket on the table, then takes the single bootee from it.

Then she removes the lid from the box and lays the other bootee on the table.

No doubt about it.

They're identical.

Everything about them matches: the size,

the shape, the shade of pink yarn, the intricate scroll work in the white lace edging.

Either the bootee that turned up on Jen's bed yesterday is the long-missing partner of the one Kathleen has kept all these years . . .

Or somebody went to a tremendous amount of trouble to duplicate the original.

It would make sense that only the person who made it in the first place would be capable of doing so.

It's precisely that knowledge that makes Kathleen's blood run cold.

Robby wasn't in school again today.

He's definitely been suspended — Jen found that out this morning when she worked up the nerve to ask one of his friends leaning on the radiator in the hallway.

She figures she has at least a couple hours of freedom after detention this afternoon. She overheard Mom mentioning to Dad that she's taking Curran to the orthodontist and won't be home until at least five o'clock. Knowing Dr. Deare's reputation for being late, it will most likely be after six.

The way Jen sees it, she has two choices with what she might do with those precious unsupervised hours. She can either go over to Robby's to talk to him in person, or she can go to find her birth father.

331

The latter option wins, hands down.

After all, Robby didn't even bother to answer all her pages, much less wish her a happy birthday. Why should she knock herself out trying to see him?

Your father didn't wish you a happy birthday, either, that nagging voice has been reminding her all day. *Why knock yourself out trying to see* him?

Because she can't help it. Because curiosity has gotten the best of her. Because, quite simply, she *needs* to do this, in spite of her mother . . . or, perhaps, just to spite her mother?

No. She's doing this for herself. Really, she is.

Maybe Quint Matteson will turn out to be a great guy. Maybe he spent his whole life regretting that he gave her up. Maybe he's been trying to find her, and couldn't. Maybe he'll want Jen to go live with him.

So, on Wednesday afternoon, as her fellow detainees head for the late bus waiting out in front of the school, Jen ducks down the deserted corridor that leads to the science building. Two minutes later, she's making her way out the back exit.

All she has to do is cross the football field and cut through a narrow strip of woods, and she's on the busy highway that runs parallel to the street the school is on.

She's never taken the public transportation system in Buffalo, but she did it once or twice in Chicago, and that's a much bigger city. How difficult can this be?

She looked up the local transit routes in the Media Center during study hall this afternoon. From the shopping center across the street, she can catch a bus downtown, and from there, she can connect to one that will take her to Quint Matteson's neighborhood.

If everything goes according to schedule, she'll have an hour's worth of round-trip travel, including the final connection to the bus that will drop her on Cuttington Road. That means she'll be left with a whole hour for . . .

Well, for whatever happens when she comes face to face with her father.

If he's even at home.

Maybe she should have called first, to make sure.

But what could she say?

Hi there, I'm your long lost daughter and I thought I'd stop by and say hello?

Yeah.

Something like that would go over much better in person.

Riding the bus into the heart of the city,

Jen stares out the window at the rows of two-story frame houses broken up by the occasional school, gas station, strip mall, or church. Jen has never seen so many churches in her life, many of them Roman Catholic. There seems to be a neighborhood tavern every couple of corners, too, many with *Friday Fish Fry* or *Ten Cent Wing Night* signs in the window. There are election campaign billboards in front of countless houses, and red-and-blue Buffalo Bills flags galore.

Who would have guessed back when they moved here in April that Jen was returning to her hometown? How odd that her roots are here.

She always knew Mom grew up here, but Jen was led to believe that she had moved to the Midwest before Jen was conceived. The Carmody family is all back in Indiana, and most of Mom's family is in Chicago. Jen assumed that Grandpa Gallagher was the family's only tie to Buffalo. Now it turns out she's a native.

She doesn't feel like a native. As she boards the connecting bus on Main Street, surrounded by senior citizens and college students and strangers, some of them men who give her disconcerting stares, she feels like a little girl lost in a foreign city.

I want to go home.

No. It's too late to back out now. She'd have to wait here for the next bus back to the suburbs anyway. She's come this far; she might as well go through with her plan. If she doesn't, she'll just go home and wonder what might have happened.

As the bus heads toward Quint Matteson's neighborhood, Jen goes over various scenarios in her head. They all start out pretty much the same — with Jen ringing the doorbell and the door being opened by a man who looks exactly like her.

That's where the fantasies branch off in different directions.

In some versions, her father gathers her into his arms, holds her close, and tells her he never wanted to let her go. From there, he either asks her to live with him on the spot, or insists on driving her home and confronting Mom and Dad angrily.

Those are the happy endings — at least, as far as Jen is concerned. In all the other variations, her birth father either denies that he's ever heard of her, or he tells her to get lost and slams the door in her face.

What will she do if that happens?

What *can* she do? You can't make somebody want you, and you can't make somebody love you.

Her mother's words come back to haunt her. Rather, to taunt her.

Love is thicker than blood.

Whatever. Blood is thicker than water, and Quint Matteson's is flowing through her veins. For all Jen knows, her mother lied about his not wanting her. For all she knows, her mother never even told him she exists.

If he really didn't want her back then — if he still doesn't want her now — she needs to hear it from his own lips.

She'll never take her mother's word for anything again.

"Katie Gallagher! It's so nice to see you again!"

Kathleen forces a polite smile at Dr. Deare's receptionist, the one with whom she attended Saint Brigid's years ago. She should remember her name; maybe she would, if she weren't so damned exhausted.

As Curran shuffles off toward the seating area, Kathleen says, "It's so nice to see you again, too . . ."

"Deb. Deb Mahalski," the woman supplies after an uncomfortable pause, the name provided not quite as warmly as it was the first time around. "I used to be Deb Duffy, remember?"

Doing her best to summon an expression of recognition, Kathleen says brightly, "Of course I remember. Saint Brigid's."

When you come right down to it, she doesn't remember a Deb Duffy, and she can't recall ever having seen her anywhere other than right here. Which isn't unusual, given the school's size and the fact that so many years have gone by . . .

Or is it?

Paranoia steals over Kathleen.

Who is this woman, really?

Oh, come on. Don't be ridiculous.

There's no reason at all for Kathleen to suspect her of being anything other than an old school chum and an orthodontist's receptionist. No reason to look her over with a wary eye, wondering if she could possibly have been looking into the kitchen window last night . . .

Oh, my God, Kathleen, stop it. You're really losing it. Get a grip.

Realizing the woman is watching her with an expectant expression and must have said something, Kathleen asks apologetically, "I'm sorry, what was that?"

"Your insurance card?" Deb's manner is growing less cheery by the moment. "I need to see it so that I can make a copy."

"Oh. Right." Kathleen fumbles in her

bag. "But I think you must already have it on file . . ."

"We need it each time you come in."

Have they always asked for it?

Kathleen can't remember. It just seems odd, that's all. Do they ask the other patients for their cards, too?

She glances around the waiting room and realizes that it's less jammed than usual. There are only two other patients, and they're both adults — a middle-aged woman and an elderly man. They might be here to see the chiropractor who shares the office space. Or they might be posing as patients, but they're really . . .

What?

Contract killers?

Undercover police officers?

Kathleen swallows hard, her heart beating like crazy.

"Um, did you find it?" Deb asks.

"Oh, sorry . . . here it is."

As Kathleen hands the laminated card across the desk, she tells herself that there's no connection between the phone calls, the pink bootee, the face out the window, and this woman having access to her personal information. No connection at all. It's not as though an insurance card would grant her access to a locked house.

338

Except that it wasn't always locked, Kathleen reminds herself yet again.

Damn it. How could she have been so stupid? All day, she's been thinking about the many times she left the door unlocked, running out on an errand, or to get the kids at the bus stop, or whenever Sissy comes to clean.

Anyone could have slipped into the house.

Well, she won't do that this week. She'll never do it again.

"Here's your card back." Deb hands it to Kathleen, along with a clipboard with the insurance paperwork on it. "I'll just need you to fill this out."

"I think you have our information on file?" Kathleen can't help saying.

"We need you to fill out a new set of papers each visit." The woman nods at Curran, who's taken a seat on the opposite end of the room. "Is he ready? Because we're running ahead today, so he can go right in."

"Oh, that's . . . that's great."

It's also highly unusual. In fact, Dr. Deare has never even been on time, much less ahead.

Again, she fights a flicker of paranoia. What if this whole thing is some kind of elaborate plot? What if Dr. Deare isn't an orthodontist at all, and Deb isn't a receptionist? What if Curran walks through that door and she never sees him again?

Stop it! You have to stop. That's got to be the most far-fetched thing you've come up with yet.

"Curran? Sweetie? The doctor's waiting for you," she says, pushing back panic.

"Okay."

She bends to kiss his head as he passes, and he looks up at her in embarrassment and disgust. "Mom!"

"Sorry."

Catching Deb looking at her strangely, she falters, then says, "You know how boys are. They don't like their moms kissing them goodbye in public."

"Actually, I have daughters," Deb reminds her. Another detail Kathleen couldn't be bothered to remember.

Then Deb adds, almost sympathetically, "But they don't like me to kiss them in public, either. And anyway, your son will be back soon, so . . ."

So you really didn't need to kiss him goodbye.

Feeling foolish, Kathleen says quickly, "Oh, I know he will be."

Of course he will be.

As her son disappears down the corridor behind the desk, Kathleen forces herself to settle into a chair halfway between the two strangers. Neither of them appears to notice her.

The frantic worry subsides a bit.

She turns her attention to the clipboard, filling out half the first page before it slips out of her jittery hand and clatters to the floor.

Both the strangers look up from their magazines.

Deb, who is standing at the copy machine, calls, "Are you all right?"

"I'm fine. Just clumsy."

Clumsy, and scared out of my mind.

This has to stop. She can't get through another sleepless night, or another day wondering who knows her secret . . . and how they found out.

She has to do something.

But what?

She has to tell somebody.

But whom?

The police are out of the question.

And Matt . . . well, he'll be shattered if she tells him the truth. Their family is already hanging in the balance, the tension in the house becoming unbearable.

If Matt finds out what she did . . .

Well, he might leave.

Would she even blame him?

But if he left, he might take the boys with him. Jen, too. Oh, God, he might take Kathleen's children away, and she wouldn't have a chance of getting them back. Not if anyone knew . . .

No.

Nobody can know.

Not even Matt.

There's nothing for her to do but hang on a little longer.

Hang on . . . and pray.

Quint Matteson's neighborhood isn't at all what Jen expected.

Then again, she reminds herself, she really had no idea what to expect. She only hoped — and this stretch of rundown two-and-three family houses on a treeless block bordering an industrial park is hardly what she hoped for.

As she makes her way along the uneven, litter-strewn sidewalk, she suddenly has the oddest sensation that she's being followed.

She turns her head and catches a glimpse of a figure in a long coat walking along half a block behind her.

Instantly reminded of that day on the soccer field, she feels sick to her stomach. Is it some psycho killer stalking her?

Her shoulders tense, she walks a few more

steps before she dares to turn her head again.

Whoever it was is gone.

Relax, Jen tells herself, exhaling in relief.

Is it any wonder she's a nervous wreck? She's been through hell these past few weeks, and now she's about to meet her father. She isn't sure whether she's looking forward to or dreading whatever lies ahead.

When she reaches the boxy three-story house fronted by a concrete porch with half its wrought iron railing missing, Jen double-checks the address against the slip of paper in her hand. This is definitely it . . . unless there was a misprint in the phone book. Which, of course, isn't out of the question.

She gingerly climbs the steps as a car drives by and honks. She turns to see a teen-aged boy leaning out the passenger's window of a souped-up heap, ogling her.

He gives a staccato, high-pitched "Ow!" and the car slows. He and the driver make kissing noises at her.

Jen's skin crawls. She turns her back, hoping the car will drive on.

After a few moments, it does, tires screeching down the block.

She shouldn't be here. This has to be the wrong address, the wrong neighborhood altogether.

But there are three doorbells, and a sticker beneath the third one reads *Matteson*.

So much for the phone book misprint.

Well, her father is a musician. He's probably sacrificed a lot for his art over the years. Or maybe he's living in this dump because the apartment has good acoustics, or something.

Whatever.

She's here, and she's going to see him. She'll judge for herself whether her mother was right about him being a loser.

She rings the doorbell and waits.

And waits.

No answer.

She rings again.

Waits.

Standing on her tiptoes, she peers through the window on the door. She can see a vestibule, a trio of metal mailboxes, and a stairway leading up.

When she tries the door, the knob turns, to her surprise.

But that doesn't mean she should go in. If he were up there, he'd have answered the buzzer, wouldn't he?

Unless he didn't hear it. Maybe it's not working properly. Would that be surprising, in a place like this?

Suddenly once again aware of the distinct sensation that somebody is behind her, Jen turns to look back at the street.

Nobody is there. At least, nobody she can see. Maybe someone is concealed behind a tree, or watching through a window.

Okay, now she totally has the creeps. She fights the illogical urge to take off running.

Instead, taking a deep breath, she pushes the door open and takes a step inside.

For a moment, she stands there in the silent hallway, wondering what she should do next.

Then, somewhere above, she hears keys rattling, a lock turning, a door banging. Footsteps pound down the stairs before she can react.

What if it's him?

Luckily — or unluckily? — it isn't.

It's a woman — or so she thinks at first glance, judging by the makeup, low-cut top, and short skirt. But as the stranger arrives on the first floor and steps into the glow from the bare bulb overhead, Jen realizes the so-called woman is actually a girl, probably not much older than she is.

"Hey," she says, stopping at the foot of the stairs to open the middle mailbox.

Not *hey*, as in *what are you doing here*, but *hey*, as in *hello*.

"Hi." Jen doesn't know what to do.

The girl peers into the box and finds it empty, which obviously isn't a good thing, judging by the curse word that explodes from her mouth.

"Sorry," she says, with a nod at Jen. "But I'm, like, waiting for a check. You know how it is."

"Yeah," Jen agrees, though she has no idea how it is.

The girl walks toward the door, jangling her keys.

As she passes, Jen works up the nerve to say, "Excuse me?"

"Yeah?"

"Um, do you know Quint Matteson?"

"You mean the guy who lived upstairs?"

Lived?

Okay, so he must have moved out. That's a good sign. Maybe he got a record deal or something.

"Yeah, I knew him," the girl says, peering into Jen's face in the dim light of the hall.

For a moment, Jen expects her to say something like *You're the spitting image of him! Are you the daughter he's been trying to find all these years?*

But she doesn't say that.

She says, "Wait, you mean you're looking for him?"

"Yeah. Do you know where he went?"

"You don't?"

Jen fights the urge to retort *Duh, why would I be asking you if I knew?*

"No," she says instead, politely. "Do you? I really need to find him."

The girl shrugs, wearing an odd expression. "Wow, like I really don't know how to tell you this, but Quint Matteson's dead."

Kathleen hands the clipboard back to Deb Mahalski. "Sorry it took me so long to fill it out," she says apologetically.

"That's okay. I know these forms can be a pain." Deb smiles, perhaps having forgiven Kathleen for not remembering her name.

"So, are you in touch with anybody else from the old days at Saint Brigid's?" Kathleen asks casually, needing to make sure her misgivings about the woman's purported role in her past really are just paranoia.

"Oh, sure." Deb mentions a few names that are vaguely familiar, but that proves nothing.

"How about you?" she asks Kathleen. "Who do you keep in touch with?"

"Do you remember Maeve O'Shea?"

Deb nods. "She married Greg Hudson,

didn't she? I always thought they were the cutest couple."

"Actually, they're divorced now."

"Well, that's not surprising. He used to cheat on her even back then," Deb says with a shrug. "Easy come, easy go, right?"

Uncomfortable with the swing the conversation has taken, Kathleen merely nods.

"You know what? I think it would be great if we organized a class reunion, don't you, Katie?"

God, no. She manages a tight smile.

Deb goes on, "I was just telling Father Joseph the other day that I would be willing to form a reunion committee."

Kathleen's jaw drops. "Father Joseph?"

"Don't tell me you don't remember Father Joseph?"

"No, I remember him," she murmurs, her heart pounding. "I just . . . I haven't seen him in years. I didn't know he was still . . ."

She trails off, her father's words echoing in her brain.

Father Joseph was here earlier.

To think she chalked it up to her father's senility.

"Oh, he's retired from the priesthood, but he's around," Deb informs her. "I run into him every now and then. He's as grouchy as ever, and more opinionated, too, if that's possible. And he looks exactly the same, but his hair is white. He still wears his robe and collar around town, even though he's retired. You'd think —"

"Do you know where he is?" Kathleen hears herself asking. "I'd love to get in touch with him, just to . . . you know. Just to say hello, after all these years."

"Sure." Deb scribbles something on a piece of scrap paper and hands it to Kathleen. "This is the name of the retirement home where he's living now. He just moved a few months ago. It's only a few minutes from Woodsbridge, as a matter of fact. Isn't that a coincidence?"

Kathleen murmurs that it is, indeed, a coincidence.

"So, Kathleen, we really should get together and start planning that reunion. What do you say? I'll give you a ring one day next week so we can talk about it."

"Great," she replies absently, clutching the piece of paper in her trembling fingers.

Father Joseph.

She went to him once before, when she had nowhere else to turn.

Now, after all that's happened, he's the last person she wants to face with the truth . . . but, perhaps, once again, the only one she dares to trust.

★ ★ ★

He waits until Jen is onboard the bus before he dares to emerge from the shelter of a doorway. He climbs onboard just as the folding doors are about to close, and deposits his change into the fare box.

The girl is already huddled in a seat halfway back, staring out the window. He sees her wiping at her cheek and realizes she's crying.

She doesn't even glance in his direction as he passes in the aisle, slipping into an empty seat two rows behind her, on the aisle.

As the bus lurches into motion, he watches her fish in her pocket for a tissue. She wipes her eyes, blows her nose, sniffles.

He opens his newspaper, pretending to be absorbed in it, but watching her over the top of the page.

He can see that her whole body is trembling. She's crying.

He wonders again what happened in the few minutes she disappeared inside that building. He didn't dare get any closer than to conceal himself in the shadow of an alleyway a few doors down the street. Not after he saw her turn around as though she sensed she was being followed.

Like mother, like daughter, he finds himself thinking, his lips curling into a smile.

It's warm on the bus. So warm that he unbuttons his long black overcoat. His head is sweating, and so is his neck beneath his collar.

Fifteen minutes later, the bus slows. The Cuttington Road stop is just ahead.

Jen stands up and makes her way up the aisle.

He follows, careful to stay several steps behind her.

As he reaches the front of the bus, the driver brakes and he's forced to grab a pole to steady himself. He loses his grip on his newspaper and it falls to the floor.

The doors are open. Jen is climbing off.

He bends to pick up the paper, but the woman in the front seat has already retrieved it for him.

He offers her a pleasant smile. "Thank you. That was nice of you."

"You're welcome," she says, and returns the smile as he climbs down the steps. "Have a good day, Father."

He gives a pleasant wave. "God bless you."

TWELVE

By Friday, Kathleen still hasn't heard from Father Joseph. She left two messages with the receptionist at the retirement home, using her maiden name and her cell phone number.

She left the phone on around the clock, nearly jumping out of her skin the one time it did ring. But it was only Maeve, wanting to meet for coffee.

Kathleen felt guilty turning down the invitation, especially after Maeve was so wonderful about showing up to surprise Jen with that expensive sweater on her birthday. Still, her instincts are telling her to keep her distance for a while. As much as she needed to confide in somebody, she shouldn't have told Maeve about Jen's birth and Quint Matteson.

Maeve might have once been her closest friend in the world — and all right, technically, she is again — but in some ways, Maeve Hudson might as well be a total stranger. When you come right down to it,

Kathleen doesn't entirely trust her. She never could keep a secret. For all she knows, Maeve could have mentioned that Matt isn't Jen's father to Erin and it could be all over school by now.

And if Kathleen spilled one secret, there's no guarantee that she won't accidentally slip about the other. Especially when it's weighing more heavily on her conscience with every passing day.

That's why she needs Father Joseph so desperately.

Yet the past forty-eight hours have been uneventful. At first unnervingly, but now, reassuringly, so. There have been no strange phone calls or cries in the night, no sightings of lurking strangers.

If it weren't for the pair of pink baby bootees tucked into Kathleen's top drawer, she might almost be able to stop looking over her shoulder and relax.

But the fact remains that somebody gift wrapped that bootee and left it on her daughter's bed. Somebody got into the house when they weren't here.

Unwilling, unable, to tell Matt, Kathleen had the locks changed yesterday while he was at work. She paid the locksmith in cash; Matt will never even have to know.

She simply opened the door for her husband when he arrived home last night, before he could insert his key in the lock. Then, when he was safely snoring in their bed, she crept downstairs and replaced the old house key on his ring with the new one, which looks exactly like it. She had already done the same thing with the keys they keep inside the deadbolt locks.

She feels safer now. She's even managed to catch a few hours of sleep these last two nights: a deep sleep undisturbed by nightmares or the cries of a phantom baby.

But something tells her this peaceful interlude won't last forever.

"Jen?"

Alone at a table in the far corner of the cafeteria, she looks up from her ham sandwich, startled by the familiar voice — a voice that hasn't spoken to her in weeks.

"Hi, Erin."

"Is anyone sitting here?" Erin gestures at the empty seats on either side of Jen, who shakes her head incredulously.

Erin suddenly wants to eat lunch with her? Why? She didn't say two words to Jen the other night at her birthday party. It was obvious she was only there because her mother dragged her along.

"Listen, Jen," Erin sets down her tray,

which contains only an apple and a diet Snapple, then slips into a chair, "I need to talk to you. It's kind of . . . well, I don't know if you know this, but . . ."

"Know what?"

"About Robby?"

At the mere mention of his name, the already sodden bread and ham in Jen's mouth threatens to choke her. She grabs her bottle of water, takes a gulp, asks, "What about him?"

Erin bites her lower lip. "Oh, God, Jen, I thought you might know."

"What is it, Erin?" Jen sets down the water bottle, her heart pounding.

"The cops came to the school this morning. I guess Robby's father reported him missing yesterday and, um —"

"What?"

A long pause. And then . . .

"They found his body early this morning," Erin blurts.

Jen gasps, pressing a hand to her lips. "No . . ."

"I know. I know." Erin shakes her head and shudders. "I can't believe it."

"What — what happened to him?" Her eyes are teary, but she can't cry. Not in front of Erin.

"Who knows? He was dealing. He probably got himself into some kind of trouble."

"You mean . . . he was *murdered?*" Jen asks in disbelief.

"I guess. Or maybe he just OD'd."

OD'd. Like Quint Matteson. The lump in Jen's throat tightens.

"I don't know the details," Erin goes on. "I just heard from Cammie Lenhart. Her father's a cop. When was the last time you saw him?"

Focus. Stay focused, Jen.

Feeling as though she's in a daze, she says, "Robby? I haven't heard from him in a few days, ever since . . . well, you know."

Of course Erin knows. Everybody knows that Jen got caught skipping school with Robby. Everybody knows she has detention and he was suspended. It's only a matter of time before everybody finds out about his death.

It isn't surprising, really. She knew he was wild. But there was something decent about him. Something . . .

"Are you okay?" Erin asks, touching her arm.

Jen nods, clenching her jaw to keep it from trembling, unwilling to betray her emotion.

"He didn't mention anything to you about being in any kind of trouble, did he, Jen?"

Is that why she's sitting here? Hoping to sniff out gossip to share with Rachel and the others?

With Erin, it's hard to tell. Her expression of concern seems genuine, but you never know.

"No," Jen admits, "he didn't say a word."

To her horror, she feels the tears in her eyes starting to spill over.

"Are you okay, Jen?" Erin asks again.

"I'm fine." But she isn't. Her throat aches with the painful effort of swallowing her grief. She can't let Erin see her cry; she can't let anyone at school see her cry. She's come this far without giving in to her emotions . . . all she has to do is get through today, and then she'll have the weekend to regroup.

"You don't look fine," Erin says, watching her closely. "What's up with you, Jen? Not just the Robby thing. I know we haven't talked lately, but you've seemed . . . I mean, you're definitely not yourself."

There was a time when she would have jumped at the opportunity to confide in Erin. But so much has changed in a few short weeks — and now, again, in a few short days.

Jen has never felt more alone in her life.

Her eyelids flutter involuntarily and another gush of tears is released to roll down her cheeks. She sweeps at them with her napkin, horrified that she's sitting here crying in the middle of the cafeteria. Thank God she's facing the wall; hopefully nobody will notice.

But of course Erin has noticed. Jen steals a glance at her and sees that she doesn't seem to know quite what to do. It's as though she's trying really hard to keep Jen at arm's length, but she looks like she wants to hug her or something.

"I'm fine," Jen says again, sniffling.

"No, you aren't."

"Okay, I'm not."

Erin hands her a folded napkin from her tray. "Here. You need to blow your nose."

"Thanks."

"Look, Jen, you know Robby was trouble. You said it yourself. It's not like the two of you were a couple. At least, not for that long."

Jen nods, wiping her nose with the napkin, wishing she could tell Erin that it isn't just about Robby.

"He could be really mean, Jen," Erin goes on matter-of-factly, taking a bite of her apple. Jen notices that her fingernails are perfect ovals, polished a pearly pink. She's suddenly aware of her own unpolished nails, bitten into ragged nubs in the stress of the last few days.

Jen makes a futile attempt to banish a fresh flood of tears.

"Come on, Jen." Erin almost looks alarmed. "You can't fall apart over this. You have to pull yourself together."

"I'm not crying about Robby." Jen buries her face in the napkin.

"Then what the heck are you crying about? Jesus, Jen, you're a mess."

She lifts her head miserably, shoulders still heaving with sobs. "I know. It's . . . my father's dead."

The moment the words have left her mouth and the expression of alarm crosses Erin's face, she knows she's made a huge mistake.

But it's too late to take them back.

"Aaah! You scared me!"

Stella stops short in the doorway of her daughters' bedroom as her cleaning lady spins around, vacuum cleaner in hand. Sissy's dark, overly made-up eyes are wide and frightened.

"I'm sorry, Sissy. I didn't mean to sneak up on you. I was calling from downstairs to tell you I'm home early but you were running the vacuum."

"It's okay." Sissy turns off the power and

presses a hand against her heart. "I guess I just didn't hear you, Mrs. Gattinski."

"It's Stella," she reminds her, for perhaps the tenth time since the girl started cleaning here. It's getting frustrating to keep correcting her.

It's not that she isn't used to being called Mrs. Gattinski on a daily basis, being a teacher. But Sissy's got to be close to thirty, too old to defer to her elders. She's probably accustomed to using formal titles out of respect for her employers, but Stella still isn't entirely comfortable with that, either. In fact, it took her a long time not to feel like she should be pitching in vacuuming and scrubbing alongside the cleaning lady.

"I'm sorry, *Stella*," Sissy echoes, her expression as awkward as the name sounds on her lips.

"It's okay. Well, I just wanted to let you know I was here. We had a half day today. I'm going to go get changed before I pick up the girls from day care."

"All right. Oh, the phone rang a little while ago. I think it was Mr. Gattinski. I didn't pick it up, though. He left a message."

"Thanks." Maybe he's decided to skip the banquet after all, Stella thinks hopefully.

Sissy is about to switch the vacuum on again.

"Oh, one more thing. . . ." Stella pauses in the doorway. "Did you find the note I left you this morning?"

"About not putting your jeans into the dryer? I found it, and I made sure I didn't. They're on the drying rack downstairs."

"Thanks." Stella can't help feeling embarrassed. But she already has two pairs of jeans she can no longer squeeze into. Even with the few pounds she lost courtesy of the flu this week, she can't afford to have any more waistbands shrunk in the laundry.

Envious of Sissy's slender build beneath the baggy sweats she wears to clean in, Stella says, "I also left a note stuck to the fridge, next to the monthly planner. Did you see that one?"

"Oh, no . . . I'm sorry."

"It just said that there are tons of apples in the crisper so help yourself. Oh, and there was tuna salad in there for you to have for your lunch, if you felt like it. Did you find it?"

"I brought my own sandwich, but thank you anyway. Oops, I'm so sorry!" Sissy blurts as the vacuum cleaner attachment in her hand clatters loudly to the hardwood floor.

"It's all right." Stella bends to retrieve it and hands it to her, then looks at her more closely. The girl appears agitated, fumbling with the attachment as she tries to replace it on the end of the hose.

"What's wrong, Sissy?" Stella asks. "Is everything okay?"

Sissy hesitates. "I'm sorry, Mrs. — I mean, Stella. I'm just a little jittery today, I guess. I thought I . . ." She trails off, shakes her head. "Never mind."

"You thought you what?"

"I just thought I heard something earlier, that's all. But I'm sure it was my imagination."

"What did you think you heard?"

"Footsteps."

"Footsteps?"

"Coming from downstairs. It was probably nothing."

"Oh, it must have been me. I got home almost five minutes ago and I checked my phone messages before I —"

"No, no, not just now. This was much earlier this afternoon. When I was washing the floor in the master bathroom, I could have sworn I heard somebody down here. I thought it must be you or your husband, so I called out, but nobody answered. And when I heard it again after a few minutes and I started to come down to look . . ."

"What?" Stella prods, her pulse racing.

She hasn't forgotten the wet tire treads in the garage the other day. "What happened?"

"I'm sorry, Mrs. Gattinski. I didn't mean to scare you. It was probably —"

"I'm not scared," Stella protests, not bothering to correct the *Mrs. Gattinski* this time.

"Are you sure? Because you seem a little scared and I didn't mean to —"

"I'm just concerned, that's all. What happened when you started to come down to look?" she repeats, unable to temper her impatience.

"I just thought I heard the footsteps again . . ." Poor Sissy suddenly looks as though she wishes she hadn't brought it up at all. "And then I, uh, I thought I heard a door slamming. That's all."

That's all?

Stella's mouth has gone dry. Somebody was here again, during the day?

Kurt, she thinks, her blood beginning to boil. It had to be him. Who else would be sneaking around the house in the middle of the day? He probably forgot the cleaning lady would be here. Or maybe that's why he called — to make sure she was. And when she didn't pick up, he thought the coast was clear, so he —

"Are you sure you're all right, Stella?" Sissy asks, watching her anxiously.

"I'm fine," she mutters, spinning on her heel and stalking toward the master bedroom.

"Oh my God." Erin gasps, staring at Jen in disbelief. "Your father's dead? But how — when . . . ?"

"Not *him.* My *real* father."

"What?"

Reluctantly, Jen spills the whole tragic tale, with Erin hanging on her every word. By the time she reaches the part where she found out Quint Matteson died a few months ago of a drug overdose, Erin has wrapped an arm around her shoulders and is patting her sympathetically.

"That's so, so awful, Jen. I'm really sorry."

"Thanks. I just . . . I don't know what to do."

"Well, what did your mom say when you told her?"

Jen flinches, hesitating before confessing, "I didn't tell her."

"Why not?"

"For one thing, because I promised her I wouldn't try to find him."

For another, because telling her mother

would somehow make it true.

There's a part — a tiny, ridiculously hopeful part — of Jen that refuses to accept that Quint Matteson is dead. She has no proof, only his downstairs neighbor's casual news bulletin. For all Jen knows, that girl could have been kidding around, or she could have had him mixed up with somebody else.

Okay, that might not be very likely, but there's a chance, isn't there? Especially since Jen did a search on the Internet for his obituary or a mention in the newspaper of a fatal drug overdose, and found nothing.

Which isn't proof that he's still alive . . .

But without proof, Jen can almost convince herself that he might be.

"You're not going to tell your mom about this, Erin, are you?" she asks belatedly.

After all, it's not as though they're friends, like they used to be. What would stop Erin from telling not just her mother, but the whole world, that Jen's father isn't Matt Carmody, but some druggie who OD'd?

In fact, after what Jen did to Erin, stealing Robby away, she wouldn't really blame Erin for doing something deliberately mean to get back at her.

But Erin is shaking her head. "Are you

kidding? Why would I tell my mom? She'd just run and tell *your* mom."

"So you won't tell her?"

"No way. Oh my God, my mother's the worst when it comes to gossiping. I never tell her anything anymore."

Relieved, Jen chooses to believe her.

She even dares to think that maybe now that Robby's gone . . .

Well, maybe there's a chance she and Erin can be friends again.

Will Erin forgive her for choosing Robby over their friendship?

Only one way to find out. Jen takes a deep breath and looks her in the eye. "Hey, Erin, do you think —"

Erin speaks simultaneously. "Hey, Jen, if you're not —"

They break off, look at each other, and laugh.

"What were you going to say?" Erin asks.

"You first."

"I was just going to say that if you're not busy tonight, I'm around. Maybe we can go to the mall for a while or something."

"I can't," Jen says. "I'm . . ."

Grounded, for one thing. But Erin doesn't need to know that.

"Babysitting," Jen says instead. "I'm babysitting for the Gattinskis. But can you do me a favor and not mention that to your mother, either?"

"Yeah. Not that I would, but why not?"

"My parents don't want me babysitting anymore. You know, because . . ."

"Because Mr. Gattinski is so gross?"

"Huh?"

"Don't tell me you don't know he totally cheats on his wife?"

Jen's jaw drops. "Where'd you hear that?"

"Oh, come on, Jen. You haven't heard it?"

Actually, she has. She's heard it a few times. It isn't hard to believe, either. There's something creepy about Mr. Gattinski. Lately whenever she catches him looking at her, she feels like she wants to go change into something totally unflattering. Ugh. She dreads having him pick her up and drop her off whenever she babysits there.

Still. . . . Wow. She didn't realize that rumor was all over the neighborhood. Poor Mrs. Gattinski is so, so nice. For her sake, not wanting to fuel the rumors, Jen merely shrugs and tells Erin, "No, I never heard that. Maybe it's not true."

Erin snorts. "Yeah, sure. You know, Jen, for all this crazy stuff you've been through lately, you're still pretty naive. But I mean that in a good way," she adds quickly, touching Jen's hand. "Hey, want me to come over and keep you company while you're babysitting?"

"Would you really?"

"Sure. Like I said, I'm just hanging out tonight and my mother's going out. I don't really feel like being alone after this whole thing with Robby. It's kind of creeping me out."

"Me, too." Jen shakes her head. "I can't believe he's dead."

"I know. Do you think he really was murdered?"

Jen tries, and fails, to imagine that. Who would want to hurt Robby? He was a dealer, yeah . . . but it's not like he was some shady character like in the movies.

"I don't know," she tells Erin. "But I hope not. I hope it was some kind of accident."

"Either way, he's still dead."

"Yeah."

They stare at each other in somber silence for a minute.

Then Erin asks what time she should come over to the Gattinskis' tonight.

"Around eight. Just don't tell your mother where you're going," Jen warns, "because my mother would kill me if she finds out I'm babysitting. I'm still grounded."

"How are you going to go if your parents don't know about it?"

"Easy. I'll just sneak out. I'm in my room every night with the door closed anyway. They'll never know," she assures Erin with far more confidence than she feels.

"What if they find out you're gone?"

"Whatever. I'll deal with it then. I mean, it's not like things can get much worse between me and them."

"Stella, it's me. I'm going straight from the office to the banquet tonight. I won't be home till late. Kiss the girls for me. Bye."

Bastard.

The face-off will have to wait until tomorrow, Stella concludes, pressing the erase button on the answering machine. At least that will give her a chance to figure out exactly what she wants to say, and how she wants to say it. It isn't as though she has absolute proof that he's having an affair. But considering the way the evidence keeps mounting, there's just no way that he isn't, as far as she's concerned.

Stella turns her attention away from the phone.

The master bedroom is neat as a hotel room and smells of lemon furniture polish. She glances at the clock. Does she have time to take a quick shower before she picks up the girls?

No. She barely has time to pull on a pair of jeans and run a comb through her hair. And there will be no taking a shower once the girls are home, running wild under her feet, clamoring for juice, for snacks, for attention.

Stella closes her eyes wearily, longing for a few minutes to herself, resenting the hell out of her husband. Why isn't Kurt ever here to help her?

Because he's at work. He isn't even supposed to be home at this hour of the day, remember?

Damn him. He's apparently capable of finding the time to sneak around the house during the day, when he's not supposed to be available. How ironic that he isn't ever here when she needs him, say, to tuck the girls into bed so that Stella wouldn't have to pay for a babysitter tonight?

Supposedly, he has a so-called banquet.

A banquet?

Is there really a banquet?

How tempting it is to check up on him.

Jen is coming in a few hours, so it's not like Stella can't go out. No, she's actually *supposed* to go out.

To the dance, she reminds herself. *You're*

supposed to be chaperoning a dance.

But what if she forgot all about the dance, and instead went over to the restaurant where Kurt's supposed to be? Just to make sure he's really there. On business. *Alone.*

If he is, he'll never even have to know she was there. She'll forget about confronting him tomorrow, and chalk up the footsteps and slamming doors — yes, and tire treads in the garage — to her own overly active imagination, and Sissy's, too.

But if Kurt isn't where he's supposed to be, with whom he's supposed to be . . .

Well, then, all bets are off, she concludes, catching sight of her grim-faced reflection and clenched fists in the mirror across the room. There's just no telling what she might do.

"Jen?" Kathleen knocks on her daughter's closed bedroom door.

No answer.

She frowns. Jen has been in here ever since this afternoon when she got home from school. Not that there's anything un-usual about that. Not lately, anyway. When it's absolutely necessary for her to emerge from her room, Jen sullenly goes about her business, then retreats from view as soon as she can.

"Jen!" Kathleen knocks again, reaching for the knob.

It's already turning, though, and her daughter opens the door, scowling. "What?"

"Daddy called from work and said he's taking us all out to dinner at the Como."

"Why?"

"Because it's Friday night and he doesn't want me to have to cook." Kathleen peers at her daughter. Jen's eyes are red. "Jen, have you been crying?"

"No."

She's lying. Pushing aside her worry, Kathleen reminds herself that her daughter is fourteen. When she was fourteen, she spent hours alone in her room, crying. It's hormones, along with everything else Jen has been through.

"Daddy will be home in fifteen minutes," she tells her daughter. "Do you want to get changed before we go?"

"I thought I was grounded."

"Well you have to eat, and since we're eating out, I'm assuming Dad wants you to go along."

"I doubt it. And anyway, that's all right. I'll stay here."

Kathleen frowns. The Como, which is a half hour away in Niagara Falls, is Jen's all-time favorite Italian restaurant. In fact, Kathleen suspects Matt chose that particular place for dinner out of guilt for not having made a bigger deal about Jen's birthday earlier in the week.

"I think you need to come with us, Jen."

"I can't. Mom, I feel nauseous. I've been feeling sick all day, like I'm coming down with something. Maybe I'm getting that flu everyone's had."

Kathleen reaches out to lay a hand against her daughter's forehead. "You do feel a little warm."

"Yeah, my head hurts, too. I just want to go to sleep."

"I'll stay home with you and Daddy can take the boys, then."

"No! Mom, please don't do that. I would feel terrible if you missed dinner out, and so would everyone else. I'll be fine. I'm just going to get into bed anyway."

"I don't know . . ."

"Take your cell phone. I'll call you if I need you."

"I don't like the idea of leaving you here alone if you're sick."

"You're treating me like a baby again. Please, Mom, you have to stop. You used to let me stay alone all the time when I was thirteen. Now suddenly you think I need you here to hold my hand?"

"It isn't that, Jen. It's just . . ."

Just what? The locks have been changed. And there probably isn't a safer neighborhood around.

"We'll see," Kathleen tells her daughter. "I'll talk to Daddy when he gets home."

"Whatever." Jen shrugs and closes her door.

She's right, Kathleen tells herself, retreating down the hall to change into something suitable for dinner out. *I am treating her like a baby.*

Jen's been staying alone for a few years now; she's been watching her brothers and babysitting other people's kids, for heaven's sake. How can Kathleen justify the sudden need to supervise a fourteen year old to Jen or Matt or anybody else?

They don't understand.

The pink bootee.

Okay, the pink bootee. What about it?

For all she knows, Jen wasn't even telling the truth about where it came from. Maybe she found it somewhere herself, and made up the whole story about it being a birthday present.

But where could she have found it?

And how could she have known its significance?

Round and round and round Kathleen's thoughts spin, the whole time she's changing into black jeans and a sweater, combing her hair, putting on lipstick and blusher so that she won't look quite so pale. By the time Matt pulls into the driveway, she's ready to insist on calling off the whole dinner.

She meets him down in the kitchen just as he's walking through the door, clutching a large bouquet of red, orange, and yellow dahlias.

"Hey," he says, and pulls her close. "These are for you."

"They are?" Matt never brings her flowers, unless it's their anniversary, or Valentine's Day . . . and sometimes, not even then. "What's the occasion?"

"No occasion."

A thought flits into her mind — something Maeve said about how she knew Gregory was cheating when he started bringing her flowers for no reason.

Kathleen eyes her husband, unable to muster the slightest shred of suspicion. Matt isn't the type to have an affair.

"They're beautiful," she murmurs, lifting the bouquet to her nose, absently noting that they're unscented, but she sniffs the distinct aroma of the outdoors, and her husband's musky aftershave clinging to the petals.

"I've just been thinking that you look like you need something bright and cheerful." Matt kisses her head gently.

Suddenly, she's overwhelmed by emotion. She leans against his shoulder and closes her eyes, wishing she could tell him everything.

Maybe she can.

Maybe she should.

Maybe —

"Daddy!" Riley bursts into the kitchen, Curran on his heels.

"You're home! Can we go now?" Curran asks, grabbing his navy fleece pullover from the hook by the door. "I want spaghetti and meatballs."

Matt grins. "Just give me five minutes to change out of this suit, and we'll go. You two need to go find warmer jackets, though. It's cold out there tonight."

"I'm never cold," Riley protests, reaching for his fleece that hangs beside Curran's.

"Come on, let's do what Dad says." Curran hangs both jackets on the hooks again and leads his little brother out of the room.

"Did you hear that?" Matt asks incredulously. "Kath, the boys just did exactly what

I told them to do. What's up with that?"

Too distracted to bother responding to the question, she informs him in a low voice, "Jen doesn't want to come to dinner."

Her husband's cheerful expression vanishes. "Big surprise. So let her stay home."

"But . . . do you think we should?"

"Why not? You want to force her to come with us so that she can sit and stare off into space all night, and make everyone else miserable?"

"I don't know . . . I just hate to leave her home alone."

"She's a big girl, remember?"

"She said she doesn't feel good. Maybe I should stay here with —"

"No," Matt cuts in firmly. "You are not going to stay here with her. I made a reservation for eight o'clock. I want to take you out for a nice dinner."

"You wanted to take the whole family out. She's part of the family, whether she believes she is or not."

"Do you think I don't know that? Of course she's part of the family. But until we can get her into therapy, it's doing more harm than good for all of us to be together, as far as I'm concerned. Did you call that family therapist you were going to try?"

"I left a message," she lies. "The, um, office is closed on Fridays."

"Okay." He heaves a sigh. Kathleen notices that he looks almost as weary as she feels.

All thoughts of telling him the truth have vanished from her mind. She can't tell him. Not now. Not yet.

If only there were someone who could advise her when to tell her husband, and how to tell him, and what to tell him.

Father Joseph.

Where are you? Why haven't you called me back?

The aging priest isn't the only person who can provide comfort, advice, forgiveness. But he's the only one she trusts, despite all the years that have passed, despite losing touch with him after . . .

Well, after it happened.

Matt is gripping her upper arms. "Listen, Kathleen, I really think it'll be good for us to get some time away from Jen. There's been nothing but tension in this house lately. It's not healthy, and it's not fair to anyone, especially the boys."

"But I thought you picked the Como because Jen loves it."

"We *all* love it." His shrug belies the disappointment in his eyes. "And she doesn't want to come, so . . ."

"Maybe if you ask her —"

"No. You told her we were going, right? And she said no."

"Maybe you can just tell her she has to go and that's that. Tell her you made a reservation for five and you're not changing it."

"I'm not going to force her." He thrusts the flowers into her hand. "Do you want to put these in water? I'm going up to take off this suit."

"Oh . . . sure." She takes the bouquet, listening to his footsteps climbing up the stairs, heading down the hall.

As she reaches into a high cupboard for a vase, she hears the footsteps pause abruptly and realizes Matt's standing in front of Jen's door.

Kathleen holds her breath, listening for a knock, for Matt's voice, for a door creaking open.

Nothing.

Nothing but her husband's footsteps as he retreats down the hall into the master bedroom, where the door slams loudly behind him.

With a sigh, Kathleen turns on the tap and fills the vase with water. She unwraps the bouquet and begins to place the stems in the vase, one by one, glad they aren't roses.

Roses would only remind her of that strange day at her mother's grave, when she found the thirteenth rose.

Again, she wonders who put it there.

Again, she finds her thoughts wandering back to Father Joseph.

He used to visit the cemetery with Kathleen when she was a little girl. Dad couldn't bring himself to take her; he left that up to the kindly priest.

Perhaps Father Joseph was the one who left the rose there on Tuesday.

The only thing that doesn't make sense is why he — or anybody else — would do it on that particular day.

November second.

A chill steals down Kathleen's spine.

THIRTEEN

"One more game of Uno?" MacKenzie Gattinski begs charmingly. "Please, Jen?"

Jen looks at Erin, who throws up her hands and shakes her head. "I'm so over this card game thing," she says, pushing her chair back from the kitchen table. "Anyway, aren't they supposed to be in bed by now?"

"Half an hour ago," Jen tells her, looking at the clock on the stove. "Okay, guys, let's clean up the cards and get ready for bed."

"But you promised we could play another game of Uno!" Michaela protests.

"That *was* the other game," Jen points out. "We played four times. You guys aren't even supposed to be up. It's getting really late. Let's go."

The twins hold their ground, sitting side by side in their pink pajamas, arms folded in identical stubborn refusal.

"What about our story?" Michaela asks.

MacKenzie pounces on that, chiming in, "We want a story!"

Jen sighs. "I'll read to you in bed if you both get upstairs now and brush your teeth. Okay?"

"Two stories?" MacKenzie negotiates.

"Two short ones. But only if you move it! Go!"

The girls run up the stairs, leaving Jen to stack the Uno cards while Erin wanders over to the television set in the living room.

"You think there's anything good on Pay Per View?"

"We can't order Pay Per View," Jen informs her, slipping the cards into the game box.

Maybe it wasn't such a good idea to have Erin over here while she's babysitting. She was so spooked by the idea of being alone tonight after finding out about what happened to Robby, but she probably should have checked with Mrs. Gattinski, first.

She actually meant to do just that, but Mrs. Gattinski seemed like she was in such a hurry to leave. And anyway, Jen wasn't sure Erin would really show up.

"Oh, look, Jen, that Colin Farrell movie is starting. Why can't we order it?"

"Erin, come on. We can't."

"I bet they won't even notice it's on the bill. He probably does it all the time."

"Who?"

"Mr. Gattinski. You know, he probably orders all those disgusting porn movies."

"Erin! Shhh!" Jen turns toward the front hall, half-expecting to see the girls.

"What? They can't hear me. They went up."

"Are you sure? I thought I just heard something." Jen tosses the cards into a drawer and walks into the hall.

The stairway is deserted. She can hear the twins in the hall bathroom above, running water and giggling.

Whatever she heard — and she isn't even sure what it was, just a faint sound that made her think somebody was there — must have been the house settling, or whatever it is that houses do.

Or is that just old houses?

Well, then, maybe it was just her imagination. No wonder she's paranoid, between Robby's death and now Erin talking about Mr. Gattinski in his own house. It's not as if the walls have ears, but Jen can't help feeling uncomfortable with that particular topic of conversation.

Back in the kitchen, she finds Erin looking inside the refrigerator.

"Erin! What are you doing?"

"Looking for something to eat. My mother polished off all the good stuff at home. I swear, it's like she's suddenly a bulimic or something. All she's been doing is cramming junk food down her throat."

"You're kidding." Jen has never seen Mrs. Hudson eat anything other than lettuce.

"Nope. And she's smoking again, too. Plus, I think she has a new boyfriend but when I asked her she wouldn't admit it."

"Why not?"

"Who knows? Maybe it's some married guy. Hey, maybe it's Mr. Gattinski."

"Ew."

"Oh, come on, he's cute. He's just kind of — what was that?"

"What was what?" Jen frowns at Erin, who's poised with her hand on the door of the fridge, looking toward the front of the house.

"That sound. You didn't hear anything?"

"Nope," Erin says calmly, but her expression is uncertain.

"Did you find out yet what happened to Robby?" Jen asks, now that the kids are out of earshot. It's the first chance she's had since Erin got here.

"No, nobody knows anything. And I checked to see if it was on the news at six but it wasn't."

"Did you tell your mother?"

"Are you kidding? She'd just say I told you so."

"She told you he was going to die?"

"God, no! She told me he was trouble. And so did you. But then you went and started seeing him."

"Yeah." Jen shifts her weight uncomfortably. "I know."

"Why, Jen? Was it just because I liked him and you were pissed off at me, or what?"

"No, it wasn't that," Jen tells her, feeling defensive. "It was just . . . I mean, he was the one who initiated it. And I don't know . . . I guess there was just something about him . . ."

"Yeah. There was." Erin shrugs and goes back to the fridge, pulling out a plastic carton of supermarket-style caramel apples with orange and yellow sprinkles. "You think these are any good?"

Relieved the subject of Robby has been dropped, at least for now, Jen says, "You'd better not eat them. They're probably for the kids."

"So? There are only two kids, and there are three apples in here."

"Yeah, but Erin . . ." Jen shakes her head. She sighs and stares absently at the calendar on the fridge door, where Mrs. Gattinski's neat printing on today's date reads,

Chaperone dance/Pick up Jen @ 7:30.

"Don't eat the candy apples, okay Erin? Have a regular apple. There's a bunch of those in the crisper. Mrs. Gattinski told me to help myself to as many as I want."

"Fruit? That's boring."

"It's not boring. It's healthy. Here." Jen takes a couple of apples from the crisper and puts them on the cutting board, along with Mrs. Gattinski's red-handled corer and a long paring knife.

"What am I supposed to do with that?"

"Cut up an apple. That's how I do it for the girls."

"What am I, three years old? If I want an apple, I can eat it the regular way."

"Yeah, but for some reason they taste better cut up."

"You're a nut," Erin says, but not in a nasty way. "Anyway, I don't want an apple unless it's a candy apple."

"Well, those are for the kids."

"Who's going to notice?"

"Erin, no."

"Please–please–please?"

"No–no–no."

"Meanie."

Grinning and rolling her eyes, Jen goes back into the front hall. She double checks to make sure the door is locked, just in case.

After what happened a few weeks ago, when she thought she saw a Peeping Tom out there . . .

Well, she isn't taking any chances.

It's not like she can call her Dad to come running over here this time if she gets spooked. Her parents are way up in Niagara Falls with her brothers, eating dinner at the Como.

In fact, with any luck, the restaurant will be jammed on a Friday night, and it'll take them forever to get a table. Then after they eat, maybe they'll stay to walk around the falls for a while, since it's such a nice night. Riley always begs to do that when they go to the Como.

If things go as planned, one of the Gattinskis will probably be home before Jen's family is, and they'll never know she went out.

If not, she just has to pray that her mother won't look into her room to check on her. She never should have said that about being sick. Knowing Mom, she'll be all worried and want to hurry home and get the thermometer.

As it is, Jen figured she'd probably be calling to check up on her. Good thing she had the foresight to take the phone off the hook so the line will ring busy. For once, she's glad her parents weren't willing to spring for the call waiting service.

She almost left a pillow propped in her bed beneath the blankets, too, the way people do on lame TV shows when they want to make it look like somebody's sleeping. But Jen figured she'd probably get into even more trouble if her parents found that.

This way, if they beat her home and find her room empty, she can make something up about how Mrs. Gattinski called for a sitter after they left. She can say Mrs. Gattinski was in a bind and that she felt really bad not helping her out.

Oh, who is Jen kidding?

That won't work. Not when she's supposed to be grounded. And sick.

The bottom line: if her parents get home before she does, she's in trouble.

But who cares? She's in trouble anyway.

"I'm going to go get the kids to bed," she calls to Erin. "Don't eat anything till I get back. And don't order Pay Per View."

"You know, you really need to lighten up, Jen. You're totally no fun," Erin grumbles, and it sounds like she means it.

So they're back to this?

Maybe Jen was better off when Erin wasn't speaking to her. At least then she didn't feel like such a straitlaced loser.

Jen heads upstairs, wishing things would just go back to the way they were, before . . .

Before she found out Robby is dead?

Before she found out Quint Matteson is dead?

Before she found out her father isn't her father?

Before they ever moved to Woodsbridge?

Suddenly, an overwhelming wave of nostalgia sweeps over her and she longs to be back in her old life in Indiana. She wants it so badly she has to stop near the top of the stairs and grip the railing to steady herself. Closing her eyes, she pictures her old friends, her old house, her old . . .

Family.

Mom, Dad, Curran, Riley, the way they used to be.

Her old self. Happy-go-lucky Jen, not a care in the world.

But that girl is gone forever, and so is the rest of it.

She's stuck here, stuck with a life that feels more peculiar with every passing day . . . almost as though it was meant to belong to somebody else.

It's almost time.

Jen has disappeared into the bathroom

upstairs with the two children. They're whining again, this time about toothpaste flavors. Good Lord, their mother has spoiled them rotten. It's almost tempting to shut them up once and for all . . . but that would be too messy.

The plan has already become complicated, thanks to Erin showing up here tonight. At first, it almost seemed prudent to wait, to search for another opportunity to get to Jen when she's alone and vulnerable.

But that's starting to become more and more difficult. Especially now that they've gone and changed the locks at 9 Sarah Crescent.

Very clever of Kathleen to do that — or so she believed. Has it given her a false sense of security? Does she think that simply by changing the locks she can keep at bay any threat to her cozy little world?

And did Jen assume, when she checked the front door lock just now, that she's safe because she's on this side of it?

Did it never occur to her that the danger she's instinctively bent on evading might have slipped into the house when nobody was looking?

She thought she heard something a short time ago.

Then, a few minutes later, so did Erin.

Funny . . . they both said that at times when I hadn't made a sound.

Are their ears playing tricks on them? Is hyper-vigilant paranoia conjuring footsteps and creaking floorboards where there are none?

Perhaps.

Or perhaps some primitive intuition has kicked in: the same intuition that alerts a helpless creature to a nearby predator.

What a useless instinct it is, for the unfortunate prey tends to sense its vulnerability only when it's too late.

Listen to Jen up there, singing a silly song to the girls. The water runs, stops, runs, stops. Giggling children and their unsuspecting babysitter retreat down the hall. The door is left ajar; voices float down the stairs. She's reading a story.

Good night, Moon.

Most of the words are muffled, but their lulling rhythm is recognizable even from down here.

Who would have thought I'd hear that story again? Who would have thought I had it memorized?

Even after all these years, it comes right back: the great green room, the red balloon, the quiet old lady whispering hush.

And Mother, and Father . . . snuggling on

the sofa between the two of them. All was right with the world back in the days of *Good night, Moon.*

Damn Jen for choosing that book to read tonight.

Damn her for dredging up memories better left where they belong: buried beneath decades worth of bitter resentment . . . and blood lust.

Damn her to hell.

It's time to do just that.

Time to step out of the shadows.

Good night, Moon.

Goodbye, Jen.

"Excuse me, Ma'am, can I help you?"

Stella turns to see that the restaurant hostess has left her post in the reception area and is hurrying after her.

Reluctantly pausing her stride toward the sign marked Banquet Room, Stella tells her, "I'm sorry, my husband has a meeting in there." Her icy hands clench into fists inside the pockets of her long trench coat. "He just . . . he forgot something at home and he asked me to drop it off for him."

"He's at a meeting in *there?*"

Stella nods, already knowing, just from the woman's dubious expression, that this just isn't going to happen. She's not going to open that door and walk into that banquet room and find Kurt in a meeting.

"Are you sure about that, Ma'am?"

"I thought he said this is where he'd be."

"Because there *is* a banquet in there . . ."

Hope flickers once again.

". . . for the Daughters of the American Revolution Good Citizenship awards."

Hope is extinguished.

Deep down, she knows she should have given up when she pulled up to the restaurant and failed to see Kurt's car. Between the parking lot and the door, her brain conjured up all sorts of possible reasons: he's late, he's come and gone, he got a ride with someone else, he's decided to skip the banquet and surprise her at the high school gym, he's sick, he's hurt, he's dead.

If only he were dead, damn him. Being a widow would be better than being divorced . . . wouldn't it?

If she were a widow, people would offer sympathy rather than pity.

Stella doesn't want pity.

She doesn't want sympathy, either.

Christ, Stella, what do you want?

Do you want Kurt back?

All she knows for certain is that she's already lost him. She swallows the painful truth with an enormous lump in her throat.

"Ma'am?" the hostess asks. "Are you all right?"

Stella nods, unable to speak. If she tries to speak, she'll cry, and she can't cry here. She turns her back on the stranger's sympathy — damn it, on her *pity* — and heads blindly toward the exit.

Outside, the cold November night wind whips her hair across her eyes. The strands stick to the few tears that manage to escape and are blown dry in place as she makes her way to her prized Volvo station wagon.

Will she even get to keep the car?

The wayward thought is followed by another, far more disturbing one: Will she get to keep the girls?

What if Kurt insists on dual custody?

Frantic fear takes its place alongside sorrow and humiliation.

Calm down, Stella. It hasn't come down to that. It won't come to that. Kurt won't try to take the girls away. He won't.

Slides behind the steering wheel, closes the door to shut out the wind. In the silence, she heaves a vehement whisper. "I hate you."

The wrath is directed toward Kurt as much as it is toward herself. How did she become this person? This frumpy, put-upon, cheated-upon suburban housefrau?

What the hell happened to the beautiful, confident blonde with a lifetime of endless possibilities ahead?

Bowing her head in despair, she jabs her key into the ignition. What now?

Not just for the rest of her dismal life, but in the immediate future? Where the hell is she going to go now?

Should she drive around aimlessly, looking for her husband?

Should she go to the school and chaperone the dance?

No. She can't do either of those things. She isn't ready to face her coworkers or the students or the loud music; she certainly isn't ready to face Kurt.

Despite her fantasies about confronting him earlier, she has no idea what she'll say to him now that his suspected duplicity is a reality. Will she ask him for an explanation, or a divorce? Will she pretend to believe him if he denies an affair? Will he even bother to deny it?

Again, she finds herself grasping at straws, searching for another explanation for his behavior. Terminal illness? Money problems? Embezzlement?

But deep down, she knows. What else can it be? When a suburban husband becomes withdrawn, disinterested in his wife, starts sneaking around and lying, there's only one reason.

It's got to be another woman.

Utterly, emotionally drained, Stella starts the engine and heads in the only direction she can possibly go right now: toward home.

"Okay, this time I mean it. Good night, girls."

"One last kiss?" Michaela begs, as her sister's protest is lost in an enormous yawn.

"Just one." Smiling, Jen plants a final kiss on each twin's forehead, then slips out the door, leaving it ajar.

They sure are cute. A handful, but cute.

She stops to go to the bathroom, then spends a few minutes wiping the purple globs of toothpaste out of the sink and mopping up the water that splashed on the floor.

It's amazing how exhausting it can be to get two little girls into bed. Checking her watch, she realizes she's been up here for a good twenty minutes — maybe even a half hour.

What the heck has Erin been doing downstairs all this time?

Come to think of it, Jen is surprised she didn't come up looking for her, asking if she can *pleasepleaseplease* order a movie or *pleasepleaseplease* eat the candy apples. Then again, she wouldn't be surprised if Erin just went ahead and did one or both of those things. She isn't the type to obey the rules, especially when they're set by a peer.

As Jen steps out of the bathroom, she stops to listen in the hallway. All is quiet in the room down the hall. Good. Maybe the girls are so worn out they'll go right to sleep.

She can hear the music blasting from the television set and realizes Erin has settled on MTV. Which is great, but it's too loud.

"Hey, Erin?" she calls, reaching the first floor. She raises her voice over the familiar opening strains of Mercury Rev's new video. "You want me to make some popcorn? I bet Mrs. Gattinski won't mind. I'm kind of hungry, too."

No answer.

Coming into the family room, Jen finds no sign of Erin, and the remote lying on the carpet in front of the couch.

She sighs. The least Erin could do if she drops something is pick it up. She bends to retrieve it, lowers the volume, and sets the remote on the coffee table. Erin must be in the bathroom under the stairs. She straightens a couch pillow that's precariously perched on the arm of the couch.

She hears a faint rustle of movement somewhere behind her.

"You want popcorn?" she asks again, turning toward the kitchen, expecting to see Erin there.

The kitchen, located past the counter that separates it from the family room, is empty.

"Erin?"

Silence.

But not the kind of silence that means a room is deserted.

No, it's the kind of silence Jen used to sense when she and her brothers played hide and seek in their old house. There were plenty of nooks and crannies where they could conceal themselves, but of course, she was familiar with every one of them.

She still remembers how she'd check the potential hiding places one by one, even though she always ultimately perceived, walking into a room, whether or not she was alone there. She'd either sense the emptiness, or she'd sense the stealthy, watchful presence of somebody hovering nearby, witnessing her every move as she searched — or merely pretended to, for Riley's benefit.

Jen has that same acute awareness now. Only this isn't a game.

Is it?

"Erin?"

This isn't the comfortable old house in Indiana. This is a brand-new house, a strange house full of dark, unfamiliar hiding places.

Jen tries to swallow and realizes her mouth has gone dry.

"I want to go over and see the falls now!" Riley announces as they leave the restaurant.

Kathleen's heart sinks. She knew it was coming. They never get away with a trip to the Como without driving over to look at Niagara Falls down the road.

But she's been feeling increasingly uneasy all evening. Right now, all she wants to do is get home to check on Jen. She should never have let her stay home alone tonight.

"You know what, Riley?" she says before Matt can speak. "Mommy is feeling a little too tired to see the falls tonight. Why don't we come back tomorrow, in the daylight?"

"But I like to see it at night!" Riley protests in dismay.

"Yeah, we want to see the lights," Curran chimes in.

"Are you okay, Kath?" Matt asks, touching her sleeve.

"I'm just worried about Jen," she admits in a low voice.

"You have your cell phone on, right?"

Kathleen nods.

"You told her to call if she needed us, right?"

"Yes, but —"

"She's fine, Kathleen. Let's just take the boys over to see the falls, and then we'll go home."

They've reached the car. Matt presses the key remote to unlock the doors.

"Please, Mommy?" Riley cajoles, looking up at her.

"All right," she agrees, pulling her cell phone from her pocket. "But I just want to call Jen and make sure she's okay."

Matt nods, opening her door for her. "I'm sure she's fine, but go ahead."

Sitting in the passenger's seat as Matt starts the engine, Kathleen dials their home number.

"Well?" Matt asks, hand poised on the shift.

"It's busy. She must be on the phone."

"Guess she's feeling better," he says with a wry shake of his head.

"What if she's not? What if . . . ?"

"What? She's talking to one of her friends, Kathleen. Trust me. She's fine."

She nods, her stomach churning. If the boys weren't in the backseat, all ears, she would tell Matt the truth right now.

"Can we go to the falls now?" Curran asks hopefully.

"Sure. Let's go." Matt steers out onto Pine Avenue.

Kathleen stares out the window, trying to quell her nagging fear and the unsettling realization that she didn't even go upstairs to kiss Jen goodbye before they left. The boys were already waiting in the car, and Matt rushed her out the door.

Why didn't I run back up? I always kiss her goodbye. Always.

Because you never know . . .

Kathleen shakes her head, trying to rid herself of the terrifying thought, but it persists.

Because you never know when it's going to be the last time for anything.

"Come on, Erin, this isn't funny," Jen calls, walking slowly toward the kitchen. "Where are you? I know you're hiding."

No answer.

Then she spots the apples.

They're sitting on top of a wooden cutting board on the otherwise spotless counter top. There are curls of reddish-green peel on the board, and the round core is there, too, neatly removed with one of those apple corers. One apple is cut into neat wedges, and so is half of another. The remaining peeled semicircle of that one sits waiting to be sliced.

It's as though somebody — Erin, of course, for who else would it be? — were interrupted in the midst of the chore.

"Erin? God, this is really stupid. Come out." Jen's voice sounds unnaturally high.

Trying to calm her racing pulse, she goes over to the counter and inspects the sink. The red-handled apple corer is there, white bits of fruit flesh clinging to the stainless steel cylinder, a stray seed lying in the sink beside it.

She leans over to look again at the cutting board . . .

And freezes, struck by a sudden realization.

Where's the knife?

Again, she peers into the sink.

No knife.

Heart pounding, she opens the dishwasher, quickly scans the entire contents. There are only butter knives here.

Where's the paring knife?

Oh, please, where's the knife? And where is Erin?

She calls her friend's name again, her thoughts careening wildly.

This has to be some horrible, sick joke Erin is playing. She probably thinks it's just so hilarious to scare the daylights out of wimpy Jen. Or maybe she's doing it to be mean. To get her back for stealing Robby away.

Robby.

Robby's dead.

What happened to him? Jen wonders frantically. Did he accidentally OD? Or was he in trouble with some other drug dealers?

Or was it something else. Something —

Suddenly, Jen's ears pick up on a muffled sound. The slightest rustle. It seems to come from the darkened hallway.

"Cut it out, Erin. I know you're there."

Nothing.

"Erin?" Her tone is hushed so that the twins won't hear her, yet it borders on high-pitched hysteria. She takes a step closer to the hall. Then another step. "Please, Erin, where are you?"

No answer.

I want my Daddy.

Oh, God, please.

I want my Daddy.

Jen squeezes her eyes closed, longing for her father's reassuring proximity, longing to make one phone call and have him show up at the door a split second later.

But Matt Carmody is miles away.

She's here alone in a strange house.

Alone in a strange house with Erin and two small children.

Please, God, let us be here alone.

Please —

She never finishes the thought.

Her senses explode as the sudden whoosh of moving air hits the back of her head and neck.

Something — *someone* — swoops in, and the world goes black.

It doesn't occur to Stella until she pulls onto the cul de sac that she isn't going to be able to drive Jen home tonight. The girls will already be in bed.

Well, Sarah Crescent is right around the corner. She can watch Jen from the window until she gets to Cuttington Road, and she'll tell her to call the second she gets home, just so that she knows she's arrived safely.

Stella hates to do it, but what choice does she have?

Anyway, this is the safest neighborhood around. What's the worst that can happen here?

Your husband can turn into a lying, cheating bastard, that's what.

She slows the car, passing the neighbors'

lamplit houses. Smoke wafts from a couple of chimneys, and television screens glow beyond uncurtained windows. Everybody's life seems so cozily complete on this dark November night.

Everybody's but Stella's.

As she presses the automatic garage door opener and waits for the door to rise, she catches a glimpse of something moving in her rearview mirror.

She turns her head just in time to see a tall figure disappear around the corner of the house.

What the . . . ?

For a moment, Stella is uncertain what to do. Should she get out of the car and go to see who it was?

Or should she go in and make sure Jen and the kids are all right?

Maternal instinct kicks in and she hurriedly puts the car in park, leaving it running in the driveway. As she heads toward the front door, she belatedly realizes she can't unlock it; her keys are in the ignition. She'll have to knock so that Jen can —

Stella stops short, seeing that the front door is standing wide open.

Sick apprehension sweeps over her.

Standing at the very brink of the American Falls, Kathleen is mesmerized by the torrent of dark water rushing toward the edge.

When she was a little girl, she used to stand in this very spot and imagine what it would be like to go over Niagara Falls. Every so often, somebody would try it in a barrel — or without one. Not long ago, somebody jumped in on the Canadian side, went over, and survived unscathed. But more often than not, a body would be swallowed by the rapids in the gorge below.

Just over fourteen years ago, she again stood in this very spot with that harsh reality in mind, knowing that all she'd have to do was put her leg over the rail and hurtle herself into the water.

It would put a merciful end to everything.

The horrible, aching loss.

The burden of guilt she knew she couldn't carry forever.

But as much as she longed for relief, she just couldn't do it. As painful as her life was, she couldn't bring herself to end it by her own hand. She was Catholic, and when you came right down to it, suicide was out of the question.

She never forgot Father Joseph's long ago sermon on that very topic. According to him, killing yourself meant being condemned to eternity in hell.

So there was nothing for Kathleen to do but muddle on through her living hell, praying for a miracle, for a reason to keep living.

The miracle came through. Or so she naively allowed herself to believe.

And now, here she is, trying to outrun a past that was bound to catch up with her sooner or later.

What made you think you could get away with it forever?

"Kathleen? Are you all right?"

She looks up to see her husband beside her, concern in his blue eyes. The boys are a few yards away, feeding quarters into one of those standing telescope viewers that looks like a cross between an old-fashioned movie robot and a parking meter.

She takes a deep breath. "No, Matt. I'm not okay. There's something I have to tell you."

With that, the shrill ring of her cell phone pierces the night.

"Mrs. Gattinski, you need to calm down," the police detective tells her earnestly, facing her across the kitchen table.

"I know . . . I'm trying . . ." She hugs herself, willing the violent tremors to stop,

407

knowing it's useless to try closing her eyes so she won't have to watch the cop dusting her countertops for fingerprints. She's already tried that, and the scene her mind's eye imagines is far more horrific than this. When she closes her eyes, she sees the bloodbath in the hallway, the lifeless corpse lying facedown on the living room floor, blood matting the long blond hair and staining the carpet below.

"Oh, God!" Stella wails, pressing her trembling fingers against her mouth. "Oh, God! Jen!"

"Take it easy, ma'am." The detective, whose name is Bro-something-or-other, speaks in a businesslike manner, yet his grim expression betrays that he, too, is shaken by the grisly scene in the next room.

She heard him mention to another detective that he has a daughter that age. Jen's age.

"I need to get out of here," she pleads again. "I need to go back upstairs and see my kids."

"They're fine, ma'am. I told you, our female officer is with them. She's reading to them. In a little while, we'll take you and the kids to a neighbor or a relative."

"I need to be with them now. Please."

"You don't want them to see you in this

condition, do you?"

"No, I don't," she murmurs, remembering the girls' sleepy, startled expressions when she burst frantically into their room earlier. After what she had just seen downstairs, she was overwhelmed with relief to find them safely tucked into their beds. By the time she had gathered them into her arms to attempt to reassure them through her hysteria, sirens were already screaming through the neighborhood.

Within moments, her house was crawling with police officers and paramedics. Yellow crime scene tape has been unfurled; handheld radios squawk endlessly; every inch of the scene is being photographed and measured. The phone has been ringing incessantly; a patrolman is stationed beside it. From what Stella can tell, it's the media every time. Somebody said the street is swarming with reporters as well as all the neighbors; the police have erected a barricade out front.

Through it all, sweet, innocent Jen Carmody lies dead on the floor in the living room, her throat slit from ear to ear.

Lucy gasps, sitting straight up in bed, her heart pounding.

The room is dark.

It takes her a moment to realize that Henry's side of the bed is empty.

For a moment, she's confused. Is he working nights again?

Then she remembers. He's back on days. He was here, asleep, when she slipped beneath the blankets earlier . . . how much earlier?

She glances at the bedside clock, its digits glowing florescent green in the darkness. To her surprise, it's just past ten o'clock. It feels like the middle of the night.

She sinks back against the pillow as the nightmare comes back to her in bits and pieces that make no sense. She was running from something — that much, she recalls. But it wasn't Henry. It was somebody else, somebody whose face she couldn't seem to glimpse. All she could see was the pair of gnarled, outstretched hands. Claws, really. Claws with ten sharpened blades on the tips, like something out of a slasher film.

She kept running until she found herself trapped in a blind alley, the claws coming closer and closer. Just as they were about to grasp her, she woke up.

Lucy closes her eyes, pressing her hand against the front buttons of her flannel nightgown. She can feel her heart throbbing beneath her fingers.

The nightmare was terrifyingly real.

Who was chasing her?

She scans the images in her brain, searching for a clue, wondering why it seems so important to figure it out.

After all, it was just a dream.

For a few minutes, Lucy struggles to piece it back together.

Finally, she gives up and reaches toward her bedside table. Opening a drawer, she feels around inside for her rosary beads.

Clutching them against her breast, she settles back and begins to pray, just as Father Joseph taught her.

"Did you reach Jen's parents?" Stella asks the detective, who nods somberly.

"They weren't at home, but we got a hold of them on the cell phone number you gave us."

Yes. Kathleen Carmody's cell phone. Stella can't believe that she even had the presence of mind to track down the number. It was still tucked in the drawer by the phone, scrawled on a piece of notebook paper in Jen's loopy teen girl handwriting. When she saw it, she burst into hysterical tears . . . again.

But the emotion comes and goes in sporadic fits. In moments like this, when she's feeling numb, she can almost think clearly. She can almost string rational thoughts together, in her mind and aloud.

Almost.

"Did you . . . you didn't . . . did you tell them?" she asks the detective.

"We only told them there had been an accident, and their daughter's been injured. They're on their way to the station house."

Stella buries her head in her hands, a fresh flood of tears overtaking her. She can't bear the thought of the anguish that awaits the Carmodys.

Moaning Jen's name, she pictures the girl's beautiful face, pictures her lying facedown in her own blood. When Stella was led past her the second time, they were bagging her hands to preserve forensic evidence. Stella could see Jen's grotesquely blue clenched fingers through the plastic; could see her pink fingernail polish.

Stella thinks of her own daughters safe and sound upstairs, and she thanks God again that they were spared.

Then she finds herself thinking of Kathleen Carmody. She wants to believe that somehow, Kathleen is different. That somehow, she loves her daughter less than Stella loves Michaela and MacKenzie. She

412

needs to believe that, needs to create a separation in her mind between her profound maternal love for her daughters and Kathleen's love for Jen, because the alternative is unthinkable.

If something happened to one of my children, I would lose my mind. I wouldn't survive. I wouldn't be able to go on.

Stella realizes the detective is patting her awkwardly on the shoulder.

"Mrs. Gattinski? Are you all right?"

She nods mutely, afraid to speak. If she speaks she will fall apart again.

"I just need a few minutes to ask you some questions, Mrs. Gattinski. Okay?"

She nods again. She knows he needs to question her and that he will also need to question the girls at some point. He promised that can wait, and that she can be there. He promised they'll be as gentle as possible with them.

He's been gentle with Stella, too, so far, asking her to describe exactly what she found when she came home. But there's nothing she can tell him that can possibly shed any light on Jen's murder.

"Where did you say you were this evening, Mrs. Gattinski?"

Actually, she didn't. She sidestepped the question when he initially asked it, and longs to sidestep it now.

If she tells him that she was where she was supposed to be — chaperoning a school dance — he'll check it out and find out she's lying. Then she'll become a suspect.

If she tells him she was out looking for her husband, whom she suspects of having an affair, Kurt will become a suspect.

Oh, who is Stella kidding? He's probably already a suspect, and so is she.

"Mrs. Gattinski?"

"I was . . . I was . . . I was supposed to be chaperoning a school dance . . ."

"Supposed to be?"

"Yes, but when I got there, I couldn't go in."

For whatever reason, Stella needs to protect her husband. He might be capable of some despicable acts, but murder is not among them.

"Why couldn't you go in, Mrs. Gattinski?"

"I've been sick all week . . ." Okay, good. That can be proven. She was sick at school, and then she took several days off. She even called the doctor. "And when I got to the school tonight, I was still feeling ill. I sat in my car for a while in the parking lot thinking I might feel better, but then I finally gave up and came home."

"Did you speak to anybody at the school?"

"No."

"Did anybody see you when you were there in your car?"

Oh, God. She should never have lied. What was she thinking?

"I . . . I don't know. Maybe."

It's too late to change her story now. It's too late to tell him the truth . . . isn't it?

She has an alibi, damn it. The hostess at the restaurant could vouch for her whereabouts.

But what about Kurt's whereabouts? What if he doesn't have an alibi? They'll think he killed Jen.

He might be a lying, cheating, sleazy bastard, but he's the father of Stella's children. She can't let him become a murder suspect.

"And your husband, Mrs. Gattinski? Where is he?"

She closes her eyes. Forces them open again, along her mouth, uncertain what she's going to say.

Then, before she can speak, from somewhere outside the house there's a sudden flurry of activity.

Stella looks toward the window, and so does the detective. Through the sliding glass doors that face the deck, they can see more and more searchlights arcing over the yard. Voices call out to each other, and dogs are barking.

She hears running footsteps, and then a red-faced young cop bursts through the door. "Hey, Detective Brodowiaz . . . we've got two more out in the backyard."

The detective looks startled. "Two more what?"

"Victims."

Stella gasps. Who can they be? Oh, God . . .

"One of them is still alive. It's another kid."

"A kid?"

Stella is swept by a wave of sheer panic. Illogical panic, because her girls are safe upstairs. They are, aren't they? She saw them, didn't she?

"Another girl," the cop is saying.

Oh, God. A girl. "My babies!" Stella shrieks, clutching the detective's sleeve.

"Your children are upstairs with Officer Patori, Mrs. Gattinski. They're fine. Do you have an ID on her?" he asks the cop.

"No, she's unconscious. Multiple stab wounds. She looks a lot like the kid in here. The paramedics are working on her."

"What about the second victim?"

"Dead. It's an adult male . . ."

The bottom drops out of Stella's world. Oh, God. Oh, God. Kurt.

"And Detective Brodowiaz?" the young cop goes on. "It looks like he's a priest."

In the midst of murmuring the rosary, Lucy hears a door creak open and bang shut somewhere downstairs.

Poised with the beads draped over her fingers, she stops praying. She hears Henry's footsteps crossing the living room; hears him running water in the kitchen.

So he went out. Where did he go?

Maybe he couldn't sleep and went out to get something to eat. Or a pack of cigarettes if he ran out.

Lucy turns onto her side, hoping he won't come back to bed for a long time. If he does, she'll fake sleep, just as she always does.

She learned that trick years ago.

Sometimes, she can feel him standing over her, watching her, as though he suspects that she isn't really deep in slumber.

Other times, he'll wake her. But that's only when he's in the mood for sex. Mercifully, that happens with less frequency as the years go on.

It's torture to lie with him naked and grunting on top of her, inside of her. Torture. It always has been.

How different it is to be with somebody you love, somebody who loves you. How lovely to lie encircled by a lover's tender embrace, rather than ensnared in a jealous husband's smothering grasp.

If only . . .

If only.

Lucy's life has consisted of if onlys, ever since the day she first locked eyes with *him* in Saint Brigid's. She'll never forget how her spirit soared when she spotted the flicker of interest in his gaze . . . or how it plummeted when she realized he was off-limits.

Their lust — their *love* — blossomed passionately anyway, despite — or perhaps, because of — the fact that it was forbidden.

She was so caught up in their affair that she became careless.

And she knows she will pay the price for that carelessness for the rest of her life.

Kathleen's hand is on the door handle before the police car screeches to a stop in front of the hospital.

"It won't open!" she shrieks, pulling the handle in futile desperation. "It won't open! Help me!"

One of the uniformed police officers is already jumping out of the front seat and hurrying around to open the back door from the outside.

The moment he does, Kathleen hurtles herself out and dashes toward the double doors to the ER. She can hear Matt running after her, calling her name, but she can't wait; she won't stop. She has to see her baby.

"My daughter!" she screams at the nurse on duty. "I need to see my daughter. She's hurt. They just brought her in."

"What's her name, ma'am?"

"Genevieve Carmody."

"Was she on the bus that crashed?"

Bus? Crash?

"I don't know . . . Please . . . I need to see my daughter!"

Matt is beside her now, his steadying hands on her shoulders. Kathleen shrugs them off impatiently, not wanting to be touched. She has to focus. She has to find Jen.

"My daughter," she repeats on a sob. "Please. I need to see her!"

It seems like an eternity before anybody responds.

The nurse says something she can't understand over the wild pounding of her heart, the roar of blood in her ears, the tumultuous thoughts tumbling through her brain.

She's been in this state of panic from the moment she received that shattering call on her cell phone.

She was barely coherent then, and she isn't now.

Christ, she doesn't even remember the terrifying high-speed drive from Niagara Falls to the Woodsbridge police station. She and Matt knew only that their daughter had been in some sort of accident.

That they weren't asked to go to a hospital was an ominous sign, and Kathleen knew it. As Matt grimly sped along the thruway toward the police station and the boys whimpered, frightened, in the backseat, she prayed over and over for a miracle . . .

And then, just as it did once before, a miracle happened.

When they arrived at the police station, they were informed that their injured daughter was being rushed to the hospital. Curran and Riley were whisked away by a kind female officer, and two officers volunteered to drive them to the ER, and here they are . . . still with no clue to what happened.

Another nurse appears, wearing scrubs,

her manner briskly efficient. "Come with me, Mr. and Mrs. Carmody. I'm afraid you can't see her yet, but —"

"What? Why can't we see her?" Kathleen moans, doubled over in physical pain. "Is she alive? Oh, please, God, is Jen alive?"

She can feel Matt pulling her along, realizes he's virtually holding her up as the nurse leads the way down a long corridor. Doctors, nurses, orderlies rush by, rumbling carts of equipment.

Are they all trying to help Jen?

Is it too late?

They're in a small office. Matt is helping Kathleen sink into a chair.

"Your daughter is in critical condition, Mr. and Mrs. Carmody." The nurse thrusts a clipboard at Matt. "We need your permission to —"

"Just save her. Do whatever you have to do. Save her!" Kathleen orders in a shrill voice. "What happened to her?"

"Was she in a bus crash?" Matt is asking incredulously. "The nurse said something about —"

"No, your daughter wasn't in the bus crash. That was a tour bus heading to the casino over the border, and the victims were brought here around the same time. Your daughter was injured at a neighbor's house."

"What?" Kathleen shakes her head. There has to be some mistake. Hope surges within her. "Jen is home. She's not at a neighbor's house. We left her home."

"The neighbor identified her as your daughter."

"Which neighbor?" Matt demands.

The nurse flips sheets of paper. "Her name was Stella Gattinski. Please, you need to listen to me, Mr. and Mrs. Carmody. Your daughter's condition is very critical."

"What happened to her?" Kathleen shrieks. "Tell us what happened!"

"She was attacked with a knife. I'm afraid that's all the information I have."

This isn't happening. This can't be happening.

The nurse is still speaking, but her voice seems to be fading. It's as though she's talking to somebody else, talking about somebody else. Not Jen. This can't be Jen.

"She's lost a lot of blood. We need to do a transfusion but with the bus accident our supply is running low. We've got more coming in, but if either of you wants to donate, we need you to do so right away. She's type O, which means she can only receive type O blood. Which of you —"

"I'm AB," Matt cuts in, shaking his head.

"You can only donate to type AB recipients," the nurse replies. "You must be O, Mrs. Carmody. Come with me, Mrs. Carmody."

Kathleen attempts to obey, but her legs wobble as she tries to put weight on them.

"Hurry, Kathleen," Matt urges. "She needs your blood."

She needs my blood.

The world is spinning.

"Kathleen! Hurry! Go with her!"

"Mrs. Carmody?" The nurse is hovering over her.

"I . . . I can't."

"What?" Matt's hands are on her upper arms. "What are you talking about? Jen needs your blood. You have to."

"Jen can't receive my blood either. I'm AB."

"Mrs. Carmody," the nurse says gently but urgently, "Your daughter is type O and your husband is type AB. You must be type O."

"I'm not!"

Beside her, she feels Matt stiffen. "I'm Jen's adoptive father," he tells the nurse. "If my wife is type AB, then Jen's birth father must have been O. But that doesn't matter. Just get type O blood into her from wherever you can."

The nurse murmurs something and

rushes out of the room.

Kathleen's life has careened out of control.

She hears herself apologizing to Matt, over and over.

"It's okay, Kathleen. It's going to be okay."

"No, it's not. I'm so, so sorry, Matt. I'm so sorry."

"Stop it! Why are you sorry? You can't help it. You can't help any of this. This isn't your fault."

"Yes, it is. It's all my fault."

"What are you talking about, Kathleen?"

She rakes her hands through her hair, panic welling inside of her.

She screams for release, "I want my baby. Oh, God, I want my baby."

Her husband gathers her into his arms, cradles her against his chest.

"It's going to be all right, Kathleen. Everything's going to be all right. Our baby is going to be fine."

"My baby is dead, Matt. My baby is dead." Her voice dissolves into a heartbroken wail.

"No, she isn't. Kathleen, pull yourself together. You heard the nurse. They're doing everything they can to save Jen. She's still alive."

"Jen isn't my baby, Matt."

"What the hell are you talking about?"

At long last, the truth spills out of her in a rush.

"My baby is dead. She died fourteen years ago."

PART III

DECEMBER

FOURTEEN

If Thanksgiving was a hard day to get through — a day spent alone in bed with two packs of cigarettes and a bottle of whiskey — the first of December is worse.

Milestones are always going to be hard, according to Maeve's therapist.

Fridays. Holidays. The first time for anything since Erin died.

Maeve woke earlier to find that it's snowing out, the first heavy snow of the season.

Erin loved snow. When she was a tiny girl, she would beg to go out and play in it until Maeve reluctantly gave in. She'd bundle her daughter in a snowsuit and pull her around the neighborhood on the little wooden sled Santa brought her for her first Christmas.

What ever happened to that sled? Is it somewhere in the garage, buried with the piles of junk Gregory never bothered to sort through when he moved out?

I'll look for it, Maeve tells herself, staring out the window at the gentle snowfall, exhaling a stream of smoke through her nostrils. *I'll look for it today.*

Suddenly, finding the sled seems urgent.

She has no idea why, or what she'll do with it if she finds it. She only knows that she needs to look for the goddamned sled.

She spent the better part of the weekend in the attic, hunting for Erin's christening gown for no good reason. She still hasn't found it, but she needs it. She just needs it desperately.

She makes a mental note to ask the shrink if this is normal. If, when you lose somebody, you are driven to find bits and pieces they left behind.

Then again, who cares if it's normal?

Who cares if —

A rattling of keys reaches her ears and the front door opens with a sudden swirl of wind, then closes.

Maeve hears somebody stomping their boots on the mat. It might be Gregory. He's taken to stopping over during the day. He claims he's checking in on her, making sure she's all right, but Maeve suspects that he's the one who needs to be here. He always finds an excuse to go up to Erin's room before he leaves, and sometimes, she can hear him sobbing in there.

She knows he's finally feeling guilty for

giving up on their family, for abandoning her and Erin. He's thinking that if he had stayed — if the divorce had never happened — Erin would still be here.

Maeve is thinking that, too. A thousand times a day, she thinks about how things could have been different, if only —

"Mrs. Hudson?"

Oh. It's Sissy.

Cleaning day. Well, it's about time. It seems like ages since she was here last, though it's only been a week.

Time drags by now that Erin is gone. It's been almost four weeks. Four weeks since Erin was murdered, since Maeve became a . . .

A what?

Odd that there's no word to describe what a woman becomes when she's no longer a mother. There's no identifying term for the person Maeve has become, no readily labeled group of survivors to which she suddenly belongs.

There are widows.

There are widowers.

There are orphans.

But this — the worst kind of loss a human being can face — this has no name.

Tears trickle down Maeve's cheeks.

"Um . . . Mrs. Hudson?"

She turns slowly to find Sissy standing behind her. Her thin frame is bundled into baggy sweat pants and an old flannel shirt, and there are snowflakes clinging to her dark hair and eyebrows.

"Hi, Sissy." She wipes the sleeve of her terry cloth robe across her eyes, feeling impatient. Can't Sissy see that she doesn't want to be disturbed?

"Are you okay?"

What a question. But what does she expect from a dim-witted cleaning lady?

"I'm fine, Sissy." Her tone is brittle. She turns back to the window, back to the falling snow. "Can you start with the upstairs today?"

"Sure." Sissy hesitates. "Do you want me to —"

"No!"

"I'm sorry. I just wanted to check."

"Don't touch her room. Don't even go in there! Ever!"

"I won't, Mrs. Hudson. I'm so sorry. I didn't mean to . . ." Sissy sounds like a little girl who just got caught telling her kid sister there's no such thing as Santa.

Maeve doesn't reply, just stands watching the fat flakes drift lazily toward the ground.

Her baby is in the ground. Snow is falling on Erin's grave, shrouding it in an icy blanket. Maeve shudders.

My baby.

They buried her in Saint Brigid's cemetery on a rainy Monday morning. Hundreds of people came. Maybe even a thousand.

The high school bused teachers and students over to the funeral; all those kids milling around wearing their grief as awkwardly as their black dress clothes.

All the neighbors came, including Stella and Kurt Gattinski. Maeve refused to look at them. There were other neighbors she only vaguely recognized: women she'd seen pushing strollers around the neighborhood or waiting at bus stops, men who mowed lawns and clipped hedges. They would leave the funeral and go home to their children, and Maeve hated them for it.

Mo was there, and her personal trainer, and women from her Pilates class. Quite a few of Gregory's patients showed up. His receptionist Nora, the one who hates Maeve, sobbed loudly throughout the service.

There were police officers in the crowd, including Detective Brodowiaz, who has been here to question Maeve a few times.

And there were reporters. Maeve saw the satellite trucks lining the curb, saw the cameras aimed in her direction as she and Greg got out of the limousine in front of the church, and again at the grave site. She wore sunglasses throughout the day, despite the rain. She couldn't bear to meet anybody's gaze.

At the cemetery Kathleen stood beside her, with Matt standing solemnly at her side. Kathleen held Maeve's hand the whole time, clinging so tenaciously at times that Maeve almost felt as though she herself were the one offering support.

Survivor's guilt, maybe.

Jen Carmody came home from the hospital a few days ago. She's going to be okay.

Yes, she's going to be okay, but Maeve's baby is in the cold, hard ground . . . buried in the same cemetery as the man who supposedly murdered her.

Father Joseph was found outside the house that night. On the ground beside him was the knife that was used to slit Erin's throat and ferociously stab Jen. He, too, was mortally wounded by its blade.

The police think that the elderly priest broke into the Gattinksis' home, killed Erin in the living room, and chased Jen out of the house. He and Jen struggled over the knife; she managed to get it away from him and stab him before he wounded her.

Or so Detective Brodowiaz believes.

The press has had a field day with the idea of a retired, well-known local priest as a cold-blooded killer. Most people feel that it doesn't make sense; others cite his fire-and-brimstone sermons as evidence of religious fanaticism and perhaps something much darker. The diocese issued a statement saying they were stunned and shocked, and had no record of any complaints or criminal allegations against the priest.

In the end, there was no logical explanation for why Erin and Jen were targeted. The priest's only link to the girls is that both their mothers attended Saint Brigid's School when he was the pastor there.

The detective has asked countless questions about that, but Maeve couldn't offer him anything that might help to pinpoint a motive.

Why her daughter died doesn't really matter to Maeve.

What matters is that she's gone.

What matters is that Maeve is alone. More alone than she's ever been in her life. She can't sleep, she can't eat, she can't speak.

All she can do is stare out the window at the falling snow.

After the funeral, Kathleen hugged her fiercely and said, "You know I'm here for you, Maeve. If there's anything I can do . . . anything you need . . . well, just ask. I can bring you meals, or run errands, or whatever. I'm here, and so is Matt," she added, glancing at her husband, who nodded.

"If you need anything, I'll be glad to help you, Maeve," he agreed, with the awkward hesitation of one who isn't quite sure what to offer. "If there's anything that needs fixing at your house, or . . . or if you need help with the yard or something . . ."

Meals. Errands. The house. The yard. Who cares about any of it?

But she murmured her thanks to both of them, knowing there's nothing that the Carmodys, or anybody else who offered, can do for her.

Nothing that matters.

"Jen?"

It's her mother, outside her bedroom door.

She sighs and turns her head toward the wall beside her bed, knowing her mother will knock again, call her name again. She won't go away.

She won't leave Jen alone.

All she wanted, all those weeks in the hospital, was to be left alone. But there were doctors, nurses, visitors. There was the police detective who came a few times, asking her questions she couldn't answer. Her parents hovered by her bed all day, every day, and her mother stayed there every night, too.

Some of the kids from school came. Amber and Rachel. They both wanted to talk about Erin — and about Robby. It was Rachel who told Jen that he had been stabbed, too. Just like her, and just like Erin.

But the police don't think there's any link. For one thing, Rachel said, his body was found in a Dumpster in a neighborhood frequented by drug dealers. Nobody seems very surprised about what happened to him. Not even Robby's father. According to Rachel, Mr. Warren told the police his son had promised to stop dealing.

In the end, Jen's initial grief for Robby has been overshadowed by her sorrow over Erin's death. Her sorrow — and her fright. She came so close to being a victim herself. She was viciously stabbed in the stomach and the neck; in the brutal struggle her right leg was broken and her left arm was fractured. Her face was bruised and swollen. Nobody would give her a mirror in the hospital, but she could see the shock on the faces of her classmates and the teachers who showed up to visit her in the hospital.

They were all so nice to her — so concerned and sympathetic.

The teachers didn't bring her any assignments to do. They told her not to worry about it; that she would have a tutor when she got back home so that she could catch up.

A lot of kids sent cards.

Even Garth Monroe. He sent a funny Shoebox one, and inside, he wrote *I'm sorry about Erin.*

Yeah.

Everybody is sorry about Erin.

Everybody wants to know what happened that night.

Everybody . . . including Jen.

She doesn't remember.

Dr. Calvert, the psychiatrist she's been seeing for the past few weeks in the hospital, says the trauma caused her memory blanks. Nobody knows when or if Jen's memory will return.

She hopes it never does.

The last thing she remembers is cleaning the bathroom after tucking the twins into bed. Purple toothpaste in the sink. Water on the floor. And then . . .

Nothing.

Nothing until she woke up in the hospital.

The police said a bad man attacked her

and Erin. A bad man who also happened to be a priest Mom used to know.

The police said Jen fought him off. They said she stabbed him in self-defense.

They say Jen killed him.

I killed him.

I killed someone.

"Jen?" Her mother is still knocking. "Can I come in?"

"Whatever," Jen says to the wall.

Mom opens the door. Her footsteps pad across the new beige rug.

They had Jen's room redecorated while she was in the hospital, as a surprise.

It was a surprise.

An unwelcome one.

The walls are orange, like Erin's walls.

Every time Jen looks at them, she thinks of Erin.

"I brought you some hot chocolate," Mom says. "And some cookies, just for you. Shortbread cut-outs. They're still warm from the oven."

Jen turns to see a plate on her night stand, beside a steaming mug of hot chocolate. The cookies are cut in Christmas shapes: a tree, a stocking, a star. Mom decorated them with sugar sprinkles.

"Thanks," she murmurs.

She isn't hungry. Not even for cookies.

Nostalgia sweeps over her as her mother kisses her head and, after a moment's hesitation, walks back toward the door.

Back in Indiana, Jen used to help Mom make shortbread cut-outs. They're the perfect cookie; the recipe doesn't even call for eggs — just butter, sugar, flour.

Jen loves to bake, but it's hard with her allergy. Mom has always said it's creative chemistry to tinker with cake and cookie recipes to make them egg-free. And there are other things they can make, like shortbread, gelatin, fruit desserts. Homemade cherry crisp is one of Jen's favorites. And pies — they used to make pies all the time.

Mom taught Jen how to roll out crust between two sheets of waxed paper cut to the exact size of the pie plate, how to flute the crust or crimp it.

Closing her eyes, she can still see the old kitchen, its white laminate counters dusted with flour and littered with dough scraps, stained with cherry juice and strewn with apple peels.

Apple peels.

She gasps.

"What is it, Jen?" Her mother is back beside her instantly.

"Nothing, I just . . ."

What was it?

Something about apple peels. Apples.

But the fleeting image flitted into her brain and then out again before she could grasp its significance.

All Jen knows is that an inexplicable terror has suddenly gripped her — a terror so real that she fears for her life . . . even though she knows the man who threatened it is gone for good. Gone because . . .

I killed him.

Why does she find that so impossible to believe?

Why does it feel so *wrong?*

Because I've never killed anything. Not even a spider.

But she killed a man?

It must be true, if that's what they're telling her.

She has nothing to go by but what she's been told. Nothing . . . unless her memory comes back.

Apples. Apples. Apples.

What about apples? Why can't she remember?

And what will happen if she does?

Lucy chose a different spot for their meeting this time. A different spot, and a different means of communicating with John.

She didn't dare send another letter. She can't risk having anything in writing.

So she summoned her courage, and she called the number she hasn't called in years. She dialed it from memory, wondering if it was still the same, wondering what she would say if Deirdre picked up, or if an answering machine did.

She'll never forget her relief when John's voice was the one that answered — or his obvious dismay when he realized it was her.

"Have you seen the news?" she asked him.

He said that he hadn't, but she didn't believe him. She still doesn't. How can anybody live in the Buffalo metropolitan area and not know what happened to Erin Hudson, to Father Joseph, to Jen Carmody?

But John said that he hadn't heard, and when she told him, he was silent.

"We need to see each other, John," Lucy told him guardly. "We need to talk about this in person."

"I can't, Lucy."

"You have to, John. I need you. *She* needs you. Us. She needs us. And we owe her this much. Somebody tried to kill her. Whoever it is, they're still out there."

"I can't deal with this now, Lucy —"

"You have to."

"Not now. Not . . . yet. Just give me some time, okay? I need to figure out some things."

She gave him time.

She gave him a few weeks.

Then she worked up the nerve to call him again, and he answered again. Reluctantly, he agreed to meet her.

Now here she is, waiting in a remote corner of sprawling Delaware Park on this stormy December morning. The sky is layered with charcoal-shaded snow clouds rolling in from the west, over the lake. The wind gusts and swirls with fat white flakes.

She looks over her shoulder, making sure the park is as deserted as it seems. Not a soul in sight.

Reassured, yet shivering inside her seasons-old wool winter coat, Lucy wishes she had foreseen the possibility of inclement weather. She should have selected some other spot, an indoor spot. But she couldn't change the meeting once it was set; John made her promise she wouldn't call him again.

What if he doesn't show up?

He has to. It's that simple.

She needs him now. He's the only one she can turn to, now that Father Joseph is gone.

Tears spring to Lucy's eyes.

She turns her face heavenward, blinking away the tears and the snowflakes that alight on her lashes.

"I'm sorry," she whispers. "I'm so sorry."

The media has cast him as a murderer rather than a hero. Nobody, outside of John, will ever know the real reason the elderly priest was outside the house where the girls were babysitting that night. Nobody will ever know he was guarding her with his life, bent on being her savior to the end. Nobody will know . . . unless Lucy tells.

And she'll never tell.

The phone is ringing when Kathleen returns to the kitchen, where the remnants of this morning's cookie-baking clutter the countertop and sink.

She glances at the window as she hunts around the countertop for the cordless phone.

God, she misses the Caller ID box. Matt keeps saying he'll replace it, but he hasn't gotten around to it yet.

These days, Kathleen doesn't feel like talking to anybody unless it's urgent. Which it very well might be this time.

It's snowing harder out there. Maybe the school is calling to say there'll be an early dismissal.

444

She dismisses that idea as quickly as it occurs to her. The forecast calls for only a foot of accumulation by midnight, and a few more inches by morning. That's a relatively measly storm by local standards; certainly no reason to close the schools.

Maybe it's Deb Mahalski. She keeps calling and leaving messages with Matt about rescheduling Curran's November checkup. Kathleen couldn't keep the appointment, knowing Deb would be full of questions about Father Joseph and her daughter's role in the shocking crime.

The phone rings again.

Kathleen decides not to pick it up. She doesn't want to talk to Deb Mahalski.

But what if it's her father? She hasn't heard from him yet today.

Or maybe it's the nursing home calling to say he's escaped again. It happened twice last week.

She picks up the phone. "Hello?"

"Kathleen? How is she?"

It's Matt, calling from work for the third time this morning. He's been doing that the past few days, ever since Jen came home from the hospital.

"She's still in bed. I was just up there."

"Is she sleeping?"

"Resting."

"But not sleeping?"

"No." Impatience sends her pacing across the kitchen and back again.

"Did she eat anything?"

"Not really."

"She needs to eat."

"I know she needs to eat, Matt. I know how to take care of —" She breaks off.

My daughter.

She can't say it.

Not to Matt. Not anymore.

All things considered, he took the news better than she'd have expected . . . or so it seems, in retrospect. When she told him, Jen's life was hanging in the balance. Nothing else really mattered at the time.

It wasn't until the next morning, when their daughter's condition was stabilized and they were in the hospital cafeteria getting coffee, that Matt dared to bring up the devastating secret she had revealed in that frantic moment.

She told him the whole story. When she was finished, they agreed that they would never tell another living soul. There was no reason to do so. Nobody would ever have to know — not even the police. It wouldn't change anything.

They've been walking on eggshells ever since, tiptoeing around each other's emotions and moods, doing whatever is necessary to get their children — all three of them — through this traumatic time. Both Curran and Riley have had chronic nightmares since that Friday evening in Niagara Falls; one or both of them ends up in bed with Matt and Kathleen most nights.

At first, they tried to protect their sons from the truth about what had happened to their sister and to Erin. But it was no use. The other kids were talking. In the end, Kathleen and Matt told them that a bad man tried to hurt Jen, but that he can't hurt anybody ever again.

"I'm going to try to come home early this afternoon," Matt is saying. "The snow is really starting to come down. I figure things will be quiet around here and I bet everyone will cut out early."

"This is Buffalo, Matt. It's winter. The snow doesn't put a stop to anything. People just deal with it."

After a pause, Matt says tersely, "Yeah. Well, I guess I'll just deal with it then."

"Good idea."

She sounds like a bitch. She can't help it. She doesn't want him to come home early. It's easier when he's not here.

Whenever he's around, she catches him looking at her with an expression of . . .

Not disappointment, exactly.

Not resentment, either. Not entirely.

She doesn't know what it is, but whenever she sees that look in his eyes, she feels sick inside. She doesn't want to face it again so soon.

"I'll call later." Matt's tone is curt. He hangs up without waiting for her reply.

Kathleen stands holding the phone, gazing out at the snow. The ground is carpeted now; bare tree limbs and the cedar rails of the boys' swing set are fringed with lush ice crystals.

Suddenly, the house feels overheated and eerily still. Seized by claustrophobic restlessness, Kathleen longs to be outside, breathing the winter fresh air, listening to the familiar, quiet sifting sound in the trees as the world is dusted in white.

Her thoughts turn to the last winter she spent here in Buffalo, when she was dating Quint Matteson — if that's what you could call it. Dating. Hah.

In the hospital, Jen told her that she tried to find him — that one of his neighbors told her he was dead.

Kathleen wasn't surprised. She wanted to tell Jen that it doesn't matter. That Quint Matteson is nothing to her anyway; no relation. But she couldn't say that. She just held her daughter while she unwittingly cried for her so-called father.

"Can you find out where he's buried, Mom?" Jen begged. "So that we can visit his grave?"

"Sure," Kathleen promised reluctantly. "I'll find out."

Another cemetery. Another grave to visit.

She hasn't been to Saint Brigid's cemetery since the day of Erin's funeral. She wants to go back, really she does. She just can't bring herself to do it yet.

Eventually, though, she'll venture back through the familiar stone gateposts of Saint Brigid's Cemetery. And when she does, she'll lay flowers at Erin's grave, a stone's throw from her mother's . . . and on the opposite side of the cemetery from where Father Joseph lies beside his own mother.

To think that she was going to confess her darkest secrets to him . . .

To think that he already knew. At least, about Jen.

She still doesn't know how he figured it out, or why he did what he did. None of it makes sense. But Kathleen can't accept that his stalking of Jen was random, as the police have assumed.

The detective in charge of the case told her the old priest might have been mentally ill, that he must have just snapped.

Kathleen is troubled, still, by questions that have no answers, and probably never will.

What about the baby she heard crying in the night?

What about the lone red rose on her mother's grave? Why did Father Joseph put it there? It was Detective Brodowiaz who told her about it, saying the owner of the florist shop near Saint Brigid's had come forward when the case exploded in the media. It turned out the priest had frequently come into the shop for a single red rose to lay at somebody's grave. The owner didn't know whose.

Kathleen did.

But she didn't tell the detective.

The last thing she wanted was for the police to start sniffing around her own past . . . or Mollie Gallagher's grave.

There's another nagging question, one even more pressing than the others.

Where did the pink bootee come from?

The more she mulls over that particular angle, the more convinced she becomes that there might be a logical explanation. Father Joseph must have found the stray bootee on the steps of Saint Brigid's after that fateful November night.

The night when Kathleen, mourning her own dead infant, found a baby girl abandoned on the doorstep of the church. Pinned to her pink crocheted blanket was a note that read *Please take care of my baby*.

And so Kathleen did.

Lucy watches John trudging toward her through a curtain of squalling snow. Even from this distance, he looks older than he did when she saw him a few weeks ago. Older, and wearier. His shoulders are hunched beneath his down coat; his gait is heavy.

He comes closer, and she wonders why he isn't wearing gloves or a hat; why his feet are clad in loafers. It's as though he's oblivious to the snow that's clinging to his hair and his eyebrows, almost camouflaging the stripe of white hair so like his daughter's.

Their daughter's.

Lucy named her Margaret, after the blessed saint to whom she had prayed for years. It was Father Joseph who told her about Margaret the Barefooted, who relied on prayer to help her survive years of abuse at the hands of her husband.

If it weren't for that peculiar birthmark in her eyebrow, Henry might have believed Margaret was his own child when she was born.

Lucy had promised her husband almost a year before giving birth that she was no longer seeing the man Henry had come to loathe. And she wasn't. She had already told John goodbye. There was just that one night . . .

Just one sinful night when they found their way into each other's arms one last time.

That was all it took.

When Lucy found herself pregnant, Henry called it a new beginning for them.

For nine months, with the baby growing in her womb, Lucy waited in anticipation, in dread. She rocked, she knitted, she prayed. She prayed that she was carrying her husband's child . . . though she longed with all her heart for it to be John's.

When the baby was born, she knew instantly. The little girl was the very image of Lucy's married lover, birthmark and all. Not only had God refused to answer her prayers, he had cursed the baby with blatant testimony to her parents' adultery.

Cursed her . . . or blessed her?

If it weren't for that birthmark, Lucy might never have recognized her daughter on television a few months ago.

It was the birthmark that jumped out at her, but beyond that, even, Margaret's face was the spitting image of John's.

Still, Lucy clung to a shred of doubt, unable to convince herself that her child might still be alive.

That was when she called Father Joseph. Years had passed since Lucy confessed her sins to the priest, but he hadn't forgotten her. He hadn't forgotten her extramarital affair that had resulted in a baby girl — a baby girl who lived only a few weeks after Lucy gave up custody.

Father Joseph had comforted her in her bereavement, had been there for her when nobody else was. And when he retired from the priesthood, he told Lucy to call upon him if she ever needed him again.

It was Father Joseph who tracked down the girl from the *Eyewitness* newscast and found her living in Orchard Hollow with the Carmody family.

It was Father Joseph who confirmed that Jen Carmody was, indeed, the spitting image of John — and that there was no record in the foster care system of Margaret's death on the second of November fourteen years ago.

It was Father Joseph who promised to watch over Margaret, now known as Jen Carmody, after Lucy got the anonymous note in the mail.

Yes, she's alive, it read. *But she won't be for long.*

Enclosed with the note was a photograph of Jen Carmody, apparently shot through a telephoto lens.

FIFTEEN

Walking wearily into the kitchen, Stella deposits yet another heavy cardboard carton with the others in the far corner, by the door to the garage.

"Is that it from the girls' room?" Kurt asks, his voice nearly drowned out by the ripping sound as he pulls a wide strand of packing tape across the flaps of a box on the counter top.

"There's one more. You'll have to get that one, though. It's full of their books. It's too heavy for me to lift."

He nods, focused on sealing the box before him.

Stella sniffs the air, makes a face. This kitchen where she spent so many hours now smells foreign to her, like mildew, bleach, Magic Marker, death — even if that horrible scent lingers only in her imagination.

They haven't lived in this house in almost a month — not since the night of Erin's murder. Kurt has been staying with his mother; Stella and the girls with her

455

mother. They couldn't come back here after what happened.

The bloodstains have been scrubbed from the hardwood floor, the walls have long since been painted over. The broken pane of glass in the window where the murderous fiend broke into the house has been replaced.

And yes, the smell of death has been chemically vanquished. Stella never knew there were experts who specialized in that sort of thing: cleanup crews who were called in to remove all traces of violent death. It was lucky for her — and lucky for Sissy, too, she supposes.

She hasn't seen the cleaning lady since that awful day, but a shaken Sissy called after being interviewed by the police. She said she'd told them everything she knew and that she was frightened by the thought that the killer might have been prowling around the house on that last day while she was upstairs cleaning.

The police, who have no real reason to think otherwise, believe that he might have been.

But Stella is convinced it was Kurt, sneaking in for a lunch hour tryst with his mystery woman. She hasn't asked him about it and he hasn't given her the specifics.

She wasn't about to tell even Sissy about her husband's affair. Better to let the cleaning lady think she, too, narrowly escaped the killer's grasp.

Sissy said she was praying for Jen Carmody's recovery, and for Erin Hudson's soul. She has a lot of faith for somebody who can't be much older than her early twenties.

She said she'd pray for Stella and the girls, too, when Stella told her they were moving away.

"Thanks," she told Sissy. "We need all the help we can get."

Yes, prayers are helpful. Money would be even more helpful.

Outwardly, the house is ready to be placed on the real estate market. With any luck, perspective buyers will be immune to the aura of tragedy that seems to hover in the air — and to the thought of paying more than two hundred thousand dollars to purchase the scene of a double homicide.

"Can you hand me that marker?" Kurt asks now, his attention on sealing the box before him.

She retrieves it from the table, places it in his outstretched hand. "Here you go."

"Thank you."

"You're welcome. Do you want something to drink?"

"No, thanks, I'm good."

She nods and walks to the cupboard, almost amused — if she were capable of smiling these days — by their overly civil conversation. They sound like those two ridiculously polite cartoon chipmunks.

After you.

Oh, no, no, no, I couldn't possibly.

No, I insist; you must go first.

A sound escapes Stella.

It isn't a laugh; she hasn't laughed in a month. It's more like a snort.

"God bless you," Kurt says.

Her mouth quirks again; she murmurs, "Thanks."

Stella opens a cabinet door to look for a glass, but finds that he's already packed them. She hunts through the fridge — which smells of sour milk and month-old leftover chili — and comes up with a half-full bottle of diet ginger ale.

Knowing it will be flat, she takes a sip anyway, and makes a face. It's from the night she sent him out to the store when she was so sick with that stomach bug.

It was only a month ago. God, is there anything in their lives that hasn't changed since then?

She goes to the sink and pours what's left of the ginger ale down the drain.

Kurt looks up from the box. "What's that?"

She holds up the empty bottle, waits for recognition to cross his face, is almost relieved when it doesn't.

They're long past rehashing what went wrong between them.

They handled all that in the wake of the murders; that those intense days are a blur is surely a blessing. Stella remembers only bits and pieces of the screaming arguments that erupted between them: her accusations, his denials, her threats, his confession.

Yes, he's been having an affair.

No, he doesn't love Stella anymore.

Yes, he wants to leave.

No, he doesn't want to go to marriage counseling.

So far, they're only referring to it as a trial separation. But deep down, Stella knows it's permanent. Their possessions are packed into separate sets of boxes, marked with three different destinations: his mother's, her mother's, and the storage unit they had to rent.

It might officially be a trial separation, but they agree that their only option is to sell the house. Even if they could afford to keep it and live separately for a while, the house no longer seems important to Stella. She doesn't want to live surrounded by the constant reminders, not only of her marriage, but of the grisly murders.

The last of the boxes of household stuff will be moved into storage tomorrow; their furniture on the weekend, before the listing appears. Stella has already seen it.

Orchard Hollow CH Colonial; 4000 sf, 4 BR, 2 1/2 BA, EIK, FR/Fpl., sgds to dk, MBS, att. 2C Gar, Central A/C. 1 acre level lot. Great family neighborhood. Quiet Cul De Sac.

Stella had to ask the realtor what some of the abbreviations stood for. Kurt made a bad joke, asking if MBS meant murderous bloody stains. Nobody laughed. The realtor stiffly informed him that it meant Master Bedroom Suite.

She then warned them that it's difficult to sell a house during the holidays, but not impossible.

The sooner they sell, the sooner Stella and the girls can make permanent living arrangements. She's anxious for life to get back into some sort of rhythm. As of today, she's used up the last of her personal days at work — most of them spent dealing with legal issues and reassuring the girls that everything is going to be okay.

So far, she's managed to shield them from the macabre events that transpired in the house that night while they were tucked safely into their beds upstairs. They're too young to understand; young enough, thank God, that their few curious questions about the commotion were easily brushed aside. The detective managed to question them so gently that the girls seemed to think it was a game. They giggled as they recounted what they did with Jen and Erin, and innocently asked when they would be babysitting again.

Stella doesn't have the heart to tell them the truth.

But she can't protect her children from every harsh reality. They comprehend now that their parents' marriage has splintered; that Daddy will be living someplace else for a while — perhaps forever. Now Michaela has started wetting her pants, and Mac-Kenzie chews holes in her sleeves, and it's all because Kurt has fallen out of love with Stella.

He tosses the marker aside abruptly, tells her, "I'm going up to get that last box from their room."

She nods, staring out the window into the backyard. Jen was found out there beneath

461

the lilac shrub, bleeding to death. The corpse of the man who tried to kill her lay beside her in the grass.

Case closed.

Case closed . . . but it doesn't make sense. Why would an aging priest break into Stella's house? Why would he be bent on murdering two young girls?

Stranger things have happened, according to Detective Brodowiaz. Sometimes the only motive for homicide is blood lust.

Still . . .

Sometimes, she finds herself wondering if Father Joseph really was the killer.

Sometimes, she wonders if he might have been an innocent bystander who was caught in the life-and-death struggle.

But why would an innocent bystander with no connection to this neighborhood be in a fenced backyard late at night?

And anyway . . . who else could have done it?

Stella feels Kurt's eyes on her and looks up to see him hesitating in the doorway.

"Are you okay?" he asks.

She nods.

"You sure?"

"I'm sure."

"You look upset."

He has to pick now to start caring?

Unsettled by the probing concern in Kurt's gaze, she forces herself to look her soon-to-be ex-husband in the eye, saying, "I'm not upset. This is the best thing for everyone."

"Of course it is. We can't stay here."

"I didn't just mean the move. I meant . . . the divorce."

There. She's said the word. And it isn't so bad now that it's out there.

Kurt remains silent for a minute.

She wonders if he'll reiterate what he's said all along — that this is merely a trial separation.

Then he nods, telling her, "Yeah. It's the best thing."

"Lucy." Her name escapes John's mouth on a wispy cloud of frost in the frigid air.

"Hi, John." Her body trembles with the cold and with the effort to keep from hurtling herself at him. His arms aren't open to her this time. Not like before.

There's been a change in the past few weeks since she last saw him. He's withdrawn. His eyes are ringed in blue-black circles; his mouth is a taut slash amidst a few days' growth of razor stubble.

"Thank you for coming."

He nods. Shrugs. Remains silent, his bare hands buried in the pockets of his baggy tan corduroy pants.

She blurts, "Father Joseph didn't try to kill Margaret."

She can see John's shoulders stiffen beneath his down jacket. Still, he's mute.

"In case there's any doubt in your mind, he didn't do it," she rushes on, needing him to know that, if nothing else. "He was there because I asked him to watch over her. He'd been following her around, keeping an eye on her, watching their house. Just to make sure she was safe."

"What made you think she was in danger in the first place?"

She reaches into the pocket of her coat and retrieves the anonymous note folded around the photo, hands it to him wordlessly.

He reads the note, glances at the photo. "Where did you get this?"

"It came to my house. Back in October. A few days after I found out she was still alive."

Deep down inside, Lucy believed then that Henry was the one who wrote the note.

Now, she isn't so sure. He was home in bed with Lucy the night somebody tried to murder Jen Carmody. Or was he?

She remembers waking to find his side of the bed empty. But he couldn't have been gone for very long . . . and he was home shortly after ten. It wouldn't have been enough time for him to slip across town and murder three people . . . would it?

God help them all, would it?

"You didn't tell me you got a note when I saw you last month."

"I meant to tell you, though. I just . . . I changed my mind."

"Why?"

Why? Because he shut down emotionally when she confronted him with the news that their daughter was still alive.

Because she didn't trust him.

And because she suspected then — and maybe she still does now — that John might have known all along that the baby didn't die in foster care, as his wife Deirdre told Lucy on that awful day fourteen years ago.

Why did she simply take Deirdre's word for it? Why didn't she ask for some kind of proof? A death certificate? A grave site? Something, anything, to prove that Margaret was really gone?

She didn't ask because it wouldn't make a difference. She had already signed away custody.

And she didn't ask because by then, she

465

was already planning to join her daughter.

She went home, slit her wrists, and woke in the psych ward.

Shuddering at the memory, she tugs at the band on her left glove, then at her right, pulling them higher beneath the sleeves of her coat lest John glimpse the faint pink remnants of her suicide attempt.

"Lucy?" John prods, still holding the note. "Why didn't you tell me about this before?"

He shakes it at her. Just a little. Just enough to make her look around the park, this time not to make sure there's nobody else in sight, but to hope somebody is.

The park is deserted.

Lucy takes a step back from John, feeling his eyes blazing into her.

"I don't know why I didn't tell you about it. I guess I wasn't sure it was real. Maybe I thought it was some kind of prank."

"You thought it was real enough to go to Father Joseph for help. Why didn't you come to me? Or at least go to the police?"

"Because . . ."

Because I was afraid Henry would find out. And I was afraid he would kill me.

Literally. She was afraid her husband would kill her.

He almost did the first time, after he laid

eyes on the newborn he thought belonged to him — and immediately recognized another man's genetic imprint on her tiny face.

Henry knew John, of course, if only by sight. John and his wife Deirdre attended the same church, lived in the same neighborhood, traveled in the same circles.

Lucy never knew how he discovered their affair. Perhaps in her carelessness she failed to cover her tracks; perhaps somebody saw her with John and told her husband.

When Henry found out, he beat her so badly that she couldn't show her face in public for weeks. He made it impossible for her to leave the house, and when her bruises healed, he forbade her to go anywhere without him. Even to church.

The one time she dared to sneak out to see John, she had every intention of bidding him a platonic farewell.

Platonic. Hah.

That was the night they conceived the baby and set in motion the tragic chain of events that led to this moment.

"Maybe we should go to the police now," she suggests to John, uneasiness settling over her when he shakes his head vehemently.

"It's too late now. They think the case is closed. If we go to them, they'll reopen it.

They'll think one of us had something to do with what happened."

She nods, having already arrived at the same conclusion herself. The whole thing will blow up in their faces. The media will have a field day. And Henry — well, Henry will show her no mercy. Not if he's innocent . . .

And not if he isn't.

Lucy's voice is plaintive as she asks John, "What are we going to do? Whoever tried to kill Margaret might go after her again. And we don't even know why. Who would want her dead?"

John averts his gaze.

Who, indeed?

John's wife.

Lucy's husband.

Henry wasn't there for the birth; he was working when she went into labor and she didn't call him. By the time he got to the hospital, the baby was swaddled in a clear glass isolette beside Lucy's bed.

She cowered when Henry bent over the sleeping infant, certain he would realize the instant he saw her that she didn't belong to him.

Henry went crazy, leaping on his wife like a rabid animal. A frantic nurse and several orderlies had to haul him off Lucy. When they did, her nose was broken, her ribs were fractured, and Henry was arrested.

She called John and asked him to come to the hospital the next morning.

He did. And he left with their daughter cradled in his arms, wrapped in the pink blanket and bootees Lucy had lovingly knit for her during all those months of waiting.

The sled — Erin's little wooden sled — wasn't in the garage, and it wasn't in the shed out back, either.

Maeve trudges back through the house through the mounting drifts of snow. She can hear Sissy clattering around in the kitchen and decides to move her search to the basement.

Heedless of the cobwebs in her snow-dampened hair and the mouse droppings beneath her feet, she pokes through distant corners piled high with junk.

Some is Gregory's: outdated patient files and dental school texts, forgotten sports equipment, the fancy wooden croquet set he coveted and then, when Maeve bought it for him as a Father's Day gift the year Erin was born, never used.

Maeve's castoffs are gathering dust and spider eggs down here, too: the never-unpacked sewing machine her misguided mother-in-law gave her as a wedding shower gift, the punch bowl set with twenty-four crystal cups she gave her one Christmas, the set of golf clubs Maeve bought thinking she could spend more time with Gregory if she learned how to play.

She rummages past her belongings and Gregory's, idly thinking she should toss all of it into the garbage or see if Sissy wants anything.

But that can wait. She has other business to attend to right now.

Erin's old Barbie dolls, clothes, and accessories fill two large plastic tubs. Maeve pushes them aside without opening them. She does the same with several cartons of Erin's school artwork, swallowing over a lump in her throat as she remembers how proudly Erin would place her own manilla paper scribbles beneath the refrigerator magnets when she came home from kindergarten each day.

Maeve saved the best of them, but tossed quite a few. What she wouldn't give to have them back, all of her baby's precious crayon drawings. How could she have thrown them away so blindly? Did she think Erin was immortal?

"Damn it," she whispers, wiping at the tears that are beginning to trickle.

There's no sign of the sled.

She turns away from her daughter's belongings, unprepared to keep searching. She's had enough for today.

But she can't go upstairs yet.

She can hear the distant rumbling hum of Sissy's vacuum in the kitchen on the floor above. If only she would just hurry up and finish and get out.

Maeve isn't leaving the basement until she has her house to herself again. The last thing she wants is the cleaning lady's sympathy, or worse yet, her prayers.

Prayers are a reminder of the man who killed Erin; of the God who let her die.

Maeve wipes her streaming eyes and nose on the sleeve of her black cashmere cardigan and is instantly reminded of the black cashmere pullover she bought for Jen Carmody just a few weeks ago. She remembers the tension at the dining room table that night. Tension between Kathleen and her father, between Kathleen and Matt, between their daughter and hers.

I can't stand Jen.

Erin's words. She and Jen had had a falling out, but Erin refused to tell Maeve why.

Now she'll never know what came between the girls — unless Jen chooses to tell

Kathleen. Highly unlikely.

Nor will Maeve ever know what Erin was doing at the Gattinskis that night with Jen.

You weren't supposed to be there, Maeve tells her daughter in silent despair. It's become a familiar refrain. *You lied to me. Why did you always have to lie to me?*

Yet would it have made any difference if she had known where Erin was going that night when she left? Would Maeve have foreseen danger in a night spent babysitting a few blocks from home?

Of course not.

Reaching into the pocket of her sweater for her cigarettes and lighter, Maeve searches for a place to sit down. She settles for an old webbed lawn chair, reaching up to remove it from the nails in the rafters where it's been hanging for years.

As she pulls it down something crawls across her hand.

Crying out, she drops the cigarettes, lighter, and chair, also knocking over an old straw broom that was propped against the wall.

The vacuum cleaner is abruptly silenced above, and Sissy's footsteps approach the basement door. "Mrs. Hudson? Are you all right down there?"

"I'm fine." Shuddering, she watches an

oversized centipede disappear beneath the chair on the floor.

"I thought I heard you scream."

"I'm fine," she calls, irritated. "Just finish cleaning, please, Sissy."

After a moment, the vacuum starts up again.

Maeve warily retrieves her cigarettes and lighter from the concrete floor, leaving the chair and broom where they fell. Settling onto the bottom step, she lights up and inhales a soothing stream of menthol.

There.

Better.

She takes another drag and finds herself facing a stack of high school yearbooks on a nearby shelf. So that's where they went. She hasn't seen them in ages.

For a long time, she stares at books, fighting the urge to reach for one.

At last, temptation gets the best of her.

Doesn't it always? she thinks grimly, lit cigarette clenched between her lips as she opens the yearbook from her senior year at Saint Brigid's.

She flips past the pages filled with various versions of oversized and backhanded high school girl handwriting punctuated with smiley faces, balloon letters, coded initials whose meanings Maeve has long since forgotten, signatures she'd be hard pressed to match with faces after all these years.

She gazes at her senior portrait, marveling at how much her own daughter was beginning to resemble her, sobbing out loud when she remembers that Erin will never sit for a senior portrait of her own.

She stubs out the cigarette on the basement floor and turns the pages slowly backward until she reaches Kathleen's face, frozen in time.

Well, she looks nothing like *her* daughter, Maeve notes with a bizarre twinge of satisfaction. Jen must resemble her deadbeat father. What was his name?

Quent.

Or Quinn.

Quinn something.

Maeve shakes her head, wondering how Kathleen could find herself in so much trouble and still miraculously land on her feet. To think that she was once destitute, out on the streets, carrying a druggie musician's baby.

To think that now she has it all.

Resentment stirs within Maeve.

Kathleen still has her daughter. God chose to save *her* daughter. Not Maeve's daughter.

Kathleen still has her husband.

Her loyal, loving husband.

Or is he?

Was it Maeve's imagination, or did she catch Matt staring at her the night of Jen's birthday dinner?

She remembers thinking at the time that she might have seen him stealing a glimpse, remembers wondering if his good night kiss on the cheek was more flirtatious than perfunctory.

She also remembers trying — and failing — to catch his eye afterward, then reasoning with herself that no man in his right mind would blatantly do so with his wife hovering at his elbow.

As she and Erin drove home silently that night in the darkened car, Maeve vowed to try and catch Matt alone, just to see if . . .

Well, if there was anything to her intuition. To see if Kathleen's perfect husband was as human as anybody else when it came to temptation. As human as Maeve was.

She remembers vowing to find out the answer.

Then her daughter was murdered, and life as Maeve knew it disappeared into haze of hot tears and insomnia, whiskey and cigarette smoke.

Now she's alone.

Kathleen isn't alone.

Now she has nothing.

Kathleen . . .

Kathleen has everything.

And slowly, Maeve's resentment boils over into rage.

Footsteps sound at the top of the stairs.

"Mrs. Hudson? Are you still down there?"

For a moment, she's tempted not to answer. Can't the dumb girl just leave her alone?

Then the footsteps start down the stairs, and Maeve sighs. "What do you want, Sissy?"

The girl pauses, her white sneakered feet all that is visible of her body on the top of the cellar steps. "I'm leaving now. Do you want me to lock the doors when I go?"

"Why would you? I'm here."

"I know, but I thought maybe you'd want the doors locked."

"Why?"

There's a pause. "I don't know."

"You're thinking the neighborhood might not be safe anymore, aren't you, Sissy?"

Maeve watches the girl's feet twitch anxiously, one sneaker crossing briefly over the other and then back again. "I don't . . . that's not why I —"

"You're thinking that if somebody could

slaughter my daughter in cold blood, somebody could walk through my front door and do the same thing to me. Aren't you, Sissy?"

"No, Mrs. Hudson, I didn't mean —"

"Trust me, that might be the best thing for everyone."

No reply.

Sissy shifts her weight.

"Get out of here, Sissy," Maeve says wearily. "Just go. And don't lock the doors on your way out. I'll take my chances."

"Are you sure you don't need anything else?"

What could she possibly need that Sissy could possibly provide?

Feeling utterly helpless, overwhelmed by pain, Maeve closes her eyes.

Help.

Ha. The kind of help she needs is beyond reach.

Matt Carmody's words echo in her head.

If you need anything, I'll be glad to help you, Maeve . . .

Then again . . .

Maybe there is something she needs. Something Sissy can't provide . . .

Something Matt Carmody can.

Maeve glances at her watch. He'd be at work right now. And she has the number. Kathleen proudly gave her one of his business cards back when they first moved here. Maeve slipped it into her wallet and never took it out.

"Mrs. Hudson?"

She glances up impatiently to see that Sissy is still hovering on the stairway above, shifting her weight from foot to foot.

"What?" Maeve asks sharply. "I thought I told you to go."

"You did . . . It's just, umm . . ."

Oh. Her pay.

Her thoughts focused on the phone call she's about to make to Matt Carmody, Maeve sighs and heads for the stairs.

Why can't I remember?

Jen punches her pillow in frustration, then winces at the pain that shoots down the splintered bones in her fragile arm.

Why does it matter, anyway?

It shouldn't. She'll probably be better off if she never has to relive what happened that night.

After all, it's over.

The man who tried to kill her is dead.

And I'm the one who killed him.

You'd think something like that — taking another person's life — would be etched in her mind as permanently as Jen's name is etched in the metal plates on the trophies that line the shelf overhead.

The trophies.

She stares at the shelf as though she's seeing it for the first time.

With tremendous effort, she hoists herself upright and reaches for the nearest one. It's heavier than she anticipates — almost too heavy for her to lift now, even with her good arm.

She stares at the gleaming figure of a girl kicking a soccer ball, stares at her name improbably engraved on the brass plate. *Jen Carmody.*

The trophy — and yes, even the breezy name — seem to belong to somebody else now. A carefree, confident, sturdy stranger . . . not this person whose spirit is as broken as her body, stranded on this island in a sea of pain.

Stranded in solitude she once craved, and now fears.

Why?

Why am I so afraid?

It's over. I'm safe. He's dead.

But the reassuring words she keeps repeating to herself — the same words her mother and the doctors have been telling her for weeks now — don't seem to penetrate.

Maybe it's because of all the medication

she's been on — medication that's supposed to ease the ache of her healing wounds and the mending bones of her right leg and left arm. The bitter white pills she obediently swallows every few hours seem to dull her thought processes more than the pain.

Or maybe it's not the medication at all.

Daddy isn't my father.

My brothers aren't my brothers.

My real father is dead.

Jen closes her eyes, trying to block it all out.

Think of something else.

Think of apples.

Apple peels.

Nothing.

Come on, Jen.

Think of what happened that night.

But she can't. She can't retrieve whatever it is that keeps flitting in to tease her, then darting just out of reach.

No, the one thing Jen instinctively needs to remember is lost in a haze of images she'd rather forget.

SIXTEEN

Stella's heels sound hollow on the hardwood floors as she walks one last time through the empty rooms of the first floor.

The living room is bathed in shadows now, the winter afternoon waning quickly. Stella reaches for a wall switch and flips it.

Nothing.

Oh. Right. The lamps are packed; there are no overhead lights or wall sconces in here.

Stella eyes the empty hooks on the barren white walls where framed art once hung. She wonders whether she should pull them out, or leave them for the new owners to deal with.

Leave them, she decides, reaching back to rub her aching shoulders. *All I want to do now is get the heck out of —*

"Tired?"

She jumps, spins around to see Kurt standing in the doorway.

"You scared me!" Last she knew, he was down in the basement, packing the last of his tools.

He chuckles. "Sorry. Didn't mean to sneak up on you."

She's reminded of that last day, when she did the same thing to Sissy as she cleaned the upstairs bathroom.

But Sissy was already jumpy that afternoon, having heard somebody creeping around the house earlier.

Was it Kurt?

Or the killer?

Again, Stella wonders how on earth an elderly man — a priest, no less — could possibly have committed such a heinous crime.

"Listen," Kurt says, glancing at his watch. "I have to get going. I need to be someplace in a few minutes."

"Meeting your girlfriend?" Stella hears herself ask tartly.

His tone and expression are as bland as an unseasoned potato. "Not until later."

She nods, wondering what kind of man wouldn't squirm under his wife's gaze after admitting a rendezvous with his girlfriend.

The kind of man who's hollow inside, she concludes. The kind of man who has no feelings; no concern for anybody but himself.

A psychopath.

That's what you call a person like that. Stella hasn't forgotten all those deviant psychology courses she took back in college.

No, you didn't forget what a psychopath was . . . you just forgot to make sure you weren't marrying one.

A snort escapes her.

Kurt's eyes narrow.

"What's so funny?"

Stella shrugs.

"No, really." He takes a step closer, coming into the shadowy living room with her. "What's so funny?"

"Nothing."

"Are you laughing at me?" The bland expression is gone; his eyes are ablaze with anger.

"Why? Did you say something funny?"

"You seem to think so."

"No, I don't. I'm not laughing." And she isn't. Not now. Now she's . . . well, she's frightened. Of him. It's ridiculous, but she is.

"You sure?"

"Positive."

She shouldn't be afraid of him. She lived with him for years, shared his bed, bore his children. There was a time when she would have gone to the ends of earth if he asked, a time when she would have died for him.

But that was so very long ago . . .

Or was it?

The night of Erin's murder, she lied to the police to protect Kurt. She was certain they'd be suspicious if she told them about his affair, and just as certain of his innocence.

In the murder, at least.

But there was once a time when she managed to convince herself that he wasn't cheating on her, wasn't there?

She was in denial about that.

What if she was in denial about the murder?

She stares at her husband. Her soon-to-be-ex-husband.

Suddenly, it's as though she's looking at a complete stranger.

The stuffed pork chops Kathleen baked for supper are drying out in the oven, and still there's no sign of Matt.

Darkness seemed to descend more swiftly than usual today, casting the house in shadow not long after she and the boys trudged home through the snow from the bus stop. Her feeling of claustrophobia intensified, Kathleen turned on almost every lamp in the house and flipped every outdoor switch as well. Somehow, the artificial light seemed to help dispel her restlessness along with the gloom. So did the fire she lit in the den, and the Christmas videos and DVDs she pulled out to keep the boys occupied.

Now, with the rousing piano music from *A Charlie Brown Christmas* playing reassuringly in the background, Kathleen peers anxiously through the living room window.

The front yard and the street are blanketed in snow, and it's still swirling, sparkling like glitter in the glow from the floodlights and lamppost.

Across the street, Kathleen sees one of her neighbors, undaunted by darkness or the weather, standing on a ladder stapling holiday lights beneath the gutter above his wreath-bedecked front door. A few houses down, a colorful Christmas tree twinkles already in a picture window.

"Christmastime . . . is here . . ." the Peanuts characters chorus in the next room.

Yes, it is. It seems like only moments have passed since Kathleen was contentedly sending the kids off on the bus on the first day of school, warm September sunshine on her shoulders. Now the holidays are upon them, and her world has spun out of control.

Kathleen is surrounded by the familiar trappings of her favorite season, but nothing is as it should be.

And where the hell is Matt? she wonders,

searching the street for an arc of headlights turning off Cuttington Road. Nothing but darkness, falling snow, and the rapidly disappearing tracks of a plow that went by more than an hour ago.

Why hasn't Matt called since this morning?

At first, she was relieved to have a reprieve from the frequently ringing phone and the tiresome questions about Jen's condition. But as the afternoon wore on, she found herself regretting the way she'd spoken to him earlier, wishing she'd told him to just come on home before the weather got too nasty. She even tried calling him back a few times, but only got his voice mail.

That wasn't unusual. Matt is frequently away from his desk. But he always calls her back as soon as he gets her message. *Always.*

"Mommy?"

She looks up to see Riley standing behind her, the spitting image of his daddy, bright blue eyes and dark hair.

Suddenly, she feels a pang of longing for Matt, for the way things used to be between them. How can they ever go back to that now?

We can't, she realizes, and grief sweeps over her. *We'll never be the same. He'll never trust me again.*

Jen will never trust me again, either. And she doesn't even know the whole story. If she ever finds out . . .

"Mommy?" Riley says again. "I'm hungry. Can I have a snack?"

"We're going to eat soon, sweetie. The second Daddy gets home."

"Well, when is he coming?"

"Any time now." She glances again out the window. Still no headlights.

"Well, call him and see when," Riley orders with five-year-old authority.

"I can't. He's not at work and he doesn't have a cell phone."

Which is his own damn fault. He had one in Indiana, provided by his company. That's not one of the perks of his new job, though. And when Kathleen suggested that they add another phone to their existing cell plan, he stubbornly refused — just as he refused to get one for Jen.

Now, anger — unreasonable or not — rises to mingle with Kathleen's worry about her husband. What if something happened to him?

"Why do we have to wait for Daddy to eat?" Riley wants to know. "Why can't we start without him? We used to eat without him all the time back home."

Back home.

Kathleen sighs. "This is home now, Riley."

"Oh yeah. I forgot."

"And we wait for Daddy because it's nice to eat dinner as a family."

"Well, Jen doesn't have to eat dinner as a family."

"That's because she got hurt. But she's almost better, and when she is, she'll eat with us again."

"I want to eat now," he whines.

"I said we'll eat soon."

He stamps his foot. *"Now!"*

Kathleen opens her mouth to scold him, then thinks better of it. He's just a hungry little boy, caught in the middle of a domestic drama.

"Okay, Riley. You and Curran can eat now if you can't wait."

"What about you?"

She leads the way back to the kitchen, saying, "I'll eat with Daddy."

Not that she has any appetite.

Where, she wonders again, is her husband?

Nobody will ever miss the broom from Maeve Hudson's basement.

Most likely, nobody will miss Maeve Hudson, either. Not for a long time.

It could very well be several days before

anybody discovers her corpse hanging from the sturdy pole in her walk-in closet, where she tried to hide once she sensed the danger she was in.

Fitting that she died there among the trappings of her life — fashionable clothes, designer shoes. Who knew an imported Italian leather belt would make such a perfect noose . . . or that its owner would give up the fight almost willingly in the end, seeming to welcome death?

That certainly made things easier for me.

No sign of forced entry. No sign of a struggle.

That's what the police report will say when Maeve's body is discovered.

By then, of course, the whole thing will be over. Nobody will connect her death with her daughter's murder, or Jen Carmody's murder.

No, people will assume she was a grieving mother who couldn't live without her child. A logical suicide . . . though there was no note. It was tempting to try to write one, imitating Maeve's distinct handwriting. That would have been a necessity, had her death been planned.

But it wasn't. It just happened, Maeve Hudson becoming an unforseen obstacle in the path.

In the end, it was better not to leave a note; better to leave well enough alone. Plenty of people kill themselves without writing a final farewell or explanation. Who would Maeve even address if she wrote such a note, anyway? She's divorced, her daughter is dead.

Kathleen, maybe? Would she have addressed a suicide note to her loyal best friend?

An interesting idea . . . but it's too late.

Back to the broom.

How clever was I to think of running back for the broom, then dragging it along behind me through the snow as I left?

Every footprint leading away from the Hudson home was swept neatly away without a trace. Now the broom handle is splintered into kindling, the bristles already crackling on the hearth.

Like her daughter, like the others who got in the way, Maeve Hudson didn't have to die. She should have left well enough alone.

She should have looked through me, not at me, in those final moments of her life.

It was my fault, too. I let my guard down. I got too comfortable and forgot to be who I'm supposed to be, just for a split second. But that's all it takes.

In any case, analyzing the catalyst of

Maeve Hudson's death is useless now that the deed is done. Now, there are far more important things to think about.

It's time.

Time to finish the job that should have been accomplished fourteen years ago.

Time for Jen Carmody to die as she should have all those years ago.

You came so close to doing it then . . . so, so close . . .

It was the perfect opportunity. They were alone together in the nursery.

The baby gazed up from her crib with trusting blue eyes — newborn navy blue eyes that would one day change to brown beneath the telltale pale streak in her left eyebrow.

If the child made a sound when the pillow came down over her face, it was muffled by the thick bulk of down pressed against her nostrils and nose.

Sugar and spice and everything nice.

Those were the words that were embroidered in pink thread on the white pillow.

Sugar and spice and everything nice . . .

That, supposedly, is what little girls are made of.

What a joke.

The baby's tiny body writhed frantically in the crib as oxygen was cut off, putting up a vehement fight for her life. But of course she was no match for the strong hands that held her down.

Another few seconds, and she'd have been dead.

But it didn't happen that way.

Instead, there were footsteps in the hall, a familiar voice calling the baby's name, the sound of a door opening . . .

It was too late to hide.

Too late to do anything but stand by helplessly as infant CPR was administered.

It was excruciating to witness the feverish effort to save the baby's life. Excruciating to hear the raging accusations, the threats, the despair that followed.

And then . . .

The baby was gone.

It didn't matter where. All that mattered, at first, was that she was gone, for good.

Gone and forgotten, just as if she really had died.

Just as you intended.

If only . . .

No. No need for if onlys. Not now. Not ever again.

Tomorrow is the day. It should have happened fourteen years ago; then it should have happened a month ago.

Once again, things went horribly wrong.

It should have been so easy. And it was, at first.

Erin Hudson never even turned around as she sliced apples at the counter, never seemed to sense that somebody was behind her. Somebody who was watching her every move from behind the hideous rubber monster mask, waiting for just the right moment to pounce.

Then she set the knife down . . . and that was it.

It was easy. So easy to reach in with a gloved hand and snatch the knife, warning her that she'd die if she made a sound.

She didn't make a sound.

She died anyway, her white throat splitting open as neatly as apple skin beneath the sharp blade.

Five minutes later, Jen walked down the stairs, right into the trap.

But unlike her friend, she didn't mutely obey orders. No, she put up a struggle, fighting, scratching, screaming.

Then came the sound of shattering glass, and the old man who seemed to come out of nowhere like some bizarre superhero dressed in a white collar instead of a cape.

In the chaotic aftermath of that shocking moment, Jen made her escape, fleeing out the back door and into the night.

She didn't get away. Almost, but not quite.

She was surprisingly tenacious, as tenacious as the surprisingly strong old priest. He managed to get the knife away, battling ferociously to save the girl's life even as his own was cut — quite literally — viciously short.

Then it was Jen's turn, once again. She was badly wounded, not just from the knife, but from the struggle. Her leg was bent at a grotesque angle. She stood and tried to run, but couldn't put weight on it. She fell again, her eyes gazing up just as they had fourteen years ago from her crib.

But this time, thanks to the mask, there was no recognition in her eyes. There was no trust, either.

This time, there was only stark terror.

Just like before, all it would have taken was another few seconds . . .

But headlights swung into the driveway before the job could be finished. There was nothing to do but run, leaving Jen and the old priest for dead.

In the end, though the girl survived, the priest's presence was more help than hindrance. His fingerprints were all over the knife. So were Jen's.

Mine weren't.

Nobody ever suspected that another person was there the night of the murders. There was no evidence. No reason. Especially after the media took the Killer Priest angle and ran with it. The papers were full of tales of deviant men of the cloth: evil disguised as good. Psychiatrists were interviewed and agreed that it wouldn't be the first time a seemingly sane person had lived an exemplary life, then suddenly snapped and gone on a homicidal spree.

It would be amusing to watch if it weren't so infuriating. Twice, Jen Carmody has managed to evade her destiny. Then she spent weeks in the hospital, frustratingly out of reach.

But she's home now.

And the third time will be the charm . . .

After a long, hot bath complete with bubbles, a magazine, and a glass of merlot, Kathleen walks into the den to find Matt dozing peacefully on the rug in front of the dying fire. The room is lit only by the flickering hearth and the drapes are open to the floodlit crystalline wonderland beyond the glass.

Her body relaxed from the hot water and wine, cozy in flannel pajamas and a terry cloth robe, the last thing she wants right now is a return to the heightened tension of an hour ago. It would be so nice just to pour another glass of wine and sit here watching the fire and the falling snow for a while, then go upstairs and crawl into bed.

She walks over to the fireplace and reaches for a black wrought iron poker. After moving the screen aside, she jabs the charred logs, sending sparks flying and chipping away the powdery bark to reveal red-hot wood.

"What are you doing?" Matt asks, stirring to life behind her.

"Keeping the fire going." She reaches into the kindling box and tosses several small pieces of wood onto the fire.

"I'll do it." Matt is at her side, reaching for the poker.

"I've got it."

"That's not how you do it." He takes the poker from her.

Kathleen clenches her jaw, the tension back full force. Well, what does she expect?

She should have just had it out with him earlier, when he blew in the door on a gust of snowy cold air just as she was putting the boys' dirty dinner dishes into the dishwasher.

Her instant relief that he was alive swiftly gave way to a flurry of questions about where he'd been, followed by growing anger at his unsatisfactory reply that he was at work. When she asked why he didn't call her back, he told her he didn't get the messages. And when she asked why he was home so late, he told her the roads were terrible because of the snow.

Then Jen was calling her from upstairs, asking for a glass of water and some more pain medication, and Riley and Curran were scuffling over what to watch on television. Kathleen had no choice but to drop the subject for the time being.

Now, however, she faces her husband with renewed anger and suspicion.

"So you didn't get all those messages I left on your voice mail?" she asks.

"Hmm?" He looks up from the fire. "Oh. I told you, no."

"How could you not have gotten them?"

Matt shrugs. "I guess I forgot to check the voice mail."

"You can do better than that."

"What?"

"I expected you to say the system was down because of the storm or something. You never forget to check your voice mail. You always call me back right away."

"There's a first time for everything."

"Oh, come on, Matt. You've been so worried about Jen there's no way you would have been out of contact for an entire day. You checked it and you got my messages and you were too pissed to call me back. Admit it."

She fully expects him to deny it.

Again, he surprises her. With obvious reluctance, he says, "All right, I'll admit it. I was pissed. I didn't feel like calling you back."

"How could you let me worry about you like that? I thought your car might have gone off the road or something."

She closes her eyes, blocking out the memory of an ice-slicked highway, crumpled metal, shooting flames.

Mollie Gallagher.

Loving Wife, Devoted Mother . . .

"It did go off the road," Matt is saying. "A few times."

Protective Grandmother.

"I was sliding all over the place. I should have left the office early this afternoon, when I wanted to. But . . ."

He trails off, looking back at the fire, poking it ferociously with the black iron prong.

But you told me not to come home.

His unspoken words hang as heavily between them as the wood smoke wafting in the air.

For a long time, they're silent. There's nothing to say.

Nothing but *I'm sorry*, and Kathleen can't bring herself to do that. The words would seem more trite than contrite in light of all that's happened.

Then Matt asks, quietly — too quietly — "How's Jen?"

"She's sleeping. The pain medication knocks her out."

"Did she eat anything with it?"

"No, she —"

"That medication is supposed to be taken with food, Kathleen. It says so right on the —"

"I gave her food. She didn't touch it. She said the pork chops were too dried out."

And that's all your fault, Kathleen wants to add. If Matt hadn't been so stubborn about coming home . . . if he had only answered his goddamned phone when she called him, and given her a chance to apologize before the whole thing blew up.

Yes, the dried out pork chops are his fault. Not hers.

She's to blame for the rest of it, though. All of it. The shambles of their marriage. The lies they told their daughter. The threat to Jen's life. The loss of Erin's. And, beneath it all, she's to blame for the very tragedy that triggered all the rest.

The death of her first daughter fourteen years ago.

Jen wakes up in the middle of the night to the eerie sensation that she isn't alone in her room.

Rolling onto her back, she realizes that the closet light, which she always leaves burning through the night, is off.

Jen scans the room, her eyes gradually growing accustomed to the darkness.

Is somebody standing at the foot of her bed?

Her heart begins to pound.

She sits up, a torrent panic rushing over her along with the painful physical effort as she realizes that somebody is there.

"Mom?"

"No, it's me."

Relief sweeps her at the sound of Matt Carmody's voice. She sinks back weakly against the pillows.

"You scared me."

"I'm sorry."

"What happened to my closet light?"

"What? Oh . . . it must have burned out."

She nods, then realizes he can't see her. "I guess it must have," she tells him, wanting to ask if he can replace it for her, wishing he'd offer.

There was a time when she wouldn't hesitate to ask a favor of her father. But now there's a wall between them that stilts every conversation, making even the most inane requests off limits. In the hospital, she asked her mother or the nurses to fetch water and magazines and help her to the bathroom, but she refused to ask him. On rare occasions that he was the only one in the room and she needed something, she would simply wait.

Jen glances at the digital clock on her night stand, hoping to find that it's almost morning.

No. Only two-forty-two.

She either has to ask her father to change the lightbulb, or spend the rest of the night in the dark.

Neither option appeals to her, but as long as he's here . . .

Come to think of it . . . why is he here? She often wakes to find her mother looming over her, but not him. Not now that she's home.

"Dad?" she asks, the once affectionate word sounding forced.

"Hmm?"

"What are you doing here?"

"Making sure you're okay." His silhouette shifts position; he steps closer, coming around to the side of the bed. "Mom said you didn't eat your dinner."

"It was dry and disgusting."

"Yeah, well . . . you need to eat. Especially with the pain medication. It's dangerous not to. You know better than that."

She shrugs, not caring that he can't see her in the dark. So now he's back to scolding her about everything, all the time? It was better when they weren't speaking at all.

She turns her back, facing the wall. Behind her, she feels him come closer to the bed, hears him reach for something on the night stand. Something rattles and she realizes he's picked up one of her prescription bottles. He shakes it a little, then sets it down again.

Sensing he's going to say something, she waits.

When he remains silent, she asks, "What are you doing?"

"Just checking to see if you need me to pick up a refill for your medication on my way home from work tomorrow, but you have enough."

"Oh."

Great. Now she feels guilty. Maybe he really does care — at least a little. At least enough to make sure she's not in unnecessary pain.

She hears the floor creak beneath his weight, realizes he's about to leave the room.

"Um, Dad?" she finds herself saying.

"Yeah?"

Don't do it. Don't ask him to change the bulb now. Don't show him that you're such a baby you can't get through the night in the dark.

She hesitates a long time, finally allowing herself to ask only, "Would you mind opening my window shades? I like to watch the snow."

She hears him cross the room, hears one shade snap up, and then the other, just to the left of her bed.

"Better?" he asks.

Her eyes are closed and she's still facing the wall, but she tells him, "Yeah. Thanks."

She hears him hesitate again in the doorway.

Does he want to say something else?

Does he expect her to?

Jen lies tense beneath the covers, torn between wanting him to come back to the bed, hold her close, tell her he loves her and he's still her daddy and will always be her daddy . . .

And just wanting him to just go away.

That's the part of her that gets her wish.

His steps retreat down the hall to the master bedroom, then pause again.

Is he standing in the doorway watching Mom sleeping? What is he thinking?

Finally, the door closes behind him, and she hears the faint sound of bedsprings squeaking as his weight descends.

Jen opens her eyes and rolls again onto her back.

The room is much brighter with the shades raised. Beyond the window that's closest to her bed, she can see that the snow is still falling.

It looks so peaceful out there.

She watches the snow, and, gradually, her clenched muscles begin to relax.

The worst month of her life is behind her. It's December now — a new month, the start of a new season.

Tomorrow, Jen decides, she might ask Mom to open her window a crack. The room feels too warm and stuffy. Suddenly, she craves fresh air.

Fresh air. A fresh start.

Yes, she decides, snuggling into the warm blankets again and closing her eyes, tomorrow will be a turning point. She can feel it.

SEVENTEEN

The second of December dawns cold and clear in Woodsbridge.

In the master bathroom, Kathleen clears a peephole in the fogged-over windowpane with the sleeve of her robe. She leans close to look out, shivering in the icy draft that seeps through the crack between the double-hung windows.

The world beyond the glass is breathtakingly beautiful. The hard edges of houses and branches and fences have been cushioned in soft billows of white against a backdrop of Carmody blue sky — the precise piercing shade of Matt and the boys' eyes.

Kathleen hears a plow rumbling by in the distance. From this side of the house, she can't see if Sarah Crescent has been cleared yet. Probably not. It's still early, and the cul de sac is relatively out of the way.

Maybe Matt will leave for work later than usual. Then again, maybe he'll leave earlier, to prove a point.

You don't want me around.

But she does. She wants him here . . . just not the way he has been, lately. Not brooding, and angry, and . . . and different. She wants him the way he used to be. She wants their life together the way it used to be, even if it meant being burdened by a secret she carried single-handedly. If wondering what would happen if her husband ever found out was difficult, living with the consequences is far more painful.

As if summoned by her thoughts, Matt pokes his head into the bathroom, busily knotting a tie around his neck. "Are you almost finished in here, Kathleen?"

There was a time when he would have shortened her name on the end of that question. Kath. What a difference the extra syllable makes.

Longing for his affection, unable to give any in return, she says only, "Almost."

She turns away from the window, squirts aqua gel onto her toothbrush.

He's still there. "Can you hurry it up? I need to get in here."

"I thought you were done."

"I showered. I still need to shave."

He disappears again.

There was a time when he would have laughingly joined her in the bathroom, shaving above her head as she spit into the

506

sink. But those days are gone. The chill between them this morning is as palpable as the draft permeating the window.

Kathleen brushes her teeth quickly and splashes cold water on her face. Her reflection in the mirror is gaunt, the skin around her eyes thin and sallow.

Turning her back on her sorry self, she emerges into the master bedroom, where her husband is tying a black dress shoe.

"It's all yours," she informs him, trying not to sound too snotty.

Apparently doing nothing of the sort, he murmurs a clipped "thanks" as he brushes past her.

Kathleen quickly makes the bed, retrieves the throw pillows from the chair and tosses them at the head.

Overhead, there's a rumbling sound, and then a crash outside the nearest window.

Startled, Kathleen opens the shade, knowing what it is even before she sees the heap of snow below.

If it's sliding off the roof, the temperature must be warming. Good. She isn't yet ready for the onset of winter. Maybe there will be a thaw.

She quickly opens the shade at the other window, hoping to be out of here before Matt emerges from the bathroom.

She's almost to the door when he comes out, pressing a bloody washcloth against his chin.

"What happened?"

"Nothing."

"You're bleeding."

"I cut myself."

"Is it bad?"

"No."

But it is. She can tell by the streaks of crimson on the washcloth and the way he winces as he presses on it.

"Do you want me to get you some Neosporin or something?" she offers, melting just a little.

"No. Thanks," he adds belatedly, and their eyes meet briefly before he looks away.

Kathleen shrugs and steps out into the hallway.

Behind her, Matt calls her name. Her full name, once again.

She hesitates. "What?"

"Make sure Jen eats today, will you? Those drugs she's on are heavy duty. She needs food in her system."

Kathleen rolls her eyes and says nothing.

Down the hall, she peeks into her daughter's room and finds her sound asleep. Jen doesn't even stir when she pulls the blankets up around her shoulders, nor when

Kathleen presses a kiss against her head and whispers, "I love you, baby girl."

Baby girl.

Her first baby girl is gone.

This is the daughter who matters now.

Kathleen stares down at her sleeping daughter, safe and sound in her own bed. She thinks of the child she buried fourteen years ago and of the one Maeve Hudson buried last month.

It's time to let go of the past. Time to stop letting harsh memories torture her. Time to banish toxic guilt from her life.

Today can be the turning point, if she allows it.

She has three children who need her, a husband who loves her.

At least, he *did*.

She vividly remembers the day the blue-eyed, handsome stranger laughingly bent to retrieve her baby's dropped rattle from beneath a park bench in Chicago. Surprisingly, he sat down at her side . . . and he never left it.

She always believed he was too good to be true, the second major miracle in her life.

The first, of course, was finding a baby girl on the church steps hours after she had buried her own precious child.

When she saw the pink bundle there, she

was deluded enough in her grief to actually believe it was her own dead baby come to life again, courtesy of her mother in heaven.

After all, hadn't she begged her mother, begged God Himself, to send her baby back to her? To give her another chance?

All she wanted was another chance.

She got it.

She found that baby, and she took her, and she ran. She ran all the way to Chicago, certain nobody would ever know the truth. The baby's real mother had abandoned her.

And nobody knew Kathleen's real daughter lay in a shallow grave she dug herself in the dead of night . . .

Right beside Mollie Gallagher's headstone.

Lucy is halfway out the door when Henry's voice stops her in her tracks.

"Where are you going?"

Keeping her back to him for fear he'll see the lie in her eyes, she says, "To church."

"In this weather?"

Her heart pounds. "It's not snowing."

"The roads are icy. Stay home."

With him, it's never a request.

It never has been, from the day she vowed before God to obey her husband until death do them part.

Obey.

She also promised to love and honor him — both vows she broke years ago. But leaving Henry is as out of the question now as it was then. Even if she had somewhere to go, some means of supporting herself, divorce is against her religion. And her religion is all she has left — all that's sustained her through the brutal years.

Last night, as her husband snored beside her in their bed, Lucy lay awake for hours, wondering if she really does love God and her church more than she hates Henry. She used to think so.

Now, she isn't so sure.

She isn't sure of anything except that Margaret's life is still in danger and nobody knows.

"Come on," Henry says behind her now as she hesitates on the snowy step. "All the heat's going out. Get back in here."

Lucy can't just wait helplessly for something to happen. She gave her daughter life; it's her duty to preserve it, at any cost.

She has to tell somebody about Margaret.

But whom?

The police? And have her name dragged through the press?

No. She can't let Henry find out about any of this. If he knew she saw John again, he would . . .

511

She closes her eyes, wincing at the thought of what he would do to her.

So the police can't know. But the Carmodys need to.

I have to talk to them, Lucy thinks desperately. *To her, especially. Kathleen Carmody. From one mother to another —*

"Lucy!" Henry barks from the doorway. "What the hell are you doing out there?"

She turns slowly to face the man she's grown to despise. If she tries to leave against his will, he'll drag her back in the house and beat her so badly she'll be trapped here for weeks.

So? Either way you're trapped, Lucy realizes.

But not for long now. In a few hours, he'll leave for work.

If she waits him out, Lucy can leave after he does, go right over to Orchard Hollow.

She only prays the extra few hours won't make the difference between life and death for Margaret.

Stella is running late for work, yet she stops at the Dunkin' Donuts drive-through after dropping the girls at day care. She stares hungrily at the donuts pictured on the sign, but orders only the largest coffee they have.

"Decaf?" the girl asks over the crackling speaker.

"God, no," Stella replies around a yawn.

She was up most of the night, and not just because her mother's pull-out couch is about as comfortable — and sturdy — as a plastic tubing chaise lounge.

No, she couldn't stop thinking about Kurt.

About his nameless, faceless girlfriend.

About his whereabouts the night of the murder.

What if he isn't having an affair at all?

What if he wasn't miles away when Erin was murdered and Jen attacked?

What if the priest wasn't the killer, but was trying to defend himself against the real killer?

A horn blasts behind Stella. She looks back to see an angry driver gesturing and realizes the car in front of her has pulled ahead.

"God, have some patience," she mutters, gesturing her apology to Mr. Impatience.

She takes her foot off the brake and coasts up to the window, handing over her money and accepting the coffee from the girl.

"Have a nice day."

The girl's breath is as steamy as the coffee in the cold morning air.

Stella nods, smiles grimly. "I will."

Yeah, right.

A nice day.

She hasn't had a nice day since . . .

Well, she can't remember the last time she had a nice day.

And now that she's on her own with two kids, a full-time job, and a pull-out couch to call home . . .

Well, if this isn't rock bottom, she doesn't know what is.

Oh, yes. Yes, she does.

Maeve Hudson's tear-stained face pops into her head.

The wake was a nightmare, the mass agony, the burial pure torture.

Stella wept throughout.

Kurt didn't attend.

Not even during calling hours at the funeral home. He said he was busy at work.

Is he that callous?

Or is there another reason he refused to go?

A darker reason — one nobody might ever suspect.

Nobody but the wife who learned the hard way that her trust in him was profoundly misplaced.

Jen awakens to find the sun streaming

through the window, something she hasn't seen in what feels like forever.

She rolls up onto her elbow, wincing as the joint takes the weight of her upper body. The physical therapist she saw at the hospital, Megan, promised her that eventually her arm will feel almost as good as new.

Not *as* good as new.

Almost.

Megan told Jen that her leg will heal, too. That she should be able to play soccer again with no problem by the time the next season rolls around.

Right now, Jen can't imagine running the length of a field, let alone facing the team without Erin.

But September is a long way away.

As if to punctuate that realization, the dull, rhythmic scraping thud of a snow shovel against concrete reaches Jen's ears. She winces as she hoists herself further upright in the bed, leaning toward the frost-etched window.

Dad is below, shoveling the sidewalk.

His jaw is set, as though he's angry about something.

Jen watches him for a long time, wondering what he's thinking about.

I miss you, she tells him silently, before turning away.

So much for a fresh start.

Her elbow might be almost as good as new someday, but it's pretty obvious that her relationship with the man she was led to believe was her father is permanently shattered. He said very little to her in all those endless days and nights as he and Mom hovered over her hospital bed. Though he seemed concerned, it could have been an act he was putting on for the doctors and nurses.

But he was there, she reminds herself. *He must care about me if he was there.*

Unless the big vigil was just for show.

But what about last night?

He was there, watching her, when nobody else was around to see him. Not even Jen herself. If she hadn't happened to wake up, she never would have known.

She wonders how many times in the past he stood over her bed watching her sleep . . . and why she finds the thought more eerily unsettling than reassuring.

It would be different if he were still her father.

But now that she knows he's not even a blood relation . . .

Well, he really has no business being in her room at all, when you come right down to it.

No business being in her room, and no business being in her life.

The phone rings just as Kathleen is throwing her barely touched ham sandwich into the garbage can.

"Mrs. Carmody?"

"Yes?" The voice sounds familiar, but she can't place it or the heavy southern accent.

"My name is Helen and I'm one of the nurses over at Erasmus."

No wonder the voice was familiar. She sighs.

Dad.

He's run away again.

"Yes?" she says, pacing to the window with the phone.

At least it isn't snowing again . . . yet. This morning's blue skies have long since given way to dark clouds looming in the west. With any luck, her father will turn up before the next squall.

"Mrs. Carmody, we need you to come right down here."

Come right down there?

That's a new one.

She sighs. "I'm sorry, but my daughter is home sick today, and I can't —"

"Mrs. Carmody, I'm afraid it's urgent."

"Did my father run away again?"

"I can't discuss this over the phone. We need you here in person."

Her heart stops; her thoughts race.

He's dead.

Her father is dead.

What else can it be?

"Okay," she tells the caller, "I'll be right there."

The only time Stella has ever set foot in the Woodsbridge Police Station was to drop off a donation for a Christmas toy drive a few years ago.

It's that time of year again, but this time, she bypasses the large cardboard box marked *Holiday Toy Donations* just inside the entrance.

She isn't sure why she's going to do what she's about to do.

Maybe she's a spurned wife seeking vengeance.

Maybe she's bound by conscience to come clean on the information she withheld and the lies she told Detective Brodowiaz.

Or maybe, deep down inside, she really believes Kurt had something to do with a double homicide.

All she knows is that the morning she spent in the classroom was unfair to the students. She couldn't focus on teaching a simple lesson she's taught dozens of times before, couldn't give the kids the attention they deserve.

She can't afford to jeopardize her students — nor can she afford, quite literally, to risk her job. She's going to need it more than ever.

Especially if her nagging doubts about her husband's innocence prove to be grounded in reality.

What if Kurt is a murderer?

What if he goes to prison?

Their lives will be ruined. Not just his, but hers, and her daughters'.

If Kurt is guilty, this is only the beginning of the nightmare Stella believed was drawing to a close.

The string of grim possibilities wound through her mind all morning, until her thoughts were hopelessly snarled and teaching was utterly impossible. Finally, she went to the principal's office and asked if she could take the rest of the day off to attend to personal business.

"You've already used your personal days, Stella," was the stern reply.

"I know, and I'm sorry . . . but this is urgent. I wouldn't be asking if it weren't."

So here she is, coming to the police with so-called urgent information now, almost a month after the case has been closed.

What the hell are you doing? she asks herself, even as her feet propel her directly to the desk sergeant.

He looks up promptly.

Too late to back out now.

He even recognizes her — thanks, no doubt, to all the media coverage last month. "Mrs. Gattinski? Can I help you?"

"Yes. Is Detective Brodowiaz here?"

The sargent looks at his watch. "He stepped out for lunch, but he should be back in about twenty minutes. Why don't you sit down and wait for him?"

Stella hesitates.

Okay, so it isn't too late to leave after all.

She can turn around and walk out the door — go back to school, back to her life, back to telling herself that her husband is nothing more than a selfish, cheating SOB.

Or she can have a seat and confide her suspicions in Detective Brodowiaz when he returns.

"Mrs. Gattinski?"

She looks up to see the desk sergeant gesturing at the row of chairs beneath a plate glass window.

She hesitates only another moment.

Then, slowly, she walks toward the window and sinks into the nearest seat.

"Don't worry about me, Mom," Jen says for the third time, forgetting to be sullen. "I'll be fine. Really."

"Are you sure?" Her mother, wearing her coat and boots, hovers nervously beside her bed. "Because I hate to leave you."

"Mom, the nurse said it was urgent. You have to go. What if Grandpa is . . ."

She trails off, not wanting to say it. But she knows what her mother is thinking. Why else would the nursing home ask her to come right over?

Either Grandpa is dead, or he's about to die.

Whatever the case, Mom needs to be there with him.

And Jen needs to be here for Mom. For the first time in weeks, touched by her mother's vulnerability, Jen has allowed the wall of ice she erected between them to thaw.

"Let me try to call Daddy one more time." Mom flips her cell phone open in shaking hands. "I keep getting his voice mail."

"Did you leave him a message?"

"I left two. It's been less than five minutes, but . . ."

Jen watches her mother dial, sees the

veins in her neck tensing as she waits for the line to ring a few times.

"Matt, it's me again. Listen, when you get this message, just come right home. I've got to leave Jen and I don't know how long I'm going to be gone. Somebody has to keep an eye on her and meet the boys at the bus stop. I'll call as soon as I can."

"Nobody has to keep an eye on me, Mom." Jen scowls as her mother tucks the phone into the pocket of her coat. "I'm old enough to take care of myself for a few hours."

"Not when you can't even get out of bed."

"Why would I have to get out of bed? I'll be fine."

Her mother just looks at her, shaking her head.

Jen knows what she's thinking.

About that night.

If only she could remember what happened that night.

Apples.

Something about apples.

She shakes her head, unable to grasp the thought that flits teasingly at the edge of her consciousness.

"You'd better go, Mom."

"I know. I'd better." There are tears in her mother's eyes.

"I'm sorry about Grandpa."

"Maybe it's not that. Maybe he just . . . I don't know . . . maybe he ran away again. Or maybe he's all out of underwear." Her mother's laugh is choked.

Jen smiles sadly. "I hope that's what it is."

"So do I. Do you need anything before I go? Do you want me to help you to the bathroom?"

She shakes her head. "I don't have to go."

Outside, there's a sudden rumbling, crashing sound.

Both Jen and her mother jump.

"It's just snow," her mother tells her. "Falling off the roof."

"I know."

"You looked worried for a second."

"So did you."

Mom shakes her head. "What if you have to go to the bathroom while I'm gone? You can't get there by yourself."

"I can if I crawl."

"Jen —"

"Don't worry about me, Mom. I don't have to go. I'll be fine."

"Well, Daddy will get my message and be here soon, anyway."

"Yeah. Just . . . will you turn on my radio before you go?"

"Sure."

Mom walks over to her desk, flips the switch on Jen's portable stereo. "Do you want a CD or the radio?"

"Radio," Jen says, knowing a CD would end and she'd be left in silence, knowing that a silent house would be scary.

Mom finds the f.m. station Jen likes. The familiar strains of her favorite Dave Matthews song fill the air reassuringly as her mother heads for the door. "If I don't get home for dinner, tell Daddy there's stew in the Crock-Pot. It'll be done by around six."

"I will."

Jen sighs, leaning back against the pillows again.

Stew in the Crock-Pot.

Daddy.

Her mother makes it sound as if everything is the way it used to be.

A lump rises in Jen's throat at the thought of the cozy family dinners they used to share, back when she thought they really were her family.

Maybe they can be again, she thinks, remembering that today was supposed to be her fresh start. Now that she's allowed the ice to melt a little, she can't help thinking that maybe what her parents did wasn't so awful. Maybe she can forgive them after all. Maybe they were just trying to protect her.

She jumps, seeing a shadow looming in her doorway, then breathes a sigh of relief when she realizes who it is.

"Mom. I thought you left."

"I started to, but I forgot something."

"What?"

Her mother leans over the bed, brushing her lips across Jen's cheek. "To kiss you goodbye."

Jen forces a confident smile. "Bye, Mom. And don't worry. Everything is going to be fine."

Her mother looks doubtful, but she says, "You're right. It is, isn't it?"

Jen nods, but inside, she isn't so sure.

"All right, Mrs. Gattinski. Why don't you tell me why you're really here?" Detective Brodowiaz says, steepling his fingers on the table that sits between them.

"I told you . . . I just wanted to thank you for all you did."

"People send notes when they want to say thank you. They send fruit baskets. And before you get any ideas, I hate fruit."

Stella laughs. It's a hollow sound. She tries, and fails, to break eye contact with the detective.

"You came down here to talk to me about what happened that night, didn't you." It's a statement, not a question.

Reluctantly, Stella nods.

"Did you remember something you forgot to tell me?" he asks, his tone surprisingly gentle.

She nods again.

"Why don't you tell me now, then? Since you're here, and I'm here, and all," he says, his head tilted in wry invitation.

"All right."

Stella takes a deep breath, wonders how to begin.

The detective leans back and folds his arms as though he has all the time in the world. As though this conversation is utterly casual, as though whatever she's about to say is almost incidental.

But his posture belies the shrewd intensity of his gaze.

He knows, she realizes. *He knows I lied that night. He knows my conscience is eating away at me. He knows that whatever I say is going to be a bombshell, and he's just waiting to pounce on it.*

Realizing she's still holding her breath, Stella exhales shakily, clenches her hands together to steady them. She gazes down at the fourth finger of her left hand at the faint red mark where her wedding ring used to be.

She had to soap it to get it off last night. Her ring finger, like the rest of her, is a few sizes bigger than it was when she got married.

She looks up at the detective and sees that he, too, was gazing down at her fingers.

He must have noticed her ring is gone.

Maybe not.

Oh, come on, Stella. He's a detective. Detectives notice everything.

So he knows her ring is gone, has obviously deduced that her marriage is in trouble. He's probably already put two and two together.

She might as well tell him what she came here to tell him. Right?

Still, she hesitates. She closes her eyes.

Once again, she's standing at the top of that treacherous trail at Holiday Valley, with Kurt at her side.

What's the matter? Are you scared?

Yes. She's no longer young, or naive, or stupid. But she is scared.

Scared of what will happen if she takes the plunge — but perhaps even more scared of what will happen if she doesn't.

Her mind made up, Stella opens her eyes.

She clears her throat nervously, takes a deep breath, and tells Detective Brodowiaz, "It's about my husband . . ."

★ ★ ★

Kathleen talks aloud to her mother as she drives to Erasmus, just as she did in the cemetery that night fourteen years ago.

"Just let him live until I get there, Mommy," she begs, tears streaming down her face as she clutches the wheel, easing her way toward the bottle-necked toll booths. The traffic ahead seems to move with painstaking sluggishness.

"I just want a chance to tell him how much I love him. Please . . ."

Does he know?

Does her father even know that she loves him?

The car in front of her moves.

Kathleen takes her foot off the brake.

She and her father never resolved what happened when she was pregnant, when he told her to get out. He simply showed up at her wedding, met her husband and daughter, and they moved on.

Rolling forward toward the toll booth, she nearly rear-ends the car in front of her. She jams on the brakes just in time, trembling.

She shouldn't be driving. She's a basket case.

It's all too much. All of it. Jen, Matt, Erin, and now her father . . .

It's too, too much.

What if her father is already dead?

"He'll never know," she whispers, eyes fastened to the brake lights in front of her as she clenches the wheel with both hands. "He'll never know how sorry I am . . ."

Sorry? a disdainful voice echoes in her head. *Sorry for what? Why are* you *sorry? He's the one who should be sorry. He turned his back on his only child when you needed him most.*

"He is sorry." Kathleen speaks aloud in the empty car, speaks with ragged conviction. "He just doesn't know how to say it."

Still . . .

How could he have done it? How could he have told her to get out? How could he have sent her, alone and frightened and pregnant, out into the night?

She hated him for it then; she hated him even more for it once she was a parent herself. She would never turn her back on her own child. *Never.* She would never . . .

Everybody makes mistakes, Kathleen.

Even parents. Even parents who love their children so much that they would die for them.

Everybody makes mistakes.

Even me.

She's crying now, fumbling for the button on the door to lower the window, fumbling in the ashtray for change to pay the toll.

She thrusts it into the toll taker's outstretched hand, barely noticing the young man's startled expression as he glimpses her tear-soaked face.

The ramp ahead is clear.

Kathleen presses down on the gas at last, roaring onto the thruway.

John's home, like the man himself, has taken on a faded, tired appearance after all these years.

This is a working-class neighborhood not far from where Saint Brigid's used to stand. The homes here are humble but generally well cared for. John's two-story frame house sits in the middle of a row of others just like it, all of them fronted by three or four concrete steps with wrought iron rails, and glassed-in porches.

But the shrubs in front of John's house are overgrown, the neglected flowerbeds filled with brown stalks nobody bothered to cut back after they bloomed months ago. The clapboards need a paint job. One second-story shutter hangs crookedly on a single hinge. The obviously leaking gutter beneath the eaves is rimmed by jagged, dripping icicles that ominously resemble drooling fangs.

Buoyed by unexpected courage from an

inner well she had assumed was long dry, Lucy mounts the recently shoveled front steps, presses the bell, hears it ring somewhere inside.

A neighbor's dog instantly begins to bark.

Lucy waits, shivering in the cold, wondering what she'll say if Deirdre comes to the door.

Maybe I should have just gone to talk to the Carmodys alone, she thinks, shifting her weight nervously from one foot to the other.

But that didn't seem right. In the long wait for Henry to leave for work, she concluded that she owes it to John to include him in the decision to confront Margaret's parents.

Her *real* parents.

The ones who are raising her, loving her, responsible for keeping her safe.

The dog is still barking in the adjacent yard, and nobody has answered the door.

Lucy presses the bell again.

The dog grows more frenzied, hurtling itself against the chain link fence next door.

She hears a door opening over there, hears a man's voice snap, "Shut up, Ribs!"

"I'm sorry," Lucy calls across the fence to the dog's disgruntled-looking gray-haired owner.

The man shrugs. "I don't think they're home."

"I guess not."

Lucy turns away.

A thought occurs to her then, and she calls out to the man again just before he closes his door.

"John and Deirdre still live here, right?"

The man hesitates.

He lied, Lucy realizes. John lied when he told me he still lives here. Why did I trust him?

"John does," the man tells her. "With his daughter."

"What about his wife?"

The man shakes his head. "She's been dead for years."

Heading toward the nursing home at breakneck speed, Kathleen alternates between praying and talking to herself. Or maybe it's the same thing.

"Oh, please. Please, I have to get there in time . . ."

In time for what?

In time to tell her father that she loves him.

That she's sorry.

That she forgives him.

That everybody makes mistakes.

Everybody deserves to be forgiven. Even Daddy.

Even me.

"Please forgive me. Please." Kathleen chokes out the words, not sure whether she's talking to her father, or to God . . . or to herself.

Begging herself for forgiveness.

"I didn't know," she whispers, swerving to avoid a slow-moving delivery van in the right lane. "I didn't know I was pregnant."

If she had known, she would have stopped.

She did stop, the minute she realized.

From the moment she found out she was expecting a baby, she quit cold turkey. Quit drinking, quit smoking, quit drugs. She never even took an aspirin, never drank a cup of coffee, so conscious of the fragile fetus growing inside of her.

But it was too late.

Her baby girl was so tiny . . . but not too tiny, the nurses said. Not dangerously tiny. Despite Kathleen's nagging fears, little Genevieve was born seemingly healthy. She had ten fingers and ten toes, and a thatch of reddish-blond hair that reminded Kathleen of her mother.

See, Mom? she used to say, looking heavenward as she proudly cradled her newborn daughter. *See? She looks just like you.*

How she wished her mother could see her grandchild.

How she wished her father could.

She convinced herself that if he took one look at the baby, he would fall in love with her. He would take Kathleen in again, both her and the baby.

A few weeks after giving birth, Kathleen boarded a train back to Buffalo, the tiny pink bundle cradled on her lap.

"We're going home, Jen," she whispered to her daughter every so often, kissing the downy fuzz on her head. "We're going home."

She got there on All Saints Day and went right to the church to see Father Joseph. She showed him the child she'd named after his mother, and she saw the tears in his eyes as he made the sign of the cross on the baby's forehead.

He invited Kathleen to stay at the rectory that night, but she told him she had made other arrangements. He had already done too much for her. For both of them.

She brought her baby to a small motel not far from her father's house. She had worked part time near the home for unwed mothers and had saved enough money to get through a few days on her own. She was going to work up her courage to face Drew Gallagher.

"We're going home, Jen."

But she wasn't ready.

Not yet.

"Soon," she promised her baby girl as she nursed her to sleep. "Soon you'll meet your grandfather, and you know what he'll say? He'll say welcome home."

Would he have said it?

Kathleen will never know.

She fell asleep that night to pleasant dreams, her baby's warm, soft body cradled in her arms.

She woke in the morning to a mother's worst nightmare, her baby's cold, stiff body cradled in her arms.

SIDs.

That's what it was. She knows that now. Back then, all that mattered was that she woke up and her little girl was dead.

What happened after that is a blur. Everything until the cemetery is a blur.

She remembers only the guilt — the terrible, crippling guilt.

All those months before she realized she was pregnant . . . all that liquor and drugs; she was barely eating, barely sleeping. Then the certainty that when the baby came there would be something horribly wrong with her . . .

And when there wasn't, I felt as though I'd been spared. As though we'd both been spared.

She should have known better.

She should have known she would pay sooner or later. That no sin goes unpunished.

Yes, she should have known. But somehow, she didn't.

She should have learned from her mistakes. But somehow, she hadn't.

Twice in a lifetime, she managed to lull herself into a false sense of security.

Once, when tiny Genevieve was born apparently healthy.

And again, when Kathleen got her second chance at motherhood.

Well, she's finally learned her lesson.

Never again will Kathleen Carmody blindly believe in happy endings.

Mouth set grimly, foot sinking on the gas pedal, she plows full speed ahead toward whatever hell her future holds.

EIGHTEEN

Mom has been gone almost half an hour, and there's still no sign of Daddy.

Jen restlessly flips the pages of a fashion magazine Rachel brought her in the hospital.

To her surprise, she's actually getting hungry. She had to force down the cereal her mother practically force fed her for breakfast and the toast her mother insisted she eat for lunch.

Now, for the first time in a month, she feels hunger pangs stirring in her gut.

That's a good sign, she tells herself, gazing down at an impossibly skinny model wearing an impossibly short skirt.

Hunger is normal.

She can smell the beef stew her mother left in the Crock-Pot downstairs. Her mouth is actually watering.

Maybe when her father gets home she can ask him to bring her something to eat, she thinks, until she remembers that she shouldn't be asking *him* for anything.

Her feelings might have thawed toward Mom, but that's different. Different because . . .

Well, because she's my mother.

Nothing has changed with Matt Carmody. He's still not her father.

But last night, he came to check on her. He came to check on her, and he opened the shades for her. He would have changed the lightbulb, too, if she had asked.

She refused to ask.

Still . . .

Maybe you're being too hard on him, Jen thinks reluctantly. After all, he's tried to be a decent father to her. He even coached her soccer team.

Her gaze once again drifts to the trophies on the book shelf above her bed.

He wouldn't have coached girls' soccer if he didn't love her. Right?

Shaking her head, she turns the page of the magazine.

The U2 song on the radio ends. The DJ announces that it's one o'clock.

"Coming up in the next half hour, we continue our lunch box blocks with Phish and Blink 182, so stick around. Now Mercury Rev's latest release opens up the one o'clock hour."

His voice gives way to opening guitar

chords that slam into Jen like a wall of falling snow from the roof, bringing an icy chill that steals her breath away.

That song . . .

It was playing.

On MTV.

When she came downstairs.

The song was playing, and she went into the kitchen, and Erin had been peeling apples.

The apple corer was there.

No knife.

There was no knife.

Jen clutches her head, her thoughts racing frantically.

The knife was gone.

And then . . .

Then somebody was there.

Somebody in a rubber Halloween mask.

And the priest . . .

"He tried to save me. Oh, my God. He tried to —"

She presses her hand against her mouth, her fingers colder than a tombstone.

It's all coming back to her.

They were wrong. All of them.

It wasn't the priest. He didn't kill Erin . . .

"And I didn't kill him."

Jen squeezes her eyes shut, remembering the figure in the mask looming over her . . .

even as another sound reaches her ears.

The faintest of sounds, nearly drowned out by the music on the radio, but there, as real as her sudden memory of that night: a floorboard creaking somewhere below.

Back in her car, Lucy instinctively steers toward Woodsbridge, knowing what she has to do now.

John.

Oh, God, John. Why didn't you tell me?

No. It's not just that he didn't mention it. He lied.

Omission of information is one thing. It's almost forgivable.

Outright lying is unforgivable.

What was it that he said that day in the coffee shop, when Lucy asked about his wife?

That she was fine.

Deirdre isn't fine. She's dead.

Why would he lie?

It was an accident, the neighbor told Lucy impatiently, as his agitated dog barked and lunged repeatedly at the chain link fence. A fall down the stairs.

Deirdre. Dead. All these years.

If Lucy had known . . .

No. It wouldn't have changed anything. She's still married, even if John is not.

He knows she would never divorce Henry, just as she always knew John would never divorce Deirdre. He wouldn't leave her and their daughter. It was that simple.

How Lucy resented John's wife for that. For a lot of things.

She was married to the man Lucy loved; she was going to be the mother of Lucy's precious baby.

John told her that Deirdre was understandably upset at first, but that she accepted the child, had agreed to raise Margaret as her own. The one condition was that Lucy stay out of their lives.

What could Lucy say? How could she argue?

Deirdre had taken in her husband's illegitimate child. She was a better person than Henry . . . or so Lucy believed.

It was John's wife who answered the phone the day Lucy worked up her nerve to call and find out how her daughter was.

"I thought you promised you would leave us alone," Deirdre snapped into the phone.

"I just wanted to check on Margaret. Please . . . how is she?"

There was a pause.

"We had to send her to foster care," Deirdre said.

"What?"

"It just wasn't working out. It was too hard on me. On Susie. Our family was falling apart. So John put her into foster care . . . and she died. I'm sorry."

It was a token apology; one Lucy barely heard and didn't acknowledge.

Her baby was dead.

Why would Deirdre have lied about her death?

Why would John have lied about Deirdre's?

None of it makes sense.

And yet . . .

And yet, deep down, Lucy is starting to realize that it might.

In a way, it might make perfect sense.

Her pulse racing along with the car, Lucy drives madly toward 9 Sarah Crescent, praying that John doesn't get there first.

Kathleen careens into the parking lot at Erasmus Home for the Aged, pulls into a blue handicapped spot by the front entrance, and leaps from the driver's seat.

"Hey!" a voice calls. "You can't park there!"

Kathleen ignores the elderly man sitting on a bench in front of the nursing home, racing past him toward the wide double doors.

"You can't park there!" he calls again. "Look at you! You're not handicapped!"

A wall of stale, cabbage-scented heat hits her as she bursts into the lobby. She rushes to the front desk, where a startled-looking and unfamiliar receptionist looks up from the *National Enquirer.*

"Yes?"

"I'm Kathleen Carmody," she says breathlessly. "Drew Gallagher's daughter?"

"Yes?"

"You called," Kathleen tells the woman, even as she glances at her name badge and sees that she isn't Helen; she's Gaile.

"Somebody called," Kathleen amends, "and said I had to get right over here. Something's wrong with my father."

"All right . . . wait here." Clearly puzzled, the receptionist disappears for a few moments, leaving Kathleen to battle a growing sense of panic.

Time is running out.

She can feel it.

Why is that woman taking so long?

You'd think they'd have alerted the receptionist to what's happening upstairs. You'd think they'd have told her Kathleen was coming, and why.

At last the woman returns, a nurse at her side. Kathleen recognizes her at once.

Betty, who was named after Betty Crocker.

"Mrs. Carmody —"

"I came as soon as they called. Is he . . . ?"

"He's fine."

Fine?

There must be some mistake.

"How can he be fine?" Kathleen asks, feeling as though she's stepped into an episode of the *Twilight Zone*. "Where is he?"

Betty looks just as puzzled as the receptionist. "He's upstairs eating Jell-O. I just saw him."

"But . . ." Her mind whirling, Kathleen clings to the desk for support. It's so warm in here she can barely think straight. Could she have possibly imagined the phone call? Suddenly, she's riddled with uncertainty.

"Why are you here, Mrs. Carmody?" Betty asks gently.

"Because . . . they called and said something was wrong."

"Who said it?"

"The nurse. Helen. She had a southern accent."

Betty and the receptionist exchange a blank glance.

"Mrs. Carmody," Betty is shaking her head, "I don't know who you spoke to, but there are no nurses here with southern accents, and none named Helen."

"Who's there?" Jen calls faintly, her heart pounding in dread as she listens to the footsteps treading up the stairs. "Daddy?"

No answer.

She shrinks back into her bed, chilled and trembling.

The footsteps pause outside her door.

Then, slowly, it creaks open.

Jen braces herself to come face to face with the monster in the rubber mask again.

Then the crack in the door widens and she sees a familiar face behind it.

"Sissy! Oh, God, you scared the crap out of me." Relief courses through her as she sinks back against the pillows at the sight of her mother's cleaning lady.

"I'm sorry. You scared me, too. I didn't know anybody was home." Sissy, clad in her usual sweats and white sneakers, steps into the room, a ski jacket slung over her arm. "Usually nobody's around when I come to clean."

"How did you get in?" Jen asks, wondering if her mother forgot to lock the house in her haste to leave. If she did, anybody could have snuck in. Anybody could be hiding, wearing a rubber mask, waiting to pounce . . .

"I have a key," Sissy tells her.

Okay, so the killer hasn't snuck in yet, Jen assures herself. She's safe, and she's no longer alone.

"Are you here all alone? Where's your mother?"

"She had to go check on my grandfather."

"And your father's at work?"

"Yes. Listen, as long as you're here, would you mind doing me a favor?"

"Sure." Sissy steps closer to the bed. "What is it? And how are you feeling?"

Jen dismisses the question with a shrug and says impatiently, "I just need you to bring me the cordless phone. I have to make an important call."

She'll dial 9-1-1 and ask to be put in touch with the police station. She'll tell whoever answers that she needs to talk to Detective Brodowiaz. She has to tell him that Father Joseph wasn't the one who tried to kill her — that whoever it was got away.

"Who do you have to call?" Sissy asks.

"Just . . . it's kind of personal. And I can't get out of bed. My leg is still really messed up."

"It stinks being in bed, doesn't it?" Sissy asks, bending over to pick up a clutter of tissues Jen haphazardly aimed for the waste-paper basket these last few days. "I was in bed last year for two weeks and I thought I was going to lose my mind."

"Really?" Jen asks impatiently, watching the cleaning lady straighten the chair in front of Jen's desk.

"Yeah, I had the flu. Did you ever have the flu?"

Jen shrugs. "I don't know. Maybe. Look —"

"I get it every year," Sissy cuts in, coming closer to the bed. "Every single year. People ask me why I don't just get a flu shot, you know? But I can't. For one thing, I hate needles."

Needles.

"I hate them too." Jen closes her eyes, finding herself back in the hospital, being poked and prodded painfully. There's still an angry black and blue scar on her upper wrist from the IV.

"But it isn't just that," Sissy goes on.

The mattress sinks and Jen opens her eyes to see Sissy perched on the edge of her bed.

"Mmm hmm." Jen doesn't want to be impolite, but she wishes the cleaning lady would just shut up and go get the goddamned phone already.

"Is that why you don't get your flu shot?" Sissy asks. "Because you're afraid of needles?"

"No, it's because I'm allergic to eggs."

"That's such a coincidence, Margaret." Sissy leans in to pierce Jen's eyes with an unexpected glare. "So am I."

"Detective Brodowiaz?" A young police officer pokes his head into the room. "You need to take a phone call."

He gestures at Stella. "Can't you see I'm in the middle of —"

"It's urgent, Detective."

Brodowiaz mutters a curse and excuses himself from the room, promising he'll be back momentarily.

Stella nods, grateful for the reprieve.

She leans back in the uncomfortable wooden chair and rakes her fingers through her hair, massaging her scalp with her fingertips.

Christ. What is she doing here, really?

Does she honestly believe Kurt has something to do with the murder?

Detective Brodowiaz asked her that very question a short time ago.

Her reply?

I wouldn't be here if I didn't believe it was possible, Detective.

But he didn't seem convinced.

As he continued to question her, Stella realized what he was thinking.

That she was a spurned wife looking for

vengeance against her cheating husband.

She wanted to tell Detective Brodowiaz that there are easier ways of doing that. She could slash all of his clothes, or . . . or have an affair herself.

But making him the prime suspect in a homicide?

After a few minutes, the door opens again; the detective strides back into the room.

"Mrs. Gattinski, I think we've covered everything. Unless you have anything else to tell me, I'm going to have to cut this short."

"You're not taking me seriously, are you?" Stella asks. "You don't think my husband had anything to do with this case. You think I'm here to get back at him for what he did to me."

"Mrs. Gattinski —"

"Let me tell you something, Detective. Kurt is very good at making people think he's innocent. It took me ten years to figure out that he's not. I can't believe you aren't even going to —"

"We checked out your husband a month ago, Mrs. Gattinski."

Stunned, she asks, "You . . . you did?"

"Did you honestly think we would leave loose ends in a murder investigation?"

"But . . . I guess I'm surprised that I didn't know."

"You didn't know because he wouldn't tell you. And neither would we. Your marriage is your business. Checking alibis is ours. Your husband told us where he was that night. We looked into it. There are reliable witnesses who can corroborate his story. He's not a suspect."

"Oh."

She can think of nothing else to say until he's halfway to the door again.

Then she calls after the detective, "Where was he? That night, I mean."

The man hesitates, then flashes a sympathetic look. "You'll have to ask him, Mrs. Gattinski."

She nods, knowing she won't.

It doesn't matter now.

Their marriage is over.

Kurt is a philanderer, but he isn't a killer.

Case closed.

At least, as far as Stella is concerned.

Slowly, she makes her way out of the room as sirens begin to wail ominously outside.

Kathleen's cell phone rings as she's heading down the thruway in the left lane at eighty miles an hour.

Her first thought is that she can't answer it. Not at this speed. She has to focus on the road, on getting herself back to Jen in one piece.

Her next thought is that she has to answer it. What if it's Detective Brodowiaz calling back?

She fumbles for the phone on the passenger's seat where she tossed it after she hung up with him a few minutes ago. It isn't there.

It rings again and she locates it on the floor beside the passenger's side door. Keeping one hand on the wheel and her eyes on the road, she swoops down to retrieve it, praying that it's the detective again; then praying that it isn't.

He promised he'd get a patrol car right over to the house.

If he's calling back, he might have good news . . .

Or he might have tragic news.

But isn't it too soon for him to be calling her back at all?

Maybe it's Jen.

But she wouldn't be able to get to the phone . . . which, Kathleen has been trying to assure herself, is why there was no answer when she tried to call home.

Bearing down on a double semi in her

lane, she flips open the phone, blindly jabbing at buttons until she hits the right one.

"Hello?" she yells into the receiver.

"Kathleen?"

"Matt!"

"Are you okay?"

She breaks into tears. "Matt, where the hell have you been?"

There's a pause. Then he says tightly, "With the police."

The word is like a cannonball launched directly at her, slamming into her and obliterating fragile hope.

"No!" Kathleen wails, instinct alone guiding the struggle to keep the car between the white lines even as her emotions swerve out of control. "Please, no. Not Jen."

Oh, God. The police. She's too late. The police are with Matt, telling him their daughter is —

"Kathleen," Matt's urgent voice rises above the roar of panic sweeping through her, "what are you talking about? It's Maeve. Not Jen."

"What?"

"Maeve's dead."

"But . . ." Foot on the brake, heart still accelerating, Kathleen instinctively steers into the right lane.

Bewildered, she tries to focus on what

Matt is telling her, all the while thanking God that it wasn't Jen; then blaming God for stealing her friend.

"She killed herself."

Oh, Maeve. No.

"Gregory found her this morning. The police came to question me because — because . . . Kathleen, you have to believe me. I had nothing to do with this."

"Matt . . . what are you talking about?"

"Maeve . . . she called me. At work. Yesterday. They must have hit redial on her phone."

"Who?"

"The police, the detectives, whoever — they found out she called me, and they came down here to talk to me."

"Matt, you're not making any sense. Maeve called you at work? What did she —"

"Kathleen, I swear, nothing happened between us."

"What?"

Yesterday. Matt was late getting home. He was acting so cagey, so distant this morning . . .

"Kathleen, she killed herself. Or maybe she didn't. All I know is that I had nothing to do with it. I wasn't there. I told her I couldn't —"

"Were you having an affair with Maeve?"

553

"No! Christ, Kathleen, aren't you listening to a word I'm saying? Do you actually think that I would —"

"I don't know what you would do, Matt, and right now I don't care. Jen is in trouble."

"In trouble? What happened?"

"I can't explain. Just get home, Matt. Get over there now. Please, Matt. Hurry."

"I can't go anywhere, Kathleen."

"Why not?"

"The police —"

She doesn't stay on the line long enough to listen to what he has to say. Disconnecting the call, she throws the phone, shaking in fury, in terror.

Maeve is dead . . . and the police are questioning Matt?

Do they think her husband is capable of murder?

Do you?

Chilled to the bone, Kathleen presses the gas pedal once again, speeding toward home.

The winding streets of Orchard Hollow are quietly deserted at this hour on a wintery weekday. Most parents are at work; most children are in school; most stay-at-home mothers are cozily inside their large houses watching over napping babies and toddlers.

Pulling up in front of 9 Sarah Crescent, Lucy spots a familiar car parked in the driveway.

John's car.

"Oh, God, no," she whispers, throwing the gear into Park and jumping out of her own car.

She breaks into a frantic run, halfway to the front door when she realizes that the car in the driveway isn't empty.

John is there, behind the steering wheel, looking as stunned to see her as she is to see him.

He rolls down the window and leans out.

"What are you doing here?"

They say it in unison.

John begins to speak, but Lucy won't let him.

Seething with barely controlled rage, she blurts, "It was you. You tried to kill Margaret."

"No."

"Yes. Don't lie. No more lies, John."

"Lucy, what are you —"

"You were the one who wanted her dead, John. You were the one who killed Father Joseph because he tried to protect her. And now . . . what? You're sitting here spying on her house?"

"No! Not spying. I — I just got here. I was about to get out of the car when you pulled up."

"Well, why are you here? To finish the job? I swear to God, John, you'll have to do it over my dead body."

"No, Lucy." His voice is ragged; his face is etched in despair. "I would never hurt you, and I'd never hurt her. She's my daughter. She's my baby girl. I'd do anything to protect her . . . you know that."

His fervent tone sends a chill down her spine. She wants to believe him. She so wants to believe him. But she can't ignore the lies.

"You promised me that fourteen years ago, when you took her from the hospital that day. You promised you'd keep her safe. And then . . . what? What the hell happened, John?"

He remains silent.

"Deirdre told me she was dead. You knew she wasn't, didn't you? You knew, and you let me believe it for all those years."

"I thought it was the best thing, Lucy, for all of us. You couldn't keep her. Not with Henry. And I couldn't keep her, either. Not with —"

He breaks off; Lucy finishes the sentence for him.

"Deirdre."

He remains silent.

"You told me Deirdre wanted to raise her. You told me she accepted her."

"She did! She did accept her, Lucy."

"Then why did you put her in foster care?"

John takes a deep breath. "I didn't put her in foster care. Do you know what happens to kids in that system, Lucy?"

She doesn't.

But she knows that he does. She'll never forget the horror stories he told her about his own childhood — stories that made her cry for the frightened, abused little boy he'd once been.

"I couldn't do that to her," he tells Lucy. "So I — I brought her to the church."

"To the *church?*" she echoes in disbelief. "What are you talking about?"

"I left her on the steps at Saint Brigid's with a note. I figured God would watch over her, and Father Joseph would see that somebody —"

"Why didn't you tell me?"

"I was afraid to. I was afraid you'd insist on keeping her, and I was afraid of what Henry might do to her. To both of you. And I couldn't keep her either. She wasn't — she wasn't safe with me."

"Why? She was your daughter, John. You

just said you would do anything to protect her."

"You don't understand."

"I'm trying." She looks into his eyes, frightened of what she sees there. "Did Deirdre try to hurt her, John? Did Deirdre try to hurt our baby?"

"No." His voice is a strangled whisper.

"You're lying."

"No. Not Deirdre."

"Then who? You?" She holds her breath, anticipating the answer, trying and failing to see the man before her as capable of hurting anyone, much less a helpless child.

"No, Lucy. Not me."

She's so relieved to hear his answer — and to realize that she believes it — that she almost misses the rest of it.

But she doesn't miss it. And the single, whispered word — just a name — sends a fresh storm of foreboding roaring through her.

"Susie."

"Who are you?" Jen asks incredulously, staring into the crazed eyes that seem oddly, hauntingly familiar.

"You know who I am. I'm Sissy."

Jen shakes her head. That's not why she's familiar, this insane woman whose face is mere inches from Jen's. It's something else. Something . . .

"Don't you remember me, Margaret?"

Margaret? Who's Margaret? And why —

"I'm your big sister."

What?

Jen shakes her head, whispers, "I don't have a sister."

"Sure you do. You mean you don't remember?"

"Sissy —"

"Sissy. Isn't that perfect? That's what he started calling me after he brought you home."

"Who?"

"Daddy. Who else?"

Daddy. The word lands hard in her gut, bringing with it a fierce longing.

I want my Daddy. Please, Daddy. Please come and save me. Please. She's insane, and she's going to hurt me.

Shaking beneath the blankets, envisioning Matt Carmody bursting into the house at any moment, Jen resolves to keep the lunatic talking.

Ask questions. Hurry. Before she does something crazy.

Jen settles on the first thing that pops into her mind.

"Is his name Quint?"

"Whose name?"

"Your — our — father's name," she forces herself to say.

"Quint? No. Not Quint. It's John. And I'm Susie. Susie-Q — that's what he always called me. Until he showed up with you."

She's deluded. She has Jen mixed up with someone else. Margaret, whoever that is.

"When you came along, he started calling me Sissy, when he bothered to talk to me at all. He said that was what you would call me, when you were old enough. Sissy. He was so wrapped up in his wittle tiny new baby girl," she says in a mimicking singsong tone, her face a grotesque caricature.

Oh, God. Keep her talking. Ask questions. Go along with it.

"How did you happen to come work for my mom?"

"Oh, that's the best part," Sissy says, obviously quite pleased with herself. "I stuck a flyer in the Hudsons' mailbox advertising my services."

The fliers. Jen recalls the September night she ran into Sissy on Sarah Crescent with a handful of them.

She gave me one, she remembers incredulously. Even back then, she was trying to work her way in. Still . . .

560

"Maeve just happened to hire you?" Jen asks in disbelief.

"Oh, it was a real coincidence. Her cleaning lady, Marta, just happened to have broken her leg the same day. It was a hit-and-run accident."

Her wild laughter is inhuman. Jen realizes with a chill that Marta's accident was no accident.

"I put my fliers in the Gattinskis' mailbox, too, after I knew you were babysitting there," Sissy is saying. "And Stella hired me, too, just like a charm. I planted the seed in Maeve's head about needing more work and the next thing I knew, your mother decided to get a cleaning lady."

Jen feels sick, thinking about her mother unwittingly inviting a killer into their home.

"You know what's amazing?" Sissy asks. "None of you — not even your mother — ever looked closely enough at me to realize that I look like you. It's not as though there isn't a resemblance, if you really look. Just . . . nobody ever really looked at me."

She trails off.

Jen stares at her, feeling as though she's looking at a twisted caricature of her own face.

Sissy looks up suddenly and catches her.

Her eyes narrow maliciously.

"How old were you when . . . when I was born?" Jen asks quickly.

Sissy laughs bitterly. "About your age. Isn't that ironic, Margaret? I was fourteen when you showed up to ruin my life. And now you're fourteen, and here I am to do the same for you."

"I didn't mean to ruin your life, Sissy."

"Don't call me that! It isn't my name!"

And Margaret isn't mine, Jen wants to hurl back at her. Yet, wincing at Sissy's harsh tone, she understands that she has to control her fury along with her fear.

She murmurs only, "I'm sorry."

"You should be. If it weren't for you, everything would have been fine."

"It will be fine, I promise. I won't —"

"You're right, it will be. Because you're not going to get another chance to steal him away from me."

"I don't want to steal him," Jen protests, struggling to keep from crying. "I don't even know him. Really. I don't want to know him. I have my own father."

And she does.

In that instant, she comprehends that Matt Carmody is her father in every way that counts. And if she can just hang on long enough, he'll be here to get her out of this.

Sissy is shaking her head, sneering. "Do you really think I believe you? Why would you stay here with him when you can be with your real parents?"

"I would never leave my mother," Jen protests feebly, her mind spinning. "Not even to be with my real father." She almost chokes on the phrase. Who's lying about her father's identity? Her mother? Or Susie?

Is he Quint or John?

Is he dead or alive?

"She isn't your mother."

Jen stares at Sissy. Now what is she talking about?

"So you really didn't know." Sissy's expression is gleeful.

"Know what?"

"Kathleen isn't your mother."

Stay calm, Jen. Don't listen to her. She's insane. You know she's insane.

And yet . . .

Something has clicked into place. Something Jen realizes she might have already sensed, deep down.

Sissy is saying, "She's not your mother any more than he's your father. But I'm definitely your big sister. Do you believe me, Margaret?"

"Yes," Jen croaks, still not sure what she believes.

"No, you don't. But I've got proof. You know how you can tell?"

Jen shakes her head mutely.

Sissy spits on her fingers and wipes her hand across her left eyebrow. She holds up her hand and Jen sees that her fingertips are smudged with black.

"Mascara," she explains.

Confused, Jen shifts her gaze from Sissy's hand to her face.

Then she sees it.

As Kathleen races toward home, she goes over and over the phone call. Not the call with Matt. The first call. Right now, every ounce of her being has to remain focused on Jen. Otherwise, she'll lose her mind. She really will.

So . . .

Helen.

The accent.

The voice that seemed so familiar . . .

Why?

She just assumed she'd heard it before while she was visiting her father at Erasmus, but obviously that isn't it.

So where did she hear it?

She hasn't been to the south in years; she hasn't run across anyone with a southern accent here in ages.

The only thing that makes sense to her is that the accent might have been fake. Perhaps it was the caller's attempt to disguise a voice Kathleen might otherwise recognize.

"Mrs. Carmody, we need you to come right down here."

Whoever called her with that false message had access to the intimate details of Kathleen's life. They knew about her father. Knew his name, knew where he was. Knew, too, that it would take a life-or-death situation to drag her away from her daughter's side after all that had happened.

"Maeve Hudson was surprised, too," Sissy tells Jen conversationally, gesturing at the pale hairs that are barely visible now that the makeup is wiped away. "I got careless yesterday when I used a towel to dry my hair and get the snow off my face. That's what happens when you get careless, you know, Margaret? You give yourself away."

Jen nods, gulping back fear.

"At first she didn't even notice. She was too busy rummaging around the house. And then do you know what she did?"

Jen shakes her head.

"She called Matt. She made me stand there in the kitchen waiting while she went to get her purse. She made me wait for my money while she called him. I bet you didn't know she was in love with him, did you?"

"No," Jen whispers. "I didn't know."

"So anyway, Maeve hung up the phone and she was crying. And she saw me standing there, and you know what happened then?"

She pauses.

Jen makes a futile attempt to find her voice.

"I said, do you know what happened then?" Sissy snarls.

"No," is all Jen can manage, a single high-pitched sound that is more a whimper than a word.

"She saw that scar in my eyebrow. That's what happened. And she got suspicious. She shouldn't have started asking questions, Margaret. Bad things happen when you ask too many questions."

"What happened to Maeve?" Jen asks, a sick feeling taking hold in the pit of her stomach.

Sissy laughs shrilly. "What do you think?"

The bootee.

The thought strikes Kathleen out of the blue, and she clenches the steering wheel with all her might.

Oh, God. She should have told Detective

Brodowiaz about the bootee. And the phone calls. The baby crying . . .

She'll tell him as soon as she sees him. She'll tell him the whole story.

But then Jen will find out the truth. Jen will know that Kathleen isn't her mother. That she stole her away . . .

But somebody left her there. On the church steps. She was abandoned.

I didn't steal her. I found her. I found her, and I did what the note asked me to do.

In her grief-stricken state that night, it was the only thing she was capable of doing. Hadn't she just come from the cemetery, where she had buried her own dead child with her bare hands in the wet earth beside her mother's grave?

What were you thinking? Why didn't you call the police when you found the baby dead?

She's asked herself that question a thousand times since that night, and the answer has never been clear.

All she knows is that she was in no condition to make rational decisions.

Blaming herself and her unhealthy early pregnancy for her baby's inexplicable death, she pleaded with God — and with her mother — to give her another chance. To send her baby back to her.

As the shock wore off and despair took

over, she found her way to the church, knowing she had to confess to Father Joseph what she had done.

Then she saw the pink bundle on the church steps.

"What happened to Maeve? Hmmm." Sissy grins at Margaret. "Here's a clue. Like mother, like daughter. Have you ever heard that old saying?"

The girl is silent, but the expression on her face speaks volumes. She's scared out of her mind.

Just like Maeve was right before she died. Erin, too.

Yes. Like mother, like daughter.

"You know," Sissy comments conversationally, "that's one thing my mother never said. She loved to spew old sayings at me. You name a cliché, and she said it. But not that one. She never said 'like mother like daughter.' At least, not about me and her. I was always Daddy's girl, you know? You know?" she repeats vehemently when there's no answer.

Margaret's head bobs a little, in either a shrug or a nod. Clearly, she's all but paralyzed with fear. Sissy relishes the feeling of utter control, enjoying this whole experience even more than she anticipated.

With the others, it wasn't about enjoyment. Nor was it about control. It was more about eliminating obstacles.

First April. Then Robby. Then Erin. Then Maeve Hudson, who popped up unexpectedly, like a construction zone located right before an on-ramp. One last roadblock before smooth sailing to that final destination.

She didn't even have to die. It was her own damned fault. In the three months Sissy worked for her, the bitch never once looked right at her. But that day, she did.

Not right away.

First, she made Sissy wait for her pay while she hunted down the telephone and made her call to Matt Carmody.

She took the phone into the next room, whispering, but Sissy heard every word she said . . . and she could easily imagine every word Matt said. The key one being "no."

After she hung up the phone, Maeve looked almost surprised to find Sissy still there.

"What are you waiting for?" she snapped.

"My pay."

Maybe it was something in Sissy's tone that made Maeve glance up sharply at her. Her gaze went right to her left eyebrow.

Sissy knew what must have happened

before she even caught sight of her own reflection in the mirror over Maeve's shoulder. The wet snow had washed away the makeup covering her scar. Maeve saw the smudge; saw the lighter hair in Sissy's brow.

Somehow, in that instant, she had the presence of mind to put two and two together. Sissy watched the lightbulb go on behind Maeve's startled eyes.

"You . . . you're . . ." She faltered then, before she spoke the last coherent words of her life. "Who are you?"

"Can't you guess?"

Maeve shook her head, frightened, clearly sensing danger, yet confused.

"You're afraid," Sissy noted, amused. "Just like your daughter was."

For a moment, Maeve stared in mute horror. Then she ran. First, she tried to go for the door, but Sissy was in the way, so she turned and raced up the stairs. She disappeared into the master bedroom, locked the door, and cowered in her closet.

Fool.

Didn't she know how flimsy the locks are in this fancy new construction?

Didn't she know she didn't have a chance?

That the rows of clothes and the thick insulation and the falling snow muffled her screams?

Maybe she did know. Maybe that's why Sissy managed to quickly overpower her despite all those hours Maeve spent at the gym.

She was strong, but Sissy was stronger. She was determined, but Sissy was more determined.

Still, it took longer than it had to. Sissy expected Maeve's neck to snap, but it didn't. Thanks to her Pilates classes and strength training, her bones and muscles were strong and supple. She strangled to death as Sissy watched in fascination, pulling on the other end of the belt with all her might.

In the end, Maeve Hudson actually seemed to welcome death. Her struggle with the makeshift noose was as short-lived as the horrible gasping sounds emitting from her slender throat as she spun slowly from the closet rod.

"Like mother, like daughter," Sissy repeats, smiling at Margaret. "Know what I mean?"

For a few breathless moments, gazing at the pink bundle on the church steps, Kathleen had believed it was the miracle she'd sought. She believed it was her baby girl, returned to her.

By the time she realized that the baby wasn't Jen — her cherished, lost Jen — she knew she would keep her anyway. She knew it was a sign from God.

How could you believe that?

Kathleen thumps the steering wheel in fury at her delusional former self, even as some part of her pipes up in defense.

You couldn't help it. You were young, and alone, and you were out of your mind with grief.

And . . .

And you knew you could get away with it.

That, perhaps, is the worst part of all.

Nobody knew her baby had died.

Nobody knew the baby had been left at the church.

Nobody . . .

Except whoever left her there in the first place.

Again, Kathleen thinks about the pink bootee.

About the person who cared enough to knit the delicate pink blanket and bootees.

Whoever it was might not be the person who wants her dead . . .

But what if they want her back?

Kathleen shudders, so distracted by the frightening thoughts running through her mind that she nearly passes the turnoff to Cuttington Road and Orchard Hollow.

"Oh my God. You killed Maeve?"

But it isn't a question. Jen *knows*.

Another thought occurs to her then; she blurts it aloud. "You killed him, too, didn't you?"

"Robby?" Sissy gives a self-satisfied nod. "Yup. Him, too."

"Robby?" Jen gasps in horror.

No. Oh, no. Oh, Robby.

"Let me guess . . ." Sissy peers into her face. "You weren't talking about Robby?"

"No, I . . ." Jen swallows hard, thinking of poor Robby. "I meant Quint."

"Who?"

"Quint Matteson. They said he OD'd. Did you —"

"No." Sissy laughs. "Sorry, I had nothing to do with that. Whoever he is." With exaggerated patience, she adds, "He's not your father, Margaret. Your father is John. *Our* father is John. Remember?"

Mute with fear, Jen stares at the woman claiming to be her sister. Stares at the scar in her eyebrow.

Following her gaze, Sissy runs her fingertips almost lovingly along her brow. "My mother always called it the mark of the devil. She was a religious fanatic, you know? She thought it meant my father was cursed, and when I came along I guess she thought I was, too. And then he brought you home. You were all dressed in pink that day. Pink bootees, and a blanket . . . oh, that reminds me. Did you get the birthday gift I left for you?"

The pink bootee. Oh, God.

"Yes," Jen whispers.

"It fell off your foot that day when they took you away. I saw my mother pick it up off the floor and throw it into the garbage. But I took it out. It was my souvenir." Sissy laughs.

"You know, my mother flipped out when she first saw you, Margaret. She said you were the spawn of the devil. She said he had to get rid of you. He said he didn't want to. But I did."

Sissy retrieves something from the folds of her coat.

"Remember this?" she asks, holding it up.

Jen stares at the white pillow with pink embroidery.

Sugar and Spice and Everything Nice . . .

"Remember it?" Sissy demands again.

Jen shakes her head, manages to find her voice. "No. No, I don't . . ."

"He bought it for you. He bought lots of

things for you. Little pink ruffly dresses, and a stuffed lamb, and an Ashton-Drake doll. I always wanted one, but he said they were too expensive. And then he bought one for you. And he said I was too old to play with it."

"I don't like dolls. I never liked dolls," Jen whispers.

Lost in her memories, Sissy ignores her. "After you left, I thought he'd give me the doll, but he didn't. He threw it away. I guess he didn't want me to have it because of what I did."

"What . . . what did you do?"

This time, the sound of Jen's voice seems to snap Sissy back to the present.

"I was naughty. Really, really naughty," she says, leaning closer and whispering conspiratorially, "Want to know what I did?"

No. Please, the only thing I want is for you not to hurt me. Please . . .

Jen nods, praying harder than she's ever prayed in her life.

"You really want me to tell you?"

Daddy, where are you?

"Yes."

"How about if I just show you instead?"

With that, Sissy raises the pillow and brings it down over Jen's face.

"Susie wanted to hurt the baby?" Lucy echoes in disbelief, staring at John.

"She tried. Deirdre found her . . . she was trying to smother Margaret in her crib."

Lucy buries her face in her hands, shaking her head. Her baby. Her poor baby.

"Deirdre did CPR. She saved her, Lucy. And she made me promise not to tell. We both knew that if we told anybody, Susie's life would be ruined."

"She tried to kill a helpless baby, John!"

"I know, but you have to understand . . ." He takes hold of Lucy's upper arms, holding her, as though he won't let go until he makes her see. "Susie was my baby, too. She was my baby first. And she was fine before Margaret came along. Deirdre and I knew that she'd be fine if things could just go back to the way they were."

"So you left a helpless baby on the steps of the church? Why didn't you come to me?"

"You couldn't keep her."

"If I knew what had happened, I'd have found a way to —"

"I couldn't tell you what happened, Lucy. Deirdre and I swore we'd never tell a soul about Susie. And we never did. I never did. Not even . . ."

"What?" she presses, when he trails off,

his expression haunted. "What is it?"

He takes a deep breath, his hands painfully tightening on her arms, almost as though he's clinging to a lifeline.

"Deirdre never forgave Susie. Neither did I, but she . . . it was different with Deirdre. She always thought Susie had the devil in her, from the moment she was born. The more time went by, the more tense things were between them. And then one day . . ."

"What? One day, what?" Lucy demands when he falls silent once again.

"Deirdre fell down the stairs. I was out when it happened. Susie was, too. At least, that's what she said."

"You didn't believe her."

"I did at the time. But I started to wonder. And then . . . then, a few months ago, I found the pictures."

"What pictures?"

He reaches into his pocket, takes out a stack of photographs and hands them to her silently.

Lucy gasps.

Flipping through them, she stares in disbelief at a series of snapshots of Jen Carmody, shot through a telephoto lens.

"Susie sent me the letter. My God, John. You knew, and you didn't —"

"I couldn't. Lucy, she's still my daughter. She's my baby."

"So is Margaret," she bites out.

"I know that." He nods in weary resignation. "That's why I'm here. I wanted to warn her parents before I went to the police. But it looks like nobody's home."

"Then let's go right to the police," Lucy says simply.

He nods, opens his mouth. Before he can speak, the air is filled with the faint sound of approaching sirens.

Jen writhes on the bed, panic taking hold as she realizes that her time is running out.

Her lungs burn with the futile strain for air as Sissy presses the pillow over her face in a ruthless death grip.

In another few seconds, it will be over.

Oh, Daddy. Oh, Mom. Please . . .

I'm sorry.

She'll never have the chance to tell them how much she loves them.

That she knows how much they love her.

Images fly through her mind.

Is this what happens when you die? You see your life flashing before you like a movie montage?

Mom coming back to kiss her goodbye.

Dad coaching soccer —

Soccer.

Jen releases her hold on her captor's viselike arm.

Feeling her way blindly, she reaches for the trophy.

The one she pulled from the shelf earlier.

The one that should still be on the bed.

Even as her fingers close over the cold metal, she remembers how heavy the trophy was. Heavy enough to kill somebody . . . but too heavy for her to lift.

Now, with her oxygen rapidly depleting, she'll need a miracle to turn it into a weapon. She can't breathe, she can't see, she can't move.

But you have to. It's your only hope. It's the only way you'll get through this, so you can tell them . . .

Mom.

Dad.

Curran.

Riley.

With a miraculous surge of adrenaline-driven strength and a fierce will to live, Jen swings the trophy upward with all her might.

Kathleen sees the red lights of the police cars in front of the house from Cuttington

Road. She pulls as close as she can, then abandons her car, pulls the keys from the ignition, and takes off running toward her home.

A knot of people are on the front lawn and steps: several uniformed officers, an unfamiliar couple, and Detective Brodowiaz.

"What happened?" Kathleen asks breathlessly, reaching his side. "Is Jen okay?"

"We've knocked and rung the bell. There's been no answer, but we can't find any evidence of a break in."

"She can't answer the door; she can't get out of bed." Frantic, Kathleen fumbles trying to jam the right key into the lock, getting it in and then turning it the wrong way in her haste to get it open.

"Relax, Mrs. Carmody." Detective Brodowiaz lays a reassuring hand on her shoulder. "Nobody broke in while you were gone. Chances are your daughter is safe upstairs."

"Whoever it was might have a key," Kathleen flings at him. "Whoever it was has been in the house before."

She throws the door open at last and races into the house, screaming her daughter's name.

"Mom?"

She's alive.

"Jen!" Kathleen shrieks, taking the stairs three at a time.

Thank you, God.

Thank you, Mommy.

She's alive.

Bursting into her daughter's bedroom, the first thing Kathleen sees is the blood-soaked bed.

"Jen! No!"

But it isn't Jen's blood.

Her daughter *is* alive. Alive but covered in blood that belongs to a lifeless figure draped across the bed.

The skull is cracked; the brown hair is matted with red clots. But the face, eyes open and staring at a grotesque angle, is intact.

Intact, and hauntingly familiar.

Stunned, Kathleen realizes why she recognized the voice on the phone.

"Oh, God," she breathes in disbelief.

It doesn't make sense. Nothing makes sense. Why?

"Oh, God. Sissy . . ."

"Mommy," Jen sobs.

Footsteps pound on the stairs, in the hall, all around them.

"Mommy, I'm so sorry."

Police officers swarm the room, guns drawn.

In the eye of the storm, Kathleen sinks onto the bed and gathers her baby into her arms, holding her close, rocking her. "It's all right, Jen. It's going to be all right. I'm here. Mommy's here."

She strokes Jen's hair, her hands sticky with blood.

Blood.

A long time ago — a lifetime ago, it seems — she told Jen about blood . . .

And about love.

"Mommy," Jen sobs. "Mommy. She hurt Maeve. Somebody has to go over there."

Maeve.

Matt.

Oh, Matt . . . I'm sorry. I'm so sorry I doubted you . . .

"Mommy, she tried to —"

"Shhh . . . It's over, sweetheart. That's all that matters now. We're going to be okay."

"There's so much blood . . ."

Blood.

Yes.

Love, Kathleen told Jen a long time ago, *is thicker than blood.*

Cradling their daughter in her arms, Kathleen whispers, "We really are going to be okay."

EPILOGUE

May

Something wet and white lands on Kathleen's hand as she climbs out of the car. She looks down at it, then up at the milky sky in disbelief.

It's snowing.

Snowing on the second Sunday in May.

Kathleen shakes her head, smiling as she buttons her jacket and pulls up the collar against the cold.

"Mom, is that . . . ?"

"Yes," she tells her daughter, who has climbed out of the passenger's seat and come to stand behind her, shivering.

"First a blizzard on Easter, and now this. I can't believe it."

"I can." Laughing, Kathleen reaches out to tug at the zipper pull of her daughter's open ski jacket, raising it to her chin. "Welcome to Buffalo. I can remember one year when it snowed on Memorial Day."

"That's not funny."

"Maybe not, but it's true."

"I think we should move to Florida," Jen

grumbles, as Kathleen opens the backseat to remove the long, shiny white boxes there. "It feels like it's been winter forever. I can't stand it."

It does, Kathleen thinks, her smile fading. It does feel like it's been winter forever. Endless months of police investigation, complicated when the decomposing body of April Lukoviak was discovered. Endless therapy sessions and fervent prayers as Kathleen — as all of the Carmodys — came to terms with the past.

It hasn't been easy. At first, it was downright traumatic, especially for Jen, who was forced to accept the shock that neither Matt nor Kathleen are her birth parents.

There were times, especially in the beginning, when she would rant and scream at Kathleen, and at Matt. She called them strangers, she called them liars, she called them far worse. Then one day, at last, when Jen was home with a terrible cold and Kathleen was straining homemade chicken soup at the sink, she came into the kitchen and she simply asked why.

"Why did you do it?"

Kathleen took a deep breath, knowing they had reached a turning point. Here, at last, was a question. A question instead of an accusation, a curse, a threat.

A question that, thank God, she could answer honestly and with all her heart.

"Because when I picked you up from the church steps and I looked down into your face, I knew that you needed me as badly as I needed you," Kathleen told her daughter. "Somewhere inside I knew it was wrong, but I didn't care. When I saw you, at first glance I thought you were my daughter. And then, when I realized that you weren't . . . well, somehow, you still were. Does that make any sense at all?"

"No," Jen said, but she was crying. And laughing.

And so was Kathleen.

And the tears and the laughter, like the chicken soup, helped with the healing.

So her daughter has learned to forgive.

And so, in the long, bleak months since December, has Kathleen.

Most importantly, she's forgiven herself.

She's also forgiven John for not coming forward sooner about Susie.

And she's forgiven Lucy, now living in a shelter for battered women, for not fighting to keep her baby girl so long ago.

They both want to play a role in Jen's life when — and if — she's ready to see them. At first, she claimed she never would be, but lately, she's been hinting that she might change her mind. That maybe she's forgiven them, too.

"It's freezing out here," Jen announces, dragging Kathleen's thoughts back to the present. "I wish it would stop snowing."

"So do I."

Like her daughter, Kathleen is more than ready for a new season. Ready to put the brutal winter behind them, once and for all.

She hands Jen one of the boxes, takes the other in her own arms, and locks the car.

"Come on," she says, leading the way down the path. "This won't take long."

Saint Brigid's Cemetery is busier than usual today, despite the weather. Kathleen can see small knots of people, many dressed in their Sunday best, gathered at quite a few graves. There are urns and wreaths of feminine-hued flowers at others.

Their first stop is a large granite stone shaped like a cross.

There, Kathleen begins to open her box, but Jen stops her.

"I want to do it," she tells her mother.

Swallowing over a lump in her throat, Kathleen watches her daughter remove a dozen red roses from the green tissue inside the florist's box and lay them at Father Joseph's grave beside the stone marked with her name, and his mother's. Genevieve.

They kneel together and pray silently.

"Thank you," Jen whispers at the end, echoing Kathleen's heartfelt sentiment for the man who honored Mollie Gallagher's memory by bringing roses to her grave all these years . . . and then saved her granddaughter's life.

Lucy told her that he never mentioned having known Kathleen in the past, nor did he mention that she had named her daughter after his mother. He had to wonder what had happened to the first Genevieve — the baby he blessed on All Saint's Day fourteen years ago. He made the sign of the cross on her forehead; he knew there was no scar on her eyebrow then.

He must have wondered what happened to Kathleen's baby; he must have wondered how and why she was switched for Lucy's baby. He must have wondered, must have doubted, must have had his suspicions, and yet, when he understood that there was danger he watched over Genevieve Carmody.

He wasn't a vicious monster stalking Jen; he was her guardian angel.

From the moment Kathleen uncovered the truth about Father Joseph's role in the tragedy, she wondered how she ever could have doubted him.

It was the fear. The fear, and the grief, and the guilt. They can do terrible things to a person if their burden is carried around for very long. They can arouse suspicion and mistrust of even those who are closest or most deserving of trust.

Like Father Joseph.

Or . . .

Or Matt.

But that's different, Kathleen reminds herself. *You never thought Matt would hurt Jen. You knew he loved her.*

You just weren't so sure he loved you.

But it all makes sense now that she knows why he acted so oddly, why he wouldn't return her calls that snowy day in December.

He was afraid that if he did, he would be compelled to tell her about the call he'd received from her best friend.

That Maeve had called to proposition her husband on that last day of her life is no longer surprising to Kathleen.

Fear and grief can do terrible things to a person.

That Matt turned her down and chose not to tell Kathleen was never surprising in the first place. He wanted to protect his wife from her best friend's betrayal.

That's Matt. Protective. Loyal. Loving.

Too good to be true. How many times has she thought that about him over the years?

But it *is* true. She has everything she always wanted.

Almost everything.

"Let's go," she says, touching Jen's sleeve.

They get to their feet. Walking in somber silence, her daughter at her side, Kathleen carries the second box to the far corner of the cemetery. They come to a stop beneath the oak tree, whose spreading branches are pale green with tender new leaves.

Kathleen removes the dozen roses from the box in her arms and sets them at the base of the tombstone.

Mollie Gallagher.

Mollie Gallagher.

Loving Wife, Devoted Mother, Protective Grandmother.

She had the last two words etched into the stone just before the holidays, after she visited the stone monument company just outside the cemetery gates, next door to the florist shop.

Protective Grandmother.

You really were, she silently tells her mother, touching the recent engraving she considers her last Christmas present to Mollie Gallagher. *You've protected her —*

and my secret — all these years.

But in the end, the sins of her past weren't meant to stay buried — and neither were the remains of her infant daughter.

The makeshift grave was exhumed not long after the police investigation began. The baby's remains were examined, then released to Kathleen, who was mercifully cleared of any potential charges.

Genevieve Gallagher Carmody was laid to rest in a tiny white coffin in a plot beside her grandmother's grave, beneath a carved marble angel that lists only her name and the dates of her birth and death.

Tears sting Kathleen's eyes as she takes the final red rose from her box and props it against her firstborn's tombstone.

"Are you okay, Mom?" Jen's arms encircle her in warmth.

Kathleen nods, wiping the tears with her sleeve.

For a long time, they stand staring down at the tiny angel.

Then Kathleen takes a deep breath. "We should go," she says. "Daddy and the boys are probably back from their secret shopping mission by now, and they were going to go get Grandpa so he can come out for dinner with us."

"Before we go, I have to run over to Mrs.

Gattinski's to drop off the Mother's Day presents the girls made for her. We did clay handprints. I promised I'd have them wrapped and ready this afternoon."

When Stella Gattinski and her daughters moved into the apartment at nearby Orchard Arms, Kathleen doubted Jen would be willing to do much babysitting there.

It took her a while, but, ultimately, she opted to take back her old weekly job. Stella, in the throes of a messy divorce, frequently expresses her gratitude when she and Kathleen take their regular early morning walks around the neighborhood.

Stella likes to say, "I don't know what I'd do without Jen."

Kathleen doesn't know, either . . . but she's well aware that she came perilously close to finding out.

"Are you ready, Mom?" Jen asks quietly, giving Kathleen's arm a gentle pat.

"I'm ready."

She touches the marble angel one last time, then bends to press her lips against the cold granite of Mollie Gallagher's gravestone.

"Happy Mother's Day, Mom," she whispers softly. "I love you."

At her side, her daughter — who greeted Kathleen first thing this morning with those very same heartfelt, precious words — puts a reassuring arm around her shoulder.

"Hey! The snow's stopped," Jen tells her, looking up in wonder.

Kathleen follows her gaze. Overhead, a gleam of golden sunshine and a patch of bright blue sky are poking through the dense ceiling of gray.

"I guess you got your wish," she tells Jen with a smile.

"We both did."

Truer words, Kathleen decides, have never been spoken.

Arm in arm, mother and daughter head toward home.